The Three

Love in a Cottage, and ~~O...~~

Francis A. Durivage

Alpha Editions

This edition published in 2023

ISBN : 9789357949750

Design and Setting By
Alpha Editions
www.alphaedis.com
Email - info@alphaedis.com

Contents

PREFACE.

The volume here submitted to the public is composed of selections from my contributions to the columns of the American press. The stories and sketches were written, most of them, in the intervals of relaxation from more serious labor and the daily business of life; and they would be suffered to disappear in the Lethe that awaits old magazines and newspapers, had not their extensive circulation, and the partial judgment of friends,—for I must not omit the stereotyped plea of scribblers,—flattered me that their collection in a permanent form would not prove wholly unacceptable. Some of these articles were published anonymously, or under the signature of "The Old 'Un," and have enjoyed the honor of adoption by persons having no claim to their paternity; and it seems time to call home and assemble these vagabond children under the paternal wing.

The materials for the tales were gathered from various sources: some are purely imaginative, some authentic, not a few jotted down from oral narrative, or derived from the vague remembrance of some old play or adventure; but the form at least is my own, and that is about all that a professional story-teller, gleaning his matter at random, can generally lay claim to.

Some of these sketches were originally published in the Boston "Olive Branch," and many in Mr. Gleason's popular papers, the "Flag of Our Union," and the "Pictorial Drawing-Room Companion." Others have appeared in the "New York Mirror," the "American Monthly Magazine," the New York "Spirit of the Times," the "Symbol," and other magazines and papers.

Should their perusal serve to beguile some hours of weariness and illness, as their composition has done, I shall feel that my labor has not been altogether vain; while the moderate success of this venture will stimulate me to attempt something more worthy the attention of the public.

FRANCIS A. DURIVAGE.

THE GOLDSMITH'S DAUGHTER.

A LEGEND OF MADRID.

Many, many years ago, in those "good old times" so much bepraised by antiquaries and the *laudatores temporis acti*,—the good old times, that is to say, of the holy office, of those magnificent *autos* when the smell of roasted heretics was as sweet a savor in the nostrils of the faithful, as that of Quakers done remarkably brown was to our godly Puritan ancestors,—there dwelt in the royal city of Madrid a wealthy goldsmith by the name of Antonio Perez, whose family—having lost his wife—consisted of a lovely daughter, named Magdalena, and a less beautiful but still charming niece, Juanita. The housekeeping and the care of the girls were committed to a starched old duenna, Donna Margarita, whose vinegar aspect and sharp tongue might well keep at a distance the boldest gallants of the court and camp. For the rest, some half dozen workmen and servitors, and a couple of stout Asturian serving wenches made up the establishment of the wealthy artisan. As the chief care of the latter was to accumulate treasure, his family, while they were denied no comfort, were debarred from luxury, and, perhaps, fared the better from this very frugality of the master. Yet in the stable, which occupied a portion of the basement story of his residence,—the other half being devoted to the *almacen*, or store,—there were a couple of long-tailed Flemish mares, and a heavy, lumbering chariot; and in the rear of the house a garden, enclosed on three sides with a stone wall, and comprising arbors, a fountain, and a choice variety of fruits and flowers.

One evening, the goldsmith's daughter and her cousin sat in their apartment, on the second story, peeping out through the closed "jalousies," or blinds, into the twilight street, haply on the watch for some gallant cavalier, whose horsemanship and costume they might admire or criticize. Seeing nothing there, however, to attract their attention, they turned to each other.

"Juanita," said the goldsmith's daughter, "I believe I have secured an admirer."

"An admirer!" exclaimed the pretty cousin. "If your father and dame Margarita didn't keep us cooped here like a pair of pigeons, we should have, at least, twenty apiece. But what manner of man is this phœnix of yours? Is he tall? Has he black eyes, or blue? Is he courtier or soldier?"

"He is tall," replied Magdalena, smiling; "but for his favor, or the color of his eyes, or quality, I cannot answer. His face and figure shrouded in a cloak, his *sombrero* pulled down over his eyes, he takes up his station against a pillar of the church whenever I go to San Ildefonso with my duenna, and watches me till mass is ended. I have caught him following our footsteps. But be he gentle or simple, fair or dark, I know not."

"A very mysterious character!" cried Juanita, laughing, "like unto the bravo of some Italian tale. Jesu Maria!" she exclaimed, springing to the window, "what goodly cavalier rides hither? His mantle is of three-pile velvet, and he wears golden spurs upon his heels. And with what a grace he sits and manages his fiery genet! Pray Heaven your suitor be as goodly a cavalier."

Magdalena gazed forth upon the horseman, and her heart silently confessed that the praises of her cousin were well bestowed. As the cavalier approached the goldsmith's house, he checked the impatient speed of his horse, and gazed upward earnestly at the window where the young girls sat.

"Magdalena!" cried the mischievous Juanita, "old Margarita is not here to document us, and I declare your beauty shall have one chance." As she spoke she threw open the blind, and exposed her lovely and blushing cousin to the gaze of the cavalier.

Ardently and admiringly he gazed upon her dark and faultless features, and then raising his plumed hat, bowed to his very saddle bow, and rode on, but turned, ever and anon, till he was lost in the distance and gradual darkening of the street.

"Mutual admiration!" cried the gay Juanita, clapping her hands. "Thank me for the stratagem. Yon cavalier is, without a doubt, the mysterious admirer of San Ildefonso."

Don Julio Montero—for that was the name of the cavalier—returned again beneath the casement, and again saw Magdalena. He also made some purchases of the old goldsmith, and managed to speak a word with his fair daughter in the shop; and in spite of the duenna, billets were exchanged between the parties. The very secrecy with which this little intrigue was managed, the mystery of it, influenced the imagination of Magdalena and increased the violence of her attachment, and loving with all the fervor of her meridian nature, she felt that any disappointment would be her death.

One evening, as her secret suitor was passing along a narrow and unfrequent street, a light touch was laid upon his shoulder, and turning, he perceived a tall figure, muffled in a long, dark cloak.

"Senor Montero," said the stranger, "one word with you." And then, observing that he hesitated, he threw open his cloak, and added, "Nay, senor, suspect not that my purpose is unfriendly; you see I have no arms, while you wear both rapier and dagger. I merely wish to say a few words on a matter of deep import to yourself."

"Your name, senor," replied the other, "methinks should precede any communication you have to make me, would you secure my confidence."

"My name, senor, I cannot disclose."

"Umph! a somewhat strange adventure!" muttered the young cavalier. "However, friend, since such you purport to be, say your say, and that right briefly, for I have affairs of urgency on my hands."

"Briefly, then, senor. You have cast your eyes on the daughter of Antonio Perez, the rich goldsmith?"

"That is my affair, methinks," replied the cavalier, haughtily. "By what right do you interfere with it? Are you brother or relative of the fair Magdalena?"

"Neither, senor; but I take a deep interest in your affairs; and I warn you, if your heart be not irretrievably involved, to withdraw from the prosecution of your addresses. To my certain knowledge, Magdalena is beloved by another."

"What of that, man? A fair field and no favor, is all I ask."

"But what if *she* loves another?"

"Ha!" exclaimed the cavalier. "Can she be sporting with me?—playing the coquette? But no! I will not believe it, at least upon the say so of a stranger. I must have proofs."

"Pray, senor, have you never observed upon the lady's fair arm a turquoise bracelet?"

"Yea, have I," replied the cavalier; "by the same token that she has promised it to me as a *gage d'amour.*"

"Do you recognize the bracelet?" cried the stranger, holding up, as he spoke, the ornament in question. "Or, if that convince you not, do you recognize this tress of raven hair—this bouquet that she wore upon her bosom yesternight?"

"That I gave her myself!" cried the cavalier. "By Heaven! she has proved false to me. But I must know," he added, fiercely, "who thou art ere thou goest hence. I must have thy secret, if I force it from thee at the dagger's point. Who art thou? speak!"

"Prithee, senor, press me not," said the stranger, drawing his cloak yet closer about him, and retreating a pace or two.

"Who art thou?" cried the cavalier, menacingly, and striding forward as the other receded.

"One whose name breathed in thine ear," replied the other, "would curdle thy young blood with horror."

Julio laughed loud and scornfully.

"Now, by Saint Iago! thou art some juggling knave—some impish charlatan, who seeks to conceal his imposture in the garb of mystery and terror. Little knowest thou the mettle of a Castilian heart. Thy name?"

The stranger stooped forward, and whispered a word or two in the ear of his companion. The young man recoiled, while his cheek turned from the glowing tinge of health and indignation to the hue of ashes; and, as he stood, rooted to the spot in terror and dismay, the stranger threw the hem of his cloak over his shoulder, and glided away like a dark shadow.

Julio's heart was so far enlisted in favor of Magdalena, that it cost him a severe struggle to throw her off as utterly unworthy of his attachment, but pride came to his rescue, and he performed his task. He wrote a letter, in which, assigning no cause for the procedure, he calmly, coldly, contemptuously renounced her hand, and told her that henceforth, should they meet, it must be as strangers.

This unexpected blow almost paralyzed Magdalena's reason. It was to be expected of her temperament that her anguish should be in proportion to her former rapture. At first stunned, she roused to the paroxysm of wild despair. Henceforth, if she lived, her life, she felt, would be an utter blank. Passion completely overmastering her reason, she resolved to destroy herself. This fearful resolution adopted, her excitement ceased. She became calm— calm as the senseless stone; no tremors shook her soul, no remorse, no regret.

She was seated alone, one evening, at that very window whence she had first beheld her false suitor, and bitter memories were crowding on her brain, when the door of her apartment opened, and closed again after admitting her old duenna, Margarita. The old woman approached with a stealthy, cat-like step, and sitting down beside the maiden, and gazing inquisitively into her dim eyes, said, in a whining voice, intended to be very winning and persuasive,—

"What ails my pretty pet? Is she unwell?"

"I am not unwell," replied Magdalena, coldly, rousing herself to the exertion of conversing, with an effort.

"Nay, my darling," said the old woman, in the same whining tone, "I am sure that something is the matter with you. You look feverish."

"I am well, Margarita; let that suffice."

"And feel no regret for the false suitor, hey?"

Magdalena turned upon her quickly—almost fiercely.

"What do you know of him?"

"All! all!" cried the old woman, while her gray eyes flashed with exultation.

"Then you know him for a false and perjured villain!" cried the beautiful Spaniard.

"I know him for an honorable cavalier; true as the steel of his Toledo blade!" retorted the duenna. "I speak riddles, Magdalena, but I will explain myself. Do you think I can forget your insults, jeers, and jokes? Do you think I knew not when you mocked me behind my back, or sought to trick me before my face? You little knew, when you and your gay-faced cousin were making merry at my expense, what wrath you were storing up against the day of evil. But I come of a race that never forgets or forgives; there is some of the blood of the wild Zingara coursing in these shrivelled veins—a love of vengeance, that is dearer than the love of life. I watched your love intrigue from the very first. I saw that it bade fair to end in happiness. Don Julio was wealthy and well born, and his intentions were honorable. After indulging your romantic spirit by a secret wooing, he would have openly claimed you of your father, and the old man would have been but too proud to give his consent. Now came the moment for revenge. I traduced you to your lover, making use of an agent who was wholly mine. Trifles produce conviction when once the faith of jealous man is shaken. A few toys—a turquoise bracelet, a lock of hair, a bunch of faded flowers—sufficed to turn the scale; and now, were an angel of heaven to pronounce you true, Don Julio would disbelieve the testimony. Ha, ha! am I not avenged?"

"And was it," said Magdalena, in a low, pathetic voice,—"was it for a few jests,—a little childish chafing against restraint, that you wrecked the happiness of a poor young girl,—blighted her hopes, and broke her heart? Woman—fiend! dare you tell me this?" she cried, kindling into passion with a sudden transition. "Avaunt! begone! Leave my sight, you hideous and evil thing! But take with you my bitter curse—no empty anathema! but one that will cling to you like the garment of flame that wraps the doomed heretic! Begone! accursed wretch—hideous in soul as you are abhorrent and repulsive in person."

Cowed, but muttering wrathful words, the stricken wretch hurried out of the apartment, into which Juanita instantly rushed.

"Magdalena, what means this?" she cried. "I heard you uttering fearful threats against old Margarita. Calm yourself; you are strangely excited."

"O Juanita, Juanita!" cried Magdalena, the tears starting from her eyes, and wringing her fair hands. "If you knew all—if you knew the wrong that woman has done me; but not now—not now; leave me, good cousin,—leave me!"

"You are not well, dearest," said Juanita; "take my advice, go to bed and repose. To-morrow you will be calm, and to-morrow you shall tell me all."

"To-morrow! to-morrow!" muttered Magdalena. "Well, well; to-morrow you will find me!"

"Yes; I will waken you, and sit at your bedside, and laugh your griefs away. Good night, Magdalena!"

"Farewell, dearest!" said the heart-stricken girl; and Juanita left the chamber.

Before a silver crucifix, Magdalena knelt in prayer.

"Father of mercies, blessed Virgin, absolve me of the sin—if sin it be to rush unbidden to the presence of my Judge! My burden is too great to bear!"

She rose from her knees, took from a cupboard a goblet of Venetian glass, and a flask of Xeres wine. Into the goblet she first dropped the contents of a paper she took from her bosom, and then filled it to the brim with wine. She had already stretched forth her hand to the fatal glass, when she heard her name called by her father.

"He would give me a good-night kiss," said the wretched girl. "I must receive it with pure lips. I come, dear father,—I come."

Scarcely had she left her chamber when the old duenna again stole into the room.

"If I could only find one of the gallant's letters," she muttered to herself, "I could arm her father's mind against her; and then if madam tried to get me turned away, she would have her labor for her pains. What have we here? A flask of Xeres, as I live! So ho, senorita! Is this the source of your inspiration when you berate your betters? I declare it smells good; the jade is no bad judge of wine!"

As she spoke, the old woman, who had no particular aversion to the juice of the grape, hurriedly drank off the contents of the goblet, and immediately filled it up again from the flask.

"There! she'll be no wiser," said she, with a cunning leer. "And now I must hurry off. I would not have the young baggage find me here for a month's wages!"

Margarita effected her retreat just in time. Magdalena returned, after having, as she supposed, seen her poor father for the last time.

Had not despair completely overmastered the reason of the poor girl, she would have shrunk from the idea of committing suicide. But misery had completely, though temporarily, wrecked her intellect. She felt no horror, no remorse at the deed she was about to commit. With a steady hand she raised the goblet to her lips, and then drank the fatal draught, as she supposed it, to the last dregs.

"I must sleep now," she said, with a deep sigh. "I shall never wake again." And throwing herself, dressed as she was, upon her couch, she soon fell into a deep slumber.

How long her senses were steeped in oblivion, she could not tell. But she was awakened by shrill screams, and started to her feet in terror.

"Where am I?" she exclaimed. "Are those the cries of the condemned? Am I indeed in another world?"

"But louder and louder came the shrieks, and now she recognized the tones as those of the old duenna. Deeply as the woman had wronged her, Magdalena's feminine nature could not be insensible to her distress. She sprang down the stairway, and now stood by the bedside of the duenna, over which Juanita was already bending.

"What *is* the matter?" she exclaimed.

"The wine! the wine! the flask of Xeres! the Venetian goblet! I am poisoned!" cried the old woman, as she writhed in agony.

The truth instantly flashed on the preternaturally-sharpened intellect of Magdalena. Her own immunity from pain confirmed the fatal supposition.

"Good God!" she cried, in tones of unutterable anguish, "I have killed her!"

The exclamation caught the keen ear of the malignant hag, suffering as she was. She raised herself up on her elbow, and pointing with her skinny finger to the horror-stricken girl, she screamed,—

"Yes, yes; you have murdered me! Send for a leech, a priest, an officer of justice! Do not let that wretch escape! She gave me a poisoned draught! she knew it—she confesses it! Ha, ha! I shall not die unavenged!"

These fearful words caught the ear of Don Antonio, as, having hastily dressed himself, he rushed into the room. They caught the ear, too, of a curious servitor, who flew to the alguazil before he summoned priest and chirurgeon.

In less than an hour afterwards, the old beldam had breathed her last, but not before she had made her false deposition to the officer of justice; not before she had learned that a paper containing evidence of poison had been found in Magdalena's room; not before she had seen the hapless girl arrested; and then she died with a lie and a smile of hideous triumph on her lips.

We cannot attempt to describe the anguish of the old goldsmith, and the despair of Juanita, as they beheld Magdalena torn from their arms to be carried before a judge for examination, and thence to be cast into prison. Believing in her innocence, and confident that it would be established in the eyes of the world, they longed for the dread ordeal of the trial. The hour came, but only to crush their hearts within them. The guilt was fixed by circumstantial evidence on the unfortunate Magdalena. Poor Juanita was forced to testify to the facts of a quarrel between her cousin and the hapless duenna, and to violent language used by the former to the latter. A paper which had contained poison had been found in the apartment of the accused. Her own hasty confession of guilt, the dying declaration of the victim added

"—confirmation strongAs proofs of Holy Writ."

Magdalena was condemned to die. In that supreme hour, when her protestations of innocence had proved of no avail, the film fell from the organs of her mental vision. Knowing herself guilty of premeditated suicide, she saw in the established charge of murder a dreadful retribution. To make her peace with Heaven in the solitude of the prison cell, was now all that she desired. She had proved the worthlessness of life, and now she prepared herself to die. But her tortures were not ended. Julio, her lost lover, demanded an interview with her, and when, after listening to her sad tale, he renewed his vows of love, and expressed his firm belief in her innocence, earth once more bloomed attractive to her eyes; life became again dear to her at the very moment she was condemned to surrender it. Her execution was fixed for the next day, at the hour of noon. At that hour, she was to take her last look of her father, her cousin, her lover—the last look of God's blessed earth.

The morning came. She had passed the night in prayer, and it found her firm and resigned. In the heart of a true woman there lies a reserve of courage that shames the prouder boast of man. She may not face death on the battle-field with the same defying front; but when it comes in a more appalling form and scene, she shrinks not from the dread ordeal. When man's foot trembles on the scaffold, woman stands there serene, unwavering, and self-sustained.

One hour before the appointed time, the door of Magdalena's cell opened, and a tall figure, wrapped in a dark cloak, with a slouched hat and sable plume, stood before her. It was the same who had gazed on her so often in the church of San Ildefonso, the same who had encountered Julio in the narrow street with proofs of her alleged falsity.

"Is the hour arrived?" asked Magdalena, calmly.

"Nay," replied the stranger, in a deep tone. "Can you not see the prison clock through the bars of your cell door? Look; it lacks yet an hour of noon."

"Then, sir, you come to announce the arrival of the holy father,—of my friends."

"They will be here anon," said the stranger.

"I do not," said Magdalena, in the same calm tone she had before employed, "see you now for the first time."

"Beautiful girl!" cried the stranger; "no! I have for months haunted you like your shadow. Your fair face threw the first gleams of sunshine into my heart that have visited it from early manhood. I love you, Magdalena!"

"This is no hour and no place for words like these," replied the captive, coldly.

"Nay!" cried the stranger, with sudden energy. "Beautiful girl, I come to save you!"

"To save me!" cried Magdalena, a sudden, wild hope springing in her breast,"—to save me! It is well done. Believe me, I am innocent. You have bribed the jailer to open my prison doors; you have contrived some means of evasion. I know not—I care not what. I shall be freed! I shall clasp my father's knees once more. I shall go forth into the blessed air and light of heaven. God bless you, whoever you are, for your words of hope!"

"You shall go forth, if you will," replied the stranger; "but openly, in the face and eyes of man. At my word the prison bars will fall, the keys will turn, the gates will be unbarred. I have a royal pardon!"

"Give it me! give it me!" almost shrieked Magdalena.

"It is bestowed on one condition: that you become my wife."

"That I become your wife!" repeated Magdalena, as if she but half comprehended the words. "Forsake poor Julio! And yet the bribe, to escape a death of infamy, to save my father's gray hairs from going down to a dishonored grave! Speak! who are you, with power to save me on these terms?"

The stranger tossed aside his sable hat and plume, and dropped his cloak, and stood before her in a rich dress of black velvet, trimmed with point lace, a broadsword belted to his waist. He was a man of middle age, of a fine, athletic figure, and handsome face, but there was an indescribable expression in his dark eyes, in the stern lines about his handsome mouth, that affected the gazer with a strange, shuddering horror.

"Peruse me well, maiden," said the stranger. "I am not deformed. I am as other men. If there be no glow in my cheek, still the blood that flows through my veins is healthy and untainted. Moreover, though I be not noble, my character is stainless. If to be the wife of an honest man is not too dear a purchase for your life, accept my hand, and you are saved."

"Who are you?" cried Magdalena, intense curiosity mastering her even in that moment.

"I am the executioner of Madrid!" replied the stranger.

Magdalena covered her face with her hands, and uttered a low cry of horror.

"I am the executioner of Madrid!" repeated he. "I have never committed crime in my life, though my blade has been reddened with the blood of my fellow-creatures. Yet no man takes my hand,—no man breaks bread or drinks wine with me. I, the dread minister of justice, a necessity of society, like the soldier on the rampart, or the priest at the altar, am a being lonely, abhorred, accursed. Yet I have the feelings, the passions of other men. But what maiden would listen to the suit of one like me? What father would give his daughter to my arms? None, none! And, therefore, the state decrees that when the executioner would wed, he must take to his arms a woman doomed to death. I loved you, Magdalena, hopelessly, ere I dreamed the hour would ever arrive when I might hope to claim you. That hour has now come. I offer you your life and my hand. You must be my bride, or my victim!"

"Your victim! your victim!" cried Magdalena. "Death a thousand times, though a thousand times undeserved, rather than your foul embrace!"

"You have chosen. Your blood be on your own head!" cried the executioner, stamping his foot. "You die unshriven and unblessed!"

"At least, abhorred ruffian," cried Magdalena, "I have some little time for preparation! The hour has not yet arrived."

"Has it not?" cried the executioner. "Behold yon clock!"

And as her eyes were strained upon the dial, he strode out of the cell, and seizing the hands, advanced them to the hour of noon. Then, at a signal from his hand, the prison bell began to toll.

"Mercy; mercy!" cried Magdalena, as he rejoined her. "Slay me not before my time!"

But the hand of the ruffian already grasped her arm, and he dragged her forth into the corridor.

At that moment, however, a loud shout arose, and a group of officials, escorting the goldsmith and Julio, waving a paper in his hand, rushed breathlessly along the passage.

"Saved, saved!" cried Magdalena. "Hither, hither, father, Julio!"

The executioner had wreathed his hand in her dark, flowing tresses; already his dreadful weapon was brandished in the air, when it was crossed by the bright Toledo blade of the young cavalier, and flew from his grasp, clanging against the prison wall.

"Unhand her, dog!" cried Julio, "or die the death!"

Sullenly the executioner released his hold, and sullenly listened to the royal pardon.

Magdalena was soon beneath her father's roof,—soon in the arms of her cousin Juanita. Long did she resist the importunities of Julio; for though innocent in fact, judicially she stood convicted of a capital offence. But as time rolled on,—as her innocence became the popular belief,—she finally relented, accepted his hand, and beneath the beautiful sky of Italy, forgot, or remembered only as a dream, the perils and sorrows of her early life.

PHILETUS POTTS.

A BIOGRAPHICAL SKETCH.

Philetus Potts is dead. Like Grimes, he was a "good old man!" A true gentleman of the old school, he clung to many of the fashions of a by-gone period with a pertinacity, which, to the eyes of the thoughtless, savored somewhat of the ludicrous. It was only of late years that he relinquished his three-cornered hat; to breeches, buckles, and hair powder he adhered to the last. He was also partial to pigtails, though his earliest was shorn from his head by a dangerous rival, who cut him out of the good graces of Miss Polly Martine, a powdered beauty of the past century, by amputating his cue; while his latest one was sacrificed on the altar of humanity—but thereby hangs a tale.

If Mr. Potts was behind his age in dress, he was in advance of it in sentiment. In his breast the milk of human kindness never curdled, and his intelligent mind was ever actively employed in devising ways and means to alleviate the sufferings of humanity, and to change the hearts of evil doers. His comprehensive kindness included the brute creation as well as mankind, in the circle of his active sympathy.

We remember an instance of his sympathy for animals. We had been making an excursion into the country. It was high noon of a sultry summer day; eggs were cooking in the sun, and the mercury in the thermometer stood at the top of the tube. Passing out of a small village, we passed a young lady pleasantly and coolly attired in white, and carrying a sunshade whose grateful shadow melted into the cool, clear olive of her fine complexion.

Mr. Potts sighed, for she reminded him of Miss Polly Martine at the same age; and Polly Martine reminded him of parasols by some recondite association. Mr. Potts remembered the first umbrella that was brought into Boston. He always carried one that might have been the first, it was so venerable, yet whole and decent, like an old gentleman in good preservation. It was a green silk one, with a plain, mahogany handle, and a ring instead of a ferrule, and very large. Discoursing of umbrellas, we came upon a cow. Mr. Potts was fond of cows—grateful to them—always spoke of them with respect. This particular cow inhabited a small paddock by the roadside, which was enclosed by a Virginia fence, and contained very little grass, and no provision for shade and shelter. So the cow stood in the sunshine, with her head resting on the fence, and her tongue lolling out of her mouth, and her large, intelligent eyes fixed on the far distance, where a herd of kine were feasting knee-deep in a field of clover, beside a running brook, overshadowed by magnificent walnut trees.

"Poor thing!" said Mr. Potts; and he stopped short and looked at the cow.

The cow looked at Mr. Potts. One had evidently magnetically influenced the other.

"She is a female, like the lady we encountered," said Mr. Potts, "but," added he, with a burst of feeling, "she has no parasol!"

The assertion was indisputable. It was a truism, cows are never provided with parasols,—but then great men are famous for uttering truisms, and we venerated Mr. Potts for following the example.

"It is now twelve o'clock!" said Mr. Potts, consulting his repeater. "At half past four, the shadow of the buttonwood will fall into this poor animal's pasture. Four hours and a half of torture, rendered more painful by the contemplation of the luxuries of her remote companions! It is insufferable!"

Then Mr. Potts, with a genial smile on his Pickwickian countenance, expanded his green silk umbrella, mounted the fence, on which he sat astride, and patiently held the umbrella over the cow's head for the space of four and a half mortal hours. The action was sublime. I regret to add that the animal proved ungrateful, and, when Mr. Potts closed his umbrella on the shadow of the buttonwood relieving guard, facilitated his descent from the Virginia fence by an ungraceful application of her horns to the amplitude of his venerable person.

It was in the summer following, that the incident I am about to relate occurred. It was fly-time,—I remember it well. We were again walking together, when we came to a wall-eyed horse, harnessed to a dog's meat cart, and left standing by his unfeeling master while he indulged in porter and pipes in a small suburban pothouse, much affected by Milesians. The horse was much annoyed by flies, and testified his impatience and suffering by stamping and tossing his head. Mr. Potts was the first to notice that the poor animal had no tail,—for the two or three vertebræ attached to the termination of the spine could hardly be supposed to constitute a tail proper. The discovery filled him with horror. A horse in fly-time without a tail! The case was worse than that of the cow.

"And here I am!" exclaimed the great and good man, in a tone of the bitterest self-reproach, "luxuriating in a pigtail which that poor creature would be glad of!"

With these words he produced a penknife, and placing it in my hands, resolutely bade me amputate his cue. I did so with tears in my eyes, and placed the severed ornament in the hands of my companion. With a piece of tape he affixed it to the horse's stump, and the gush of satisfaction he felt at seeing the first fly despatched by the ingenious but costly substitute for a tail, must have been, I think, an adequate recompense for the sacrifice.

I think it was in that same summer that Mr. Potts laid before the Philanthropic and Humane Society, of which he was an honorable and honorary member, his "plan for the amelioration of the condition of no-tailed horses in fly-time, by the substitution of feather dusters for the natural appendage, to which are added some hints on the grafting of tails with artificial scions, by a retired farrier in ill health."

During the last year of his life, Mr. Potts offered a prize of five thousand dollars for the discovery of a harmless and indelible white paint, to be used in changing the complexion of the colored population, to place them on an equality with ourselves, or for any chemical process which would produce the same result.

Mr. Potts proposed to substitute for capital punishment, houses of seclusion for murderers, where, remote from the world, in rural retreats, they might converse with nature, and in the cultivation of the earth, or the pursuit of botany, might become gradually softened and humanized. At the expiration of a few months' probation, he proposed to restore them to society.

A criminal is an erring brother. The object of punishment is reformation, and not vengeance. Hence, Mr. Potts proposed to supply our prisoners with teachers of languages, arts and sciences, dancing and gymnastics. Every prison should have, he contended, a billiard room and bowling saloon, a hairdresser, and a French cook. Occasionally, accompanied by proper officers, the convicts should be taken to the Italian Opera, or allowed to dance at Papanti's. The object would be so to refine their tastes that they should shrink from theft and murder, simply because they were ungentlemanly. Readmitted to society, these gentlemen would give tone to the upper classes.

But Mr. Potts has gone in the midst of his schemes of usefulness. The tailless quadruped, the shedless cow, the unwhitewashed African, the condemned felon, the unhappy prisoner, actually treated as if he were no gentleman, in him have lost a friend. When shall we see his like again? Echo answers, Probably not for a very long period.

THE GONDOLIER.

O, rest thee here, my gondolier,
Rest, rest, while up I go,
To climb yon light balcony's height
While thou keep'st watch below.
Ah! if high Heaven had tongues as well
As starry eyes to see—
O, think what tales 'twould hate to tell
Of wandering youths like me.

MOORE.

The traveller of to-day who visits Venice sees in that once splendid city nothing but a mass of mouldering palaces, the melancholy remains of former grandeur and magnificence; but few tokens to remind him that she was once the queen of the Adriatic, the emporium of Europe. But at the period of which we write the "sea Cybele" was in the very zenith of her brilliancy and power.

It was the season of carnival, and nowhere else in Italy were the holidays celebrated with such zest and magnificence. By night millions of lamps burned in the palace windows, rivalling the splendors of the firmament, and reflected in the still waters of the lagoons like myriads of stars. Night and day music was resounding. There were regattas, balls, and festas, and the entire population seemed to have gone mad with gayety, and to have lost all thought of the Council of Ten, the Bridge of Signs, and the poniards of the bravoes.

On a bright morning of this holiday season, a group of young gondoliers, attired in their gayest costume, were sitting at the head of a flight of marble steps that led up from one of the canals, waiting for their fares. A cavalier and lady, both gayly attired, and both masked, had just alighted from a gondola and passed the boatman on their way to some rendezvous.

The gondolier who had conducted them, an old, gray-headed, hard-looking fellow, had pocketed his fee, nodded his thanks, and pushed off again from the landing.

"There goes old Beppo," said one of the gondoliers on shore. "He will make a good day's work of it. I can swear I saw the glitter of gold in his hand just now."

"Yes, yes!" said another. "Let him alone for making his money. And what he makes, he keeps. He's a close-fisted old hunks."

"And what is he so scrimping and saving for?" asked a third. "He is unmarried—he has no children."

"No—but he is to be married," said the first.

"How! the man's past sixty."

"Yes, comrade, but he will not be the first old fellow who has taken a young wife in his dotage. Have you never heard that he has a young ward, beautiful as an angel, whom he keeps cooped up as tenderly as a brooding dove in his tumble-down old house on the Canal Orfano? Nobody but himself has ever set eyes on her to my knowledge."

"There you're mistaken, Stefano," said a young man, who had not hitherto spoken. He was a fine, dashing, handsome young fellow of twenty-six, in a holiday suit of crimson and gold, with a fiery eye, long, curling locks, and a mustache as black as jet.

"Let's hear what Antonio Giraldo has to say about the matter!" cried his companions.

"Simply this," said the young man. "I have seen the imprisoned fair one—the peerless Zanetta—for such is her name. She is lovely as the day; and for her voice—why—*Corpo di Bacco*! La Gianina, the prima donna, is a screechowl to *my* nightingale."

"*Your* nightingale! Bravo!" cried Stefano, in a tone of mocking irony. "What can you know about her voice?"

"Simply this, Master Stefano," replied the young gondolier. "When floating beneath her window in my gondola, I have addressed her in such rude strains of melody as I best knew how to frame. She has replied in tones so liquid and pure that the angels might have listened."

"By Heaven! the fellow's in love!" cried Stefano.

"Long live music and love!" cried Antonio. "What were life worth without them?"

"You're in excellent spirits!" cried Stefano.

"And why shouldn't a man be, on his wedding day?"

"Mad as a march hare," cried Stefano.

"Mark me," said Antonio. "That girl shall never marry old Beppo—my word for it. She hates him."

"She'll elope with some noble, then."

"To be cast off to wither when he is tired of her charms? No! the bridegroom for Zanetta is a gondolier."

"With all my heart," said Stefano. "But come, comrades, it is no use waiting here. Let us to our gondolas, and row for St. Marks. You'll come with us, Antonio."

"Not I—my occupation's gone."

"How so?"

"I have sold my gondola."

"Sold your gondola."

"Ay—that was my word."

"But why?"

"I wanted money."

"Your gondola was the means of earning it."

"Very true—but I had occasion for a certain sum at once."

"And why not have recourse to our purses, Antonio? Light as they are, we would have made it up by contributions among us."

"I doubted not your kindness—but my self-respect would not permit me to ask your aid. Good by, comrades; we shall meet again to-morrow."

"To-morrow. *Addio!*"

There was a brilliant masquerade that evening at the palazzo of Count Giulio Colonna. Invitations had been issued to all the world, and all the world was present. The finest music, the richest wines, the most splendid decorations were lavished on the occasion. Perhaps, among that brilliant company, there was more than one plebeian, who, under cover of the masque, and employing the license common at these saturnalia, had intruded himself unbidden.

Old Beppo, the gondolier, was in attendance at the vestibule of the palace, feasting his avaricious eyes on the glimpses of wealth and luxury he noted within doors, when a gentleman in rich costume, and wearing a mask, beckoned him to one side, and desired a moment's interview.

"Do you know me?" was the first question asked by the stranger.

"No, signor," replied the old gondolier.

"Do you know these gentlemen?" asked the mask, slipping a couple of gold pieces into the miser's hand.

"Perfectly," replied the boatman, grinning. "What are your lordship's commands?"

"Is your gondola in waiting?"

"Yes, signor. It lies below, moored to the landing."

"'Tis well; hast thou any scruples about aiding in a love intrigue?"

"None in the world, signor."

"Then I'll make a confidant of you."

"I will be all secrecy, signor."

"Briefly then, gondolier," said the mask, "I am in love with a very charming young person."

"Well."

"Well—and this young person loves me in return."

"Good; and you are going to marry her."

"Not so fast, gondolier. She has an old guardian, who, at the age of sixty, or more, has been absurd enough—only think of it—to propose to marry her himself."

"The absurd old fool!" cried Beppo, not without some twinges, for he thought of his own projects with regard to Zanetta.

"Now, then," said the mask, "I have resolved to run away with her to-night. I have the opportunity—for she is here in the Palazzo Colonna. Now will and can you aid me? I will recompense you liberally."

"Ah! my lord—your lordship has come to the right market," said the old sinner. "I'm used to affairs of this kind. Has your lordship a priest engaged?"

"I have not."

"Then I can recommend one. Hard by is a chapel dedicated to Our Lady, where there is a very worthy man, accustomed to affairs of this kind, who will tie the knot for a moderate fee, without asking any impertinent questions."

"His name?"

"Father Dominic."

"Good! he is the man for us—and you are the prince of gondoliers. Get your gondola ready, and I will rejoin you at the foot of the stairs with the lady in a moment."

Old Beppo hastened to prepare his gondola, and while so doing, muttered to himself,—

"Well, well—this is a good night's work. I'm getting old, and I must soon retire from business. Every stroke of luck like this helps on the day when I shall call Zanetta mine. So, there's another old fool to be duped to-night! Serve him right! Why don't he keep his treasure under lock and key, as I do? But men will never learn wisdom. Here they come."

The young cavalier reappeared upon the marble steps, leading a lady, masked and veiled, but whose elastic step and graceful bearing seemed to designate her as one moving in the highest circles. The young lovers took their seats in the centre of the light craft, and drew the curtains round them, while Beppo pushed off, and his vigorous oar soon sent the shallop dancing over the waters of the lagoon. After a few moments the motion ceased, and Beppo informed his patron that they had arrived at their place of destination. After making the boat fast, the gondolier landed, and entered the small chapel which stood on the brink of the canal. In a few moments he returned, and informed the masked cavalier that all was prepared. The gentleman then handed out the lady, and both entered the chapel, Beppo keeping guard without, to prevent or give notice of any intrusion.

The marriage ceremony was performed very rapidly by Father Dominic, for he was just going to bed when the gondola arrived, and was duly anxious to despatch his business, that he might consign his wearied limbs to rest.

"Is it all over?" whispered Beppo, in the ear of the cavalier, as he came out with his lady.

"All right," replied the mask, in the same tone of voice. "But one thing perplexes me. I have no place that I can call my home, to-night. The lady will be missed; my palace will be watched—I should incur the risk of swords crossing and bloodshed, if I sought to take her thither, to-night."

"If my house were not so very humble," said the gondolier, hesitatingly.

"The very thing," said the mask, joyfully. "No matter how humble the roof, provided that it shelter us. To-morrow we can arrange matters for flight, or for remaining."

"Then get into the gondola, my lord, and I will row you thither in a few minutes."

The party reëmbarked, and soon reached the gondolier's residence. After fastening his craft, he unlocked his door; and striking a light, conducted his distinguished guests up stairs. As he passed one of the chamber doors, the old gondolier, addressing the masked lady as he pointed to it, said,—

"You have made a moonlight flitting, to-night, signora, and I wish you joy of your escape. But if you had been as safely kept as a precious charge I have in this room, you would never have stood before the altar to-night, with your noble bridegroom."

"You forget that 'love laughs at locksmiths,'" said the cavalier.

At the door of their apartments, the old man, before bidding them good night, pausing, said,—

"Pardon me, signor, but I would fain know the name of the noble cavalier I have had the honor of serving to-night."

"You shall know to-morrow," replied the mask. "*Buona notte*, Beppo. Remember it's carnival time."

The next morning Beppo was up betimes, anxious to learn the mystery connected with the married couple. He was not kept long in suspense. His patron of the preceding evening soon made his appearance, but masked as before.

"Beppo!" said the stranger, "you rendered me an inestimable service last night."

"You rewarded me handsomely, signor, and I shall never regret it."

"Give me your word then, that you will never upbraid me with the service I imposed on you."

"I give you my word," said the old man, surprised; "but why do you exact it?"

"Because," said the stranger, raising his mask, "I am no Venetian noble, but simply Antonio Giraldi, a gondolier like yourself."

"You! Antonio Giraldi! And the lady—?"

"Was your ward, Zanetta. You locked her chamber door, and took the house key with you—but a ladder of ropes from a lady's balcony is as good as a staircase; and as I told you last night, 'love laughs at locksmiths.'"

Of course old Beppo stormed and swore, as irascible old gentlemen are very apt to do in similar circumstances, but he ended by forgiving the lovers, as that was the only act in his power. He not only forgave them, but gave up his gondola to the stronger hands of Antonio, and settled a handsome portion on Zanetta; nor did he ever regret his generosity, for they proved grateful and affectionate, and were the stay and solace of his declining years. Such is the veritable history of a carnival incident of the olden days of Venice.

THE SURRENDER OF CORNWALLIS.

A MILITARY SKETCH.

It was a great day for Dogtown, being no other than the anniversary of the annual militia muster; and on this occasion not only the Dogtown Blues were on parade upon the village green, but the entire regiment of which they formed a part, commanded by the gallant Colonel Zephaniah Slorkey, postmaster and variety-store keeper, was to engage in a sham fight, representing the surrender of Cornwallis. There was no attempt at historical costume, but it was understood that Slorkey, with his cowhide boots and rusty plated spurs, his long, swallow-tailed blue coat, and threadbare chapeau with a cock's tail feather in it, mounted on his seventy-five dollar piebald mare, promoted from the plough and "dump cart," was the representative of General Washington. Major Israel Ryely, his second in command, a native of the rival village of Hardscrabble, was to figure as Lord Cornwallis; and the selection was the more appropriate, since the private relations of these two great men were any thing but amicable, and they espoused opposite sides in politics. Dr. Galenius Jalap, an apothecary and surgeon of the regiment, a man with a hatchet face, hook nose, and thin, weeping whiskers, the color of sugar gingerbread, undertook the character of La Fayette at very short notice, and a very dim conception of the character he had.

The entire population of Dogtown and Hardscrabble turned out to witness the stupendous military operations of the day. On the American side were the Dogtown Blues, with four companies of ununiformed militia, armed with rifles, fowling pieces, and rusty muskets, and typifying the continental army. Their artillery consisted of two light field pieces, served by a select band of volunteers. These pieces were posted on an eminence commanding the entire plain. At the foot of this hill, Colonel Slorkey drew up his troops in line of battle, his left wing protected by an impassable frog pond, and his right resting on a large piggery, whose extent prevented the enemy from turning his flank in that direction.

On the descent of an opposing eminence, likewise strengthened by two guns, Major Ryely placed the Hardscrabble Guards, the Sheet Iron Riflemen, the Mudhollow Invincibles, the Dandelion Fireeaters, and the Scrufftown Sharpshooters. A thousand bright eyes, from the commanding eminences, looked down on the serried ranks of bayonets, the brazen-throated artillery, the panoplied plough horses, the plumed commanders, the rustling banners, and all the "pomp, pride, and circumstance of glorious war."

Preliminaries being thus settled, the commanding officers put spurs to their horses, and met in the centre of the plain, there saluting with their scythe-blade swords.

"Major Ryely," said the colonel, rising in his stirrups, "the follerin' are the odder of pufformances: we open with eour artillery—you reply with yourn. Under kiver of eour guns we advance to the attack. You do the same to meet us—firin' like smoke. Arter a sharp scrimmedge you retire—send us a flag of truce with terms—and finally lay down your arms."

The major bowed till his ostrich feather touched the mane of his wall-eyed plough horse, then turned bridle, and regained his ranks at a gait something between a stumble and a rack. The representative of General Washington rejoined his men at a hard trot, rising two feet from his saddle at every concussion of his bony steed.

"Fellur sogers!" roared the temporary father of his country; "yonder stands Cornwallis and his redcoats—only they haint got red coats, partickerlarly them in blue swaller-tails. We air bound to lick 'em—hurrah for our side! Go inter 'em like a thousand of bricks fallin' off 'n a slated rufe. The genius of Ammerikin liberty, in the shape of the carnivorous eagle, soarin' aloft on diluted pillions, seems to mutter *E Pluribus Unum*—we are one of 'em! Hail Columby happy land! Sing Yankee Doodle that fine tune—cry havock! and let looset the dogs of war."

Then commenced the horror of the sham fight. The continental guns opened in thunder tones. The British artillery hurled back their terrific echoes. Bang! bang! boom! boom! The canopy of heaven was stained with the sulphurous smoke. The drummers rattled away on their sheepskins—the fifers distended their cheeks till they resembled blown bladders. In the midst of all this noise and tumult, the undaunted Slorkey, and the indomitable Jalap, rushed to and fro, with clanking scabbards, and brandished scythe blades, twin thunderbolts of war.

"Forrard march!" roared Slorkey. With the yell of demons, his fierce followers advanced to the onset, firing their blank cartridges with desperate valor.

Equally alert were Major Ryely and his followers.

"Their swords were a thousand, their bosoms were one."

Their faces begrimed with powder, their eyes gleaming with ferocity, they descended to the plain—an avalanche of heroes. The soul of Headly would have swelled within him had he seen them.

For more than one hour that deadly consumption of blank cartridges endured, and then Ryely and his troops retired in good order.

"Boys," said the major, "old Slorkey wants us to gin out—send a flag of truce—a white pocket handkerchief on a beanpole—and propose to surrender. But it goes agin my grit for Hardscrabble to cave in to Dogtown, when we could knock the hindsights off 'em, if we was only a mind to."

"Hurray for the major!" responded the Hardscrabblers.

"I've got a grudge agin the kurnil," said the major, "and if you'll stand by me, I'll take it out of 'em. What say?"

"Agreed!" was the spontaneous response.

While Slorkey was waiting for the covenanted flag of truce, he saw the hated Ryely rise in his stirrups, and heard his stentorian voice roar out the word, "Charge!"

A deafening shout answered his appeal. In an instant Hardscrabble and its allies were down on Dogtown and its defenders. The latter stood it for a moment, but Ryely knocked the colonel off his horse, the surgeon had his nose pulled, the Dogtown Blues justified their name by their looks, and, seized with a sudden panic, fled—fled ingloriously from their native training field. The audacious outrage was consummated—history was violated—and General Washington was beaten by Cornwallis.

Dire were the threats against Ryely uttered by the colonel, as he was carried home on a shutter; nothing short of a court martial was his slightest menace. But no court martial ever took place. The military pride and glory of Dogtown were wounded to the quick; the force of popular opinion compelled Slorkey to resign, and to consummate his chagrin, his treacherous rival was chosen colonel of the regiment. So unstable are human honors— so ungrateful are republics.

THE THREE BRIDES.

Towards the close of a chilly afternoon, in the latter part of last November, I was travelling in New Hampshire on horseback. The road was solitary and rugged, and wound along through gloomy pine forests and over abrupt and stony hills. Several circumstances conduced to my discomfort. I was not sure of my way; I had a hurt in my bridle hand, and evening was approaching, heralded by an icy rain and a cold, searching wind. I felt a sinking of spirits which I could not dispel by rapid riding; for my horse, fatigued by a long day's journey, refused to answer spur and whip with his usual animation. In an hour after, I was convinced that I had mistaken my road, and night surprised me in the forest. I had been in more unpleasant situations; so I adopted my usual expedient of letting the reins fall upon my courser's neck. He, however, blundered on, with his nose drooping to the ground, stumbling every moment, though ordinarily as surefooted as a roebuck. So we plodded on for a mile, while the landscape grew darker and darker. At length, finding my horse less intelligent or more despairing than myself, I resumed the rein, and endeavored to cheer my brute companion. To tell the truth, I stood in need of something exhilarating myself. The sombre air of the eternal pines struck a deathly gloom to my heart, as one by one they seemed to rise on my path, like threatening genii extending their scathed limbs to meet me. The rain, fine and cold, bedewed me from head to foot, and I question if a more miserable pair of animals ever threaded their way through the mazes of an enchanted forest. I thought of the comfortable home I had left for my forlorn pleasure excursion, of that cheerful hearth around which my family were gathered, of wine, music, love, and the thousand endearments I had left behind, and then I gazed into the recesses of the shadowy wood that closed about me, almost in despair. I began to dread the apparition of some giant intruder, and was seriously meditating the production of a pair of pistols, when my quick glance caught the glimmer of distant lights, twinkling through some opening in the trees, and darting a beam of hope upon the wanderer's soul. My reins were instantly grasped, and my rowels were struck into the sides of my charger. He snorted, pricked up his ears, erected his head, and sprang forth in an uncontrollable gallop. Up hill and down hill I pricked my gallant gray; and when the forest was past, and his hoofs glinted on the stones of a street leading through a small village, I felt an animation that I cannot well describe. A creaking signboard, swinging in the wind on rusty irons, directed me to the only inn of the village. It was a two-story brick building, standing a little back from the road. I drew rein at the door, and dismounted my weary nag. My loud vociferations summoned to my side a bull dog, cursed with a most unhappy disposition, and a hostler whose temper was hardly more amiable. He took my horse with an air of surly indifference, and gruffly directed me to the bar room.

This apartment was tenanted by half a dozen rough farmers, rendered savage and morose by incessantly imbibing alcohol; and by the proprietor of the tavern, a bluff man, with a portly paunch, a hard gray eye, and a stern Caledonian lip. He welcomed me without much frankness or cordiality, and I sank into a wooden settle, eyed by the surly guests of mine host, and the subject of sundry muttered remarks. The group, as it was lighted up by the strong red glare of the fire, had certainly a bandit appearance, which, however delightful to a Salvator Rosa, was by no means inviting to a traveller who had sought the bosom of the hills for pleasure. After making a few remarks, which elicited only monosyllables in answer, I relapsed into silence; from which, however, I was soon aroused by the entrance of the surly hostler, who in no very gracious manner informed me that my horse was lame, and likely to be sick. This intelligence produced a visit to the stable, and the conviction that I could not possibly resume my journey on the ensuing day; which was somewhat disagreeable to a man who had taken up a decided prejudice against the inn and all its inmates.

Having succeeded in procuring a private room and a fire, I ignited an execrable cigar, (ah, how unlike thy *principes*, dear S.,) and endeavored to lose myself in the agreeable occupation of castle building while supper was preparing. Alas! my fancy came not at my call. I had lost my power of abstraction—the realities around me were too engrossing. Ere the dying shriek of a majestic rooster had ceased to sound in my ear, his remains were served upon my table, together with a cup or two of very villanous gunpowder tea, and a pitcher of cider, with coarse bread and butter *ad libitum*. Supper was soon despatched, and in answer to a bell, lightly touched, a vinegar-visaged waiting-maid, of the interesting age of forty-five, entered and removed the scarcely touched viands—the *rudis indigestaque moles*. I ventured to address her, with a request that I might be supplied with a few books, to enable me to while away the evening. I anticipated a literary feast from the readiness with which she rushed from the room; but she reappeared, bringing only Young's Night Thoughts, (very greasy,) a volume of tales with the catastrophes torn out, a set of plays consisting only of first acts, and an odd number of the Eclectic Magazine. This was sufficiently provoking; but I read a few pages, and tried a second cigar, and made the tour of the apartment, examining a family mourning-piece worked in satin, a genealogical tree done in worsted, and a portrait of the mutton-headed landlord and his snappish wife. I counted the ticks of the clock for half an hour, and was finally reduced to the forlorn expedient of seeing likenesses in the burning embers. When the clock struck nine, I rang for slippers and a guide to my bed room, and the landlord appeared, candle in hand, to usher me to my sleeping apartment. As I followed him up the creaking staircase, and along the dark upper entry, I could not help regretting that fancy was unable to convert him into the seneschal of a baronial mansion, and the room to which I was going a haunted chamber. It seemed as if my surly host had the power of divining what was passing in my mind, for when he had ushered me into the room, and placed the candle on the light stand, he said,—

"I hope you'll sleep comfortable, for there ain't many rats here, sir. And as for the ghost they say frequents this chamber, I believe that's all in my eye, though, to be sure, the window does look out on the burial ground."

"Umph! a comfortable prospect."

"Very, sir; you have a fine view of the squire's new tomb and the poorhouse, with a wing of the jail behind the trees. And I've stuck my second-best hat in that broken pane of glass, and there's a chest of drawers to set against the door; so you'll be warm and free from intrusion. I wish you good night, sir."

All that night I was troubled with strange dreams, peopled by phantoms from the neighboring churchyard; but a *bona fide* ghost I cannot say I saw. In the morning I rose very early, and took a look from the window, but the prospect was very uninviting. The churchyard was a bleak, desolate place, overgrown with weeds, and studded with slate stones, bounded by a ruinous brick wall, and having an entrance through a dilapidated gateway. One or two melancholy-looking cows were feeding on the rank herbage that sprang from the unctuous soil, spurning many a *hic jacet* with their cloven hoofs. But afar, in the most distant part of the field, I espied the figure of a man who was busily occupied in digging a grave. There was something within that impelled me to stroll forth and accost him. I dressed, descended, and having ordered breakfast, left the inn, clambered over the ruinous wall, and stood within the precincts of the burial-place. The spot had evidently been used for the purposes of sepulture for a number of years, for the ground rose into numerous hillocks, and I could hardly walk a step without stumbling upon some grassy mound. Even where the perishable gravestones had been shattered by the hand of time, the length of the elevations enabled me to judge of the age of the deceased. This slight swell rose over the remains of some beloved child, who had been committed to the dust with only the simple ceremonies of the Protestant faith, bedewed by the tears of parents, and blessed by the broken voice of farewell affection. This mound, of larger dimension, was heaped above the giant frame of manhood. Some sturdy tiller of the soil, or rough dweller in the forest, perhaps cut off by a sudden casualty, had been laid here in his last leaden sleep—no more to start at the rising beam of the sun, no more to rush to the glorious excitement of the hunt, no more to pant in noonday toil. Over the whole field of the dead there seemed to brood the spirit of desolation. Stern heads, rudely chiselled, from the grave stones, and frightful emblems met the eye at every turn. Here was none of that simple elegance with which modern taste loves to invest the memorials of the departed; no graceful acacias, or nodding elms, or sorrowing willows shed their dews upon the turf—every thing spoke of the bitterness of parting, of the agony of the last hour, of the passing away from earth—nothing of the reunion in heaven!

I passed on to where the grave digger was pursuing his occupation. He answered my morning salutation civilly enough, but continued intent upon his work. He was a man of about fifty years of age, spare, but strong, with gray hair, and sunken cheeks, and certain lines about the mouth which augured a propensity to indulge in dry jest, though the sternness of his gray eye seemed to contradict the tacit assertion.

"An unpleasant morning, sir, to work in the open air," said I.

"He that regardeth the clouds shall not reap," replied the grave digger, still plying his spade. "Death stalks abroad fair day and foul day, and we that follow in his footsteps must prepare for the dead, rain or shine."

"A melancholy occupation."

"A fit one for a moralist. Some would find a pleasure in it. Deacon Giles, I am sure, would willingly be in my place now."

"And why so?"

"This grave is for his wife," replied the grave digger, looking up from his occupation with a dry smile that wrinkled his sallow cheek and distorted his shrunken lips. Perceiving that his merriment was not infectious, he resumed his employment, and that so assiduously, that in a very short time he had hollowed the last resting-place of Deacon Giles's consort. This done, he ascended from the trench with a lightness that surprised me, and walking a few paces from the new-made grave, sat down upon a tombstone, and beckoned me to approach. I did so.

"Young man," said he, "a sexton and a grave digger, if he is one who has a zeal for his calling, becomes something of an historian, amassing many a curious tale and strange legend concerning the people with whom he has to do, living and dead. For a man with a taste for his profession cannot provide for the last repose of his fellows without taking an interest in their story, the manner of their death, and the concern of the relatives who follow their remains so tearfully to the grave."

"Then," replied I, taking a seat beside the sexton, "methinks you could relate some interesting tales."

Again the withering smile that I had before observed passed over the face of the sexton, as he answered,—

"I am no story teller, sir; I deal in fact, not fiction. Yes, yes, I could chronicle some strange events. But of all things I know, there is nothing stranger than the melancholy history of the three brides."

"The three brides?"

"Ay. Do you see three hillocks yonder, side by side? There they sleep, and will till the last trumpet comes wailing and wailing through the heart of these lone hills, with a tone so strange and stirring, that the dead will start from their graves at its first awful note. Then will come the judgment and the retribution. But to my tale. Look there, sir; on yonder hill you may observe a little isolated house, with a straggling fence in front, and a few stunted apple trees on the ascent behind it. It is sadly out of repair now, and the garden is all overgrown with weeds and brambles, and the whole place has a desolate appearance. If the wind were high now, you might hear the old crazy shutters flapping against the sides, and the wind tearing the gray shingles off the roof. Many years ago, there lived in that house an old man and his son, who cultivated the few acres of arable land which belong to it.

"The father was a self-taught man, deeply versed in the mysteries of science, and, as he could tell the name of every flower that blossomed in the wood and grew in the garden, and used to sit up late of nights at his books, or reading the mystic story of the starry heavens, men thought he was crazed or bewitched, and avoided him, and even hated him, as the ignorant ever shun and dread the gifted and enlightened. A few there were, and among others the minister, and lawyer, and physician of the place, who showed some willingness to afford him countenance; but they soon dropped his acquaintance, for they found the old man somewhat reserved and morose, and, moreover, their vanity was wounded by discovering the extent of his knowledge. To the minister he would quote the Fathers and the Scriptures in the original tongues and showed himself well armed with the weapons of polemical controversy. He astonished the lawyer by his profound acquaintance with jurisprudence; and the physician was surprised at the extent of his medical knowledge. So they all deserted him, and the minister, from whom the old man differed in some trifling points of doctrine, spoke very slightingly of him; and by and by all looked upon the self-educated farmer with eyes of aversion. But he little cared for that, for he derived his consolation from loftier resources, and in the untracked paths of science found a pleasure as in the pathless woods! He instructed his son in all his lore—the languages, literature, history, philosophy, science, were unfolded, one by one, to the enthusiastic son of the solitary. Years rolled away, and the old man died. He died when a storm convulsed the face of nature, when the wind howled around his shattered dwelling, and the lightning played above the roof; and though he went to heaven in faith and purity, the vulgar thought and said that the evil one had claimed his own in the thunder and commotion of the elements. I cannot paint to you the grief of the son at his bereavement. He was, for a time, as one distracted. The minister came and muttered a few cold and hollow phrases in his ear, and a few neighbors, impelled by curiosity to see the interior of the old man's dwelling, came to his funeral. With a proud and lofty look the son stood beside the departed in the midst of the band of hypocritical mourners, with a pang at his heart, but a serenity on his brow. He thanked his friends for their kindness, acknowledged their courtesy, and then strode away from the grave to bury his grief in the privacy of his deserted dwelling.

"He found, at first, the solitude of the mansion almost insupportable, and he paced the echoing floors from morning till night, in all the agony of woe and desolation, vainly imploring Heaven for relief. It came to him first in the guise of poetic inspiration. He wrote with a wonderful ease and power. Page after page came from his prolific pen, almost without an effort; and there was a time when he dreamed (vain fool!) of immortality. Some of his productions came before the world. They were praised and circulated, and inquiries were set on foot in the hope of discovering the author. He, wrapped in the veil of impenetrable obscurity, listened to the voice of applause, more delicious because it was obtained by stealth. From the obscurity of yonder lone mansion, and from this remote region, to send forth lays which astonished the world, was, indeed, a triumph to the visionary bard.

"His thirst for fame was gratified, and now he began to yearn for the companionship of some sweet being of the other sex, to share the laurels he had won, to whisper consolation in his ear in moments of despondency, and to supply the void which the death of his old father had occasioned. He would picture to himself the felicity of a refined intercourse with a highly intellectual and beautiful woman, and, as he had chosen for his motto, *What has been done may still be done*, he did not despair of success. In this village lived three sisters, all beautiful and all accomplished. Their names were Mary, Adelaide, and Madeleine. I am far enough past the age of enthusiasm, but never can I forget the beauty of those young girls. Mary was the youngest, and a fairer-haired, more laughing damsel never danced upon a green. Adelaide, who was a few years older, was dark haired and pensive; but of the three, Madeleine, the eldest, possessed the most fire, spirit, cultivation, and intellectuality. Their father was a man of taste and education, and, being somewhat above vulgar prejudices, permitted the visits of the hero of my story. Still he did not altogether encourage the affection which he found springing up between Mary and the poet. When, however, he found that her affections were engaged, he did not withhold his consent from her marriage, and the recluse bore to his solitary mansion the young bride of his affections. O sir, the house assumed a new appearance within and without. Roses bloomed in the garden, jessamines peeped through its lattices, and the fields about it smiled with the effects of careful cultivation. Lights were seen in the little parlor in the evening, and many a time would the passenger pause by the garden gate to listen to strains of the sweetest music, breathed by choral voices from the cottage. If the mysterious student and his wife were neglected by their neighbors, what cared they? Their endearing and mutual affection made their home a little paradise. But death came to Eden. Mary fell suddenly sick, and, after a few hours' illness, died in the arms of her husband and her sister Madeleine. This was the student's second heavy affliction.

"Days, months, rolled on, and the only solace of the bereaved was to sit with the sisters of the deceased, and talk of the lost one. To Adelaide, at length, he offered his widowed heart. She came to his lone house like the dove, bearing the olive branch of peace and consolation. Their bridal was not one of revelry and mirth, for a sad recollection brooded over the hour. Yet they lived happily; the husband again smiled, and, with a new spring, the roses again blossomed in their garden. But it seemed as if a fatality pursued this singular man. When the rose withered and the leaf fell, in the mellow autumn of the year, Adelaide, too, sickened and died, like her younger sister, in the arms of her husband and of Madeleine.

"Perhaps you will think it strange, young man, that, after all, the wretched survivor stood again at the altar. But he was a mysterious being, whose ways were inscrutable, who, thirsting for domestic bliss, was doomed ever to seek and never to find it. His third bride was Madeleine. I well remember her. She was a beauty, in the true sense of the word. It may seem strange to you to hear the praise of beauty from such lips as mine; but I cannot help expatiating upon hers. She might have sat upon a throne, and the most loyal subject, the proudest peer, would have sworn the blood within her veins had descended from a hundred kings. She was a proud creature, with a tall, commanding form, and raven tresses, that floated, dark and cloud-like, over her shoulders. She was a singularly-gifted woman, and possessed of rare inspiration. She loved the widower for his power and his fame, and she wedded him. They were married in that church. It was on a summer afternoon—I recollect it well. During the ceremony, the blackest cloud I ever saw overspread the heavens like a pall, and, at the moment when the *third bride* pronounced her vow, a clap of thunder shook the building to the centre. All the females shrieked, but the bride herself made the response with a steady voice, and her eyes glittered with wild fire as she gazed upon her bridegroom. He remarked a kind of incoherence in her expressions as they rode home-ward, which surprised him at the time. Arrived at his house, she shrunk upon the threshold: but this was the timidity of a maiden. When they were alone he clasped her hand—it was as cold as ice! He looked into her face.

"Madeleine," said he, "what means this? your cheeks are as pale as your wedding gown!" The bride uttered a frantic shriek.

"My wedding gown!" exclaimed she; "no, no—this—this is my sister's shroud! The hour for confession has arrived. It is God that impels me to speak. To win you I have lost my soul! Yes—yes—I am a murderess! She smiled upon me in the joyous affection of her young heart—but I gave her the fatal drug! Adelaide twined her white arms about my neck, but I administered the poison! Take me to your arms: I have lost my soul for you, and mine must you be!"

"She spread her long, white arms, and stood like a maniac before him," said the sexton, rising, in the excitement of the moment, and assuming the attitude he described; "and then," continued he, in a hollow voice, "at that moment came the thunder and the flash, and the guilty woman fell dead upon the floor!" The countenance of the narrator expressed all the horror that he felt.

"And the bridegroom," asked I; "the husband of the destroyer and the victims—what became of him?"

"*He stands before you!*" was the thrilling answer.

CALIFORNIA SPECULATION.

Mose Jenkins did not take the California fever when it first broke out; for he was, as he acknowledged himself, "slow-motioned," and his skull was of such formidable thickness, that it required a good many months for an idea to penetrate into his brain. In the interim, he delved and digged away on a corner of his father's farm, having leased the land of the old gentleman, and purchased his time of the same respectable individual for the purpose of working it. But to work a farm where the rocks are so near together, that the sheep's noses have to be sharpened before they can graze between them, is not a very profitable business; and Mose, by dint of hard thinking, arrived at the conclusion that there might possibly be some other occupation less laborious and quite as lucrative.

"Confound these granite rocks!" he exclaimed, one day, as he was ploughing, after he had broken his trace chains for a second time; "they hev another kind er rocks in Calliforny. Jehosaphat! If I was only *thar*. There a fellur hez to dig; but he gets pretty good wages—five thousand dollars a month is middlin', not to say fair."

In short, Mose Jenkins made up his mind to go to San Francisco, having got the wherewithal to carry him in a packet to the land of promise. Fearful of opposition, he communicated his project neither to the author of his days, the venerable Zephaniah Jenkins, nor to the beloved of his heart, Miss Prudence Salter, a cherry-cheeked damsel in a state of orphanage; but wrote down to a friend in Boston to secure a passage. He reserved his communications to the very last moment, when he was all ready for starting. His father gave him his blessing; Prudence was more difficult to manage.

"It's a breach of promise case," said she, "I don't believe you mean to marry me arter all."

"Yes, I do, ye silly critter," said Mose. "I'll come and make you Mrs. Jenkins; but I want to get the rocks first."

"Ain't there rocks enough here?" asked Prudence, simply.

"Pooh! I mean the rocks what folks carries in their pockets, an' treats every body with—all sollid gold."

"I don't believe half them stories," said Prudence, contemptuously.

"They're as true as gospil," said Mose, "'cause I see it in a paper. And there's Curnil Hateful Slowboy, that went from here last year—you'd ort to know him, Prudence, coz he was one of your old beaux—wall, now, they say he's one of the richest men in Calliforny. I tell you I'm bound to make my fortin' there."

"And so am I," said Prudence, resolutely.

"You!" exclaimed Mose.

"Yes. I'm bound to go, too; and I'll follow you in the next ship, else you'll be green enough to marry one of them 'ere Ingine gals."

"Prudence, you're spunk!" exclaimed Mose, in terms of the warmest admiration. "Good by! And I swow I'll marry you jest as soon as you set foot in Calliforny."

Not to amplify on details, our adventurer landed there safely, and was, of course, like all verdant voyagers, much surprised at the tariff of prices subjected to his notice. The porter who carried his trunk to the hotel charged him ten dollars; and though that same hotel was a leaky tent, a plate of tough beef was charged seventy-five cents, and a watery potato fifty. Business was very dull, too, at the moment of his arrival; the accounts from the mines were disastrous, and every thing announced an approaching crisis. Moses confided his griefs to Colonel Hateful Slowboy, his fellow-townsman, who was really one of the richest men in California, winding up with lamentations over the expected arrival of Prudence, whom he had promised to marry.

"What kin I do with a wife," said he, "when I can't support myself, even?"

"Very true," said the colonel. "Now, if it were me, the case would be very different."

"Prudence done all the courtin' herself, curnil," said our hero, sulkily. "I never should have offered if it hadn't been for her. I kinder like 'er pretty well, though: she's a sort of pretty nice gal."

"Well, Mose," said the colonel, "what do you say to giving up your claim?"

"Eh?" said Mose, pricking up his ears.

"What'll you take for your right and title—cash down—no questions asked?"

"Wall, I dunnow," said Mose, opening his jackknife and picking up a chip. "Prudence is a pretty nice gal, as you said, curnil."

"As *you* said, Mr. Jenkins."

"Wall, it's all the same. The critter's very fond of me and so be I of her. I had plaguy hard work, I tell you, to get her consent."

"Come, come," said the colonel, "you want to drive a hard bargain with me. I'm willing to give you a fair price, say twenty thousand; but I don't want to be swindled."

"Say twenty-five thousand and take her, curnil."

"No—twenty."

"Cash down?"

"Cash down."

"Done."

"The money's ready whenever Prudence is."

In a few days another ship from Boston came in, and Prudence was among the first to land. Mose met her with very little ardor, the colonel remaining in the background. After some little conversation, the young lady reminded her lover of their agreement.

"I can't do it, Prudence; I've swore off—I've jined the old bachelor society."

"But you promised me," screamed Prudence.

"Can't help that; you can't get a verdict here for breaches of promise; there ain't no law here; every body goes on his own individual hook."

"You cruel monster, why can't you marry me?"

"'Cause."

"'Cause what?"

"'Cause," said Mose, retreating to a safe distance, "*I've traded you away!*"

Colonel Slowboy was at hand to catch the fair one as she came near falling. He was her old beau, and he knew the weak points of her character; moreover he had splendid red whiskers and a million of money—she married him, partly from ambition and partly from revenge.

The moment they were united, Moses set sail for the United States, with his twenty thousand dollars, and arrived back safely. When asked how he had accumulated such a sum in so short a time, he answered, "trading," and when questioned about the prospects of the El Dorado, would answer, with a grin, that it was a "great country for women." And this was the end of his California speculation.

THE FRENCH GUARDSMAN.

With the army of Marshal Saxe, encamped near Fontenoy ready to give battle to the allies, there were not a few ladies, who, impelled by a chivalric feeling, or personally interested in the fate of some of the combatants, had followed the troops to witness the triumph of the French arms. Their presence was at once the incitement and reward of valor, for what soldier would not fight with tenfold gallantry when he knew that his exploits were witnessed by the eyes of her he loved as wife, mistress, or mother, and whose safety or honor, perhaps, depended on his prowess?

Among those most distinguished for their beauty was the youthful Heloise, the lovely daughter of the Baron de Clairville, a French general officer. The *beaux yeux* of the demoiselle had enslaved more than one young officer, but of the host of suitors none could boast with reason of encouragement, except Henri de Grandville, and Raoul, Count de St. Prix, both commanding companies in the French Guards. Both were handsome and accomplished young men, and both had yet their spurs to win upon the field of battle. They had been fast friends until the pursuit of the same lady had created a sort of estrangement between them. Little was known of Henri de Grandville previous to his reception of his commission in the guards. He had been brought up by his mother in an old provincial chateau, and though his manners and education were those of a gentleman, still he seemed but little acquainted with the world, and above all ignorant of the lighter accomplishments of the courtier. Perhaps this very simplicity of manner and frankness of character, contrasting so strangely with the fashionable affectations of the court, endeared him to his comrades, and strongly prepossessed Heloise de Clairville in his favor. His rival was of a different stamp. Raoul de St. Prix was a dashing, brilliant officer, brave as steel, but fond of dress, reckless, dissipated, and extravagant. Yet his faults were those of his age, and belonged to the circumstances by which he was surrounded. The Baron de Clairville, while he left his daughter free to make her election, yet, as a plain, blunt soldier, rather than a courtier, secretly inclined to favor the pretensions of Henri. Still, his treatment of the two young guardsmen was the same, for they gave equal promise of military gallantry.

It was on the eve of the battle of Fontenoy that Henri sought an interview with Heloise, who occupied a gay pavilion near her father's tent. He found her alone and weeping.

"Mademoiselle," said he, "you are unhappy. Will you permit a friend to inquire the cause of your sorrow?"

"Can you ask me, Monsieur de Grandville! Of the thousands of brave men who lie down to-night in peaceful slumber, how many sleep their last sleep on earth! How many eyes, that will witness to-morrow's sun arise, will be closed forever before it goes down at evening! O, what a dreadful business is this trade of war! My poor father, he never cares for himself, he never asks his men to go where he is unwilling to lead. I fear for his safety in the deadly conflict of to-morrow."

"If the devotion of one faithful follower can save him, lady," answered Henri, "be assured of his safety. I would pour out the blood in my veins as freely as water to shield the father of Heloise de Clairville."

"But you—you—Henri—Monsieur de Grandville—you think nothing of your own life."

"If I fall," answered the young soldier, "my poor mother will weep bitterly for her only son, though he perish on the field of honor. But who else will shed a tear for the poor guardsman?"

"Henri!" exclaimed the young girl, reproachfully, and the soft eyes she raised to his were filled with tears.

"Is it possible?" cried the young soldier. "Can my fate awaken even a momentary interest in the heart of the loveliest, the gentlest of her sex? Ah, why do you render life so dear to me at the moment I must peril it?"

"Believe me," answered Heloise, drying her tears, "that I would not hold you back, when honor beckons you. It is to such hands as yours that the honor of the golden lilies is committed. I am the daughter of a soldier, and though these tears confess my sex, I honor bravery when it is displayed in a good cause. I honor the soldier as much as I detest the duellist."

"Then listen to one whose sword was never stained with his brother's blood. I had thought to go to the field with my secret concealed in my own breast, but something impels me to speak out. I love you, Heloise—I have dared to love—to adore you."

The fair girl blushed till her very temples were crimsoned over with eloquent blood. The young soldier threw himself at her feet, and taking the fair hand she abandoned to him, covered it with kisses; nor did he rise till he had received confirmation of his new-born hopes, and knew that, for good or ill, the heart of Heloise was irrevocably his. Finally, he was compelled to tear himself away, but he carried to his tent a feeling of delicious joy which steeled his mind against all thought of the chances of the morrow.

The moments passed away in delirious revery, but at length he was interrupted by St. Prix.

The count was in the worst of humors—his brow was dark with passion, and he threw himself into a seat, and flung his plumed hat on the table with an energy that betrayed the violence of his emotions.

"What's the matter, Raoul?" asked Henri. "Has Saxe changed his plans? Do we fall back instead of advancing?"

"No, thank God! there will be plenty of throat-cutting to-morrow, and the French Guards have the post of honor."

"Thank Heaven!" exclaimed Henri, joyfully.

"You seem in excellent spirits to-night, Captain Henri de Grandville."

"I wish I could say as much of you, Captain Raoul de St. Prix."

"Tell me the cause of your felicity."

"Enlighten me respecting your ill humor."

"Willingly, on condition that you will explain your satisfaction."

"Agreed."

"Well, then—you know the marked preference—marked preference, I say—always shown me by Mademoiselle Heloise de Clairville."

"I will not dispute with you—go on."

"You must have been blinded by absurd hopes not to have noticed it; every officer in the army looked to me as the *futur* of the lady. Well, sir, encouraged and led on by this siren, I made my proposals to her to-night. *Ventre St. Gris!* I had engaged to settle with my creditors out of her marriage portion."

"Go on—go on—this is excellent, St. Prix."

"Well, sir, she rejected me—me, the Count de St. Prix. A prior engagement, forsooth! I wish to Heaven I knew the fellow! Before sunrise he should have more button holes in his doublet than ever his tailor made."

"Captain St. Prix," replied Henri, "you have not far to look. In me behold the fortunate suitor. Come, come; confess that your pride, and not your heart, was engaged in the affair. The game was fairly played; the stakes are mine."

"This trifling will not pass muster with me, sir," said the count, sternly. "Know—if you knew it not before—that Raoul de St. Prix never fixed his eye on a prize that he did not obtain, or missing it, failed to punish his successful rival. You are a soldier, and you understand me, sir," he added, touching his sword knot with his gloved hand.

"This is midsummer madness, Raoul," answered Henri, with good temper. "Had I been unsuccessful, painful, fatal as the disappointment would have been, I should have resigned the lady to you without a struggle."

"That shows the difference between a gentleman and a *parvenu*," retorted St. Prix.

"A *parvenu!*" cried De Grandville, starting to his feet.

"Yes. Who knows you? Whence came you? You are an intruder in our ranks."

"I bear the king's commission."

"Yes, and have not courage enough to sustain it. I have defied you to your teeth, and you refuse to fight."

"My principles are opposed to duelling. In the words of the lady whose preference honors me, 'I honor the soldier as much as I detest the duellist.' Besides, has not the marshal strictly forbidden duels in the camp? Conscience, reason, authority, every consideration forbids my acceptance of the challenge."

"Then," said St. Prix, "you shall submit to an indignity that disgraces a French gentleman forever." And raising his sheathed sword, he struck De Grandville with the flat of the scabbard.

Henri's sword instantly flashed in the lamplight, and St. Prix drawing his rapier, they were instantly engaged in deadly combat. Both were expert swordsmen, and while one fought with the ferocity of hatred and disappointment, the arm of the other was nerved by a sense of wrong. The metallic ring of their blades was unintermitted, for neither paused to take breath, but, with teeth set and eyes glaring, thrust, parried, advanced, and fell back in the fierce ardor of the combat. At last, De Grandville, seeing an opportunity, sent his adversary's blade whirling through the air, and drawing back his weapon, prepared to thrust it through his breast.

"Strike!" said St. Prix; "you have vanquished me in love and in arms, and there is nothing left me but to die."

"Die, then, but on the field of battle, brave Raoul," said de Grandville, "and since I have deprived you of your sword, take mine; I shall be honored by the exchange."

"Hold!" said a stern voice; and turning, Henri beheld with confusion the countenance of Marshal Saxe, who, attended by a file of musketeers, had entered the tent at the close of the duel. "You will give up your sword to this officer, Captain de Grandville," added he, pointing to a commissioned officer by whom he was accompanied. "Count de St. Prix, you will pick up your weapon, also, and surrender it. Officers who forget themselves so far as to seek each other's lives upon the eve of battle, with the enemy before them, are unworthy of command. This is matter for the provost marshal."

And the old soldier seated himself at the table, and eyed the offenders angrily and sternly.

"May it please your excellency," said St. Prix, "I alone deserve to suffer. I insulted the gentleman, and forced him to fight."

"Forced him to fight?" said the marshal. "Hadn't he read the orders of the day?"

"I do not claim your clemency, marshal," said Henri. "I committed this fault with my eyes open. But a man cannot always command his passions."

"That's true, my lad. But what were you fighting about?"

"A woman, your excellency," said St. Prix.

"A woman! fools! a woman that's not to be had without fighting for isn't worth having. Well, well—boys will be boys. I pardon you on two conditions. In the first place, you must shake hands." Henri and Raoul advanced and joined their hands. "And in the next place, that you give a good account of yourselves to-morrow. *Sacre nom de Dieu!* I can ill spare two lads of spirit from the guards. And now," said the marshal, rising, after restoring their swords to the officers, "good night, gentlemen; and plenty of hard knocks to-morrow."

The next day witnessed one of those terrible encounters, whose sanguinary prints make a more indelible impression on the page of history than the records of the more generous deeds of peaceful life. The greatest gallantry was displayed on both sides, and on the part of the French no officers were more distinguished for their valor than the two guardsmen whose encounter on the previous evening we have just related. Raoul de St. Prix, in the early part of the engagement, fell sword in hand at the head of his company, thus meeting with honor a fate he had earnestly desired. Henri de Grandville, in the course of the day, found himself in command of the regiment, every officer of higher rank having fallen. When the carnage had ceased, he laid a stand of captured colors at the feet of the commander-in-chief, and was complimented by Marshal Saxe at the head of the army, receiving assurance that his gallantry should be at once reported to the king.

Flushed with triumph, the young guardsman flew to the presence of his mother, to receive her embrace and recount in modest terms the story of his deeds. She rejoiced in his safety, and sympathized with his joy. But all at once, as he made her the confident of other hopes, and enlarged on the prospect of his speedy union with Heloise de Clairville, her countenance changed, and her eyes became suffused with tears.

"Dear Henri," said she, "I knew nothing of this. Why did you not sooner apprise me of this fatal passion?"

"Fatal passion, dear mother! Why do you thus characterize the love I bear to the purest, the most beautiful of her sex?"

"She is, indeed, all that you paint her, Henri; but you must learn the hard task of renouncing your hopes. You can never marry her."

"And why so? Do you refuse your consent?"

"Alas! no. But the Baron de Clairville—"

"He regards me with a favorable eye. I have reason to think he knows of my attachment to his daughter, and approves of it. Even now, his congratulations had a marked meaning, which could hardly be ambiguous."

"But a fatal, an insurmountable barrier lies between you and the object of your hopes."

"Do not keep me in suspense," cried the young soldier, "Explain this mystery, I implore you."

"Have you fortitude to listen to a dreadful secret, the possession of which has well nigh destroyed the life of your mother?"

"God will give me strength to bear any stroke," replied Henri. "Thanks to your instruction and example, I have schooled myself to suffer, unrepining, whatever Providence, in its infinite wisdom, sees fitting to inflict. If I have a soul for the dangers of the field, I have also, I think, the courage to confront those trials that pierce the heart with keener agonies than any the steel of a foeman can inflict. Fear not to task me beyond my strength."

"I will be as brief as possible," said the lady. "Your father, Henri, was of noble birth and possessed of fortune. My own share of the world's goods was small, and yet it was on this pittance alone that we were sustained, till the exertions of a generous friend procured you, under the name of De Grandville, (my maiden name,) a commission in the guards."

"Then De Grandville was not the name of my father."

"No—he belonged to the noble house of Montmorenci. The early years of our married life were passed in happiness that I always feared was too great to be enduring. It was brought to a bitter and miserable end. Deadly enemies—for the best and noblest have their foes—conspired against your father, and he was accused—falsely accused, mark me—of treason to his king and country. I will not tell you by what forgery and perjury he was made to appear guilty—but he was convicted—and sentenced—"

"Sentenced!"

"Ay, sentenced, and suffered. He died by the hands of *Monsieur de Paris!*"

"*Monsieur de Paris!*"

"The executioner!"

Henri uttered a piercing cry, and covered his face with his hands. He remained a long time in this attitude, his frame convulsed by the agonies of grief, while his mother watched, with streaming eyes, the effect of her communication. At length he removed his hands, and raised his head. His countenance was deadly pale,—the only indication of the train of emotions which had just convulsed him,—but his look was firm and high.

"Mother," said he, pressing her hand, "I thank you. It was better to learn this dreadful secret from your lips than from the words of another. Henceforth we will live for each other—we shall have a common sorrow and a common fate. I pray you to excuse me for a few moments. I will soon rejoin you, but I have first a duty to perform."

The young guardsman passed from his mother's presence to that of the Baron de Clairville.

"Welcome, welcome! my brave boy," said the old soldier. "You have fairly won your spurs."

"Sir, you flatter me," replied Henri, gravely.

"Not at all. Saxe himself says that more distinguished gallantry never fell beneath his notice."

"You think then, baron, I can claim a post of honor and danger in the next engagement?"

"You can lead the Forlorn Hope if you like."

"Enough, baron. I came to ask your forgiveness."

"My forgiveness!"

"Yes, sir, for having wronged you unconsciously so lately as last evening."

"Wronged me, and how, strange boy? you talk in riddles."

"Last evening, sir, on the eve of battle, which might well, considering what followed, have been my last of life, I sought your daughter. Her manner, some unguarded words she dropped, emboldened me to declare a secret which I had hitherto kept fast locked in my breast. I threw myself at her feet, and told her that I loved her."

"And she—"

"Confessed that she loved me in return."

- 42 -

"Henri! my boy—my son—my hero! this news makes me young again! it gladdens my old heart like the shout of victory upon a stricken field. Is this your offence? I freely pardon it."

"You know not all, baron. You knew that I was a poor and obscure soldier of fortune."

"The man who has distinguished himself as you have done this day, might claim the hand of an emperor's daughter."

"Baron, between me and Heloise there lies a black shadow—a memory—a horror, which forbids our meeting. The very name I bear does not belong to me."

"And how may you be named, young man, if not De Grandville?"

"Henri de Montmorenci," replied the young soldier.

"De Montmorenci!" cried the baron. "That is a noble and historic name. The house of Montmorenci has been well represented in the field."

"*And on the scaffold!*" added Henri, with deep emotion.

"The scaffold!" exclaimed the baron. "Yes, yes; I remember now a dreadful tragedy. But *he* suffered unjustly."

"No matter," answered Henri. "The ignominious punishment remains a stain upon our escutcheon. Men will point to me as the son of a condemned and executed traitor. Could I forget for a moment the tragedy which has rendered my poor mother an animated image of death, the finger of the world would recall my wandering thoughts to the horrors of the fact. The scaffold, with all its bloody paraphernalia, would rise up before me."

"Henri, you are too sensitive," said the baron. "The best and bravest of France (alas for our history!) have closed their lives upon the scaffold. I believe your father innocent. If it were otherwise, you have redeemed the honor of your race. You deserve my daughter's hand—take her and be happy."

"Make her the companion of my agony! Never."

"Come with me," said the baron; "her smiles shall dispel these gloomy fantasies."

"No, no! urge me not," said the young guardsman. "Let me return to my poor mother. She has need of all my consolation. I renounce forever my ill-fated attachment. Heaven, for its own wise purposes, has chosen to afflict me. Farewell, baron; I thank you for your kindness—your generous friendship. You and Heloise will soon learn that Henri de Montmorenci is no more.

After the next battle, if you seek me out, you will find me where the French dead lie thickest on the field."

"Noble-hearted fellow!" cried the baron, when Henri had left him. "He ought to be a field marshal."

"Marshal Saxe requests your immediate presence, baron," said an aide-de-camp, presenting himself with a salute.

"Monsieur de Baron," said the commander-in-chief, when De Clairville had obeyed the summons, "I have chosen you to carry my despatches to the king; you will find yourself honorably mentioned therein, and I think the favor of royalty will reward your merit."

The baron bowed low as he received the despatches from the hand of the marshal, and was soon ready for the journey, first taking a hasty farewell of his daughter, whom he commended to the care of Madame de Grandville, (or rather Montmorenci,) during his absence.

In five days thereafter, he reported himself to the marshal, and was then at liberty to attend to his private concerns. He found Heloise in the company of Henri and his mother, and the gloom depicted on their countenances presented a singular contrast to the radiant joy that sparkled in the eyes and smiled on the lips of the genial and warm-hearted old soldier. He kissed his daughter, saluted Madame de Grandville, and then, shaking the young guardsman warmly by the hand, exclaimed,—

"Good news, Henri; I bring you a budget of them. The king has heard of your gallantry, and inquired into your story."

"Heaven bless him!" exclaimed the mother.

"The memory of your father," continued the baron, "has been vindicated by a parliamentry decree affirming his innocence. His forfeited estates are restored to his family; and I bring you, under the king's seal, your commission as full colonel in the French Guards, and letters patent of nobility, *Count* Henri de Montmorenci!"

Henri and his mother were nearly overwhelmed by this good news; while Heloise clung to her father's arm for support.

"No fainting, girl," said the happy baron. "That will never do for a soldier's wife. Here, take her, count, make her happy—and let us hear no more of your volunteering on Forlorn Hopes—at least, during the honeymoon."

We need not add that the baron's injunctions were implicitly obeyed.

PERSONAL SATISFACTION.

Mrs. Tubbs had been a very fine woman—she was still good looking at the period of which we write, but then—

"Fanny was younger once than she is now,
And prettier of course."

She had been married some years. Tubbs was a gentleman farmer, and lived out in Roxbury, when land was cheaper there than it is now, and a man of moderate means could own a few acres within three miles of Boston State House. On retiring from the wholesale West India goods business, he had purchased a little estate in the vicinity of the Norfolk House, and raised vegetables and other "notions" with the usual success attendant upon the agricultural experiments of gentlemen amateurs; that is, his potatoes cost him about half a dollar a peck, and his quinces ninepence apiece. He had a greenhouse one quarter of a mile long, and kept a fire in it all the year round, at the suggestion of a rascally gardener, whose brother kept a wood and coal yard. We could tell some droll stories about Tubbs's gardening, if they were to the purpose. We will mention, however, that when he went into the vegetable business he was innocent as a lamb, and verdant as one of his own green peapods, and of course he made some curious mistakes. He was not aware that the infant bean, like the pious Æneas, was "in the habit of carrying its father on its back," and so thinking that nature had made a mistake, he reversed the order of the young sprouts, and reinterred the aged beans. This was one of his many blunders. However, we have nothing to do with his gardening. We have said he was innocent as a lamb, but he was by no means so pacific; on the contrary, his temper was as inflammable as gun cotton— the slightest spark would set it in a blaze.

To return to Mrs. Tubbs, whom we have most ungallantly left in the lurch since the first paragraph. She had been into Boston one day, shopping, and returned home in the omnibus. She sat between two young men. The one on her right was modest and well-behaved, while the other was entirely the reverse. He might have been drinking—he might have been partially insane—these are charitable suppositions; but at all events, he had the impertinence to address Mrs. Tubbs in a low tone, audible only to herself. He muttered some compliment to her appearance—talked a little nonsense—inoffensive in itself, but intolerable as coming from a stranger. Mrs. Tubbs made no reply, but she was glad to spring from the conveyance when the driver pulled up at the Norfolk House. To her great joy she espied the faithful Tubbs, attired in a *blouse*, and wheeling a barrow full of gravel down Bartlett Street, with all the dignity of a gentleman farmer, conscious of being a useful, if not an ornamental, member of society. She accosted him with,—

"Tubbs, love, I've got something to tell you."

Tubbs relinquished the handles of the barrow, and sat down in the gravel.

"Mr. Tubbs!" screamed the lady, "you've got your best pantaloons on."

"Never mind, my dear; out with your story, for I'm busy."

"Mr. Tubbs! I've been insulted!"

Mr. Tubbs's head instantly became as red as one of his own blood beets.

"Who is the miscreant?" he yelled, jumping up.

"A young man who sat next to me in the omnibus."

"Describe him!"

"Dark hair and eyes, with a black stock, light waistcoat, dark-colored coat and pantaloons—"

"Which way did he go?" interrupted Mr. Tubbs.

"Into the hourly office."

"'Tis well! Mrs. T., I'll have his heart's blood!"

"Now, T., be calm!" interposed his better half.

"Mrs. T., I will be calm," was the dignified reply, "calm as the surface of Mount Ætna, on the eve of an eruption. Farewell, love, for a moment. Have an eye to the wheelbarrow while I have a settlement with this scoundrel!"

With these words, Tubbs marched up the hill. He entered the hourly office, and looked round him. His first glance lighted on a young man who answered the description given by Mrs. Tubbs; but he wished to make assurance doubly sure, and so he accosted him politely,—

"Fine growing weather, sir."

"Yes, sir," replied the stranger.

"Peas are doing finely," said Mr. Tubbs.

"Indeed!"

"If the weather holds, we can plant corn next week."

"Indeed!"

"Pray, sir," continued Tubbs, "did you come out in the last coach?"

"I did, sir."

"Was there a lady in the coach?"

"There was, sir. I recollect a lady sat next to me."

"You scoundrel! what did you mean by insulting my wife?"

This question was followed by a blow, which sent the young gentleman sprawling on the floor. Tubbs stood him up, and knocked him down again and again, like a man practising on a single pin in a bowling alley. The sufferer showed some fight, but Tubbs's blood was up, and he hammered down all opposition. The drivers looked on in admiration to see "Old Tubbs vollop the chap as had insulted his wife," and so he had it all his own way. He dragged the offender out of the office, and finished him off on the sidewalk. He was engaged in this laudable occupation, when his better half, tired of mounting guard over the wheelbarrow, appeared upon the field.

"Mr. Tubbs!" she screamed.

"Wait a minute, my dear. I've only done one side of his head."

"But, Mr. Tubbs! *That wasn't the man!*"

Tubbs suspended operations, and stood fixed in horror. The remains of the injured individual were taken into the hourly office. Then came remorse and apologies unaccepted and unacceptable—a lawyer's letter—an action for assault and battery, and heavy damages. The real offender had escaped, and was never heard of; the victim was the well-behaved young gentleman, who had sat on Mrs. Tubbs's right. Her description, which had answered for both, had occasioned the dilemma, which, while it proved an expensive lesson to Mr. Tubbs, was also an effectual one, and saved him from many a rash and hasty action, and induced him ever afterwards to adopt Colonel Crockett's golden maxim, *"Be always sure you're right, then go ahead."*

THE CASTLE ON THE RHINE.

In one of those old feudal castles, which, perched, like eagle nests, upon the picturesque hills that overhang

"The wide and winding Rhine,"

and with their crumbling and ivy-grown towers, arrest the eyes of the delighted traveller, as he views them from the deck of the gliding steamer, there dwelt, some years ago, the Baron Von Rosenburg and his lady Mathilde. The baron was a very proud man, and continually boasting of his descent from a "long and noble line of martial ancestors," gentlemen who were wont, in the "good old times," to wear steel on head, back, and breast, and each of whom supported a score of retainers in his feudal castle. Where the money comes from to support a princely housekeeping, when the head of the family has no property or employment, is sometimes a mystery nowadays; but no such doubt attached to the resources of the baron's ancestors. These gentlemen, when short of provisions, would sally forth at the head of their followers, and capture the first drove of cattle they encountered, without stopping to inquire into the ownership. Sometimes they made excursions on the river, and levied contributions on the little barks of traders who often carried valuable cargoes from one Rhine town to another.

But the privileges of the robber knights and bandit nobles were sadly shorn by the progressive spirit of modern civilization. With a total disregard of the immunities of chivalry, modern legislators declared that it was as great a crime for a baron to seize on a herd of cattle as for a peasant to steal a sheep. Hence the great families along the Rhine went into decay. The castles were dismantled, many noble names died out, very few remained, the representatives of the ancestral glory of olden times.

Among them was the baron. He had been a soldier and a courtier in his youth, had spent some time abroad, and was about forty when he married a lady of the same age, and settled down in the old family castle of Rosenberg. Here he lorded it over the surrounding valley, the simple inhabitants of which, though exempt from all feudal obligations, yet in some sort regarded themselves as vassals of the baron. They made him presents of fish, accompanied him to the chase, and lent him a willing hand, whenever he required assistance at the castle.

The baron, though he had the wherewithal to live comfortably enough, was yet a poor representative of the race he sprang from. His army consisted of a few farm servants, his cavalry of a ploughboy on a cart-horse, and his navy of a fishing boat. But, on the whole, he was happy. He passed his days either in trimming his vines or hunting, and his evenings in poring over mildewed parchments or books of heraldry, hunting up long pedigrees, and puffing a monstrous meerschaum till the atmosphere was as dense as the interior of a smokehouse. The lady Mathilde embroidered from morning till night.

They had, however, a common source of grief. Fate had not blessed them with children. The lady yearned for the companionship of a daughter; the baron mourned at the prospect of the extinction of his name for want of a male heir.

It was while pondering on this subject one day, as they were strolling out together, that the baron and his lady came upon the cottage of an old soldier named Karl Mueller, who cultivated a little vineyard not far from the castle.

The old man was seated on a bench before his door, smoking, and so deeply plunged in revery, that he was not aware of the approach of visitors till the baron touched him on the shoulder.

"In a brown study, Karl?" said the baron.

"I have enough to think about," returned the soldier "I'm getting old, and one thing troubles me."

"What's that, my good fellow?"

"Why, you see, baron, I'm not alone here."

"Not alone?"

"No, sir—I—have—I have a little child here."

"I never knew you were married, Karl."

"Nor was I, your honor. For I always thought an infantry soldier ought to be in marching order, and never have more baggage than he could carry in his knapsack. No, no; the child is none of mine."

"But it is related to you," said the baroness.

"It is my grandchild, madam," replied the soldier, fixing his eyes on the lady; "and the child of as brave a man as ever faced the fire of the enemy. He might have been a field marshal, for the matter of that. I saw him at Oberstadt when the hussars went down to charge the enemy's light cavalry. Faith, madam, they made daylight shine through their ranks. Their curved sabres cut them up as the sickle does the corn. I saw him, the girl's father, madam, go into that affair with the hussars; but he came not out safe. It was pitiful to see his uniform all dabbled with blood, as he lay on the ground, and to see his pale lips quivering, as he prayed for water. I gave him the last drop in my canteen, and I swore I'd protect the child. But I fear I'm getting too old for the task."

The baroness, whose eyes were filled with tears, turned to her husband, and asked,—

"Shall we not give a shelter to the child of a brave man?"

The baron nodded, and the proposal was accepted by Karl, who retired into his cottage, and immediately reappeared, bringing forth a beautiful girl of ten, with fair hair and blue eyes, and a form of graceful symmetry.

"A girl! nonsense!" said the baron, in a tone of disappointment. But the baroness folded the child in her arms with rapture. The child responded to the caresses of the lady with equal ardor.

So the little Adelaide was soon domesticated in the castle which her frolic spirit filled with gayety. The baroness renewed her youth in gazing upon hers, and the baron never scolded her, even when she took his pipe out of his mouth, or rummaged among his parchments.

As she grew up to womanhood, she became more serious and thoughtful. She was anxious to learn every thing touching her father, but on this subject the baroness could give her no information; and Karl, her grandfather, seemed equally averse to speaking of it. When hard pressed, he promised to speak out at some future time.

One day she was summoned in great haste to the cottage of old Karl. The old man had suddenly been taken ill, and required the presence of his granddaughter. It was evident, at a glance, that he was on his death bed.

"Adelaide," said he, "forgive me, before I die, that I may depart in peace."

"Forgive you, dear grandfather! am I not deeply indebted to you?"

"I should have reposed more confidence in you; I should have spoken to you about your parents."

"My father?" asked Adelaide.

"Was a brave and good man. But of your mother—your good mother—she was—"

Here a spasm interrupted his utterance, and he lay back on his pillow gasping for breath. After a brief space he seemed to revive again, and made strong efforts to express himself, but his breath failed him. He motioned to Adelaide to fetch him writing materials, and while she held a sheet of paper on a book before him, he essayed with feeble fingers to trace a sentence with a pen. But the rapid approach of death foiled all his endeavors to communicate a secret that evidently lay close to his heart; and while the young girl bent over him in an agony of grief, he gently sighed away his last. The baron and baroness found their *protégée*, an hour afterwards, still sorrowing by the bedside of her early friend and protector. With gentle violence they removed her from the chamber of death, and took her home to the castle, where they gave directions to the proper persons to take charge of the old soldier's remains, and inter them with that decent respect which was due to his character and station. Among his effects was found a will, in which he made Adelaide his heiress, bequeathing to her his little landed estate, and a small sum in gold, the produce of his toil and frugality. This event cast a gloom over the spirits of the young maiden, from which, however, her religious persuasions, the attention of her friends, and the elasticity of her youth, eventually relieved her.

The old castle on the Rhine was gay once more, when Rudolph Ernstein, a nephew of the baron, a gay young captain of hussars, whose gallantry and beauty had given him reputation at Vienna, came to pay a long visit to his uncle. He was a high-spirited and accomplished young man, had served with distinction, was a devoted admirer of the ladies, and one of those military Adonises who are born to conquest. He was charmed to find domesticated beneath the old roof tree so fair and lovable a girl as Adelaide, and of course did his best to render his society agreeable to her. He sang to her songs of his own writing, to airs of his own composition, accompanied on his guitar; he told her tales of strange lands that he had visited, of cavalry skirmishes in which he had participated, sketched her favorite scenes in pencil, and offered to teach her the newest dances in vogue at Vienna. He was a dangerous companion to a young girl whose imagination needed but a spark to kindle it, and for a time she indulged in the wild hope that she had made a conquest of Rudolph. But then her reason told her, that even if he loved her, it would be impossible for a young man of family to offer his hand to an almost portionless girl, about whose origin a veil of mystery seemed wrapped. The names of her parents, even, had never been disclosed to her, by the lips of probably the only man who knew her history, and those lips were now cold and mute in death. Hence the little gleam of sunshine which had for a moment penetrated her heart was speedily quenched in a deeper darkness than that which reigned in it before, and she could not help viewing the visit of Rudolph as an ominous event.

One morning, she was witness to a scene which dashed out the last faint glimmering of hope. They were all seated at a huge oaken table, from which the servants had just removed the apparatus of the morning meal.

"Rudolph," said the baron, after lighting his pipe,—an operation of great solemnity and deliberation, and taking a few whiffs to make sure that its contents were duly ignited,—"Rudolph, do you know why I sent for you to Rosenburg?"

"Why, sir," replied the hussar, "I suppose it was because you really have a sort of regard for an idle, good-for-nothing fellow, whose redeeming quality is an attachment to a very kind old uncle, and whose nonsense and good spirits are perhaps a partial compensation for the trouble he gives every body in this tumble-down old castle."

"Tumble-down old castle!" exclaimed the baron, in high dudgeon, the latter part of the soldier's speech cancelling the former; "why, you jackanapes, it will stand for centuries. It resisted the cannon of Napoleon, and it bids defiance to the battering of time. Yes, sir, Rosenburg will stand long after your great-great-grandchildren are superannuated."

"I am not likely to be blessed in the way you hint at, uncle," said the soldier, carelessly. "I am likely, for aught I see, to die a bachelor."

"Nonsense!" said the baron. "What's to become of your family name? Do you think I will allow it to die out, like the Pumpernickels, the Snaphausens, and the Ollenstoffenburgers? No, boy. I sent for you to tell you that I have contracted for your hand with my friend the Baron Von Steinberg."

"Really, sir, you dispose of me in a very cavalier way."

"That's because you're too careless or lazy to look out for yourself," retorted the baron. "But then you can have no possible objection to the present match. The fair Julia is just twenty—eyes, you dog—lips, you rascal—a shape, you blockhead, to bewitch an anchorite. And then she has the gelt—the money, my boy."

"A commodity of which I happen to be minus," said the soldier.

"Arn't you my heir?" asked the baron.

"You are very kind," said the hussar, with a slight sigh.

He glanced at Adelaide, but he read no sentiment on her calm and pensive countenance.

"She's as cold as a glacier on the Donderberg!" he muttered to himself.

"Well, sir—you haven't given me an answer," said the baron, impatiently.

"My dear uncle," said the soldier, jumping up, and snatching his fowling-piece, "it's a glorious morning for sport; and I'm much mistaken if I don't add a half dozen brace of birds to your bill of fare to-day."

"But the fair Julia Von Steinberg?" said the baron.

"O! I forgot," said Rudolph. "I'm entirely in your hands. Do with me as you please. My profession, you know, has given me habits of obedience. I suppose I must sacrifice myself. Good morning."

And away he went to enjoy his sport upon the mountains.

"Young, lovely, and rich!" said poor Adelaide, with a sigh, when she had regained her room. "If this be true, she is indeed worthy of Ernstein. He will love her—they will be happy—and I—I can but wish them joy, and die."

There was great preparation in the castle Von Rosenburg, that day week, for the reception of the prospective bride. Every thing was cleaned and furbished up, from battlement to dungeon keep. An old flag with the family arms was hoisted from the rampart, and the butler, who had served in the wars of the Alliance, mounted an old swivel on the ramparts with the intention of firing it off, on the approach of the old family carriage of the Von Steinbergs, Captain Rudolph Von Ernstein, in his splendid hussar uniform, looked the beau ideal of a soldier lover. Even the baron was rejuvenated by a court suit that had not seen the light since the nuptials of Maria Louisa and the Emperor Napoleon.

At last the carriage appeared. The villagers and hangers on of the establishment hurrahed in the court yard as it drew up, the old butler applied the match to the priming of the swivel and was prostrated by the discharge, while the baron came near tumbling over his sword in his eagerness to welcome his old friend and his old friend's daughter.

The Baron Von Steinberg alighted and bowed his thanks; while Captain Rudolph handed out the lovely Julia. As her light foot touched the pavement, Adelaide advanced to offer a bouquet; at one glance she appreciated the exquisite beauty of her rival, and dropping the flowers, retired to an obscure corner of the court yard to conceal her anguish and despair.

The festive train swept into the castle. All was gayety and uproar within doors. The baron could scarce contain the transports of his joy; and Von Steinberg was equally excited. The excitement, however, seemed to be too much for the fair Julia, whose cheek was paler than the satin robe she wore, while Rudolph, perhaps from sympathy, was uneasy and agitated.

At last the bell of the castle was rung for dinner, and the party proceeded to the great hall. But Adelaide did not make her appearance. Search was made for her; she was not in her apartment. An angry flush overspread the brow of old Rosenburg at this announcement, and after some minutes passed in waiting for her appearance, he ordered dinner to be served without her. The repast was not a very gay one, notwithstanding the efforts of the master of the house to make it so. Night had long fallen, and Adelaide did not reappear. The family, from being vexed, now became alarmed, and it was determined to go in search of her. Rudolph and the baron went forth with two servants and torches to scour the woods, after vainly searching through the castle. One of the men went on in advance. He had been gone but a short time when he came back speechless with grief and amazement. Rudolph and his uncle pushed forward through the thickets, and on the banks of a small stream, dammed up to form a lake, they found the bonnet and shawl of the missing girl.

"Good God!" exclaimed Rudolph, "she has destroyed herself. I have noticed a strange wildness in her appearance for several days past; in a fit of mental aberration she has wandered away, and here found her death."

A piercing scream was heard at this moment. The baroness, who had followed them, had recognized the garments of Adelaide.

"My child! my child!" she shrieked, "my own! my beautiful! she is no more."

"This is worse and worse," said the baron, wringing his hands. "This will make us all mad."

But at this moment a boat was seen approaching. It was the miller, who brought with him the body of Adelaide, dripping as it had been drawn from the water. He laid her fair form upon the bank. The baroness, who could not be restrained, threw herself beside her, and kissed her pale lips. Rudolph, too, seized the cold hands.

"She lives!" he exclaimed. "She is not lost to us!"

"Rudolph—dear Rudolph!" murmured the poor girl.

"My child! my child! she lives!" cried the baroness.

And it was indeed so. She had thrown herself into the water, indeed, but the miller, who happened to be at hand, had flown to her rescue, and she was now, by the united efforts of her friends, restored to consciousness.

"Dear, dear Adelaide!" cried the baroness; "your life repays me now for all my sufferings. Yes, dearest, you are my own, my only child. Yes, baron," she added, noticing the incredulous expression of her husband—"the supposed death of a daughter has wrung from a mother's heart the despairing cry that betrayed her secret. In former days, I married, secretly, Colonel Schonfeldt, a brave soldier of the emperor, against whom my parents cherished a deadly enmity. He fell upon the field of battle, and this poor girl, the fruit of our love, was committed to the hands of strangers, till such time as I could take her to my heart. I avow it without shame, nor can you, baron, whose noble qualities won my heart, reproach me with the love I bear this dear girl."

"She is my child now," said the baron, "as well as yours. Let us take her back to the castle; she is a precious charge."

"I will see to her," said Rudolph, "and it shall not be my fault if she ever have another protector."

So the party regained the castle, where Von Steinberg and Julia were anxiously awaiting their return.

When Adelaide had been carefully attended to, Rudolph sought his uncle and guests in the great hall.

"Miss Julia Von Steinberg," said the soldier, "since confessions are the order of the night, I must place mine on record. I met you to-day in obedience to orders, believing my heart was my own. The event of to-night has told me too truly that I had unconsciously lost it. But I am a man of honor, and if you will accept my hand without my heart, it is yours."

"Captain Ernstein," replied the beauty, "I thank you for your frank confession. I cannot possibly accept your hand without your heart. Nay—do not frown, father—I have a secret for your ear, and if you do not wish to wreck your daughter's happiness, you will urge me no further."

Von Steinberg frowned, and pshawed, and pished, and then, clearing his voice, addressed the baron.

"Come, Von Rosenberg," said he, "confess that we have been acting like a couple of old fools, in trying our hand at match making—it is a business for the young people themselves, and not for old soldiers like us. Say, shall we reduce the mutineers to obedience, or shall we let them have it their own way?"

"Circumstances alter cases," answered the baron. "When I proposed for Julia's hand, I didn't know my wife had a daughter to marry. And if that were not the case, I am inclined to think the secret alluded to by the young lady, would prove an insuperable obstacle to the ratification of our treaty."

This secret was no other than a love affair between the fair Julia and a certain count who had waltzed with her at the baths of Baden-Baden, the preceding summer. We are glad to say that the flirtation thus happily commenced ended in matrimony. As for Rudolph, he was shortly after united to the fair Adelaide, on which occasion the baron gave such a rouse as the old towers of Von Rosenberg had not known since the rollicking days of its first feudal masters. It was illuminated at every window and loophole, so that the waters of the Rhine rolled beneath it a sea of fire, or as if their channels were overflowed with generous Asmanshausen; and the old butler discharged his swivel so many times that he had to be taken down from the battlements and drenched with Rhenish to preserve his life.

Thus ended all that is worthy commemorating in the modern history of the Castle on the Rhine.

LOVE IN A COTTAGE.

"Tell me, Charley, who is that fascinating creature in blue that waltzes so divinely?" asked young Frank Belmont of his friend Charles Hastings, as they stood "playing wallflower" for the moment, at a military ball.

"Julia Heathcote," answered Charles, with a half sigh, "an old flame of mine. I proposed, but she refused me."

"On what ground?"

"Simply because I had a comfortable income. Her head is full of romantic notions, and she dreams of nothing but love in a cottage. She contends that poverty is essential to happiness—and money its bane."

"Have you given up all hopes of her?"

"Entirely; in fact, I'm engaged."

"Then you have no objections to my addressing this dear, romantic angel?"

"None whatever. But I see my *fiancée*—excuse me—I must walk through the next quadrille with her."

Frank Belmont was a stranger in Boston—a New Yorker—immensely rich and fashionable, but his reputation had not preceded him, and Charley Hastings was the only man who knew him in New England. He procured an introduction to the beauty from one of the managers, and soon danced and talked himself into her good graces. In fact, it was a clear case of love at first sight on both sides.

The enamoured pair were sitting apart, enjoying a most delightful *tête-à-tête*. Suddenly Belmont heaved a deep sigh.

"Why do you sigh, Mr. Belmont?" asked the fair Julia, somewhat pleased with this proof of sensibility. "Is not this a gay scene?"

"Alas! yes," replied Belmont, gloomily; "but fate does not permit me to mingle habitually in scenes like this. They only make my ordinary life doubly gloomy—and even here I deem to see the shadow of a fiend waving me away. What right have I to be here?"

"What fiend do you allude to?" asked Miss Heathcote, with increasing interest.

"A fiend hardly presentable in good society," replied Belmont, bitterly. "One could tolerate a Mephistophiles—a dignified fiend, with his pockets full of money—but my tormentor, if personified, would appear with seedy boots and a shocking bad hat."

"How absurd!"

"It is too true," sighed Belmont, "and the name of this fiend is *Poverty*!"

"Are you poor?"

"Yes, madam. I am poor, and when I would fain render myself agreeable in the eyes of beauty—in the eyes of one I could love, this fiend whispers me, 'Beware! you have nothing to offer her but love in a cottage.'"

"Mr. Belmont," said Julia, with sparkling eyes, and a voice of unusual animation, "although there are sordid souls in this world, who only judge of the merits of an individual by his pecuniary possessions, I am not one of that number. I respect poverty; there is something highly poetical about it, and I imagine that happiness is oftener found in the humble cottage than beneath the palace roof."

Belmont appeared enchanted with this encouraging avowal. The next day, after cautioning his friend Charley to say nothing of his actual circumstances, he called on the widow Heathcote and her fair daughter in the character of the "poor gentleman." The widow had very different notions from her romantic offspring, and when Belmont candidly confessed his poverty on soliciting permission to address Julia, he was very politely requested to change the subject, and never mention it again.

The result of all this manœuvring was an elopement; the belle of the ball jumping out of a chamber window on a shed, and coming down a flight of steps to reach her lover, for the sake of being romantic, when she might just as well have walked out of the front door.

The happy couple passed a day in New York city, and then Frank took his beloved to his "cottage."

An Irish hack conveyed them to a miserable shanty in the environs of New York, where they alighted, and Frank, escorting the bride into the apartment which served for parlor, kitchen, and drawing room, and was neither papered nor carpeted, introduced her to his mother, much in the way Claude Melnotte presents Pauline. The old woman, who was peeling potatoes, hastily wiped her hands and face with a greasy apron, and saluted her "darter," as she called her, on both cheeks.

"Can it be possible," thought Julia, "that this vulgar creature is my Belmont's mother?"

"Frank!" screamed the old woman, "you'd better go right up stairs and take off them clothes—for the boy's been sent arter 'em more'n fifty times. Frank borried them clothes, ma'am," she added to Julia, by way of explanation, "to look smart when he went down east."

The bridegroom retired on this hint, and soon reappeared in a pair of faded nankeen pantaloons, reaching to about the calf of the leg, a very shabby black coat, out at the elbows, a ragged black vest, and, instead of his varnished leather boots, a pair of immense cowhide brogans.

"Now," said he, sitting quietly down by the cooking stove, "I begin to feel at home. Ah! this is delightful, isn't it, dearest?" and he warbled,—

"Though never so humble, there's no place like home."

Julia's heart swelled so that she could not utter a word.

"Dearest," said Frank, "I think you told me you had no objection to smoking?"

"None in the least," said the bride; "I rather like the flavor of a cigar."

"O, a cigar!" replied Belmont; "that would never do for a poor man."

And O, horror! he produced an old clay pipe, and filling it from a little newspaper parcel of tobacco, began to smoke with a keen relish.

"Dinner! dinner!" he exclaimed at length; "ah! thank you, mother; I'm as hungry as a bear. Codfish and potatoes, Julia—not very tempting fare—but what of that? our aliment is love!"

"Yes, and by way of treat," added the old woman, "I've been and gone and bought a whole pint of Albany ale, and three cream cakes, from the candy shop next block."

Poor Julia pleaded indisposition, and could not eat a mouthful. Before Belmont, however, the codfish and potatoes, and the ale, and cream cakes disappeared with a very unromantic and unlover-like velocity. At the close of the meal, a thundering double knock was heard at the door.

"Come in!" cried Belmont.

A low-browed man, in a green waistcoat, entered.

"Now, Misther Belmont," he exclaimed, in a strong Hibernian accent, "are ye ready to go to work? By the powers! if I don't see ye sailed to-morrow on the shopboard, I'll discharge ye without a character—and ye shall starve on the top of that."

"To-morrow morning, Mr. Maloney," replied Belmont, meekly, "I'll be at my post."

"And it'll be mighty healthy for you to do that same," replied the man as he retired.

"Belmont, speak—tell me," gasped Julia, "who is that man—that loafer?"

"He is my employer," answered Belmont, smiling.

"And his profession?"

"He is a tailor."

"And you?"

"Am a journeyman tailor, at your service—a laborious and thankless calling it ever was to me—but now, dearest, as I drive the hissing goose across the smoking seam, I shall think of my own angel and my dear cottage, and be happy."

That night Julia retired weeping to her room in the attic.

"That 'ere counterpin, darter," said the old woman, "I worked with these here old hands. Ain't it putty? I hope you'll sleep well here. There's a broken pane of glass, but I've put one of Frank's old hats in it, and I don't think you'll feel the draught. There used to be a good many rats here, but I don't think they'll trouble you now, for Frank's been a pizinin' of 'em."

Left alone, Julia threw herself into a chair, and burst into a flood of tears. Even Belmont had ceased to be attractive in her eyes—the stern privations that surrounded her banished all thoughts of love. The realities of life had cured her in one day of all her Quixotic notions.

"Well, Julia, how do you like poverty and love in a cottage?" asked Belmont, entering in his bridal dress.

"Not so well, sir, as you seem to like that borrowed suit," answered the bride, reddening with vexation.

"Very well; you shall suffer it no longer. My carriage awaits your orders at the door."

"Your carriage, indeed!"

"Yes, dearest, it waits but for you, to bear us to Belmont Hall, my lovely villa on the Hudson."

"And your mother?"

"I have no mother, alas! The old woman down stairs is an old servant of the family."

"Then you've been deceiving me, Frank—how wicked!"

"It was all done with a good motive. You were not born to endure a life of privation, but to shine the ornament of an elegant and refined circle. I hope you will not love me the less when you learn that I am worth nearly half a million—that's the melancholy fact, and I can't help it."

"O Frank!" cried the beautiful girl, and hid her face in his bosom.

She presided with grace at the elegant festivities of Belmont Hall, and seemed to support her husband's wealth and luxurious style of living with the greatest fortitude and resignation, never complaining of her comforts, nor murmuring a wish for living in a cottage.

THE CAREER OF AN ARTIST.

I woke up one morning and found myself famous.—BYRON.

Julian Montfort was a farmer's boy; bred up to the plough handle and cart tail. His father and mother were plain, honest people, of hard-working habits and limited ideas, and without the slightest dash of romance in their temperaments. Their house, their lands were unprepossessing in appearance. The soil was impoverished by long and illiberal culture; and old Montfort had a true old-fashioned prejudice against trees. Instead of smiling hedgerows, with here and there a weeping elm or plumy evergreen to cast their graceful shadows upon the pasture land, his acres were enclosed with harsh stone walls, or an unpicturesque Virginia fence with its zigzag of rude rails. The farmer had an equal prejudice against books, "book larnin', and book-larned men." Of course, with these ideas, Julian's education was limited to a few quarters' schooling under an old pedagogue, whose native language was Dutch, and who never took very kindly to the English tongue. Besides, teaching was only an episode with him; for his vocation was that of a clergyman, and he held forth on Sundays in alternate Dutch and English to his little congregation—as is still the custom in many of the small agricultural parishes in New York State, where the scene of our veritable story lies.

Our hero, young Julian, early began to show a restiveness under the training he received, which sadly perplexed his plain matter-of-fact father. The latter could not conceive why the boy should sometimes leave his plough in the furrow, and sit upon a hillock, gazing curiously and admiringly upon a simple wild flower. He knew not why the youth should stand with his eyes fixed upon the western sky when it was pavilioned with crimson, and gold, and purple; or later yet, when, one by one, the stars came timidly forth and took their places in the darkening heaven. He shook his head at these manifestations, and confidently informed his help-mate that he feared the boy was "not right"—significantly touching, as he spoke, that portion of his anatomy where he fondly imagined a vast quantity of brain of very superior quality was safely stowed away, guarded by a sufficient quantity of skull to protect it against any accident. Neither he nor the good wife imagined, for a moment, that Julian was a genius, and that his talent, circumscribed by circumstances, was struggling for an outlet for its development.

At last the divine spark within him was kindled into flame. An itinerant portrait painter came round, with his tools of trade, and did the dominie in brown and red, and the squire's daughter in vermilion and flake white, and set the whole village agog with his marvellous achievements. Julian cultivated his acquaintance, received some secret instructions in the A B C of art, and bargained for some drawing and painting materials. His aspirations had at length found an object. Long and painfully he labored in secret; but his advances were rapid, for he took nature as a model. At last he ventured to display his latest achievement—a small portrait of his father. It was first shown to his mother, and filled her with astonishment and delight. It is the privilege of woman, however circumstanced, to appreciate and applaud true genius. Of course, Moliere's housekeeper occurs to the reader as an illustration. The picture was next shown to the old man. He gazed at it with a sort of silent horror, puffing the smoke from his pipe in short, spasmodic jerks, and slowly shaking his head before he spoke.

"Do you know it, father?" asked the young artist.

"Know it!" exclaimed the old man. "Yes—yes—I see myself there like I was lookin' into a glass. There's my nose, and eyes, and mouth, and hair; yes, and there's my pipe. It ain't right—it can't be right—it's witchcraft. Satan must ha' helped you, boy—you couldn't never ha' done it without the aid of the evil one."

This was a sad damper. But just then the dominie luckily happened in to take a pipe with his parishioner. He pronounced the work excellent, and satisfied his old friend's doubts as to the honesty of the transaction. Julian blessed the old man in his heart for the comfort he afforded.

And now the fame of the young painter flew through the village. The tavern keeper ordered a head of General Washington for his sign board, the old one—originally a portrait of the Duke of Cambridge with the court dress painted out—not satisfying some of his critical customers. And for the blacksmith, Montfort painted a rampant black horse, prevented from falling backward by a solid tail. The stable keeper also gave him orders for sundry coats of arms to be depicted on wagon panels and sleigh dashers, so that the incipient artist had plenty of orders and not a little cash.

But he soon grew tired of this local reputation. He panted for the association of kindred spirits; for the impulse and example to be found in some great centre of civilization; for refinement, fame—all that is dear to an ardent imagination. And so, one morning, he announced his intention of seeking his fortune in the city of New York.

His mother was sad, but did not oppose his wishes; his father shook his head, as he always did when any thing was proposed—no matter what. The old gentleman seemed to derive great pleasure from shaking his head, and no one interfered with so harmless an amusement.

"Goin' to York, hey?" said he, emitting sundry puffs of smoke. "The Yorkers are a curious set of people, boy. I read into a paper once't about how they car' on—droppin' pocket books, and sellin' brass watches for gold, and knockin' people down and stompin' onto 'em."

"But the dominie thinks I might make money there," said the young man.

"O, then you'd better go. The dominie's got a longer head than you or I, boy," said the old man.

"Yes, father," said the youth, kindling with animation. "In New York I am sure to win fame and fortune. I shall come back, then, and buy you a better farm, and hire hands for you, so that you won't be obliged to work so hard— and you can set out trees."

"Hain't no opinion of trees," said the old man, shaking his head.

"Well, well, father, you shall have money, and do what you like with it; for my part I shall be content with fame."

"Fame! what is that?" said the old man, laying down his pipe in bewilderment.

"Fame! Do you ask what fame is?" exclaimed the romantic boy. But he paused, convinced in a moment of the perfect futility of attempting to convey an idea of the unsubstantial phantom to the old man's intellect. Perhaps the old farmer was the better philosopher of the two.

But Julian gained his point, and departed for the great city—the goal of so many struggles, the grave of so many hopes. He was at first dazzled by the splendors of the artificial life, into the heart of which he plunged; and then, with a homesick feeling, he sighed for that verdurous luxury of nature he had left. He missed the trees—for he thought the shabby and rusty foliage of the Battery and Park hardly worthy of that name. But, in time to save him from utter disappointment and heart sickness, there opened on his vision the glorious dawning of the world of art. He passed from gallery to gallery, and from studio to studio, drinking in the beauties that unfolded before him with the eyes of his body and his soul. He was enraptured, dazzled, enchanted. Then he settled down to work in his humble room, economizing the scanty funds he had brought with him to the city. Like many young aspirants, he grasped, at first, at the most difficult subjects. He constantly groped for a high ideal. He would fly before he had learned to walk. With an imperfect knowledge of architecture and anatomy, and a limited stock of information, he would paint history—mythology. He sought to illustrate poetry, and dared attempt scenes from the Bible, Shakspeare, and Milton. He failed, though there were glimpses of grandeur and glory in his faulty attempts.

Then he turned back, with a sickening feeling, to the elements of art, distasteful as he found them. It was hard to pore over rectangles and curves, bones and muscles, angles and measurements, after sporting with irregular forms and fascinating colors. He tried portraiture, but he had no feeling for the business. He could not transfigure the dull and commonplace heads he was to copy. He had not the nice tact that makes beauty of ugliness without the loss of identity. He could not ennoble vulgarians. The sordid man bore the stamp of baseness on his canvas. His pictures were too true; and truth is death to the portrait painter.

He began to grow morbid in his feelings, and was fast verging to a misanthrope. His clothes grew shabby, and looked shabbier for his careless way of wearing them. He was often cold and hungry. There were times when he viewed with envy and hate the evidences of prosperity he saw about him. He railed against those pursuits of life which made men rich and prosperous. He began to think with the French demagogue, that "property was a theft," and to regard with great favor the socialistic doctrines then coming into vogue. The American social system he pronounced corrupt and rotten, and deserving to be uprooted and subverted. And this was the rustic boy, who, a few months before, had left his home so full of hope, and generous feeling, and high aspiration.

There were times when he yearned for the humble scenes of his boyhood. But he was too proud to throw up his pencils and palette, and go back to the old farm house; and so he found a vent for his home feeling in painting some of the scenes of his earliest life—the rustic dances, the huskings, the haymakings, and junketings with which he was so familiar.

One of these pictures—a rustic dance was the subject—he sent to a gilder's to be framed. He had consecrated three dollars to this purpose, and went one day to see how his commission had been executed. He found the picture framer, who was also a picture dealer, in his shirt sleeves, talking with a middle-aged gentleman, who was praising his performance.

"Really a very clever thing," said the gentleman, scanning the painting through his gold-bowed eye glasses.

"The composition, coloring, and light and shade, are admirable; but the life, animation, and naturalness of the figures make its great charm. Ah, why don't our artists study to produce life as it exists around them, and as they themselves know it and feel it, instead of giving us the gods and goddesses of a defunct and false religion, and scenes three thousand miles and years away?"

"Mr. Greville," said the picture framer, "allow me to make you acquainted with the artist, Mr. Montfort; he's a next-door neighbor of yours—lives at No ——, Broadway."

"Mr. Montfort," said the gentleman, warmly shaking the hand the artist shyly extended, "you found me admiring your work. And I'm sure I did not know I had so talented a neighbor. I shall be glad to be better acquainted with you. I presume your picture is for sale."

"Not so, sir," replied the artist, coldly. "It is a reminiscence of earlier and happier days. It was painted for my own satisfaction, and I shall keep it as long as I have a place to hang it in. It is a common mistake, sir, with our patrons, to suppose they can buy our souls as well as our labor."

Mr. Greville's cheek flushed; but as he glanced at the shabby exterior and wan face of the artist, his color faded, and he answered gently—

"Believe me, Mr. Montfort, I am not one of the persons you describe—if, indeed, they exist elsewhere but in your imagination. I should be the last person to fail in sympathy for the high-toned feelings of an artist; for in early life I was thought to manifest a talent for art—and, indeed, I had a strong desire to follow the vocation."

"And you abandoned it—you turned a deaf ear to the divine inspiration—you preferred wealth to glory—to be one of the vulgar many rather than to belong to the choice few. I congratulate you, Mr. Greville, on your taste."

"You judge me harshly, Mr. Montfort," replied the gentleman, pleasantly. "I am hardly required to justify my choice of calling to a perfect stranger; and yet your very frankness induces me to say a word or two of the motives which impelled me. My parents were poor. An artist's life seemed to hold no immediate prospects of competence. They to whom I owed my being might die of want before I had established a reputation. I had an opportunity to enter commercial life advantageously. I prospered. I have lived to see the declining days of my parents cheered by every comfort, and to rear a family in comfort and opulence. One of my boys promises to make a good artist. Fortunately, I can bestow on him the means of following the bent of his inclination. Instead of being an indifferent painter myself, I am an extensive purchaser of works of art, so that my conscience acquits me of any very great wrong in the course I adopted."

Montfort was silent; he was worsted in the argument.

"Mr. Montfort," pursued the gentleman, after a pause, "my evenings are always at my disposal, and I like to surround myself with men of talent. I have already a large circle of acquaintances among artists, musicians, and literary men, and once a week they meet at my house; I shall be very happy to see you among us. To-night is my evening of reception—will you join us?"

Proud and shy as he was, Montfort could not help accepting an invitation so frankly and pleasantly tendered. He promised to come.

"One favor more," said Mr. Greville. "You won't sell that picture. Will you lend it to me for a day or two?"

"I cannot refuse you, of course, Mr. Greville."

"If you have the slightest objection, say so frankly," said the kind-hearted merchant.

"I have not the slightest objection, Mr. Greville. It is entirely at your disposal."

Mr. Greville was profuse in his thanks.

"Shall I send it to your house?" said the picture framer.

"No, Mr. Tennant," replied the merchant. "It is too valuable to be trusted out of my hands. I am personally responsible, and I fear that I am not rich enough to remunerate the artist, if any harm happens to it."

With these words, bowing to the artist, Mr. Greville took the picture carefully under his arm, and left the shop, Montfort soon following.

"Well, I declare," said the picture framer, when he was left alone, "artists is queer animils, and no mistake. Neglect 'em, and it makes 'em as mad as a short-horned bull in fly time; coax 'em and pat 'em, and they lets fly their heels in your face. Seems to me, if I was an artist, I shouldn't be particular about being a hog, too. There ain't no sense in it. Now, it beats my notion all to pieces to see how Mr. Greville could talk so pleasantly and gentlemanly to that dratted Montfort, and he flyin' into his face all the time like a tarrier dog. I'd a punched his head for him, I would—if they'd had me up afore the Sessions for saltin' and batterin'. Consequently it's better to be a pictur' framer than a pictur' painter. Cause why?—a pictur' framer is a gentleman, and a pictur' painter is a hog."

There was a good deal of truth in what Mr. Tennant said, mixed up with a good deal of uncharitableness. But what did he know of the *genus irritabile vatum*?

Evening came; and after many misgivings, Montfort, in an eclectic costume, selected from his whole wardrobe, at a late hour, ventured to emerge from his humble domicile, and present himself at the rosewood portal of his aristocratic neighbor. He soon found himself in the dazzling drawing room, bewildered by the lights, and the splendor of the decoration and the furniture. Mr. Greville saw his embarrassment, and hastened to dispel it. He shook him warmly by the hand, and presented him to his lady and daughter, and then to a crowd of guests. A distinguished artist begged the honor of an introduction to him, and he soon found himself among people who understood him, and with whom he could converse at his ease. Though he was lionized, he was lionized by people who understood the sensitiveness of artistic natures. They flattered delicately and tastefully. Their incense excited, but did not intoxicate or suffocate. In one of the drawing rooms the gratified artist beheld his picture placed in an admirable light, the cynosure of all eyes, and the theme of all lips.

"I am certainly very much indebted to you for placing it so advantageously," said the artist to his host. "It owes at least half its success to the arrangement of the light."

"Do you hear that, Caroline?" asked Mr. Greville, turning to his beautiful daughter, who stood smiling beside him.

"I was afraid I had made some mistake in the arrangement," said the beautiful girl, blushing with pleasure.

Montfort attempted a complimentary remark, but his tongue failed him. He would have given worlds for the self-possession of some of the *nonchalant* dandies he saw hovering around the peerless beauty. He was forced to content himself with awkwardly bowing his thanks.

In the latter part of the evening, one of the rooms was cleared for a dance. Montfort was solicited to join in a quadrille, and a beautiful partner was even presented to his notice; but he wanted confidence and knowledge, and he had no faith in the integrity of the gaiter shoes he had vamped up for the occasion, so that he was forced to decline. This incident revived some of his morbid feelings that had begun to slumber, and he caught himself muttering something about the "frivolities of fashion."

He thought to make his exit unnoticed; but Mr. Greville detected him, and urged him to repeat his visit.

The next day, during his reception hours, several visitors called—an unheard-of thing. They glanced indifferently at his mythological daubs, but were enthusiastic in their praises of his rustic subjects. The day following, more visitors came. He was offered and accepted four hundred dollars for one of his cabinet pictures. In a word, orders flowed in upon him; he could hardly paint fast enough to supply the demand. He became rather fastidious in his dress—patronized the first tailors and boot makers, cultivated the graces, and took lessons in the waltz and polka. At Mr. Greville's, and some of the other houses he visited, he was remarked as being somewhat of a dandy. And this was Montfort the misanthrope—Montfort the socialist—Montfort the agrarian.

An important episode in his career was an order to paint the portrait of Miss Caroline Greville. He had already had three or four sittings, and the picture was approaching completion; then the work suddenly ceased. Day after day the artist pleaded engagements. At the same time he discontinued his visits at the house.

Mr. Greville, somewhat offended, called on Montfort for an explanation. He found his daughter's picture covered by a curtain.

"My dear sir," said he, "how does it happen that you can't go on with that picture? My wife is very anxious about it."

"I can never finish it," said the artist sadly.

"How so, my young friend?"

"Mr. Greville, I will be frank with you. I love your daughter; I, a poor artist, have dared to lift my eyes to the child of the opulent merchant. I have never in look or word, though, led her to divine my feelings—the secret is in my own keeping. But I cannot see her day after day—I cannot scan her beautiful and innocent features, or listen to the brilliant flow of her conversation, without agony. This has compelled me, sir, to suspend my work."

"Mr. Julian Montfort," said the merchant, "you seem bent—excuse me—on making yourself miserable. You are no longer a poor artist; you have a fortune in your pencil. Your profession is now a surer thing than mine. There is no gentleman in the city who ought not to be proud of your alliance; and if you can make yourself acceptable to my daughter, why, take her and be happy."

How Julian sped in his wooing may be inferred from the fact that, at a certain wedding ceremony in Grace Church, he performed the important part of bridegroom to the bride of Miss Caroline Greville; and after the usual quantity of hand shakings, and tears, and kisses, and all the usual efforts to make a wedding resemble a funeral as much as possible, Mr. and Mrs. Montfort took passage in one of the Havre steamers for an extensive tour upon the European continent.

When they returned, Mr. Montfort's reputation rose higher than ever, of course, and he made money with marvellous rapidity. He is now as well known in Wall Street as in his studio, has a town and country house, is a strong conservative in politics, and talks very learnedly about the moneyed interest. He has made some efforts to transplant his good old father and mother to New York; but they prefer residing at his villa, and taking care of his Durham cattle and Suffolk pigs, and seeing that his "Cochin Chinas" and "Brahma Pootras" do not trample down the children when they go out to feed the poultry of a summer morning.

SOUVENIRS OF A RETIRED OYSTERMAN IN ILL HEALTH.

Samivel, my boy, always stick to the shop; and if ever you become a *millionhair*, like me, never be seduced by any womankind into enterin' fash'nable society, and moving among the circles of *bong tong*. (I have been obligated to study French without a master; 'cause the Upper Ten always talks in bad French, and so a word or two will slip in onawares, even ven talking to a friend—just as a bad oyster will sometimes make its way into a good stew, spite of the best artist.)

I envies you, Samivel. You don't know what a treat it is to me to be admitted confidentially behind the counter, and to find myself surrounded once more by these here congenial bivalves. I can't escape from old associations. Oysters stare me in the face wherever I go. They're fash'nable, Samivel, and it's about the only think in fash'n as I reg'larly likes.

The other day we gave a *derjerner*, (that's French for brekfax, Samivel,) which took place about dinner time, and consisted of several distinguished pussons of the city, and three or four Hungry'uns as came over in the last steamer—reg'lar rang-a-tangs, vith these 'ere yaller anchovies growin' onto their upper lips. The old ooman, or madame, as she calls herself, was on hand to receive—but I was out of the way. She was mightily flustered, for she know'd I could talk a little Dutch, and she wanted me for to interpret with the Hungry'uns.

So she speaks up werry sharp, (the old ooman can speak werry sharp by times,) and says to my youngest, a boy,—

"Where on airth *can* your father be?"

"O, daddy's in the sink room," says the young 'un, "a openin' eyesters."

The whole *derjerner* bust into a hoss larff—for these Upper Ten folks, Samivel,—betwixt you and me and the pump, my boy,—ain't got no more manners than hogs. The child was voted an *ongfong terriblee*—but it wor a fack. I had went down into the sink room, as a mere looker-on in Veneer, and I seen one of my *employees* a making such botchwork of openin', hagglin' up his hands, and misusin' the oysters, than I off coat, tucked up sleeves, and went to work, and rolled 'em off amazin'—I tell you. The past rushed back on me—the familiar feel of the knife almost banished my dyspepsy—I lived—I breathed—I vas a oysterman again. Did I ever show you them lines I wrote into my darter's album? No. Vell, then, 'ere goes:—

TO AN UNOPENED OYSTER.

Thou liest fair within thy shell;
Thy charms no mortal eye can see;
And so, as Lamprey[A] says, of old
Was Wenus lodged—the fairest she.

But beauties such as yourn and hern
Were never born unseen to waste;
Like her, you're bound to come to light,
To gratify refinement's taste.

The fairest of the female race
To Ilium vent with Priam's boy;
So the best oysters that I see
Are sent by railroad off to Troy.

Sleep on—sleep on—nor dream of woe
Until the horrid deed be done—
Then out and die, like Simile,[B]
In thy first glance upon the sun.

[A] Probably Lempriere.

[B] Semele (?)

Well, and 'ows bizness, Samivel? You've got a good stand, and you're bound to succeed. But beware of the Cracker-Fiend. I'll tell you about him.

There vas a chap as used to *patronize* me that vas one of the hungriest customers you ever did see. He was werry shabbily dressed, and he looked for all the world like the picturs I've seen of Shakspeare's "lean and hungry Cashier."

He used to come in, give his order, (generally a stew,) and then go and set down in a box and drop the curting. It allers looks suspicious for a customer to drop his curting *afore* you bring him the oysters—*arterwards* it's all perfectly proper, in course. Afore the stew was ready, he would call out—

"Waiter! crackers!"

The boy would hand him a basket; but when his stew was set before him, there warn't no crackers in *his* box.

So ve put him on a allowance of a dozen crackers, which is werry liberal, considerin' as pickles and pepper-sarce is throw'd in gratis. But he used to step out quietly and snake baskets of crackers outen other boxes, so's the other customers, as alvays conducted themselves like perfick gen'lemen, vas all the time a singing out, "Waiter! plate of crackers."

Then we kept a boy a-watching of him, so's to keep him in his box till he'd eat his oysters, and then you had to keep a werry sharp eye on him ven he was paying, and you vas a-makin' change, els't you'd hev all the crackers took off the counter.

One day arter he vas gone, ve found all the crackers missin' from one side of the room. Of course, ve suspected he done it, but how he done it vas as much a puzzle as the Spinks.

Next day, arter ve got him into his box, ve vatched and listened. Ve heard a queer kind of sound, like a man trying to play the jewsharp vith his boots; and, sir, ve detected the cracker-fiend a climbin' over the partitions into the neighborin' boxes, and a collarin' all the crackers he could come acrost.

Perhaps you think I vent into him like a knife into a Prince's Bay. But I didn't do no such think. I treated him werry perlite, and gin him two dollars, a keg of crackers, and a jar of pickled oysters, on condition he'd go and patronize some other establishment. Keep an eye open for him, Samivel.

Be generous, Samivel, but don't carry generosity to XS, for an antidote I'm about to relate, out of my pusnol experience, illustrates the evil effex of excessive philanthrophy.

A little gal used to come into my shop to buy oysters. I seen she was some kind of a foreigner, so I set her down for Dutch—as them vas the only foreigners I vas acquainted vith at the time. I artervards discovered she was French. She was werry thin, and as pale as a soft-shelled clam; there was a dark blue color under her eyes, like these here muscle shells. At first, she used to buy ninepence worth of oysters. Arter a while it came down to fourpence; and one day she only vanted two cents vorth. I asked her who they vas for, and she said,—

"For my grandfather; he is very sick, sare."

I followed her, and found out where her grandfather lived. So one night I opened four gallons of prime New Yorkers, put 'em in a kettle, took a lot of crackers and soft bread, and started for the Frenchman's. The little gal came to the door, and showed me up stairs. The poor old customer was all alone, in bed, and yaller as a blanket. He start up ven he see us, and exclaimed,—

"Ah! mon Dieu! Antoinette, priez le gentilhomme de 'asseoir."

The leetle gal offered me a stool, but I didn't set down.

"Mounseer," said I, in some French manufactured for the occasion, "I havey broughtee you sommey oysteries," and I showed him the kittle, with the kiver off.

I thought his eyes kind of vatered at the sight, but he sighed, and turnin' to the leetle gal, said,—

"Antoinette, dites à Monsieur, que je n'ai plus d'argent—pas un sou."

I guessed it was something about money, so afore the leetle gal could translate it, I sang out,—

"I don't want no money, Mounseer; these here are free gratis, for nothin' at all. I always treats my customers once in a while."

That was a lie, Samivel—but never mind, I gin him a dozen, and the old fellur seemed to like 'em fust rate. Then I offered him some more, but he hung back. However I made him swallow 'em, and offered some to the leetle gal.

"After grandpapa," said she.

So I offered him some more.

"No more, I zank you; I 'ave eat too moosh."

I know'd he was only sogerin' out of delixy. So I says as perlite as possible,—

"None of that, old fellur—catch hold. I fetched 'em for you, and I'm bound to see you eat 'em."

"Sare, you are *too* kind," said he; and he vent to vork again. Arter a spell, he stopped.

"Don't like 'em—hey?" says I, pretendin' to be mad.

"I sall prove ze contraire," said he, in a kind of die-away manner, and he went into 'em agin.

Presently, he gin over, and fell back on his piller murmurin'—

"Sare, you are too good."

I gin the balance to the leetle gal, and told her to come round in the mornin', and I'd fill her kittle for her, adding that her grandfather would be all straight in the mornin'.

Samivel! he *vas* all straight in the morning, but just as stiff as a cold poker. The last two or three dozen finished him; his digestion wasn't strong enough for 'em, and he know'd it, but he eat himself to death out of politeness. The French are certingly the perlitest people on the face of the yairth.

Howsever, I see him buried decently, and I adopted the leetle gal. She was well brung up and educated, and she larned my darters French—the real Simon Pure—for she was a Canadian, and her grandfather came from Gascony. But his fate vos a orful lesson. Benevolence, like an oyster-roast, is good for nothink if it's over done. And now, Samivel, my boy, *a-jew*, for I have a *sworray* this evenin', and receive half Beacon Street. *A-jew.*

THE NEW YEAR'S STOCKINGS.

"Never crosses his t's, nor dots his i's, and his n's and v's and r's are all alike!" said, almost despairingly, Mr. Simon Quillpen, the painstaking clerk of old Lawyer Latitat, as he sat late at night, on the last day of the year, digging away at the copy of a legal document his liberal patron and employer had placed in his hands in the early part of the evening. "Thank Heaven!" he added, laying down his pen, and consulting a huge silver bull's eye which he pulled from a threadbare fob, "I shall soon get through this job, and then, hey for roast potatoes and the charming society of Mrs. Q.!" And with this consolatory reflection, he resumed his work with redoubled energy.

Mr. Quillpen was a little man; not so very little as to pass for a phenomenon, but certainly too small to be noticed by a recruiting grenadier sergeant. His nose was quite sharp and gave his mild, thin countenance, particularly as he carried his head a little on one side, a very bird-like air. He trod, too, gingerly and lightly, very like a sparrow or a tomtit; and, to complete the analogy, his head being almost always surmounted by a pen, he had a sort of crested, blue-jayish aspect, that was rather comical. Quillpen had a very little wife and three very little children, Bob, Chiffy, and the baby; the last the ultimate specimen of the *diminuendo*. It was well for them that they were so small, for Quillpen obtained his *starvelihood* by driving the quill for Mr. Latitat at four hundred dollars a year, to which Mrs. Quillpen added, from time to time, certain little sums derived from making shirts and overalls at the rate of about ten cents the million stitches.

Whether Mr. Latitat was able to pay more was a question that never entered the minute brain of Simon Quillpen; for he had so humble an opinion of his own merits, and was always so contented and cheerful, that he regarded his salary as enormous, and was wont playfully to sign little confidential notes Crœsus Quillpen and Girard Quillpen, and on rare convivial occasions would sometimes style himself Baron Rothschild. But this last title was very rarely indulged in, because it once sent his particular crony, a chuckle-headed clerk in the post-office, into a cachinnatory fit which was "rayther in the apoplectic line."

"To return to our muttons." Simon dug away at his copying with an occasional reverential glance at a certain low oaken door, opening into the *penetralia* of this abode of law and righteousness, behind which oaken door, at that very moment, sat Mr. Lucius Latitat, either deeply engaged in the solution of some vast legal problem, or calculating the interest on an outstanding note, or consulting with chuckling delight a list of mortgages to be foreclosed.

Well—Quillpen finished his document, wiped his pen on a thick velvet butterfly, laid it in the rack above the ink, pushed back his chair from the table, withdrew the cambric sleeve from his right arm, and smoothed down his wristbands, having first put on his India rubber overshoes. The fact is, he was very anxious to get home, and he could not go without first seeing Mr. Latitat. The idea of knocking at Mr. Latitat's door on business of his own never once occurred to him. He would do that for a client, but not for himself. So he ventured on a series of low coughs, and finding no notice was taken of them, he dropped the poker into the coalhod, the most daring act he had ever perpetrated. The slight noise thus produced crashed on his guilty ears like thunder, or rather with the roar of a universal earthquake. Slight, however, as it was, it brought out Mr. Latitat from his interior.

"What the deuse are you making such a racket for?" he exclaimed in tones that thrilled to the heart of his employee; then, without waiting for an answer, he slightly glanced at the table, and asked, "Have you got through that job?"

"Yes'm—I mean, yes'r" replied the quivering Simon.

"Well, then, you can go. I'm going myself. You blow out the lights and lock the room. And mind and be here early to-morrow morning. Nothing like beginning the New Year well. Good night."

"Mr. Latitat, sir!" cried Quillpen, with desperate resolution, as he saw the great man about to disappear—"please, sir—could you let me have a little money to-night?"

"Why! what do you want of money?" retorted the lawyer. "O! I 'spose you have a host of unpaid bills."

"No, sir; no, sir; that's not it," Simon hastened to say. "I hain't got narry bill standing. I pay as I go. Cash takes the lot!"

"None of your coarse, vulgar slang to me!" said Latitat. "Reserve it for your loose companions. If not to pay bills, what for?"

"Please, sir,—we, that is Mrs. Q. and myself, want to put something in the children's stockings, sir."

"Then put the children's legs in 'em!" said the lawyer with a grin. "I make no payments to be used for any such ridiculous purposes. Good night. Yet stay—take this letter—there's money in it—a large amount—put it in the post-office with your own hands as you go home."

"And you can't let me have a trifle?" gasped Simon.

"Not a cent!" snarled the lawyer; and he slammed the door behind him, and went heavily down the stairs.

"I wonder how it feels to punch a man's head," said Simon, as he stood rooted to the spot where Mr. Latitat left him. "It's illegal—it's actionable—there are fines and penalties provided by the statute: but it seems as if there were cases that might justify the operation—morally. But then, again—what good would it do to punch his head? Punching his head wouldn't get me money—and if I was to try it, on finding that the licks didn't bring out the cash, I might be tempted to help myself to the cash, and that would be highway robbery; and when the punchee ventured to suggest that, the puncher might be tempted to silence him. O Lord! that's the way these murders in the first degree happen; and I think that I was almost on the point of taking the first step. I really think I look a little like Babe the pirate," added the poor man, glancing at his mild but disturbed features in the glass; "or like Captain Kidd, or leastways like Country McClusky—a regular bruiser!"

Sitting down before the grate, and stirring it feebly with the poker, he tried to devise some feasible plan for supplying the vacuum in his treasury. He might borrow, but then all his friends were very poor, and particularly hard up—at this particular season of the year. The bull's eye watch might have been "spouted," if he had foreseen this contingency; but every avuncular relative was now at this hour of the night snug abed to a dead certainty. Purchasing on credit was not to be thought of, and the only toy shop which kept open late enough for his purchases, was kept by a man to whom he was totally unknown. Time galloped on, meanwhile, and the half-hour struck.

"I'll slip that letter in the post-office, and then go home," said Simon sorrowfully, rising as he spoke, and grasping his inseparable umbrella.

"Hallo! shipmate! where-away?" cried a hoarse voice. And Mr. Quillpen became aware of the presence of an "ancient mariner," enveloped in a very rough dreadnought, and finished off with a large amount of whiskers and tarpaulin.

"I was going home, sir," replied Simon, with the deferential air of a very little to a very big man.

"Ay—going to clap on hatches and deadlights. Well, tell me one thing—where-away may one find one Mr. Latitat—a shore-going cove, a regular land-shark, d'ye see?"

"This is Mr. Latitat's office, sir," said Simon.

"Ay—and is he within hail?"

"No, sir, he has gone home."

"Slipped his cable—hey? just my luck! Well, one might snooze comfortably on this here table—mightn't he? You can clear out, and I'll take care of the shop till morning."

"That would be perfectly inadmissible, sir," said Simon, "the idea of a stranger's sleeping here!"

"A stranger!" cried the sailor. "Why, shipmate, do you happen to know who I am? Look at me! Don't you find somewhat of a family likeness to Lucius in my old weather-beaten mug? Why, man-alive, I'm his brother,—his own blood brother! You must a heard him speak of me. Been cruising round the world in chase of Fortune, but could never overhaul her. Been sick, shipwrecked, and now come back as poor as I went. But Lucius has got enough for both of us. How glad he'll be to see me to-morrow, hey, old Ink-and-tape?"

Simon had his doubts about that matter, but told the sailor to come in the morning, and see.

"That I will," said the tar, "and start him up with a rousing Happy New Year! But I say, shipmate, I don't want to sleep in the watch-house. Have you never a shilling about your trousers?"

Simon answered that he hadn't a cent.

"Why, don't that brother of mine give you good wages?"

"Enormous!" said Simon.

"What becomes of it all?"

"I spend it all—I'm very extravagant," said Simon, shaking his head. "And then, I'm sorry to say, your brother isn't always punctual in his payments. To-night, for instance, I couldn't get a cent from him."

"Then I tell you what I'd do, shipmate," said the sailor, confidentially. "I'd overhaul some of his letters. Steam will loosen a wafer, and a hot knife-blade, wax. I'd overhaul his money-letters and pay myself. Ha! ha! do you take? Now, that letter you've got in your fin, my boy, looks woundy like a dokiment chock full of shinplasters. What do you say to making prize of 'em? wouldn't it be a jolly go?"

"Stand off!" said Simon, assuming a heavy round ruler and a commanding attitude. "Don't you come anigh me, or there'll be a case of justifiable homicide here. How dare you counsel me to commit a robbery on your own brother? I wonder you ain't ashamed to look me in the face."

"A chap as has cruised as many years as I have in the low latitudes ain't afraid to look any body in the face," answered the "ancient mariner," grimly. "I made you a fair offer, shipmate, and you rejected it like a long-shore jackass as you are. Good night to ye."

Much to his relief, the sailor took himself off, and Simon, after locking and double locking his door, went to the post-office and deposited the letter with which he had been intrusted. As he lived a great way up on the Neck, he did not reach home until after all the clocks of the city had struck twelve, so that he was able to surprise his little wife, who was sitting up for him, with a "Happy New Year!"

He cast a rueful eye at the line of stockings hung along the mantel-piece in the sitting room, and then sorrowfully announced to his wife his failure to obtain money of Mr. Latitat.

"There'll be nothing for the stockings, Meg," said he, "unless what the poor children put in ours."

"I am very sorry," said his wife, who bore the announcement much better than he anticipated; "but we'll have a happy New Year for all that."

Simon's roasted potatoes were completely charred, he had been detained so late; but there was a little meal in the centre of each, and charcoal is not at all unhealthy. He went to bed, and in spite of his cares, slept the sleep of the just.

A confused babbling awoke him at daylight. Master Bobby was standing on his stomach, Miss Chiffy was seated nearly on his head, and baby was crowing in its cradle. Happy New Years and kisses were exchanged. "O, dear papa and mamma!" cried Bobby, "what a beautiful horse I found in my stocking!"

"And what a beautiful wax doll, with eyes that move, in mine," said Chiffy,—"and such a splendid rattle and coral in baby's. Now, pray go down and see what there is in yours."

"This is some of your work, little woman," whispered Simon to his wife. But the little woman denied it emphatically. Much mystified, he hurried down to the breakfast room. The children had made the usual offering of very hard and highly-colored sugar plums; but in each of the two large stockings, stowed away at the bottom, was a roll of bank notes, five hundred dollars in each.

"Somebody wants to ruin us!" cried Simon, bursting into tears. "This is stolen money, and they want to lay it on to us."

"All I know about it," said Mrs. Quillpen, "is, that last night, just before you came home, a sailor man came here with all these things, and said they were for us, and made me promise to put them in the stockings, as he directed, and say nothing about his visit to you."

"A sailor!" cried Simon—"I have it! I think I know who it is. Good by—I'll be back to breakfast directly."

Simon ran to the office, and found, as he anticipated, Mr. Latitat there before him.

"A happy New Year to you, sir," said he. "Have you seen your brother?"

"I have not," replied Mr. Latitat.

Simon then told him all that happened on the preceding night; the apparition of the sailor,—the temptation,—the money found in the stockings, in proof of which he showed the thousand dollars, and stating his fears that they had been stolen, offered to deposit the sum in his employer's hands.

"Keep 'em, shipmate; they were meant for you!" exclaimed Mr. Latitat, suddenly and queerly, assuming the very voice and look of the nautical brother of the preceding evening.

While Simon stared his eyes out of his head, Mr. Latitat informed him that he had no brother—that he had disguised himself for the purpose of putting his clerk's long-tried fidelity to a final test, and, that sustained triumphantly, had rewarded him in the manner we have seen. He told how, disgusted in early life by the treachery and ingratitude of friends and relations who had combined to ruin him, he had become a misanthrope and miser; how the spectacle of Simon's disinterested fidelity, rigid sense of honor, self-denial and cheerfulness, had won back his better nature; and he wound off, as he shook Quillpen warmly by the hand, by announcing that he had raised his salary to twelve hundred dollars per annum.

The good news almost killed Simon. "Please your honor," said he, endeavoring to frame an appropriate reply,—"no—that ain't it—please your excellency—you've gone and done it—you've gone and done it! I was Baron Rothschild before, and now—no—I can't tell what I am—it isn't in no biographical dictionary, and I don't believe it's in the 'Wealth of Nations!'"

"Well, never mind," said Latitat, laughing, "go home and tell Mrs. Q. the office won't be open till to-morrow, and that I shall depend on dining with you all to-day."

THE OBLIGING YOUNG MAN.

"Cars ready for Boston and way stations!" shouted the conductor of a railroad train, as the steamhorse, harnessed for his twenty mile trip, stood chafing, snorting, and coughing, throwing up angry puffs of mingled gray and dingy vapor from his sturdy lungs. "Cars ready for Boston and way stations!"

"O, yes!" replied a brisk young man, with a bright eye, peculiar smirk, spotted neckcloth, and gray gaiters with pearl buttons. "Cars ready for Boston and way stations. All aboard. Now's your time—quick, or you'll lose 'em. Now then, ma'am."

"But, sir," remonstrated the old lady he addressed, and whom he was urging at the steps of a first class car.

"O, never mind!" replied the brisk young man. "Know what you're going to say—too much trouble—none whatever, I assure you. Perfect stranger, true—but scriptural injunction, do as you'd be done by. In with you—ding! ding!—there's the bell—off we go."

And so in fact they did go off at forty miles an hour.

"But, sir," said the old lady, trembling violently.

"I see," interrupted the OBLIGING YOUNG MAN; "want a seat—here it is—a great bargain—cars full—quick, or you'll lose it."

"But, sir," said the old lady, with nervous trepidation, "I—I—wasn't going to Boston."

"The deuce you weren't. Well, well, well, why couldn't you say so? Hullo! Conductor! Stop the cars!"

"Can't do it," replied the conductor. "This train don't stop short of Woburn watering station."

"Woburn watering station!" whimpered the old woman, wringing her hands. "O, what shall I do?"

"Sit still; take it easy—no use crying for spilt milk; what can't be cured must be endured. I'll look out sharp; you might have saved yourself all this trouble."

Away went the cars, racketting and oscillating, while the obliging young man was looking round for another recipient of his good services.

"Ha!" he muttered to himself. "There's a poor young fellow quite alone. Lovesick, perhaps; pale cheek—sunken eye—never told his love; but let—Shakspeare—I'm his man! Must look out for the old woman. Here we are, ma'am, fifteen miles to Lowell—out with you—look out for the cars on the back track. Good by—pleasant trip!"

Ding dong, went the bell again.

"Hullo! here's her bundle! Catch, there—heads! All right—get on, driver!"

And having tossed a bundle after the old woman, he resumed his seat.

"Confound it!" roared a fat man in a blue spencer. "You're treading on my corns."

"Beg pardon," said the obliging young man. "Bad things, corns,—'trifling sum of misery new added to the foot of your account;' old author—name forgotten. Never mind—drive on!"

"But where's my bundle?" asked the fat man. "Conductor! Where's my bundle? Brown paper—red string. Saw it here a moment since."

The conductor knew nothing about it. The obliging young man did. It was the same he had thrown out after the old woman.

"You'll find it some where," he said, with a consolatory wink. "Can't lose a brown paper bundle. I've tried—often—always turned up; little boy sure to bring it. 'Here's your bundle, sir; ninepence, please.' All right—go ahead!"

Here the obliging young man took his seat beside the pale-faced youth.

"Ill health, sir?"

"No, sir," replied the pale-faced youth, fidgeting.

"Mental malady—eh?"

The young man sighed.

"See it all. Don't say a word, man! Cupid, heart from heart, forced to part. Flinty-hearted father?"

"No, sir."

"Flinty-hearted mother?"

"No, sir."

"Flinty-hearted aunt?"

The lovesick young man sighed, and nodded assent.

"Tell me the story. I'm a stranger—but my heart is here, sir." Whereupon the obliging young man referred to a watch pocket in his plaid vest, and nodded with a great deal of intelligence. "Tell me all—like to serve my fellows—no other occupation; out with it, as the doctor said to the little boy that swallowed his sister's necklace."

The lovesick youth informed the obliging young man that he loved and was beloved by a young lady of Boston, whose aunt, acting as her guardian, opposed his suit. He was going to Boston to put a plan of elopement into operation. He had prepared two letters, one to the aunt renouncing his hopes, to throw her off her guard; the other to the young lady, appointing a meeting at the Providence cars. The difficulty was to get the letters delivered. This the obliging young man readily undertook to do in person. Both the aunt and niece bore the same name—Emeline Brown; but the aunt's letter was sealed with black, the niece's with red wax. The letters were delivered with many injunctions to the obliging young man, and the two new-made friends parted on the arrival of the cars in Boston.

The Providence cars were just getting ready to start, when, amid all the bustle and confusion, a pale-faced young man "might have been seen," as Mr. James, the novelist, says, nervously pacing to and fro, and occasionally darting into Pleasant Street, and scrutinizing every approaching passenger and vehicle. At last, when there was but a single moment to spare, a hack drove up furiously, and a veiled lady hastily descended, and gave her hand to her expectant admirer.

"Quick, Emeline, or we shall lose the train!"

The enamoured couple were soon seated beside each other, and whirling away to Providence. The lady said little, but sat with downcast head and veiled face, apparently overwhelmed with confusion at the step she had taken. But it was enough for young Dovekin to know she was beside him, and he poured forth an unbroken stream of delicious nonsense, till the train arrived at its destination.

In the station house the lady lifted her veil. Horror and confusion! It was the aunt! The obliging young man had delivered the wrong letter.

"Yes, sir," said Miss Brown, "I am the person whom you qualified, in your letter intended for my niece, as a 'hateful hag, in whose eyes you were throwing dust'. What do you say to that, sir?"

"Say!" replied the disconsolate Dovekin. "It's no use to say any thing; for it is my settled purpose to spring over the parapet of the railroad bridge and seek oblivion in a watery grave. But first, if I could find that obliging young man, I'd be the death of him."

"No you wouldn't," said the voice of that interesting individual, as he made his appearance with a lady on his arm. "Here she is—take her—be happy. After I'd given the notes, mind misgave me—went back to the house—

found the aunt gone—niece in tears—followed after—same train—last car—here she is!"

"I hope this will be a lesson," said Dovekin.

"So it is. Henceforth, I shall mind my own business; for every thing I've undertaken lately, on other folks' account, has gone amiss. Come, aunty, give your blessing—let 'em go. Train ready—I'm off—best of wishes—good by. Cars ready for Boston and way stations!—all aboard."

The aunt gave her blessing; and this was the last that any of the party saw of the *Obliging Young Man.*

EULALIE LASALLE.

A STORY OF THE REIGN OF TERROR.

O, what was love made for if 'twas not for this,The same amidst sorrow, and transport, and bliss?

MOORE.

The fanaticism of the French revolutionists had reached its height; the excitable population, intoxicated with power, and maddened by the vague dread of the retribution of despair, goaded on by profligate, ferocious, or insane leaders, was plunging into the most revolting and sanguinary excesses. The son of St. Louis had ascended to heaven, the beautiful and unfortunate Marie Antoinette had laid her head upon the block, the baby heir of the throne of the Capets was languishing in the hands of his keepers, and the Girondists, the true friends of republican liberty, were silenced by exile or the scaffold. In short, the Reign of Terror, the memorable sway of Robespierre, hung like a funeral pall upon the land which was fast becoming a vast cemetery. The provincial towns, faithful echoes of the central capital, were repeating the theme of horror with a thousand variations. Each considerable city had its guillotine, and where that instrument of punishment was wanting, the fusillade or the mitraille supplied its place.

At this crisis, Eugene Beauvallon, a young merchant of Toulouse, presented himself one morning in the drawing room of Mademoiselle Eulalie Lasalle, an orphan girl of great beauty and accomplishment, to whom he had long been betrothed, and whom he would ere this have married but for the political troubles of the period. Eulalie was a graceful creature, slenderly and symmetrically formed, with soft blue eyes, and an exceedingly gentle expression, which was indicative of her character. She seemed too fair and fragile to buffet with the storms of life, and ill fitted to endure its troubles, created to be the idol of a drawing room, the fairy queen of a boudoir.

Eugene was a handsome, manly fellow, of great energy and character. The revolution surprised him in the act of making a fortune; the whirlwind had stripped him of most of his property, but had yet left him liberty and life. He had contrived to avoid rendering himself obnoxious to the sansculottes without securing their confidence. The tri-colored cockade which he wore in his hat shielded him from the fatal epithet of aristocrat—a certain passport to the guillotine.

Beauvallon then seated himself beside Eulalie, who was struck with the radiant expression of his countenance, and begged to know the reason of his joyous excitement.

"I have good news to tell you," he said, gayly; "but we are not alone," he added, stopping short, as his eyes rested on the sinister face of an old woman, humbly attired, who was busily engaged in knitting, not far from the lovers.

"O, don't mind poor old Mannette," said Eulalie. "The poor old creature is past hearing thunder. It is a woman, Eugene, I rescued from absolute starvation, and she is so grateful, and seems so desirous of doing something to render herself useful, that I am mortified almost at her sense of the obligation."

"I hope she has not supplanted your pretty *femme de chambre*, Julie, of whom you threatened to be jealous. My admiration, I hope, has not cost the girl her place."

"O, dear, no! I couldn't part with Julie!" replied Eulalie, laughing gayly. "But come, you must not tantalize me—what has occurred to make you so gay, at a time when every true Frenchman wears a face of mourning?"

"The Marquis de Montmorenci is at liberty."

"At liberty? How happened it that the Revolutionary Tribunal acquitted him?"

"Acquitted him! Eulalie, does the tiger that has once tasted the blood of his prey permit him to escape? Is Robespierre more lenient than the beast of prey? No, Eulalie, he escaped by the aid of a true friend. He fled from Paris, reached Toulouse, and found shelter under my roof!"

The cheek of Eulalie turned ashy pale. "Under your roof!" she faltered. "Do you know the penalty of sheltering a fugitive from justice?"

"It is death upon the scaffold," answered the young merchant, calmly. "But better that a thousand times than the sin of ingratitude; the sin of turning a deaf ear to the claims of humanity."

"My own noble Eugene!" exclaimed the young girl, enthusiastically, pressing her lover's hand. "Every day increases my love, my respect for you, and my sense of my own unworthiness. But you will never have to blush for the inferiority of your wife."

"What do you mean, dearest?" inquired Eugene, with alarm.

"This is no time for marriage," said Eulalie, sadly. "Images of death and violence meet our eyes whichever way they turn. We were born, Eugene, in melancholy times, and our loves are misplaced. We shall meet hereafter; on this earth, I fear, our destinies will never be united."

"Prophetess of evil!" said Beauvallon, gayly. "Your rosy lips belie your gloomy augury. No, Eulalie, this dark cloud cannot forever overshadow the land—even now I think I can see glimpses of the blue sky. *Le bon temps viendra*,—the good time is coming,—and then, Eulalie, be sure that I will claim your promised hand."

The conversation of the lovers had been so animated and interesting that they did not notice the moment when old Mannette had glided like a spectre from the apartment.

Beauvallon lingered a while,—"parting is such sweet sorrow,"—and finally reluctantly tore himself from the presence of Eulalie, promising to see her again on the ensuing day, and let her know whatever had transpired in the interim.

As he approached the street in which his store and house were situated, he heard the confused murmur of a multitude, and soon perceived, on turning the corner, that a very large crowd was collected outside his door. There were men and women—many of the former armed with pikes and sabres—the latter, the refuse of the populace, who appeared like birds of evil omen at every scene of violence and tumult.

A hundred voices called out his name as he approached, and menacing gestures were addressed to him by the multitude.

"Citizens," said the merchant, "what is the meaning of all this?"

"You shall know, traitor," shrieked a palsied hag of eighty, whose lurid eyes had already gloated on every public execution that had taken place in Toulouse. "Here is Citizen Dumart of the revolutionary committee—ah, *he* is a true friend of the people—he is no aristocrat in disguise! *Vive le Citoyen Dumart!*"

"Long live Citizen Dumart! Down with the aristocrats!" shouted a hundred voices.

The Citizen Dumart was a sallow-faced man, dressed in rusty black, wearing an enormous tri-colored cockade in his three-cornered hat, with a sash of the same color girt around his waist. His bloodshot eyes expressed a mixture of cowardice with ferocity. He was flanked by a couple of pikemen as hideous as the Afrites of Eastern romance.

"Citizen Beauvallon," said he, in a voice whose tremor betrayed his native timidity, "I arrest you in the name of the revolutionary committee of Toulouse. Citizen Beauvallon, it is useless to resist the authority of the representatives of the people; if you have any concealed weapons about you, I advise you to surrender them. You see I stand here protected by the arms of the people."

"I have no weapons," replied Beauvallon. "I have no sinister designs. I know not why I am arrested. Acquaint me with the charge, and confront me with my accusers."

"Seize upon the prisoner!" cried Dumart to his satellites. And he breathed freer when he saw the merchant in the gripe of two muscular ruffians, whose iron hands compressed his wrists as if they were manacles.

"Away with him!" screamed the hag who had spoken before. "Away with him to the revolutionary committee! Down with the aristocrats!"

Followed by the imprecations of the crowd, Beauvallon was conducted to the town house, and in a very few moments was placed at the bar of the revolutionary committee—a body invested with the power of life and death. On his way thither he had found means to speak a word to an acquaintance in the crowd, and to beg him to inform Eulalie of what had happened.

So soon as he had heard the accusation read, and knew that he was charged with the crime of aiding the Marquis de Montmorenci, a fugitive from justice, he felt that his situation was indeed critical; but mingled with his astonishment and dread was a curiosity to learn whence his denunciation could have proceeded—who could have lodged the information against him. He was not long kept in suspense, for the witness brought on the stand to confront him was no other than Mannette, the supposed deaf servant of Eulalie Lasalle, who had overheard his confession of the morning, and hastened to denounce him. Though his sentence was not immediately pronounced, and the decision of his case was deferred till the next day, Beauvallon felt that his doom was sealed.

He was conveyed to a house in the vicinity of the town hall for confinement, as the prisons were all overstocked. His jailer was a man whom the merchant had formerly befriended, and whose heart was not inaccessible to emotions of pity, though he was above bribery, and evidently determined to execute his duty to the letter.

"I have a favor to ask of you, my friend," said the prisoner, slipping a golden louis into his hand.

"If it is one that I can grant without violating my duty," replied the jailer, returning the money to Beauvallon, "I will do so for the sake of old times, but not for gold."

Beauvallon explained that he wished to send a note to Mlle. Lasalle, requesting her to visit him in prison—an interview which would probably be their last, and the jailer undertook readily to see the missive delivered, and to permit the visit. The note having been despatched, Beauvallon sat down to wait for the arrival of his mistress.

The sad hours passed away,—but though he learned from the jailer that his errand had been performed, no Eulalie made her appearance.

"She forsakes me!" he muttered bitterly. "The wounded deer is abandoned by the herd, and an unfortunate man is shunned by his fellows. Well, the dream was pleasant while it lasted—the regret of awakening can scarce be tedious—a few hours, and all the incidents of this transitory life will be forgotten. But Eulalie—whom I loved better than my life itself—it is hard to die without one word from thee."

When on the following day Beauvallon was again taken before the revolutionary committee, he looked anxiously around the court room to see if he could discover the face of Eulalie among the spectators, many of whom were women. But he was disappointed. Her absence convinced him that she had abandoned him, and wholly absorbed by this reflection, he paid no attention to the formula of his trial. He was condemned to death, the sentence to be executed on the following day.

"Mr. President," said he, rising, "I thank you, and I have merely one favor to ask. Anticipate the time of punishment—let it be to-day instead of to-morrow—let me go hence to the scaffold."

"Your request is reasonable," replied the president, in a bland voice, "and if circumstances permitted, it would afford me the greatest pleasure to grant it. But the guillotine requires repair, and will not be in a condition to perform its functions until to-morrow, at which time, Citizen Beauvallon, at the hour of ten, A.M., you will have ceased to exist. Good night, and pleasant dreams!"

This sally was received with roars of applause, and the unhappy prisoner was reconducted to the place of confinement.

That night was a sleepless one. Beauvallon's arrest, his speedy trial and condemnation, the desertion of Eulalie, had followed each other with such stunning rapidity, that, until now, he had hardly time to reflect upon the dismal chain of circumstances—now they pressed upon his attention, and crowded his mind to overflowing. At midnight, as he lay tossing on his bed, upon which he had thrown himself without undressing, he thought he heard a confused noise in the apartment of the next house adjoining his. The noise increased. He placed his hand upon the wall, and felt it jar under successive shocks. Suddenly a current of air blew in upon him, and at the same time a faint ray of light streamed through an opening in the partition.

"Courage!" said a soft voice. "The opening enlarges. Now, Julie!"

Julie! Beauvallon was sure he heard the name, and yet uncertain whether or not he was dreaming.

"Julie!" he exclaimed, cautiously.

"Yes, monsieur—it is Julie—sure enough," answered a pleasant voice.

"Then you, at least, have not forgotten me."

"No one who has once known you can ever forget you. Courage! you will soon be free. Aid us if you can."

"Then you are not alone?"

"Have patience, and you will see."

His own exertions, added to those of his friends without, soon enabled the prisoner to force his way into the next house; but there disappointment awaited him. Two soldiers in the uniform of the *gensdarmerie* stood before him.

"*On ne passe par ici*,—you can't pass here,"—said one.

"What cruel mockery is this?" cried Beauvallon. "Is it not enough that I am condemned to death, but you must subject me to an atrocious pleasantry? This is refinement of cruelty."

"It seems that our disguise is perfect, Julie," said the soldier who had not yet spoken. "Eugene does not know his best friends."

In an instant the speaker was folded in the arms of Beauvallon. It was Eulalie herself, as bewitchingly beautiful in her uniform as in the habiliments of her sex. She hurriedly explained that the moment she heard of Eugene's arrest, she prepared to meet the worst contingency. She had already converted her money into cash. Learning the place of his imprisonment, she had hired, through the agency of another person, the adjoining house, which happened to be unoccupied. The task of making an aperture in the partition was an easy one—the difficulty of passing through the city was greater. The idea of military disguises then occurred. Julie and herself had already equipped themselves, and they were provided with a uniform for Beauvallon.

Secured by this costume, the three fugitives ventured forth. In the great square of the city, workmen were busily employed in repairing the hideous engine of death, and Beauvallon passed, not without a shudder, beneath the very shadow of the guillotine, to which he had been doomed.

Seated on the cold ground, beneath the fatal apparatus, was an old woman muttering to herself.

"Good evening, citizens," said she. "We shall have a fine day for the show to-morrow. Look how the bonny stars are winking and blinking on the gay knife blade they've been sharpening. It will be darker and redder when the clock strikes ten again. Down with the aristocrats!"

The fugitives needed no more to quicken their steps. They reached the frontiers in safety, and beyond the Rhine, in the hospitable land of Germany, the lovers were united; nor did they return to France till the star of Robespierre had set in blood, and the master mind of Napoleon had placed its impress on the destinies of France.

THE OLD CITY PUMP.

Many evenings since, we were passing up State Street late at night. State Street at midnight is a very different affair from State Street at high noon. The shadows of the tall buildings fall on a deserted thoroughfare; save where, here and there, a spectral bank watchman keeps ward over the granite sepulchres of golden eagles, and the flimsier representatives of wealth. The bulls and bears have retired to their dens, and East India merchants are invisible. Newsboys are nowhere, and every sound has died away. There stands the Old State House, peculiar and picturesque, rising with a look of other days, a relic of past time, against the deep blue sky, or webbing the full moon with the delicate tracery of its slender spars and signal halliards. And there stands—no! there stood the old Town Pump. But it is no more—*Ilium fuit* was written on its forehead—it has been reformed out of office, its occupation has gone, its handle has been amputated, its body has been dissected, and there is nothing of it left.

Yet on the evening to which we alluded in the beginning, the old pump was there, and crossing over from the Merchants Bank, we leaned against its handle, as one leans against the arm of an old friend, in a musing, idle mood. Presently we heard a gurgling sound and confused murmurs issuing from its lips—"like airy tongues that syllable men's names." Anon these murmurs shaped themselves into distinct articulations, and as we listened, wonderingly, the old pump spoke:—

"Past twelve o'clock, and a moonlight night. All well, as I'm a pump. Nobody breaking into banks, and nobody kicking up rows—watchmen fast asleep, and every body quiet. But I can't sleep. No! the city government has murdered sleep! There's something heavy on my buckets, and I fear me, I'm a gone sucker! They thought I couldn't find out what they were up to—the municipal government—but I'm a deep one, and I know every thing that's going for'ard. What a jolly go, to be sure! They told me Mayor Bigelow hated proscription—but I knew it was gammon! He must follow the fashion, and Cochituate is all the go. There ain't no pumps now—it's all fountain! Pump water is full of animalculæ, and straddle bugs don't exist in pond water—of course not. Nobody ever see young pollywogs and snapping turtles floating down stream in fly-time. Certainly not! I'm getting old—of course I am; that's the talk! I've been in office too long. Well, well, I know I'm rather asthmatic and phthisicky—but nobody ever knowed me to suck, even in the driest time. These living waters have welled up even from the time when the salt sea was divided from the land, and the rocks were cloven by the hand of Omnipotence, and the sweet spring came bursting upward from the fragrant earth, and light and flowers came together to welcome the birthday of the glad and glorious gift. Here, many a century back, the giant mastodon trod the earth into deep hollows, as he moved upon his sounding path. Then came another time. In the hollow of the three hills, the Indian raised his bark wigwam, and the smoke of his council fire curled up like a mist-wreath in the forest. Here the red man filled the wild gourd cup when he returned weary from the chase or the skirmish. And here, too, the Indian maiden smoothed her dark locks, and her lustrous, laughing eyes gazed upon the image of her own dusky beauty, mirrored on the surface of the wave. By and by the red man ceased to drink of my unfailing rill. Beings with pale faces came to me to quench their thirst; bearded lips were moistened with my diamond drops; and I looked up upon iron corselet and steel hauberk, and faces harder than either. But the old Puritans gave me form and substance—a 'local habitation and a name.' The spirit of the fountain was wedded to its present tabernacle. The dwellings of men sprang up around me in the place of the departing forest. I gave them all a cheerful welcome. If the colonists worked hard, I worked harder yet. I filled their pails and cups, and revived their failing hearts, and cheered their unremitting labors. They called me their friend. The pretty girls smiled upon me, as, under pretence of levying contributions on my treasures, they chatted with young men who gathered at my side. Then came a sterner period. I heard no more love tales—no more idle gossip. Men stood here, and spoke of deep wrong, of tyranny, of trampled rights, of resistance, of liberty! That was a word I had not heard since the red man drank of my unfettered tide. One night, there was a great gathering here. There were men and boys, a multitude. There was much angry talk and much confusion. Then I heard the roll of the drum and the regular tramp of an armed force. A band of British soldiers, all resplendent with scarlet, and gold, and burnished muskets that glittered in the moonbeams, were formed into line at the command of an officer, and confronted the dark array of citizens. Then came an angry discussion—orders on the part of the commander for the multitude to disperse, which were unheeded or disobeyed. Then that line of glittering tubes was levelled. I heard the fatal word "fire!" the flame leaped from the muzzles of the muskets, and the volley crashed and echoed in the street. Blood flowed upon the pavement—the blood of citizens mingled with my waters, and I was the witness of a fearful tragedy. In after times, I heard it named the Boston Massacre. Since then, I have seen hours of sunshine and triumph, of fun and frolic, of anger and rejoicing. My waters have laved the dust that it might not soil the uniform of Washington as he rode past on his snow-white charger, amid the acclamations of the multitude. I have seen Hull and his tars pass up the street, bearing the stripes and stars in triumph from the war of the ocean. I have heard long-winded orators spout over my head in emulation of my craft, "in one weak, washy, everlasting flood." I have seen many a military, many a civic pageant. The last I witnessed was, as Dick Swiveller remarks, a 'stifler.' It was that confounded Water Celebration. Republics *is* ungrateful. I was forgotten on that occasion. Nobody drank at the old city pump. People sat on my head and stood on my nose, just as if I had no feelings. I heard a young lady in the gallery overhead say, 'Well, that horrid old pump will soon be out of the way now.' And a city father answered her, 'Of course.' It was a workin' then—treason and fate, and all them things. I knew they were going to 'put me out of my misery,' as the saying goes. I'm getting superannuated—I heard 'em say so. Sometimes an office boy tastes a drop, and then turns up his nose,—as if it wasn't pug enough before,—and says, 'What horrid stuff! the Cochituate for my money!' General Washington's canteen was filled here—and he said, 'Delicious!' when he raised it to his lips. But he was no judge, of course not. Time was when I wasn't slow but I'm not fast enough for this generation. When folks write letters with lightning, and sail ships with tea-kettles, pumps can't come it over 'em. Well, well, I'll hold out to the last—I'll make 'em carry me off and bury me decently at the city's expense, and perhaps some kind old friend will write my epitaph."

The old pump was mute—the speech was ended—its "song had died into an echo." We passed on mournful and thoughtful. Republics are ungrateful— old friends are forgotten with a change of fashion, and there is a period to the greatness of town pumps as well as the glory of individuals.

THE TWO PORTRAITS.

"Beautiful! beautiful!" exclaimed Ernest Lavalle, as, throwing himself back in his chair, he contemplated, with eyes half shut, a lovely countenance that smiled on him from a canvas, to which he had just added a few hesitating touches. It was but a sketch—little more than outline and dead coloring, and a misty haze seemed spread over the face, so that it looked vision-like and intangible. The young painter's exclamation was not addressed to his workmanship—he was not even looking at that faint image; but, through its medium, was gazing on lineaments as rare and fascinating as ever floated through a poet's or an artist's dream. Deep, lustrous blue eyes, in whose depth sincerity and feeling lay crystallized; features as regular as those of a Grecian statue; a lip melting, ripe, and dewy, half concealing, half revealing, a line of pearls; soft brown hair, descending in waves upon a neck and shoulders of satin surface and Parian firmness. Such were some of the external traits of loveliness belonging to

"A creature not too bright and good
For human nature's daily food,"

who had completely actualized the ideal of the young Parisian artist, into whose studio we have introduced our readers. The fair original, whose portrait is before us, was Rose d'Amour, a beautiful actress of one of the metropolitan theatres, who had just made her debut with distinguished success. There was quite a romance in her history. Of unknown parents, she had commenced her career—like the celebrated Rachel—as a street singer, and was looking forward to no more brilliant future, when her beauty, genius, and purity of character attracted the attention of a distinguished newspaper editor, by whose benevolent generosity she was enabled to prepare herself for the stage, by two or three years of assiduous study. The success of his protégée more than repaid the kind patron for his exertions and expenditure.

A word of Ernest Lavalle, and it shall suffice. He was the son of a humble vine dresser in one of the agricultural departments of France. His talent for drawing, early manifested, attracted the notice of his parish priest, whose earnest representations induced his father to send the boy to Paris, and give him the advantages afforded by the capital for students of art. In the great city, Ernest allowed none of the attractions, by which he was surrounded, to divert him from the assiduous pursuit of his beloved art. His mornings were passed in the gallery of the Louvre, his afternoons in private study, and his evenings at the academy, where he drew from casts and the living model. The only relaxation he permitted himself, was an occasional excursion in the picturesque environs of the French capital; and he always took his sketch book with him, thus making even his pleasure subservient to his studies. Two prizes obtained, for a drawing and a picture, secured for him the patronage of the academy, at whose expense he was sent to Italy, to pursue his studies in the famous galleries of Rome and Florence. He returned with a mind imbued with the beauty and majesty of the works of those great masters, whose glory will outlive the canvas and marble which achieved it, determined to win for himself a niche in the temple of Fame, or perish in his laborious efforts to obtain it. At this time he was in his twenty-second year. A vigorous constitution was his heritage; and his rounded cheek glowed with the warm color of health. His strictly classical features were enhanced by the luxuriance of his hair, which he wore flowing in its native curls, while his full beard and mustache relieved his face from the charge of effeminacy.

Ernest was yet engaged in the contemplation of the unfinished work—or rather in dreaming of the bright original—when a light tap was heard at his door. He opened it eagerly, and his poor studio was suddenly illuminated, as it were, by the radiant apparition of Rose d'Amour. She was dressed with a charming simplicity, which well became a sylph like form, that required no adventitious aid from art.

"Good morning, Monsieur Lavalle!" said the beautiful actress, cheerfully, as she dropped gracefully into the *fauteuil* prepared for her reception. "You find me in the best possible humor to-day, thanks to this bright morning sun, and to the success of last night. *Mon Dieu!* so many bouquets! you can't think! Really, the life of an *artiste* begins to be amusing. Don't you find it so, as a painter?"

"I confess to you, mademoiselle, I have my moments of despondency."

"With your fine talent! Think better of yourself. I hope, at least, that I have not been so unlucky as to surprise you in one of those inopportune moments."

"Ah, mademoiselle," said the painter, "if it were so, one of your smiles would dispel the cloud in a moment."

"Really!" replied the actress, gayly. "Are you quite sure there is no flattery in the remark? I am aware that flattery is an essential part of an artist's profession."

"Not of a true artist's," replied Ernest. "The aim and end of all art is truth; and he who forgets it is untrue to his high mission."

"True," said the lady. "Well, then, *faites votre possible*—as Napoleon said to his friend David—for I am anxious that this portrait shall be a *chef-d'œuvre*. I design it for a present."

"With such a subject before me," replied the painter "I could not labor more conscientiously, if the picture were designed for myself."

The sitting passed away rapidly, for the artist; and he was surprised when the lady, after consulting her watch, rose hastily, and exclaimed, "That odious rehearsal! I must leave you—but you ought to be satisfied, for I have given you two hours of my valuable time. Adieu, then, until to-morrow."

With a smile that seemed natural to her, the beautiful girl vanished, taking with her half the sunshine of the room.

The painter continued his labor of love. Indeed, so absorbed was he in his employment, that he did not notice the entrance of a visitor, until he felt a light tap on his shoulder, accompanied by the words,—

"Bravo, *mon cher*! You are getting on famously. That is Rose herself—as radiant as she appears on the stage, when the focus of a *lorgnette* has excluded all the stupid and *ennuyantes* figures that surround her."

The speaker was Sir Frederic Stanley, an English baronet, now some months in Paris, where he had plunged into all the gayeties of the season. He was a handsome man, of middle age, whose features bore the impress of dissipation.

"You know the original, then?" asked the painter, somewhat coldly.

"Know her! My dear fellow, I don't know any body else, as the Yankees say. Why, I have the entry of the *Gaité*, and pass all my evenings behind the scenes. I flatter myself—but no matter. I have taken a fancy to that picture: what do you say to a hundred louis for it?"

"It is not for me to dispose of it."

"You have succeeded so well, you wish to keep it for yourself—eh? Double the price, and let me have it!"

"Impossible, Sir Frederic. It is painted for Mlle. d'Amour herself, and she designs it for a present."

"Say no more," said the baronet, with a self-satisfied smile. "I think I could name the happy individual."

Ernest would not gratify his visitor by a question, and the latter, finding the artist reserved and *distrait*, suddenly recollected the races at Chantilly, and took his leave.

"Can it be possible," thought the painter, "that Rose has suffered her affections to repose on that conceited, purse-proud, elderly Englishman? O, woman! woman! how readily you barter the wealth of your heart for a handful of gold!"

Another tap at the door—another visitor! Really, Lavalle must be getting famous! This time it is a lady—a lady of surpassing loveliness—one of those well-preserved Englishwomen, who, at forty, are as attractive as at twenty. This lady was tall and stately, with elegant manners, and perhaps a thought of sadness in her expression. She gazed long and earnestly upon the portrait of Rose d'Amour.

"It is a beautiful face!" she said, at length. "And one that indicates, I should think, goodness of heart."

"She is an angel!" said the painter.

"You speak warmly, sir," said the lady, with a sad smile.

Ernest blushed, for he feared that he had betrayed his secret. The lady did not appear to notice his embarrassment, and passed to the occasion of her visit, which was to engage the young artist to paint her portrait—a task which he readily undertook, for he was pleased with, and interested in, his fair patroness. The picture was immediately commenced, and an hour fixed for a second sitting, on the next day. It was on that occasion that the fair unknown encountered the actress, and they retired in company.

The two portraits were finished at the same time, and reflected the greatest credit upon the artist. They were varnished, framed, and paid for, but the painter had received no orders for their final disposition, when, one morning, he was waited on by the two ladies, who informed him that they should call upon him the following day, when the two portraits would be presented, in his study, to the persons for whom they were designed. The artist was enjoined to place them on two separate easels,—that of the actress to stand nearest the door of the studio, and both to be concealed by a curtain until the ladies should give the signal for their exposure. The portrait of the English lady, we will here remark, had, by her request, been hitherto seen only by the artist. There was a mystery in this arrangement, which piqued, excessively, the curiosity of the painter, and he was anxious to witness the *denouement*.

The next day, at eleven o'clock, every thing was in readiness, and the painter awaited the solution of the mystery.

The first person who presented himself was Sir Frederic Stanley. He was very radiant.

"Congratulate me, *mon cher*," said he. "Read that."

Ernest took an open note from his hand, and read as follows:—

"Be at the studio of Ernest Lavalle, to-morrow, at eleven. You will there receive a present, which, if there be any truth in man's vows, will certainly delight you.

"Rose."

The astonishment and disappointment of Ernest was at its height, when his door opened, and the actress entered, followed by a female, closely veiled.

"You are true to your appointment, Sir Frederic," said the actress, gayly, "and your punctuality shall be rewarded."

She advanced to the farther easel, and, lifting the curtain, disclosed the features of the English lady.

"This is for you!" she said, laughing.

"My wife! by all that's wonderful!" exclaimed the baronet.

"Accompanied by the original!" said Lady Stanley, as she unveiled and advanced. "Sir Frederic! Sir Frederic! when you were amusing yourself, by paying unmeaning attentions to this young lady, I am afraid you forgot to tell her that you had a wife in England."

"I thought it unnecessary," stammered the baronet.

"How could you disturb the peace of mind of a young girl, when you knew you could not requite her affection?" continued Lady Stanley.

"It was only a flirtation, to pass the time," said Sir Frederic; "but I acknowledge it was culpable. My dear Emeline, I thank you for your present. I shall ever cherish it as my dearest possession—next to yourself."

"For you, sir," said the beautiful actress, turning to Ernest, "I cannot think of depriving you of your best effort. Take the portrait. I wish the subject were worthier." And she withdrew the curtain from her picture.

"I am ungrateful," said Ernest, in a low and tremulous tone. "Much as I prize the picture, I can never be happy without the original."

"Is it so?" replied the actress, in the same low tone of emotion; then, placing her hand timidly in his, she added, "The original is yours!"

UNCLE OBED.

A FULL LENGTH PORTRAIT IN PEN AND INK.

Uncle Obed—we omit his family name for various reasons—lived away down east, in a small but flourishing village, where he occupied a snug house, and what with a little farming, a little fishing, a little hunting, and a little trading, contrived, not only to make both ends meet at the expiration of each year, but accumulated quite a little property.

In personal appearance he was small, but muscular and wiry. He was far from handsome; a pug nose, set between a pair of gooseberry eyes, a long, straight mouth, a head of hair in which sandy red and iron gray were mixed together, did not give him a very fascinating aspect. He rarely smiled, but when he did, his smile was expressive of the deepest cunning.

Uncle Obed had one grievous fault—an unhappy propensity for acquiring the property of others—"a natural proclivity," as General Pillow says, to stealing. The Spartans thought there was no harm in stealing—in fact that it was rather meritorious than otherwise, providing that it was never found out; and both in theory and practice, Uncle Obed was a thorough Spartan. A few of his exploits in this way will serve to show his extraordinary 'cuteness.

A neighbor of his had a black heifer with a white face, which occasionally made irruptions into Uncle Obed's pasturage. One evening, Obed made a seizure of her, and tied her up in his barn. He then went to the owner of the animal.

"Mr. Stagg," said he, "there's been a cantankerous heifer a breaking into my lot, and I've been a lookin' for her, and I've cotched her at last."

"Well," said the unconscious Mr. Stagg, "I 'spose you're going to drive her to the pound."

"No, I ain't," answered Uncle Obed, with the smile we have alluded to, "I know a trick worth two of that. I'm going to kill her; and if you won't say nothing to nobody, but'll come up to-night and help me, you shall hev the horns and hide for your trouble."

"Done," said Mr. Stagg. "I'll come."

In the mean time, Uncle Obed took a pot of black paint, and covered the white face of the heifer, so as to prevent recognition. The neighbor came up at night, and helped despatch his own "critter," receiving the horns and hide for his pay, and laughing with Obed to think how cleverly the owner had been "done."

The next day he missed his heifer, and called on Obed to ask if he had seen her.

"I hain't seen her to-day," replied Uncle Obed, "but if you'll go to the tannery, where you sold that hide, and 'll just take the trouble to overhaul it, Mr. Stagg, prehaps you'll find out where your heifer is."

*Preh*aps he did.

On another occasion Uncle Obed appropriated—we scorn to charge him with stealing—a cow which had had the misfortune to lose her tail. Stepping into a tannery, he cut off a tail, and sewed it on to the fragment which yet decorated the hind quarters of the stolen animal. He then drove her along towards the next market, and having to cross a ferry, had just got on board the boat with his booty, when down came the owner of the missing cow, "bloody with spurring, fiery red with haste," and took passage on the same boat.

He eyed his cow very sharply, while Uncle Obed stood quietly by, watching the result of the investigation.

"That's a pretty good cow, ain't it?" said Uncle Obed.

"Yes," replied the owner, "and if her tail was cut off, I could swear it was mine."

Uncle Obed quietly took his knife out of his pocket, and cutting the tail short off *above* where the false one was joined on, threw it into the river.

"Now, neighbor," said he, triumphantly, "can you swear that's your cow?"

"Of course not," said the owner. "But they look very much alike."

After stealing something or other, we forget what, Uncle Obed was observed, and the sheriff was sent in pursuit of him, in hot haste, mounted on a fine and very fast horse. After a hard run, Uncle Obed halted at the edge of a rough piece of ground, pulled off his coat, and pulled down about a rod of stone wall, then quietly went to work building it up again, as if that was his regular occupation.

Presently the sheriff came riding up on the spur, and reining in, asked Obed if he had seen a fellow running for his life.

"Yes," said Obed, "I see him jest now streakin' it like a quarter hoss in *that* direction," pointing off. "But he was pretty nigh blown, and I 'xpect you can catch him in about two minnits."

"Well, just hold my horse," said the sheriff, "and I'll overhaul him."

The sheriff scrambled over the stones and through the bushes in the direction indicated, and the moment he was out of sight, Uncle Obed jumped on the horse and rode off at the top of his speed. He rode his prize to a town a good ways off, and sold the horse for a hundred and fifty dollars.

For some similar exploit, he was arrested and committed to jail in Essex county, to await his trial. But the prison being then in a process of repair, Uncle Obed, with other victims of the law, was incarcerated in the fort in Salem harbor. He made his escape, however, by crawling through the sewer, as Jack Sheppard did from Newgate prison. The sentinel on duty saw a mass of seaweed floating on the surface of the water. Now, this was nothing extraordinary, but it *was* extraordinary for seaweed to float *against* the tide. Uncle Obed's head was in that floating mass. He was hailed and ordered to swim back. He made no answer. A volley of musketry was discharged at him, but no boat being very handy, he got off and made his escape, very much after the manner of Rob Roy at the ford of Avondow.

Uncle Obed had a famous black Newfoundland dog, worth from sixty to eighty dollars. When hard up, he used to take the dog about fifty or a hundred miles from home, where he was unknown, and sell him. No matter what the distance was, the dog always came back to his old master, who realized several hundred dollars by the repeated sales of him.

Such were a few of the exploits of this departed worthy, actually vouched for by contemporaries. His passion for stealing was undoubtedly a monomania, for he was known in many cases to make voluntary restitution of articles that he had purloined, and his circumstances did not allow him the plea of necessity which palliates the errors of desperately poor rogues in every eye except that of the law.

THE CASKET OF JEWELS.

Mr. Luke Brandon was a Wall Street broker, of moderate business capacity, little education, and of plain manners, partaking of the rustic simplicity of his original employment—he was, in early life, a farmer in one of the western counties of New York. With less talent and more cunning, he might have become a very rich man, at short notice; but being brought up in an old-fashioned school of morality, he could never learn to dignify swindling by the epithet of smartness, nor consider overreaching his neighbor a "fair business transaction." Hence he plodded along the even tenor of his way, contented with moderate profits, and satisfied with the prospect of becoming independent by slow degrees.

But in an evil hour, during a fortnight's relaxation at the Catskill Mountain House, this steady and respectable gentleman, at the mature age of thirty-five, quite an old bachelor indeed, fell desperately in love with a dashing girl of twenty, the orphan daughter of a bankrupt ship chandler. Miss Maria Manners was highly educated; that is, she could write short notes on perfumed billet paper, without making any orthographical or grammatical mistakes, had taken three quarters' lessons of a French barber, could work worsted lapdogs and embroider slippers, danced like a sylph, and played on the piano indifferently well. She had visited the Catskills on a matrimonial speculation, and made a dead set at poor Brandon. Of course with his experience in the ways of women, he fell a ready dupe to the fascinating wiles of Miss Manners. She kept him in an agony of suspense for a week, during every evening of which she waltzed with a young lieutenant of dragoons, who was playing billiards and drinking champagne on a sick leave, until she could hear from a fabulous guardian at Philadelphia, and obtain his consent to a sacrifice of her brilliant prospects—nothing a year and a very suspicious account at a fashionable milliner's.

Mr. Brandon went down to the city, purchased a snug house, furnished it modestly, gave a liberal order on his tailor, and one memorable morning, might have been seen looking very uncomfortable, in a white satin stock and kids, beside a lady elegantly dressed in satin and blonde lace, while a portly clergyman pronounced his sentence in the shape of a marriage benediction.

There was a snug wedding breakfast in the new house, at which were present several eminent apple speculators from Fulton market, two or three bank clerks, and a reporter for a weekly newspaper, who consumed a ruinous amount of sandwiches and bottled ale.

Before the honeymoon was over, the bride began to display some of the less amiable features of her character. She sneered at the situation and simplicity of the establishment, and protested she was unaccustomed to that sort of style. She was perfectly sincere in this, for the defunct ship chandler had lived in a basement and two attic chambers.

By dint of repeated persecutions, she induced her husband to move into a larger house; and finally, after the expiration of many years, we find them established in the upper part of the city, in a splendid mansion, looking out upon a fashionable square, with a little marble boy in front sitting on a brick, and spouting a stream of Croton through a clam shell.

One morning, Mr. Brandon came home about eleven o'clock. On entering his front door, he beheld, lounging on a sofa, with the *Courrier des Etats Unis* in his hand, Claude, the handsome French page of Mrs. B.

"Where is Mrs. B.?" asked the elderly broker.

"Madame is in her boudoir," replied the page; "but," he added, seeing his master move in that direction, "I do not know whether she is visible."

"That I will ascertain myself, young gentleman," replied the broker, with a slight shade of irony in his tone. "But tell me, is there any one with her?"

"Only M. Auguste Charmant," said the page.

"That confounded Frenchman!" muttered the plebeian broker. "My Yankee house is turned topsyturvy by these foreigners. There's a French cook, and a French chambermaid, and the friend of the family is a Frenchman. I don't know what I'm eating, and I hardly understand a word that's said at my table. Sometimes, by way of change, they talk Italian instead of French. One might as well associate with a stack of monkeys. Out of the way, jackanapes."

"Monsieur," said the page, with true Gallic dignity, "I was about to proceed to announce monsieur."

"Monsieur can announce himself," replied Brandon, with the grin of a hyena; and proceeding up stairs, he entered the boudoir without knocking.

Mrs. Brandon was lounging on a *fauteuil*, in an elegant morning toilet— literally plunged and embowered in costly Brussels lace. Her delicate, bejewelled fingers were playing with the petals of an exquisite bouquet. Thanks to a good constitution, a life of ease, an accomplished milliner and an incomparable dentist, the fair Maria, though the mother of a marriageable girl, was still a lovely and fascinating woman, and Brandon, as he gazed on her superb figure, almost forgave her absurd ambition and her ruinous extravagance. Still, when he glanced at his own anxious, emaciated, and careworn features, in the splendid Versailles mirror that hung opposite, his transitory pleasure gave way to stern and bitter feelings. He merely nodded to his wife, and bowed coldly to her companion, a young man attired in the height of fashion, with dark eyes and hair, and the most superb mustache imaginable.

"Ah! my dear Meestare Brandon," said the dandy, "give me your hand. I congratulate you on such a *bonne fortune*—such good luck as has befallen you."

"Explain yourself, sir," said the broker.

"*Avec plaisir.* I have secured for you a box at the opera for the whole season—and for only five hundred dollars."

The broker whistled.

"Really nothing," said Mrs. Brandon; "only think—the best troupe we have yet had—a new *prima donna* and a new *basso.*"

"Fiddlestick!" said the matter-of-fact husband. "What does it amount to?"

"Brandon," said the lady with a true maternal dignity, "reflect upon the importance of the opera to the education of your daughter."

"Nonsense!" said the broker, angrily. "My daughter Julia would please me much better if she cultivated a little common sense, and adopted the plain, republican manners fitted to the eventualities of her future life, instead of aping foreign fashions, and doing her best to denationalize her character."

Monsieur Auguste Charmant shrugged his shoulders, Mrs. Brandon clasped her hands, and the former, rising said,—

"*Au revoir*, madame, *au plaisir*, Monsieur Brandon. I will bid you good morning, and leave you to the pleasures of a conjugal *tête-a-tête.*"

Mr. Brandon rose and paced the room to and fro for several minutes after the departure of the Frenchman, narrowly eyed by Mrs. Brandon, who was anticipating a "scene," and preparing to meet it. In these contests the victory generally rested with the lady. The broker finally opened the door, and finding the page with ear glued against the keyhole, quietly took that young gentleman by the lobe of his left ear, and leading him to the head of the staircase, advised him, as a friend, to descend it as speedily as possible, before his gravitation was assisted by the application of an extraneous power. This accomplished, he returned to the boudoir, and locking the door, sat down beside his wife. The latter playfully tapped his cheek with her bouquet, but the broker took no notice of the coquettish action, and gloomily contemplating his gaiters, as if afraid to trust his eyes with the siren glances of his partner, commenced:—

"Mrs. B., I want to have some serious talk with you."

"You never have any other kind of small talk," retorted the lady. "You have a rare gift at sermonizing."

Mr. Brandon passed over the sneer, and continued:—

"You alluded just now to Julia; it is of her I wish to speak. Let me remind you of her future prospects, and ask you whether it be not time to change your system of educating her, and prepare her for a change of life. You will remember then, that, two years ago, with the consent of all parties, she was engaged to Arthur Merton, a very promising young dry goods merchant of Boston."

"Only a retail merchant," said Mrs. Brandon.

"A promising young merchant, the son of my old friend Jasper Merton. It was agreed between us that I should bestow ten thousand dollars on my daughter, and Merton an equal sum upon his son. In case of the failure of either party to fulfil the engagement, the father of the party was to forfeit to the aggrieved person the sum of ten thousand dollars. This very week, I expect my old friend and his son to ratify the contract. You know with what difficulty, owing to the enormous expenses of our mode of life, I have laid aside the stipulated sum; for in your hands, the hands of the mother of my child, I have lodged this sacred deposit."

"Very true," said the lady, "and it is now in my secretary, under lock and key. But what an odious arrangement! How the contract and the forfeit smell of the shop!"

"Don't despise the smell of the shop, Maria," said the broker, smiling gravely, "it is the smell of the shop that perfumes the boudoir."

"And then Arthur Merton is such a shocking person," continued the lady; "really, no manners."

"To my mind, Maria," said the broker, "his manners, plain, open, and frank, are infinitely superior to those of the French butterfly who is always fluttering at your elbow."

"And if he is always fluttering at my elbow," retorted the lady, "it is because you are always away."

"That is because I always have business," said the broker. "If we lived in less style, I should have more leisure. Ah! Maria! Maria! I fear that we are driving on too recklessly; the day of reckoning will come—we seem to be sailing prosperously now, but a shipwreck may terminate the voyage."

"Not while I have the helm," said the lady. "Listen to me, Brandon. You know little of the philosophy of life. To command success, we must seem to have obtained it. To be rich, we must seem so. You have done well to follow my advice in one particular. You have taken a very prominent part in the present presidential canvass. There cannot fail to be a change of administration, and while you have been making yourself conspicuous in public, I have been electioneering for you in private. I have been feasting and petting the men who hold the winning cards in their hands. It is not for mere ostentation that I have invited to my *soirées*, the Hon. Mr. A., and Judge B., and Counsellor C."

"I don't see what you're driving at," said the broker.

"O, of course not. But when you find yourself a *millionnaire*, and all by the scheming of your wife, perhaps, B., you'd think there was some wisdom in what you are pleased to call my fashionable follies. But to make the matter plain—a change of administration occurs—you are the confidential friend of the secretary of the treasury—your talents as a financier are duly recognized—you have the management of the most important loans and contracts—you have four years, perhaps eight, to flourish in, and your fortune is made."

"Ah!" said the broker, doubtfully.

"If such success attends you, and there can be no doubt of it, how painful would be your reflections, if you thought that you had sacrificed your daughter's future in an alliance with a petty trader. I have arranged a brighter destiny for her—a marriage with a foreign nobleman."

"I'd rather see her the wife of a Yankee peddler."

"Out upon you!" cried the lady. "I tell you, your opposition will have little weight, Mr. B. Come to my *soirée* this evening, and I will present you to Count Alfred de Roseville, an exile from France for political offences—only think, B., he was the intimate friend of Henry V."

"And who vouches for this paragon?"

"Our friend, Auguste."

"*Your* friend, Auguste, you mean."

"I mean M. Charmant, the friend of the family."

"And what does Julia think of this Phœnix?"

"She adores him."

"Alas! how her gentleness of nature must have been perverted! Well, well, Maria, in spite of myself, I cannot resolve to humble your pride, or thwart your schemes. I believe you love me and your daughter. Yet you are playing a desperate game—remember, our all is staked upon the issue."

"And I'll await the hazard of the die," replied Mrs. B., as she kissed her husband fondly, and dismissed him with a wave of the hand.

When Brandon came down into the hall, he was thunder-struck at meeting there three persons, whose appearance, after what had just passed up stairs in the boudoir, might well be considered inopportune. The first was uncle Richard Watkins, a relative of Mr. Brandon's, who resided in the country, and had become immensely rich by land speculations, and the others were Mr. Merton and his son. A pile of baggage announced that they were not mere callers.

"Give us your hand, Luke," said uncle Richard, extending his enormous brown palm, "you ain't glad to see me, nor nothin', be you? Brought my trunk, valise, carpet bag, and hatbox, and cal'late to spend six weeks here. How's the old woman and the gal—pretty smart? Well, that's hearty."

The broker shook the old man by the hand, and then turned to welcome with the best grace he could his friend Merton, and his proposed son-in-law.

"You know what *we've* come for," said the elder Merton, with a sly wink.

"Pray walk into the drawing room," said the broker, and 'on hospitable thoughts intent,' he threw wide the door, and the party entered.

Ah! unlucky Brandon! why didst thou not summon the French page to announce thy guests? Thou hadst then been spared a scene that might have figured in a comedy, and came near furnishing material for a tragedy.

An elegant young man was kneeling at the feet of an elegant young lady. The former was Count Alfred de Roseville, the latter Miss Julia Brandon. The count started to his feet, the young lady blushed and shrieked. The count was the first to recover his voice and self-possession. Rushing to the broker, he exclaimed in broken English,—

"O, my dear monsieur, how I moost glad to see you—your daughter—Mees Julie—she 'ave say—yais—yais—yais—to my ardent love suit—and now I have the honneur to salute her respectable papa."

"O, father," said the terrified girl, "it was with mother's knowledge and consent."

Brandon could not speak a word.

"This lady, sir," said Merton, fiercely, advancing to the count, "is my affianced bride."

"Your bride—eh?" cried the count, "when she has just come to say—yais—to my ardent love suit!"

"What does the gal say? what does the gal say?" asked uncle Richard, interposing.

"Speak, Julia," said her father, sternly, "and weigh well your words. I will not force you to fulfil a contract against your will—the penalty and contingency of such a refusal have been provided for—but pause before you reject the son of my old friend for a foreigner—a man with whom you can have had but a few days' acquaintance."

Julia averted her eyes, and blushed scarlet, but placed her hand in that of the count just as her mother entered the apartment.

"Enough," said young Merton, "I am satisfied. Come, father, let us retire—our presence here is only a burden. O, Julia!" he added, in a tone of deep feeling, "little did I expect this at your hands. I have looked forward to this meeting with the fondest hope. It is past—farewell—may you be happy."

"I shall be very happy to see you again—nevair!" said the count.

"O, as to that," said young Merton, approaching him, and addressing him in a low tone, "I think *you*, at least, have not seen the last of me, monsieur. At any rate, you shall hear from me soon."

"I 'ave not nozzin to do nor not to say viz *canaille*," said the count.

"Then, perhaps, it will be more agreeable to you, sir, to be horsewhipped in Broadway," said Merton.

"Me! horsevhip! me! the friend of Henri V.! horreur!" cried the count.

"Very good, monsieur, I have presented the alternative. Where may you be found?"

"*Hôtel de Ville*—City Hotel."

"*Au plaisir*, then *Count* Alfred de Roseville," said Merton, glancing at the card the Frenchman handed him. "Come, father."

"Mr. Brandon, I shall wait on you at your counting room in the course of the forenoon," said Mr. Merton, senior; "we have an account to settle together."

And the father and son bowed themselves out of the room. Julia was so much agitated at the events which had just transpired, that she was compelled to retire to her room. Uncle Richard and Mr. and Mrs. Brandon remained upon the field of battle.

"Well, Maria," said the broker, "the first act of the comedy has been played, in which you have assigned me a very insignificant and low-comedy part, but I don't think either of us has made a very distinguished figure in it. I hope the last act will redeem the first."

The lady reddened, but made no reply.

"Let us foot up the column to see what amount is to be carried forward," continued the broker. "Here's an old friendship dissolved—a worthy young man broken hearted—a suspicious suitor introduced into my family, and ten thousand dollars to be paid on demand. A very pretty morning's work."

"It will come out right," said Mrs. Brandon.

"As the boy remarked when he was gored by the cow's horn," observed uncle Richard, philosophically, as he extended his length upon an ottoman, including his boots in the enjoyment of the comfort of cut velvet.

"I leave uncle Richard to your care, madam," said the broker, "while I go down in town to ascertain the value of my new son-in-law's paper upon 'change."

On an evening not long after the above scenes, the broker's house was brilliantly lighted up from basement to attic. Through the open hall door, at the head of the flight of marble steps, servants in livery were seen receiving the shawls and hats of the guests, as carriage after carriage deposited its brilliant contents at the house of the financier. Mingled with the black coats of the gentlemen, and the gossamer attire of the ladies, were seen the brilliant uniforms of officers of the army and navy. The crowd poured into the magnificent ball room, where, flanked by her husband, and by the indefatigable Monsieur Charmant, the lovely hostess received her guests with an elegance of manner truly aristocratic. The delicious waltzes of Strauss, performed by a German band, floated through the magnificent rooms. Glistening chandeliers poured down a flood of soft light on the fair faces and the polished ivory shoulders of the ladies. It was a scene of enchantment, and Mrs. Brandon revelled in the splendor that surrounded her and the incense that was offered. She was pleased at the distinguished appearance of her husband, pleased to see her daughter hanging on the arm of the French count, pleased at every thing but one. One object alone, like the black mask at the bridal of Hernani, marred the festivity, and created a discord in the midst of the harmony—that was uncle Richard, walking up and down the ball room in a meal-colored coat and cowhide boots.

Various efforts were made to get possession of uncle Richard and lead him away into captivity. A whist table was suggested in an anteroom, an Havana was proposed in the library, but he "didn't want to play cards, and had just quit smoking," and so he paraded his coat and boots before the company, the "observed of all observers."

Mrs. B. made the best of it, whispering confidentially that he was a distant connection, immensely rich, partially insane, but perfectly harmless. O, how dazzling was Mrs. Brandon that evening, in the beauty of her person and of her attire! She wore diamonds that were valued at ten thousand dollars.

In the midst of the brilliant festivities, Mr. Brandon was suddenly summoned from the ball room. He presently returned, looking very pale, and beckoned his wife, who followed him into the library. Mr. Merton, senior, was there, with a very stern expression on his countenance.

"What's the matter?" asked Mrs. Brandon.

"The matter," said her husband, "is simply this—Mr. Merton leaves town to-night for Philadelphia, on special business, and having occasion for a large sum of money, requires the immediate payment of the ten thousand dollars which are due him for our violation of the marriage contract."

"Yes, madam," said Mr. Merton, "and I called on your husband for it, and he referred me to you as having the deposit in your possession."

"Wouldn't to-morrow do as well?" asked the lady anxiously.

"No, madam, my necessity is urgent."

"Go, Maria," said the broker, "and bring the money instantly. A debt like this admits of no postponement."

"Alas! alas!" stammered the poor woman, "I have not this money by me. Surely, Mr. Brandon, you must be able to command it."

"Not one dollar, madam," said the broker. "I would have spared you this explanation to-night, but you have brought it on yourself. This is our last night of factitious splendor—my affairs are in inextricable confusion—losses have this day come to light which complete my ruin—and to-morrow the world will know me as a bankrupt."

Mrs. Brandon wrung her hands and sobbed bitterly.

"But that is a grief for to-morrow," said the broker, sternly. "There is music and dancing, champagne and flowers, in the next room—enough glory for to-night. But this business of Mr. Merton's requires instant attention. What have you done with the ten thousand dollars? Have you dared to squander it?"

"No, no," said Mrs. Brandon earnestly. "I am not so bad as that. I deposited it with Sandford, the jeweller, of whom I hired the casket of jewels to deck myself to-night."

"Mr. Merton," said the broker, calmly, "I shall have to trouble your patience a little while longer. I will write instantly to Mr. Sandford, late as it is, and bid him bring the money here at once."

After despatching the note, Brandon and his wife returned to the ball room. O, how insipid to the lady's ear seemed now the babble of her guests! The flowers had lost their perfume—the music its divine influence. Yet, with the serpent of remorse and anguish gnawing at her heart, she was forced to smile and seem happy and at ease. A half hour passed in this way seemed an age of torture; and when the messenger despatched by her husband had returned and summoned them again to the library, it gave her inexpressible relief.

"O, Mr. Sandford!" she exclaimed to the jeweller, who was now added to the party, "how happy I am to see you! There is your casket—and here are your diamonds!" and she tore the jewels from her neck, ears, and wrists, and offered them to the jeweller.

"Madam," said the jeweller, gravely, after having examined the gems, "these are not the articles I furnished you. I lent you a set of diamonds—these are paste!"

"What is the meaning of this?" asked the broker sternly.

"I know not. I cannot explain. O, Luke! Luke! I am innocent!" and Mrs. Brandon sunk fainting into a chair.

When she had recovered her senses, Mr. Brandon asked,—

"Did you make this arrangement in person?"

"No," she replied; "it was through the mediation of Mr. Charmant."

"Let's send for him," said Merton.

"Stay," said the broker; "an idea has occurred to me. I have observed at times that this Monsieur Charmant had a good deal to say to your French page, my good lady."

"It was he that recommended Claude," said Mrs. Brandon.

"Then we will have Claude before us," said the broker.

Claude soon made his appearance.

"Claude," said Mrs. Brandon, "do you know any thing about this casket of jewels?"

The boy changed color, but shook his head.

"Now, my Christian friend," said the broker, "you need not tell us what you know about the jewels, if you are unwilling; but in case of your refusal, I shall send for a police officer, who will, undoubtedly, drum the whole affair out of you."

The threat had the desired effect. The boy confessed that Charmant and De Roseville were impostors—that they were not even Frenchmen, but a brace of London thieves, who had picked up a knowledge of French during a professional tour on the continent, and who had emigrated to America for the purpose of introducing their art among our unsophisticated countrymen. Charmant had been a jeweller, and this enabled him to counterfeit the gems obtained of Mr. Sandford, which he purposed disposing of at the first favorable opportunity. The boy believed that Charmant had them about him at that moment. In England, Charmant was known as French Jack, and Roseville as Rusty Joe.

"Go back to the ball room," said Mr. Merton to Brandon, "and take your wife with you. Mr. Sandford, you stay by the boy. I'll go for an officer."

Brandon and his lady returned to the ball room, the latter somewhat relieved, but mortified at the deceptions which had been practised on her.

In a few minutes a burly member of the police, with a very thick stick, and a very red handkerchief knotted round his neck, made his appearance, to the astonishment and consternation of the guests, amid whom the host and hostess alone testified no excitement or alarm.

"Sarvant, ladies and gentlemen, sarvant," said the legal functionary, scraping his right boot, and plucking desperately at the brim of his hat. "Don't let me interrupt yer innercent amusement—sorry to intrude, as the bull said when he rushed into the china shop—but business before pleasure—now then, my hearty! how are you?"

The last words were accompanied by a vigorous blow on the shoulder of M. Auguste Charmant, who was at that moment paying his attentions to a belle from Union Square.

"*Monsieur me parle-t-il?*" exclaimed the dandy, with well-feigned astonishment.

"O, nix the lingo, French Jack," said the officer, "or leastways patter Romany so's a cove can understand you. Fork over them are dimonds—or else it will go harder with you. The boy's peached, and the game's up—you were spotted long ago."

With a smothered curse, French Jack dived his hand into his vest pocket and produced the stolen jewels. While this was enacting, the count had been quietly stealing to the door, but the vigilant officer had an eye upon his movements, and a hand upon his shoulder before he could escape.

"Now I've got the pair of you," said the worthy man, chuckling apoplectically in the folds of his red handkerchief. "Now, don't ride rusty, Joe—for there's a small few of us outside with amazin' thick sticks, that might fall on your head and hurt you, if so be you happened to be rambustical."

"Curse the luck!" muttered the thief, as with his companion he marched off.

It may well be imagined that the scene dispersed the party in a hurry. They took French leave, like birds scattered by a sudden storm. Julia was carried to bed in hysterics, accompanied by her mother. Merton and the jeweller had disappeared, the three rogues had been taken into custody, and only Brandon and uncle Richard

———"trod aloneThe banquet hall deserted."

"Well, uncle," said the broker, bitterly, "the game's up. I have been ruined, stock and fluke, by letting my wife have her own way, and to-morrow I shall be a bankrupt."

"No you won't," said uncle Richard.

"Yes I shall," said the broker, angrily. "And Julia, abandoned by her lover, will be broken hearted."

"No she won't," said uncle Richard.

"Who's to prevent it?" asked the broker.

"Uncle Richard," replied that personage. "What's the use of a friend, unless he's a friend in need. I've got plenty of money, and neither chick nor child in the world. I'll meet your liabilities with cash. Young Merton loves Julia in spite of her temporary alienation—he will gladly take her back. The rogues will get their deserts. Your wife, sick and ashamed of her fashionable follies, will gladly gin' up this house and the servants. You'll buy a little country seat on the Hudson, and I'll come and live with you."

As every thing turned out exactly as uncle Richard promised and predicted, we have no occasion to enlarge on the fortunate subsiding of this "sea of troubles."

ACTING CHARADES.

But, masters, remember that I am an ass; though it be not written down, yet forget not that I am an ass.—SHAKSPEARE, *Much Ado about Nothing.*

Many of our readers have doubtless witnessed, or perchance participated in, the amusement of acting charades—a divertisement much in vogue in social circles, and if cleverly done, productive of much mirth. To the uninitiated, a brief description of an acted charade may not be unacceptable. A word of two or more syllables is selected, each part of which must make sense by itself—as, for instance, the word inspector, which would be decomposed, thus; *inn spectre.* The company of performers would then extemporize a scene at a public house, leaving the spectators to guess at the first syllable, *inn.* The second scene would represent the terror occasioned by the apparition of a phantom, and give the second part of the word spectre. The third scene would represent the whole word, and would perhaps be a brigade inspector reviewing his troops, giving occasion for the humors of a Yankee militia training. Much ingenuity is required in the selection of a word, and in carrying out the representation, with appropriate dialogue, &c.

Acting charades generally turns a house topsy turvy; wardrobes and garrets are ransacked for costumes and properties; hats, canes, umbrellas, and firearms are mustered, and old dresses that haven't seen the light for forty years are rummaged out as disguises for the actors in these extempore theatricals.

In a certain circle in this city there was a knot of clever young people, of both sexes, strongly addicted to acting charades, and very happy in their execution. But they were unfortunately afflicted by an interloper,

"Whose headWas not of brains particularly full,"

one of those geniuses who have a fatal facility for making blunders. Yet, with a pleasing unconsciousness of his deficiencies, he was always volunteering his services, and always expected, in this matter of acting charades, to be intrusted with the leading parts.

One evening the usual coterie was assembled, charades were proposed, as usual, and the little knot of performers retired to the back drawing room, dropping the curtain behind them, and prepared for their performance, congratulating themselves that Mr. Blinks, the name of the marplot, was not on hand to spoil their sport. They selected the word *catastrophe,* and the curtain went up.

A very pretty and lively young lady, who had been abroad, gave a very happy imitation of the almost inimitable Jenny Vertpré, in the French vaudeville of the "Cat metamorphosed to a Woman," in that scene where she betrays her original nature. She purred, she frolicked, she pounced on an imaginary mouse, caught it, tossed it up in the air, and went through all the manœuvres of a veritable grimalkin. When the curtain fell, amidst roars of laughter and applause, the first syllable—cat—was whispered from mouth to mouth, among the audience.

At this moment the hated Blinks arrived in the green-room.

"What are you up to? Acting charades—eh? By Jove! I'm just in time. You must give me a part—can't get along without me. What's the word?"

"No matter," said the young lady who had played the cat, with a wicked smile of intelligence. "Prompter, ring the curtain up. All you've got to do, Mr. Blinks, is to walk across the stage."

"But where's my dress?"

"What you have on. Appear in your own character."

The curtain went up, and Blinks stalked across with his accustomed air of intolerable stupidity. Amidst smothered laughter, the audience guessed the second syllable of the charade—*ass*.

The curtain went up for the third time. A group of Indian chiefs were located in a wigwam. A young brave entered, distinguished by the eagle plume and wampum belt, the bow and hatchet, and threw down at the feet of the eldest warrior a bundle of the scalps he had brought back from battle. A hum of approbation rose from the assembly. The curtain fell. The word *trophy* had been thus indicated. The whole word was then represented by an appropriate scene from the close of a popular tragedy, and the spectators, cheering the performance, called out *catastrophe* to the actors.

"Well, they made out to guess it," said Blinks, when the curtain had fallen, for the last time. "But now it's all over, you made one confounded blunder."

"What was that?" asked the wicked young lady.

"You didn't act the second syllable."

"No?"

"No! indeed!" said Blinks, with a look of intense cunning. "You had *cat* and *trophy*—but where was the *ass*?"

"O, indeed!" said the young lady.

"You see, ladies and gentleman," said Blinks, enjoying his triumph, "you can't get along without me. If I'd been here in the beginning, you'd have had the ass."

"We certainly should," said the young lady, winking to her companions, who could hardly suppress their laughter.

"And I move we repeat this charade to-morrow night," said Blinks—"and mind, I'm the ass."

"Of course."

"I'll get a costume and disguise myself."

"Disguise yourself!" echoed his tormentor—"for Heaven's sake, don't do that—they'd never guess it."

The next night the charade was ass-ass-in, and Blinks went on for the first two syllables. He was perfectly at home—"Richard himself again!" and the wicked young lady, in complimenting his performance, declared it was "*perfectly natural.*"

THE GREEN CHAMBER.

In my younger days, "ghost stories" were the most popular narratives extant, and the lady or gentleman who could recite the most thrilling adventure, involving a genuine spiritual visitant, was sure to be the lion or lioness of the evening party he enlivened (?) with the dismal details. The elder auditors never seemed particularly horrified or terror-stricken, however much gratified they were, but the younger members would drink in every word, "supping full of horrors." After listening to one of these authentic narratives, we used to be very reluctant to retire to our dormitories, and never ventured to get into bed till we had examined suspicious-looking closets, old wardrobes, and, indeed, every nook and corner that might be supposed to harbor a ghost or a ghoul.

Fortunately for the rising generation, these tales have gone out of fashion, and though some attempts to revive the taste have been made—as in the "Night Side of Nature"—such efforts have proved deplorable failures. The young people of to-day make light of ghosts. The spectres in the incantation scene of "Der Freyschutz" are received with roars of laughter, and even the statue in Don Giovanni seems "jolly," notwithstanding the illusive music of Mozart. We were about to remark that the age had outgrown superstition, but we remembered the Rochester knockings, and concluded to be modestly silent.

One evening, many years since—it was a blustering December evening—the wind howling as it dashed the old buttonwood limbs in its fury against the parlor windows of the country house where a few of us were assembled to pass the winter holidays, we gathered before a roaring fire of walnut and oak, which made every thing within doors as cheery and comfortable as all without was desolate and dreary. The window shutters were left unfastened, that the bright lamplight and ruddy firelight might stream afar upon the wintry waste, and perhaps guide some benighted wayfarer to a hospitable shelter.

We shall not attempt to describe the group, as any such portrait painting would not be germane to the matter more immediately in hand. Suffice it to say, that one of the youngsters begged aunt Deborah, the matron of the mansion, to tell us a ghost story,—"a real ghost story, aunt Deborah,"—for in those days we were terribly afraid of counterfeits, and hated to hear a narrative where the ghost turned out in the end to be no ghost after all, but a mere compound of flesh and blood like ourselves.

Aunt Deborah smiled at our earnestness, and tantalized our impatience by some of those little arts with which the practised story-teller enhances the value and interest of her narrative. She tapped her silver snuffbox, opened it deliberately, took a very delicate pinch of the Lundy Foot, shut the box, replaced it in her pocket, folded her hands before her, looked round a minute on the expectant group, and then began.

I shall despair of imparting to this cold pen-and-ink record of her story the inimitable conversational grace with which she embellished it. It made an indelible impression on my memory, and if I have never before repeated it, it was from a lurking fear that—though the old lady assured us it was "not to be found in any book or newspaper"—it might have found its way into print. However, as twenty years have elapsed, and I have never yet met with it in type, I will venture to give the outlines of the narrative.

Major Rupert Stanley, a "bold dragoon" in the service of his majesty George III., found himself, one dark and blustering night in autumn, riding towards London on the old York road. He had supped with a friend who lived at a village some distance off the road, and he was unfamiliar with the country. Though not raining, the air was damp, and the heavy, surcharged clouds threatened every moment to pour down their contents. But the major, though a young man, was an old campaigner; and with a warm cloak wrapped about him, and a good horse under him, would have cared very little for storm and darkness, had he felt sure of a good bed for himself, and comfortable quarters for his horse, when he had ridden far enough for the strength of his faithful animal. A good horseman cares as much for the comfort of his steed as for his own ease. To add to the discomfort of the evening, there was some chance of meeting highwaymen; but Major Stanley felt no uneasiness on that score, as, just before leaving his friend's house, he had examined his holster pistols, and freshly primed them. A brush with a highwayman would enhance the romance of a night journey.

So he jogged along; but mile after mile was passed, and no twinkling light in the distance gave notice of the appearance of the wished-for inn. The major's horse began to give unmistakable evidence of distress—stumbling once or twice, and recovering himself with difficulty. At last, a dim light suddenly appeared at a turn of the road. The horse pricked up his ears, and trotted forward with spirit, soon halting beside a one-story cottage. The major was disappointed, but he rode up to the door and rapped loudly with the but of his riding whip. The summons brought a sleepy cotter to the door.

"My good friend," said the major, "can you tell me how far it is to the next inn?"

"Eh! it be about zeven mile, zur," was the answer, in the broad Yorkshire dialect of the district.

"Seven miles!" exclaimed the major, in a tone of deep disappointment, "and my horse is already blown! My good fellow, can't you put my horse somewhere, and give me a bed? I will pay you liberally for your trouble."

"Eh! goodness zakes!" said the rustic. "I be nought but a ditcher! There be noa plaze to put the nag in, and there be only one room and one bed in the cot."

"What *shall* I do?" cried the major, at his wits' end.

"I'll tell 'ee, zur," said the rustic, scratching his head violently, as if to extract his ideas by the roots. "There be a voine large house on the road, about a moile vurther on. It's noa an inn, but the colonel zees company vor the vun o' the thing—'cause he loikes to zee company about 'un. You must 'a heard ov him—Colonel Rogers—a' used to be a soger once."

"Say no more," cried the major. "I *have* heard of this hospitable gentleman; and his having been in the army gives me a sure claim to his attention. Here's a crown for your information, my good friend. Come, Marlborough!"

Touching his steed with the spur, the major rode off, feeling an exhilaration of spirits which soon communicated itself to the horse. A sharp trot of a few minutes brought him to a large mansion, which stood unfenced, like a huge caravansery, by the roadside. He made for the front door and, without dismounting, plied the large brass knocker till a servant in livery made his appearance.

"Is your master up?" asked the major.

"I am the occupant of this house," said a venerable gentleman, making his appearance at the hall door.

"I am a benighted traveller, sir," said the major, touching his hat, "and come to claim your well-known hospitality. Can you give me a bed for the night? I am afraid my four-footed companion is hardly able to carry me to the next inn."

"I cannot promise you a bed, sir," said the host, "for I have but one spare bed in the house."

"And that——" said the major.

"Happens to be in a room that does not enjoy a very pleasing reputation. In short, sir, one room of my house is haunted; and that is the only one, unfortunately, that I can place at your disposal to-night."

"My dear sir," said the major, springing from his horse, and tossing the bridle to the servant, "you enchant me beyond expression! A haunted chamber! The very thing—and I, who have never seen a ghost! What luck!"

The host shook his head gravely.

"I never knew a man," he said, "to pass a night in that chamber without regretting it."

Major Stanley laughed as he took his pistols from the holster pipes. "With these friends of mine," he said, "I fear neither ghost nor demon."

Colonel Rogers showed his guest into a comfortable parlor, where a seacoal fire was burning cheerfully in a grate, and refreshments most welcome to a weary traveller stood upon a table.

"Mine host" was an old campaigner, and had seen much service during the war of the American revolution, and he was full of interesting anecdotes and descriptions of adventures. But while Major Stanley was apparently listening attentively to the narrative of his hospitable entertainer, throwing in the appropriate ejaculations of surprise and pleasure at the proper intervals, his whole attention was in reality absorbed by a charming girl of twenty, the daughter of the colonel, who graced the table with her presence. Never, he thought, had he seen so beautiful, so modest, and so ladylike a creature; and she, in turn, seemed very favorably impressed with the manly beauty and frank manners of their military guest.

At length she retired. The colonel, who was a three-bottle man, and had found a listener to his heart, was somewhat inclined to prolong the session into the small hours of the morning, but finding that his guest was much fatigued, and even beginning to nod in the midst of his choicest story, he felt compelled to ask him if he would not like to retire. Major Stanley replied promptly in the affirmative, and the old gentleman, taking up a silver candlestick, ceremoniously marshalled his guest to a large, old-fashioned room, the walls of which being papered with green, gave it its appellation of the "Green Chamber." A comfortable bed invited to repose; a cheerful fire was blazing on the hearth, and every thing was cosy and quiet. The major looked round him with a smile of satisfaction.

"I am deeply indebted to you, colonel," said he, "for affording me such comfortable quarters. I shall sleep like a top."

"I am afraid not," answered the colonel, shaking his head gravely. "I never knew a guest of mine to pass a quiet night in the Green Chamber."

"I shall prove an exception," said the major, smiling. "But I must make one remark," he added, seriously. "It is ill sporting with the feelings of a soldier; and should any of your servants attempt to play tricks upon me, they will have occasion to repent it." And he laid his heavy pistol on the lightstand by his bedside.

"My servants, Major Stanley," said the old gentleman, with an air of offended dignity, "are too well drilled to dare attempt any tricks upon my guests. Good night, major."

"Good night, colonel."

The door closed. Major Stanley locked it. Having done so, he took a survey of the apartment. Besides the door opening into the entry, there was another leading to some other room. There was no lock upon this second door, but a heavy table, placed across, completely barricaded it.

"I am safe," thought the major, "unless there is a storming party of ghosts to attack me in my fastness. I think I shall sleep well."

He threw himself into an arm chair before the fire, and watching the glowing embers, amused himself with building castles in the air, and musing on the attractions of the fair Julia, his host's daughter. He was far enough from thinking of spectral visitants, when a very slight noise struck on his ear. Glancing in the direction of the inner door, he thought he saw the heavy table glide backwards from its place. Quick as thought, he caught up a pistol, and challenged the intruder. There was no reply—but the door continued to open, and the table to slide back. At last there glided into the room a tall, graceful figure, robed in white. At the first glance, the blood curdled in the major's veins; at the second, he recognized the daughter of his host. Her eyes were wide open, and she advanced with an assured step, but it was very evident she was asleep. Here was the mystery of the Green Chamber solved at once. The young girl walked to the fireplace and seated herself in the arm chair from which the soldier had just risen. His first impulse was to vacate the room, and go directly and alarm the colonel. But, in the first place, he knew not what apartment his host occupied, and in the second, curiosity prompted him to watch the *dénouement* of this singular scene. Julia raised her left hand, and gazing on a beautiful ring that adorned one of her white and taper fingers, pressed it repeatedly to her lips. She then sank into an attitude of repose, her arms drooping listlessly by her sides.

The major approached her, and stole the ring from her finger. His action disturbed, but did not awaken her. She seemed to miss the ring, however, and, after groping hopelessly for it, rose and glided through the doorway as silently as she had entered. She had no sooner retired than the major replaced the table, and drawing a heavy clothes press against it, effectually guarded himself against a second intrusion.

This done, he threw himself upon the bed, and slept soundly till a late hour of the morning. When he awoke, he sprang out of bed, and ran to the window. Every trace of the storm had passed away, and an unclouded sun was shining on the radiant landscape. After performing the duties of his toilet, he was summoned to breakfast, where he met the colonel and his daughter.

"Well, major, and how did you pass the night?" asked the colonel, anxiously.

"Famously," replied Stanley. "I slept like a top, as I told you I should."

"Then, thank Heaven, the spell is broken at last," said the colonel, "and the White Phantom has ceased to haunt the Green Chamber."

"By no means," said the major, smiling; "the White Phantom paid me a visit last night, and left me a token of the honor."

"A token!" exclaimed the father and daughter in a breath.

"Yes, my friends, and here it is." And the major handed the ring to the old gentleman.

"What's the meaning of this, Julia?" exclaimed the colonel. "This ring I gave you last week!"

Julia uttered a faint cry, and turned deadly pale.

"The mystery is easily explained," said the major. "The young lady is a sleep-walker. She came into my room before I had retired, utterly unconscious of her actions. I took the ring from her hand, that I might be able to convince you and her of the reality of what I had witnessed."

The major's business was not pressing, and he readily yielded to the colonel's urgent request to pass a few days with him. Their mutual liking increased upon better acquaintance, and in a few weeks the White Phantom's ring, inscribed with the names of Rupert Stanley and Julia Rogers, served as the sacred symbol of their union for life.

HE WASN'T A HORSE JOCKEY.

It was at the close of a fine, autumnal afternoon, that a simple-looking traveller, attired in a homespun suit of gray, and wearing a broad-brimmed, Quaker-looking hat, drove up to the door of the Spread Eagle Tavern, in the town of B——, State of Maine, kept by Major E. Spike, and ordered refreshments for himself and horse. There was nothing particular about the traveller, except his air of simplicity; but his horse was a character. The animal was at least thirty years of age, and was as gaunt as Rosinante, and would have been a dear bargain at fifteen dollars. The traveller acknowledged that he had been taken in somewhat when he bought the animal, for he "wasn't a horse jockey," and "did'nt know much about critters!" However, he added, "that if he had good luck in his trip down east, [he was agent for a Hartford Life Assurance Company,] he meant to pick up something handsome in the way of horse flesh to take home with him." After communicating his name and business, and sundry other particulars, with a frankness which, while it satisfied the curiosity, excited the contempt of Major Spike, the stranger, whom we shall call Zebulon Smith, departed.

He had a business call to make on the widow Stebbins, who lived about three miles off, in a very old, unfinished, shingled house, of immense extent, in the centre of an unfenced lot, the chief products of which were rocks, brambles, and barberry bushes.

"Keep much stock, Miss Stebbins?" said he, as, having transacted his business, he prepared to resume his journey.

"Why, no," said she; "I'm a lone woman, and hain't got no help; so I keep only a cow and that 'ere colt. I wish I could sell him, for I ain't got nobody to break him in properly."

Zebulon looked at the colt. He was a limpsey, long-legged, shaggy animal, with a ewe-neck, drooping head, and little, undecided tail, completely knotted up with burs; but then he was only five years old.

"Heow'll yeou trade, Miss Stebbins?" asked the agent. "I've a mind to take the critter, if you'll trade even, though I don't know the pints of a horse. I ain't a horse jockey. Heowever, you're a lone woman, and I want to oblige you. You hain't got nobody to break the colt for you, and here's my hoss would suit you to a T. He's a nice family hoss."

"Heow old is he?" asked Mrs. Stebbins.

"He's *risin'* six years," said Zebulon, and so he was.

"He looks pretty well along," said the widow. "How much boot will you give me?"

"Boot!" exclaimed Zebulon. "O, if you talk about boot, I'm off. I ain't no horse jockey, but I know I'm flingin' my hoss—good old hoss—away by tradin' even. But generosity and consideration for widders—specially good-lookin' ones—was allers a failin' in my family."

"I don't know as I had orter," said the widow, thoughtfully; "if Mr. Stebbins was alive, you wouldn't get the colt so cheap, for he sot every thing by him. He's sot his pedigree down in the births, deaths, and marriages, in our family Bible. He allers said, poor man, he was goin' to make a great hoss."

"That 'ere was an optical delusion," said the agent; "he warn't never a goin' to make a great hoss, and he won't never be a great hoss. I know so much, if I ain't a horse jockey. Come, now, what say? Shall I ungear, and leave my critter, or put on the string and be a travellin'?"

"You may have the colt," said the widow, bursting into tears, and retiring, unable to witness the consummation of the sacrifice.

"Come, young Burtail," said Zebulon, addressing the colt. "It's time you was sot to work. I don't know whether you ever had a collar over your darned ewe-neck or not. I don't see how any thing short of a crooked-neck squash could fit it; but I'll try mine on." And with these words he harnessed up the colt, and leaving his old "hoss" with the widow, drove on his way rejoicing.

About fifteen miles farther east, he stopped and put up at a tavern, where he made an arrangement to leave the colt for a week, hiring the landlord's horse to pursue his journey. He gave directions to have the colt fed high in the interim, to have his tail nicked and put in pulleys, his head checked up, and his coat carefully shaved according to the new practice. A very astute hostler promised that every thing should be done according to his directions, and to his perfect satisfaction.

Accordingly, in a week's time, when Zebulon came back, he hardly knew his bargain. The colt was fat as a hog. His sides shone like silver; his mane was neatly trimmed; his tail was crimped, and rose and fell in a graceful curve; and he carried his head as proudly as an Arabian.

With the metamorphosed animal in the fills, the agent drove back to the Spread Eagle, and put up for the night. In the morning, he ordered his team, and paid his bill. Major Spike, who was great on horses, standing at the front door, was struck with the appearance of his guest's "cattle."

"Been buying a new hoss?" said the major.

"Yes; I thought I'd try one, though I ain't a horse jockey," answered the agent, making an excuse to examine the buckles of his harness.

"Don't want to sell him, do you?" said the major.

"Why, no, major, I reckon not. I expect he'll suit me fust rate. I'm doin' pooty well, now, and can afford to hev' somethin' nice. I calklate to keep him."

"I don't like his color," said the major.

"Well, I do," said Zebulon, getting into his wagon. "Good mornin', major."

"Hold on," said the major. "I've got a hoss I want to show you. Jake, bring out the bay, and let Mr. Smith have a squint at him."

The hostler brought out a square-built, chunky, bay horse, in fine condition, and looking like a capital roadster.

"What do you think of *that* hoss, Mr. Smith?" asked the major, triumphantly.

"Pretty fair hoss," said the agent. "But I tell you I'm no judge of horses; I ain't a horse jockey."

"Well, now, I tell you what," said the major; "I'm a darned fool for doin' of it; but when I take a fancy, I don't mind expense to gratify it. I'm willing to swap hosses even with you."

"Even!" screamed the agent. "Now, major, that's a good one. I ain't a horse jockey. I don't know the value of the critters; but I ain't altogether a reg'lar, soft-headed, know-nothin' fool; and if I had a mind to part with this 'ere splendiferous animal, I should want boot."

"You're a hard one," said the major; "but as fur as twenty dollars———"

"Twenty dollars! get out," said the agent, indignantly. "G'lang, Bob!" and he actually started his team.

"Hold on!" roared the major. "What do you want?"

"Say forty, and I'll do it—no, I won't," said the agent.

"You said you would. It's a bargain. You said forty, didn't he, Jake?"

The hostler could not deny it.

"Well, you're the hardest customer *I* ever see!" muttered the agent, as he got out of the wagon. "This is the wust mornin's work I ever did. Let me have your old bay, and be a travellin'. You'd hev' a fellur's eye teeth afore he knowed it, ef you wanted 'em."

The major chuckled as he counted out forty dollars and handed them to the agent. He eagerly assisted the hostler to ungear the coveted horse; and when the bay was harnessed up, did not urge the agent to stop, and the latter drove off, looking as melancholy as if he had buried all his relations.

The major drove out with his new purchase that very day; but his performance did not equal his expectations. However, as an experienced horse jockey, he knew that great allowances are to be made for a green horse, and he promised to train him up to "2.50," at the least. But before one week had passed over his head, his expectations were all dashed. There was no "go" in the animal. His nose dropped to the ground, his tail slunk, and his toes dug into the gravel as if he was boring for water. The major had to confess that he had been completely taken in.

"That infernal rascal!" said he; "I wish I could catch him here again."

"You ain't very likely to," remarked Jake, the hostler, dryly.

"Why so? Do you know any thing about him? Did you ever see him before?"

"Ever see him! why, he came from the same place that I did."

"Where's that?"

"Meredith Bridge."

"Meredith Bridge!" exclaimed the landlord. "And he said he wasn't a horse jockey. O, what an ass I was."

"Very true," said the hostler.

"Any how, you never saw the horse before?" said the landlord.

"Never see the horse before!" exclaimed Jake. "Why, Lord bless you, I know'd him soonsever I sot eyes on him. He's Miss Stebbins's colt."

"And you never told me of this, you scoundrel!"

"I want a goin' to spile a trade," said the hostler. "And then I've heard you say so often that nobody could take you in on a hoss, that I thought it warnt no use."

"The cussed swindler!" said the major. "After havin' shaved every body he came across, he went and shaved a hoss, and put him off on me—*me*, the greatest hossman in the State of Maine. The next chap from Meredith Bridge that comes into these diggins, I'll get a fight out of and lick him, jest as sure as my name's Elnathan Spike!"

FUNERAL SHADOWS.

A MYSTERY.

The wind was howling and moaning through the almost deserted streets of Boston, on a chilly evening of September, as a young man of medium height and slight figure drew a faded and threadbare black cloak around him, pulled his fur cap down on his forehead to shelter his eyes from the cutting wind, and strode down Washington Street in a northerly direction, with a rapid and impatient step. Arrived at the door of a house of moderate pretensions, he entered hastily. We shall follow him to the third story, enter with him a large and wholly dark apartment, and watch him while he kindles a fire on the ample hearth stone. A pale-blue flame flickers hesitatingly among the wood, and conjures up from the walls around strange shapes and countenances bathed in the indistinct and lurid light. And now the flame grows brighter, and the heavy furniture in the apartment flings strange shadows, horizontal, diagonal, and perpendicular; and the pictures on the wall (for we are in a painter's studio) looked quite as vague and vapory as the projected shadows. It is not difficult to imagine some of these faces endowed with vitality, and so wild and startling are many of them that the wavering shadows seem to belong to them, and to be their strangely-animated limbs.

The painter lit a lamp, and then a huge meerschaum filled with fragrant tobacco, his nightly solace and daily inspiration. While the smoke wreaths slowly ascended to the ceiling, he wove his Gothic fancies, and saw, in the blue clouds that hovered over him, embryo designs and groups that he afterwards transferred to canvas.

Malise Grey was an artist of great but peculiar talent—a fine draughtsman, an admirable colorist, but his imagination was of a Gothic cast, and he delighted in strange, fantastical, and supernatural subjects. He had travelled much in Germany, and his mind was imbued with the superstitions and legends of that storied land. These he loved to illustrate with his pencil, and his walls were covered with German scenes and subjects, from the "Witches' Sabbath" to the "Castled Crag of Drachenfels." Portraits he painted from necessity, not choice; but he was too true an artist for the million. The sleek hypocrite wore not on his canvas the deceptive look of holiness that bore him on through life to wealth and honor, but the crafty, sensual smile, the libertine eye, and lips that indicated the secret phases of his character. Imbecile beauty saw her index in the painted mirror. Folly stood convicted by the pencil. It was frequently remarked, that you might learn more of a man from a glance at his portrait than from months' companionship with the original. Malise Grey was not popular—but he lived for his art, and bread and water satisfied his earthly cravings.

The meerschaum fairly smoked out, the artist drew from a dusty pile of canvases one on which he had painted a family group. It was a fancy piece. An old man lay upon his death bed, over which bent a weeping wife and a sorrowing and lovely child. The face of the latter was one of unearthly beauty, and Raphael or Titian might not have disdained the painting of those glistening blue eyes, and the falling sunbeams of that golden hair. The painter had poured out his soul upon that angelic countenance and perfect figure.

"It is my ideal," said the artist, "and, by the mystic whisper of the heart, by the bright teaching of the star that rules my destiny, by the forbidden lore of which I have drank deeply, I know that the ideal of each mind is the reflex of the actual, and with the true artist fancy is existence!"

The meerschaum was again filled, and Malise Grey contemplated his picture. The smoke wreaths rolled around it, but it shone out luminous and starlike. Its harmony was like the silent melody of the spheres, and its musical radiance dispelled the remembrance of all his sufferings, and lulled him like the melody of falling waters. When, at length, he drew his poor couch from its recess, and threw himself upon it, he left the picture full in sight, and continued to watch it by the fading firelight till its last luminous point disappeared with the blaze, and slumber closed his lids to make its memory brighter.

The next morning was clear and sparkling; the first rays of the sun were like fiery rubies on the walls of the studio.

The painter sprang to his feet. "The dream!" he cried. "My heart did not deceive me. The spirits are at work for its accomplishment."

He went forth to take his daily walk. There were times when an appalling dread of insanity smote his heart, and once the expression of a friend at the recital of one of his wildest fantasies led him into a train of reflection and self-examination which shook his very soul. For a time he forsook his studio, and went abroad into the gay world and formed fashionable acquaintances; but he went back to his lonely room and his hermit life at the expiration of a few weeks, convinced that the madness of art was preferable to the madness of society. And it was a painful thing for him to go abroad, for no one sympathized with him. His mind dwelt either on the shadowy past, or the yet more shadowy future. He held no communion with the present. So, on the occasion we have referred to, after a hurried walk, he returned to his room, the door of which he had left unlocked. A veiled lady sat before his easel. She rose upon his entrance. His heart beat high with anticipations. The lady thus addressed him:—

"Malise Grey, we have known each other in the land of dreams!" and removing her veil, she pointed with her left hand to the picture, while she extended her right to the painter. The ideal and the actual stood before him. A strange light gleamed upon the painter's mind, and he spoke as if prompted by some unseen power.

"Esther Vaughan, by this token do I know you." He took her hand, and added, "By the mystic spell that drew us to each other, I conjure you here to plight your troth to me for weal and woe."

"My father died shortly after that picture was painted," replied the maiden, "and my mother—my poor mother—soon followed him. The spirit summons commanded me to seek you out. I have obeyed."

A strange marriage was solemnized in the Old King's Chapel. The bride wore no rose or orange flower in her braided hair, and a long, black veil enveloped her from head to foot. In fact, her entire raiment, and that of the bridegroom, was of the same ghastly hue; and the ceremony was performed beneath the light of torches, which threw their funeral glare upon the mortuary tablets and reliefs that decorate the interior of the sacred edifice. As the newly-married pair were about to step into the carriage at the door, a thin figure in black approached the bride, and laid its hand upon her arm. The countenance was not visible. The bride uttered a sharp cry of pain and terror, and the figure instantly stepped back.

"Hold up your torch, there, sexton," cried the painter; "some one has insulted the bride."

A tall figure was seen stealing away through the tombstones in the churchyard, to which he had probably gained access through a breach in the wall, at that time wholly ruinous.

It is not our intention to describe the happiness of Malise Grey and his strangely-found and strangely-wedded bride. Enough to say, it was like all the circumstances that composed his existence—dream-like and strange. So vivid were his dreams and reveries, that he often wondered whether they were not the actual, and his marriage life the imaginary, part of his existence. He could not give himself up to enjoyment; and sometimes, when his young wife would have lavished on him the wealth of her innocent caresses, he turned from her moodily, and muttered, "What have I to do with a spirit bride? When the sun rises, these shadows will disperse."

Esther Grey had often solicited her husband to paint her portrait, since the likeness in the family picture showed her under the influence of grief. She wished a record of her happiness. Grey set about complying with her request. He assumed the task in a moment of inspired and fresh feeling, and went to work with heart and soul. His sketch was instantaneously executed, and then

"His touches they flew like leaves in a storm;
And the pure pearly white, and the carnation warm,
Contending in harmony, glowed."

Suddenly he threw down his pencil, and paced the apartment to and fro with rapid strides. "The doomed look!" he muttered, "the doomed look! Esther, I can paint no more to-day."

But the morrow found him early at his task. A few hours' work completed a portrait which, for fidelity of likeness, harmony of accessories, and felicity of coloring, was almost unsurpassable. Yet the painter refused to have it framed, and concealed it from view behind a curtain in his studio.

A day or two afterwards, a stranger called upon the artist. He was a tall, thin man, attired in a threadbare suit of black bombazine. He was frightfully pale. His jaws were prominent, and the sallow, shrunken skin clung close to every muscle of his countenance. His dark, sunken, and glossy eyes had an unearthly expression, and his air was melancholy in the extreme. A nameless chill came over the painter as he surveyed the aspect of his unknown visitor. The stranger coldly surveyed the productions of the artist, and honored them with a few brief comments. At length he paused before the veiled picture, and said, "This picture of your wife belongs to me."

The painter was so strong a believer in the supernatural, had been subject to so many inexplicable influences, that he felt no surprise at the stranger's naming the subject of the veiled picture without uncovering it. But he repeated, sternly, "Belongs to you? What mean you by that remark?"

"I mean it is, or will be mine, by purchase."

"Not so."

"Then you will not sell it?"

"I will not part with it at any price."

The stranger smiled, but not sneeringly or sarcastically The expression of his countenance was mournful in the extreme, and likewise unpleasant, because the parting of his shrivelled lips displayed his large, yellow teeth in unpleasant relief. He opened the door, but paused upon the threshold.

"You will not part with it?"

"Once more, no!" replied the painter.

"No matter; the original will soon be mine."

The door closed rapidly behind his noiseless steps. A vague terror shot through the soul of the artist.

When Esther Vaughan came to the dwelling of the painter, she was radiant with a health which had triumphed over sorrow and long watching, but the seeds of disease now fastened upon her frame, and she sunk under its influence, growing daily feebler. The almost distracted husband employed the best physicians in the city, and under their efforts Esther, for a while, seemed to revive. One day, in solemn conclave, they decided that the patient would live, and announced the intelligence to the poor painter, as he sat in his lonely studio, with much pomposity and emphasis. At the time of this announcement, the painter was standing opposite the open door through which the physicians had just entered. At the moment when a smile of gratified love was lighting up his intelligent countenance, his eyes, looking beyond the group of visitors, caught in the corridor those of the strange bidder for the veiled picture. The unknown shook his head slowly and mournfully, then turned and retired.

"Stop him, gentlemen," cried the painter, bursting through the group of leeches; "he is a deadly enemy!"

The physicians looked at each other, smiled darkly, and shook their heads.

"Poor Grey!" said an old doctor.

"Mad?" asked the youngest of the group.

"The cell, the chain, and scourge would be a wholesome prescription," said the first speaker.

Such were the tender mercies of science to madness in the eighteenth century.

It was a hushed midsummer night. The hum of busy footsteps had long since died away, and the twinkling lights had faded, one by one, from the huge bulk of the metropolis. To the lonely night watcher, there was enough of light in the mild effulgence of the moon to distinguish whether the pale invalid woke or slumbered; whether the repose of the dead was inviolate, or invaded by noisome things that move abroad only in darkness. And midway between life and death, so motionless that you would say she belonged to the dark realm of the latter, so lovely that the former still seemed to claim her own, lay the earth-born love of the painter, with her ethereal essence yet hovering near the beloved of her soul. The painter sat by the bedside, with her thin, pale hand clasped in his. He had listened to her last accents; he had heard her call him, in the fervor of her affection, "her beautiful, her own;" and he knew that, ere the unseen clock had recorded the death of another hour, the feeble pulse that fluttered beneath his fingers would have ceased to beat. Yet, with all this, his eyes were tearless, and his heart less heavy than in those dark dreams which had foreshadowed this event. In weal or woe, his prophetic dreams seemed even more impressive than the realities which followed them.

It appeared as if there were a magnetic influence in the touch of the dying hand; that the soul of Esther, bathed in the dawning light of the better world, had communicated a portion of its brightness to his own. So the hours wore on; the feeble pulse yet beat, but fainter and fainter. At last, through the open window which commanded a view of the east, the brightening streaks of dawn appeared; in the leaves of a solitary tree, that stood amid a wilderness of brick hard by, was heard the faint, tremulous twitter of a bird waiting but a ruddier ray to launch forth upon his dewy pinions. A smile, like a ray of light, dawned upon the countenance of Esther. She pointed to a shadowy alcove in the chamber, and the painter's eye, following the indication, detected the figure of his mysterious and prophetic visitor. But the countenance of the unknown was milder, softer; a veil of brightness had fallen upon the more repulsive lineaments, and when the broad daylight beamed into the apartment, his image melted into the ray, like a rain-drop into a sunny sea. A thrill ran through the painter's frame; he gazed upon the face of Esther; it was that of death.

An unfinished painting rests upon an easel; it is a glimpse of paradise. In the centre is a focus of almost intolerable splendor, the luminous veil of the Inconceivable and Infinite; while towards it, as if drawn by a vortex of glory, yet held in suspense when too near, hovers a cloud of radiant forms and faces, their souls, pure and beatified, beaming from their countenances, all full of adoration, intelligence, and bliss. The painter sat before it, giving the last touches with a feeble yet graceful hand. A light seemed to stream upon him from the picture, and lit up his pale, inspired countenance.

The door opened, yet the painter turned not from his task; he heard no footstep, yet he knew that the messenger—no longer feared, but hoped for—was standing at his side.

"One touch more," he said, softly. "Thus 'tis done, and bravely done!"

He turned—the mysterious messenger was truly there. But as the painter gazed, the herald's form was transfigured; his poor garments had given place to shining raiments; his countenance beamed glory and goodness; effulgent wings expanded their snowy plumage from his glorious shoulders, and on his forehead shone a star like that of morning. He touched the mortal hand that throbbed to meet his clasp; the last film fell from the painter's eye, and he saw, with ecstasy, no horrid phantom, but AZRAEL, the Angel of Death, great, beautiful, and good.

THE LATE ELIAS MUGGS,

CAPTAIN IN THE M. V. M.

Elias Muggs is no more! Hepzibah Muggs is a widow; a stranger has purchased the stock of West India goods, and the Bluetown Fusileers are commanded by the first lieutenant. These are sad changes.

It is not a little remarkable that though Captain Elias Muggs was not born in the same year as the Duke of Wellington, (though, by the way, every body else seems to have been,) yet he died about the same time. There was a striking similarity between their characters and positions. The Iron Duke was commander-in-chief of the allied forces at the battle of Waterloo, and Elias Muggs was commander of the Bluetown Fusileers. If Elias Muggs had been born on the other side of the water, he probably would have been the Duke of Wellington; and if the Duke of Wellington had been born here, he would probably have been Elias Muggs. This proposition may appear a metaphysical subtlety to obtuse minds, but to ours it seems as clear as mud.

When such a man dies, he must not be permitted to depart

"Without the meed of one melodious tear."

His loss is a national loss. Nature seems to have intended him for President of the United States, but "left him two drinks behind;" whence we may conclude that Nature is a humbug, a conclusion practically arrived at by most artists, living and dead.

Elias Muggs, from his tenderest years, was devoted to groceries and glory. His venerable schoolmistress, who has outlived her illustrious pupil, and is now supported by the town whose founders were formed by her care, and who laid the foundation of our hero's greatness by the powerful application of birch at the seat of learning, assured us, in a recent interview, that the military propensities of Muggs were developed at an early age. She observed that it was impossible to fix his attention on the classic page of Noah Webster when the Bluetown Fusileers were passing the school house with drum and fife, and that the motive of his first experiment at "hooking jack" was a desire to attend a country muster in the neighboring town. She added, that she distinctly remembered having confiscated a box of tin soldiers with which he was amusing himself, and that he threatened to "punch her eye" if she did not release the unconscious prisoners of war on *parole*. These are very important facts.

We are unable to state the precise age at which Elias entered the service— but the town clerk of Bluetown places it at twenty-one. He went through the different grades with great rapidity, and was finally chosen captain in a warmly-contested election. There is no question that he would have been elected unanimously, without difficulty, had there not existed a great doubt in the *corps* (Captain Muggs, by the way, always pronounced this word, and spelled it, *corpse*) of his ability to "treat;" whereas his adversary was distinguished for possessing a "pocket full of rocks," and a willingness "to treat every body." The success of our hero, under the circumstances, was purely owing to military merit. The moment he was chosen, he took the field at the head of his command. Admiring Bluetown gazed approvingly upon his swallow-tailed coat, his tall plume, his shining battle blade, his plated scabbard, worsted sash, and low-heeled, cowhide boots. The fair, who are ever ready to award their smiles to chivalry, were unanimous in their approval, and Deacon Dogget's daughter was heard to murmur, "O, what a pooty soger 'lias makes!" "Upon this hint he spake" a few days afterwards, and in due time they were married. But enough of that—our essay treats of war, not love.

In his "first field," Captain Muggs displayed his extraordinary knowledge of tactics. He it was who first discovered the method of "dressing" a line, by backing it up against a curbstone. He also divested military science of many pedantic terms, which tend only to confuse the young conscript, and dampen the military ardor of the patriot soldier. He substituted the brief and soldierly words of command, "haw!" "gee!" and "whoa!" for "left," "right," and "halt." His spirited "let her rip!" was an infinite improvement on the "fire" of the Steuben manual. The object of the commander is to make himself understood readily by his men, and in this Captain Muggs was perfectly successful.

The greatest commanders have been famous for their terse eloquence. Napoleon said to his troops in Egypt, "Soldiers, from the summit of these pyramids twenty centuries look down on you this day." Scott, in Mexico, said to Smith's brigade, "Brave rifles, you have been baptized in fire, and have come out steel." And Muggs, at Bluetown, after the last manœuvre, said, "Feller sogers, that 'ere was prime—and now less adjourn to the tavern and likker up at my expense." It is questionable whether any speech of Napoleon or Scott ever excited more enthusiasm.

The company adjourned to the tavern, and after plentifully refreshing with long nines, pigtail, New England, and crackers, departed with three cheers for the "cap'n." We would fain draw a veil over what followed. But a strict regard for truth compels us to "speak right out in meetin'." All great men have their weaknesses. Cæsar was not immaculate. Alexander the Great died of *mania a potu*. There was no Maine liquor law at the time of which we speak. There was not even a temperance society in all Bluetown.

Captain Muggs was in the green and salad days of youth. He was flushed with military success, young, ardent, and imprudent.

He retired to a private room with the commissioned officers of his "corps," and left a liberal order at the bar. Healths were drank, songs sung, patriotic and otherwise, more otherwise than patriotic, and the "fast and furious" fun was driven into the small hours of the morning. When the bill was presented, Captain Muggs was without funds; and his gallant subordinates, on the bare suggestion of a loan, incontinently vanished. Captain Muggs intimated something about credit. The landlord shook his head. Captain Muggs was grieved, and the landlord consulted the flytraps on the ceiling, still extending his open hand, with the palm upwards, in the direction of the officer. Finding the publican obdurate, the captain proposed to leave his uniform and equipments in pawn, and the offer was accepted.

And here let us pause to contemplate the moral greatness of this act. Those insignia of rank were as dear to Muggs as the apple of his eye. They were to him what the sceptre and crown were to Napoleon. It was like tugging at his heartstrings to unfasten the belt and sash, and lay the sword upon the table. Marsyas suffered not more when Apollo removed his skin than Muggs did when the landlord stripped off his coat and epaulets. When the hat and plume were laid upon the altar of offended Mammon, Muggs uttered a deep groan, and departed in his shirt sleeves. If we were a great historical painter, we should prefer this subject to that of Washington resigning his commission as commander-in-chief of the revolutionary army.

The same integrity distinguished Captain Muggs throughout his life. When, some years afterwards, he received a letter from a lawyer, stating that, in case he did not immediately satisfy a certain claim of five years' standing, legal measures would be adopted to enforce payment, he remitted the sum in question without a murmur.

Personal courage is not deemed indispensable to great commanders. Marlborough is said to have trembled on the battle field. It is the part of the officer to command—of the men to execute. But Muggs was as valiant as he was wise. On a field day, when a certain turbulent apple woman persisted in encroaching on the lines, Captain Muggs charged her in person, unsupported by his troops, upset her apple stall, and expelled her from the lines. Such achievements are of rare occurrence.

On every parade day, Muggs was "thar." In every sham fight he was first and foremost. He was always loudest in proclaiming the "dooty of the milingtary to support the civil power." Yet in the great riot caused by the illegal impounding of Steve Gubbins's bull, when Bluetown was divided against itself, her constabulary force and "specials" ignominiously beaten and routed, Captain Muggs, with an heroic deafness to the call of glory and the selectmen, from a reluctance to shed the blood of his fellow-citizens, refused to call out his company, and concealed himself in a hayloft till the affray was over, the pound completely demolished, and the bull rescued from the minions of the law.

The loss of such a man is irreparable. What a president he would have made! Magnanimity, self-denial, punctuality, eloquence, popularity, military glory—why, he had all the elements of success. But our heroes are fast passing away. Muggs is gone, and we must make up our minds to be governed by mere statesmen!

THE SOLDIER'S WIFE.

It was a fine night in the autumn of the year 1805, and the stars shone as brilliantly over the gay city of Paris as if they had burned in an Italian heaven. The cumbrous mass of the palace of the Tuileries, instead of lying like a dark leviathan in the shadows of the night, blazed with light in all its many-windowed length; for the soldier emperor, the idol of his subjects, that night gave a grand ball and reception to the world. Troops in full uniform were under arms, and the great lamps of the court yard gazed brightly on the channelled bayonets and polished musket barrels of the sentinels. Carriage after carriage drew up at the great portal, and emitted beautiful ladies, brilliantly attired, and marshals and staff officers blazing with embroidery; for Napoleon, simple and unostentatious in his own person, well knew the importance of surrounding himself with a brilliant court; and the people, even the rude and ragged denizens of the Faubourgs St. Antoine and St. Marceau, as they hung upon the iron railing and scanned the splendid dresses of the guests as they alighted from their carriages, were well pleased to see that a throne created by themselves could vie in splendor with the old hereditary seats of loyalty that existed in spite of the execrations of the million. They marked with pleasure the arms of some of the ancient Bourbon nobility on the panels of some of the glittering equipages, for all the aristocracy of France had not joined the banners of her adversaries.

Within the walls of the palace, in the reception room, the scene was yet more dazzling. The draperies of the throne, at the foot of which stood Josephine, more impressive from her native and winning loveliness than the splendor of the priceless diamonds that decked her brow and neck, and the emperor in the simple attire of a gentleman, with no distinctive ornament save the grand cross of the Legion of Honor: the draperies of the throne, we say, no longer presented the golden lilies of the Bourbon, but the golden bees of Napoleon—symbols of the industry and perseverance which had raised him to his rank. The eye, as it roamed around the brilliant circle, encountered few of those vapid faces which make the staple of the surroundings of an hereditary throne. Every epaulet that sparkled there graced the shoulder of a man who had won his grade by exposure, gallantry, and intellect. There was the scarred veteran of the Sambre and the Meuse, heroes who had crossed "that terrible bridge of Lodi" in the path of the French tricolor and the face of the withering fire of Austrian batteries—dim eyes that had been blighted by the burning sands of Egypt, warriors who had braved the perils of the Alps, and the dangers of the plains of Lombardy.

Somewhat apart from the brilliant circle, in the embrasure of one of the deep and lofty windows, stood a young officer, in conversation with a beautiful young woman. The latter was attired in white satin, and the rich lace veil that half hid the orange flower in her hair, and descended gracefully over her faultless shoulders, proclaimed her to be a bride. And the young soldier, her companion? The radiant pride and joy that beamed from his fine dark eye, the animation of his manner, and the tenderness of his tone, as he addressed the lady, emphatically proclaimed the bridegroom. Such, indeed, were the relations of Colonel Lioncourt and Leonide Lasalle, who had that day only lost her maiden appellation at the altar of Notre Dame.

So absorbed was the young colonel in the conversation, that it was only after he had been twice addressed that he turned and noticed the proximity of a third person.

"Sorry to interrupt you, colonel," said the new comer, a young man with dark lowering brows, deep-set eyes, and a sinister expression, heightened by a sabre cut that traversed his left cheek diagonally, "but his majesty desires to speak to you."

"*Au revoir*, Leonide," said the young colonel to his bride; "I will join you again in a few moments. The emperor is laconic enough in his communications. Meanwhile, I leave you to the care of my friend."

The emperor was already impatient, and the moment the colonel appeared he grasped his arm familiarly, and led him aside, while the immediate group of courtiers fell back respectfully, and out of earshot.

"Colonel," said Napoleon, "I have news—great news. The enemies of France will not give us a moment's repose. It is no longer England alone that threatens us. I could have crushed England, had she met me single handed. In a month my eagles would have lighted on the tower of London. Russia, Austria, and Sweden have joined her. Our frontier is threatened by half a million men. Lioncourt, you are brave and trusty, and I will tell you what I dare communicate to few. My movements must be as secret as the grave. Paris must not suspect them. What do you think I propose doing?"

"To strengthen the frontier by concentrating your troops on different points, sire."

Napoleon smiled.

"No, Lioncourt; we will beard the lion in his den. I have broken up the camp at Boulogne. I will rush at once into the heart of Germany. I will separate the enemy's columns from each other. The first division that marches against me shall be outflanked, attacked in the rear, and cut to pieces. One after another they shall fall before me. In three months I shall triumph over the coalition. I shall dictate terms of peace from the field of battle. Lioncourt, they are short sighted. They know nothing of me yet. They fancy that my heart is engaged in these frivolous pomps and gayeties with which I amuse the people—that I have become enervated by 'Capuan delights.' But you know me better. You know that my throne is the back of my war horse—that the sword is my sceptre, cannon my diplomatists. I wished for peace—they have elected war; on their heads be the guilt and the bloodshed."

He paused, out of breath with the rapidity of his utterance. Colonel Lioncourt waited respectfully till he should recommence.

"Colonel," he said, at last, in a tone of sadness, a melancholy shade passing over his fine features, "they have described me as a sanguinary monster. History will do me justice. History will attest that I never drew the sword without just cause—that I returned it to its scabbard on the earliest opportunity. Not on my soul the guilt of slaughtered thousands, of villages burned, of peasants driven from their homes, of fields ravaged, of women widowed, and children orphaned. My whole soul yearns for peace. I would build my true greatness on the promulgation of just laws, the culture of religion and intellect, the triumphs of agriculture, and the arts of peace. But I must obey my destiny. Europe must be ploughed by the sword. The struggle is between civilization and barbarism, freedom and despotism, the Frank and the Cossack. But I prate too long. Colonel, I sent for you to pronounce a hard sentence. Your regiment of hussars is already under arms. You must march to-night—instantly."

"Sire," said Lioncourt, with a sigh. "This news will kill my poor wife."

"Josephine shall console her," said the emperor. "I would have informed you earlier, but St. Eustache, your lieutenant colonel, whom I now see talking with madame, advised me not to do so."

"I thank him," muttered Lioncourt bitterly.

"You have no time to lose. I counsel you to leave the presence quietly. Let your wife learn that you have marched by a letter. Better that than the agony of parting. I know something of human, and particularly feminine, nature. Adieu, colonel. Courage and good fortune."

And so saying, the emperor glided easily back to the circle he had left. Lioncourt's brain reeled under the blow he had received. He gazed upon his wife as she stood radiant, beautiful, and unsuspicious, under a glittering chandelier, with the same feelings with which a man takes his last look of the shore as he sinks forever in the treacherous wave. In another moment he was gone. The sentries presented arms as he passed out of the palace. His orderly was in the court yard holding his charger by the bridle. The colonel threw himself into the saddle, and was soon at the head of the regiment. The trumpets and kettledrums were mute—for such were the general orders and the regiment rode out of the city in silence, broken only by the heavy tramping of the horses' hoofs, and the clanking of scabbards rebounding from their flanks. As they passed out of one of the gates, the lieutenant colonel, St. Eustache, joined the column at a gallop, and reported to his commander.

St. Eustache had been a lover of Leonide Lasalle, had proposed for her hand, and been rejected. Still, he had not utterly ceased to love her, but his desire of possession was now mingled with a thirst of vengeance. He both hated and loved the beautiful Leonide, while he regarded his fortunate rival and commanding officer with feelings of unmitigated hatred. Yet he had art enough to conceal his guilty feelings and guilty projects. While he rode beside the colonel, his thoughts ran somewhat in this vein:—

"Well, at least I have succeeded in marring their joy. Lioncourt's triumph over me was short lived. He may never see his bride again. He is venturesome and rash. We have sharp work before us, or I'm very much mistaken, and Colonel Eugene Lioncourt may figure in the list of killed in the first general engagement. Then I renew my suit, and if Leonide again reject me, there's no virtue in determination."

While the colonel's regiment was slowly pursuing its way, the festivities at the Tuileries were drawing to a close. Madame Lioncourt wondered very much at the absence of her husband, and still more so when the guests began to depart, and he did not reappear to escort her to her carriage. It was then that the empress honored her with an interview, and, with tears in her beautiful eyes, informed her of her husband's march in obedience to orders. The poor lady bore bravely up against the effect of this intelligence so long as she was in the presence of the emperor and empress; but when alone in her carriage, on her way to her now solitary home, she burst into a flood of tears, and it seemed as if her very heart were breaking. The next morning brought a short but kind note from her husband. It was overflowing with affection and full of hope. The campaign, conducted by Napoleon's genius, he thought, could not fail to be brief, and he should return with new laurels, to lay them at the feet of his lovely bride. This little note was treasured up by Leonide as if it had been the relic of a saint, and its words of love and promise cheered her day after day in the absence of her husband.

At last, news came to the capital from the seat of war. The battle of Austerlitz had been fought and won. The cannon thundered from the Invalides, Paris blazed with illuminations, and the steeples reeled with the crashing peals of the joy bells. No particulars came at first; many had been killed and wounded; but the French eagles were victorious, and this was all the people at first cared for. Lioncourt's regiment had covered itself with glory, but no special mention was made of him in the first despatches.

At last, one morning, a visitor was announced to Madame Lioncourt, and she hastily descended to her salon to receive him. St. Eustache advanced to meet her. She eagerly scanned his countenance as he held out his hand. It was grave and sombre. A second glance showed her a black crape sword knot on the hilt of his sabre. She fainted and sank upon the floor before St. Eustache could catch her in his arms. He summoned her maid, and the latter, with the assistance of another servant, bore her mistress from the apartment.

St. Eustache paced the room to and fro, occasionally raising his eyes to contemplate the rich gilded ceiling, the paintings and statuettes, which adorned the *salon*.

"Some style here!" he muttered. "And they say she has this in her own right. Lioncourt left her some funds, I fancy. Young, beautiful, rich; by Jove, she is a prize."

His meditations were interrupted by the return of Madame Lioncourt, who motioned her visitor to be seated, and sank into a *fauteuil* herself. She was pale as marble, and her eyes were red with recent tears, but her voice was calm and firm as she said,—

"I need hardly ask you, sir, if my poor husband has fallen. I could read ill news in your countenance as soon as you appeared. Were you near him when he fell?"

"I was beside him, madame. We were charging the flying Russians. Our horses, maddened with excitement, had carried us far in advance of our column, when suddenly we were surrounded by a group of horsemen, who took courage and rallied for a moment. Lioncourt was carrying death in every blow he dealt, when a Russian cavalry officer, discharging his pistol at point blank distance, shot him dead from the saddle. I saw no more, for I was myself wounded and swept away in the torrent of the fight. But he is dead. Even if that pistol shot had not slain him, the hoofs of his own troopers, as they rushed madly forward in pursuit of the enemy, would have trampled every spark of life out of his bosom."

Leonide wrung her hands.

"But you, at least, recovered his—his remains?"

"Pardon, madame. I instituted a search for our colonel's body where he fell. But the spot had already been visited by marauders. All the insignia of rank had disappeared; and in the mangled heap of stripped and mutilated corpses, it was impossible to distinguish friend from foe."

The widowed bride groaned deeply as she covered her face with her handkerchief and rocked to and fro on her seat.

"Madame," said St. Eustache, "I will no longer intrude upon your grief. When time has somewhat assuaged the poignancy of your affliction, I will again call on you to tender my respectful sympathies."

Time wore on, and with it brought those alleviations it affords to even the keenest sorrow. The assiduity of friends compelled Madame Lioncourt to lay aside her widow's weeds, and reappear in the great world of fashion. There, whatever may have been her secret sorrow, she learned to wear the mask of a smiling exterior, and even to appear gayest among the gay, as if she sought forgetfulness in the wildest excitement and most frivolous amusement.

During all this time, St. Eustache, who had got a military appointment at Paris, was ever at her side. It was impossible for her to avoid him. He escorted her to her carriage when she left a ball room; he was the first to claim her hand when she entered. He was so respectful, so sad, so humble, that it was impossible to take offence at his assiduities, and she even began to like him in spite of former prejudices. Though it was evident that the freedom of her hand had renewed his former hopes, still no words of his ever betrayed their revival; only sometimes a suppressed sigh, the trembling of his hand as it touched hers, gave evidence that could not be mistaken.

Affairs were in this condition, when a brother of Leonide, Alfred Lasalle, a young advocate from the provinces, came to establish himself in Paris. He at once became the protector and guardian of his sister, and, as such, conceived the same violent dislike to St. Eustache that Leonide had formerly entertained towards him. St. Eustache, after many fruitless attempts to conciliate the brother, gave it up in despair. Still, whenever Alfred's affairs called him away, he supplied his place with the young widow.

At this time, play sometimes ran very high in the salons of the capital; and Leonide rose from the *écarté* table one night, indebted to St. Eustache in the sum of a thousand crowns.

"Call on me to-morrow," said Leonide, with a flushed face, "and I will repay you."

St. Eustache was pretty well acquainted with the affairs of the young widow. He knew that she had been living on her capital for some time, and that she had reached the limit of her resources. He knew that it was utterly impossible for her to raise a thousand crowns in twenty-four hours. She must, therefore, he thought, cancel her debt by her hand. This was the alternative to which he had been manœuvring to bring her; therefore he entered her salon the next day with the air of a victor. He was no longer covetous of wealth; he had prospered in his own speculations, and was immensely rich; the hand of Leonide, even without her heart, was now all he sought.

Madame Lioncourt received him with the easy assurance of a woman of the world. He, on his part, advanced with the grace of a French courtier.

"You came to remind me, sir," said the lady, "that I was unfortunate at play last night."

"No, madame," said St. Eustache, "it is yourself who reminds me of it. Pardon me, I am somewhat acquainted with your circumstances. I know that you are no longer as rich as you are beautiful——"

"Sir!"

"Pardon the allusion, madam; I did not intend to insult you, but only to suggest that the payment of money was not the only method of cancelling a debt."

"I do not understand you, sir."

"Leonide, it is time that you did understand me!" cried St. Eustache, impetuously. "It is time that I should throw off the mask and assert my claim to your hand. I loved you once—I love you still. You are now in my power. You cannot pay me the money you owe me; but you can make me happy. Your hand——"

"Colonel St. Eustache," said the lady, coldly, as she rose and handed him a pocket book, "be good enough to count those notes."

St. Eustache ran over them hastily.

"A thousand crowns, madame," he said.

"Then the debt is cancelled. Never renew the proposal of this morning. Good day, sir."

With a haughty inclination of the head, she swept out of the room.

"Never renew the proposal of this morning!" said St. Eustache to himself. "A thousand furies! It shall be renewed to-night. She will be at the masquerade at the opera house. I have bribed her chambermaid, and know her dress. She shall hear me plead my suit. I have dared too much, perilled too much, to give her up so easily."

Amidst the gay crowd at the opera house was a light figure in a pink domino, attended by one in black. Not to make a mystery of these characters, they were Madame Lioncourt and her brother.

"Dear Alfred," said the lady, "I am afraid you impoverished yourself to aid me in extricating myself from the toils of my persevering suitor."

"Say nothing of it, Leonide," replied Alfred. "Your liberty is cheaply purchased by the sacrifice."

"Lady, one word with you," said a low voice at her side.

She turned, and beheld a pilgrim with scrip, staff, and cross, and closely masked.

"Twenty, if you will, reverend sir," she replied gayly. "But methinks this is a strange scene for one of your solemn vocation."

"The true man," replied the mask, "finds something to interest him in every scene of life. Wherever men and women assemble in crowds, there is always an opportunity for counsel and consolation. The pious pilgrim should console the sad; and are not the saddest hearts found in the gayest throngs?"

"True, true," replied Leonide, with a deep sigh.

"But you, at least, are happy, lady," said the pilgrim.

"Happy! Could you see my face, you would see a mask more impenetrable than this velvet one I wear. It is all smiles," she whispered. "But," she added, laying her hand on her bosom,—

"'I have a silent sorrow here,
A grief I'll ne'er impart;
It heaves no sigh, it sheds no tear,
But it consumes my heart.'"

"Can it be possible!" cried the pilgrim. "You have the reputation of being one of the gayest of the Parisian ladies."

"Then you know me not."

"I know you by name, Madame Lioncourt."

"Then you should know that name represents a noble and gallant heart—the life of my own widowed bosom. You should know that Lioncourt, the bravest of the brave, the truest of the true, lies in a nameless grave at Austerlitz, the very spot unknown."

"I too was at Austerlitz," said the pilgrim, in a deep voice.

"You were at Austerlitz!"

"Yes, madame, in the—hussars."

"It was my husband's regiment."

"Yes, madame. I was for a long time supposed to be dead. My comrades saw me fall, and I was reported for dead. Faith, I came near dying. But I fell into the hands of some good people, though they were Austrians, and they took good care of me, and cured my wounds; and here I am at last."

"Ah! why," exclaimed Madame Lioncourt, "may this not have been the fate of your colonel? Why may not he too have survived the carnage, and been preserved in the same manner? His body was never recognized."

"Very possibly Lioncourt may still be living."

"Yet St. Eustache told me he was dead."

"He is a false traitor!" cried the pilgrim. "Leonide!" cried he, with thrilling emphasis, "you have borne bad news; can you bear good?"

"God will give me strength to bear good tidings," cried the lady.

"Then arm yourself with all your energy," said the stranger. "Lioncourt lives."

"Lives!" said Leonide, faintly, grasping the arm of the stranger to support herself from falling.

"Courage, madame; I tell you the truth. He lives."

"Then take me to him. The crisis is past. I can bear to meet him; nothing but delay will kill me now!" cried the lady, hurriedly.

"He stands beside you!" said the stranger.

A long, deep sigh, and Leonide lay in the arms of the pilgrim, who was still masked. But she recovered herself with superhuman energy, and said,—

"Come, come, I must see you. I must kneel at your feet. I must clasp your hands; my joy—my love—my life!"

"Room, room, there!" cried a seneschal. "The emperor!"

"Dearest Leonide," whispered a voice in her ear, "I resolved to see you again to-night, in spite of your prohibition to renew my suit."

"Then wait here beside me; do not leave me," answered the lady, as she recognized St. Eustache.

"That will I not, dearest," was the fervent reply.

Napoleon, with Josephine leaning on his arm, advanced through the broad space cleared by the attendants, and when he had taken up a position in the centre of the hall, near Lioncourt and his bride, St. Eustache and Lasalle, gave the signal for the company to unmask. As they obeyed, and every face was uncovered, his quick glance caught the pale and handsome features of the young cavalry colonel.

"What!" he exclaimed, impetuously. "Can the grave give up its dead? Do our eyes deceive us? Is this indeed Lioncourt, whom we left dead upon the field of Austerlitz? Advance, man, and satisfy our doubts."

Lioncourt advanced, and the emperor laid his hand upon his arm.

"You are pale as a ghost, man; but still you're flesh and blood. Give an account of yourself. Speak quickly; don't you see these ladies are dying of curiosity? and, faith, so I am too," he added, smiling.

"Sire," said the colonel, "you will, perhaps, remember ordering my regiment in pursuit of the flying Russians?"

"Perfectly well; and they performed the service gallantly. Their rear was cut to pieces."

"St. Eustache and I rode side by side," pursued the colonel.

"Here is St. Eustache," cried the emperor, beckoning the officer to advance.

"My dear colonel!" cried St. Eustache, embracing his old commander.

"Go on, colonel," cried the emperor, stamping his foot impatiently.

"We hung upon the flying rear of the enemy, sabring every man we overtook. Faith, I hardly know what happened afterwards," said the colonel, pausing.

"Take up the thread of the story, St. Eustache," said the emperor; "don't let it break off here."

"Well, sire," said St. Eustache, drawing, a long breath, "as the colonel and I were charging side by side, cutting right and left, separated from our men by the superior speed of our horses, a Russian officer wheeled and shot the colonel from his saddle."

"That was how it happened, Lioncourt," said the emperor. "Now go on. Afterwards——"

"When I came to my senses, sire," resumed Lioncourt, gloomily, "I found myself in the hands of some Austrian peasants. I had been plundered of my epaulets and uniform, and they took me for a common soldier. But they carried me to their cottage, and dressed my wound, and eventually I got well."

"But where were you wounded, colonel?" asked the emperor.

"A pistol ball had entered behind my left shoulder, and came out by my collar bone."

"*Behind* your left shoulder!" cried Napoleon. "And yet you were facing the enemy. How was that?"

"Because," said the colonel, sternly, "a Frenchman, a soldier, an officer, a disappointed rival, took that opportunity of assassinating me, and shot me with his own hostler pistol."

"His name!" shouted the emperor, quivering with passion, "his name; do you know him?"

"Well.—It was Lieutenant Colonel St. Eustache!"

All eyes were turned on St. Eustache. His knees knocked together, his eyes were fixed, cold drops of perspiration stood on his forehead. But in all that circle of indignant eyes, the detected criminal saw only the eagle orbs of the emperor, that pierced to his very soul.

"Is this charge true?" asked Napoleon, quickly, quivering with one of his tremendous tornadoes of passion.

St. Eustache could not answer; but he nodded his head.

"Your sword!" cried the emperor.

Mechanically the criminal drew his sabre; he had thrown off his domino, and now stood revealed in the uniform he disgraced, and offered the hilt to the emperor. Napoleon clutched it, and snapped the blade under foot. Then, tearing off his epaulets, he threw them on the floor, stamped on them, and beckoning to an officer who stood by, gasped out,—

"A guard, a guard!"

In a few minutes the tramp of armed men was heard in the saloon, and the wretched culprit was removed.

"*General* Lioncourt," said the emperor to his recovered officer, "your new commission shall be made out to-morrow. In the mean while the lovely Leonide shall teach you to forget your trials."

The assemblage broke up. Lioncourt, his wife, and her faithful brother retired to their now happy home.

The next day was fixed for the trial of the guilty St. Eustache before a court martial—a mere formal preliminary to his execution, for he had confessed his crime; but it appeared that during the preceding night he had managed to escape.

Flying from justice, the wretched criminal reached one of the bridges that span the Seine. Climbing to the parapet, he gazed down into the dark and turbid flood, now black as midnight, that rolled beneath the yawning arch. There was no star in the sky, and here and there only a dim light twinkled, reflected in the muddy wave. Daylight was beginning to streak the east with sickly rays. Soon the great city would be astir. Soon hoarse voices would be clamoring for the traitor, the assassin, the dastard, who, in the hour of victory, had raised his hand against a brother Frenchman. Soon, if he lingered, his ears would be doomed to hear the death penalty—soon the muskets, whose fire he had so often commanded, would be levelled against his breast. All was lost,—all for which he had schemed and sinned,—the applause of his countrymen, the favor of his emperor, the love of Leonide. At least, he would disappoint Paris of a spectacle. He would die by his own act. A sudden spring, a heavy plunge, a few bubbles breaking on the black surface, and the wretched criminal was no more!

Days afterwards, a couple of soldiers, lounging into La Morgue, the dismal receptacle where bodies are exposed for identification, recognized in a pallid and bloated corpse the remains of the late lieutenant colonel of the ——th hussars.

Lioncourt learned his fate, but it threw no shadow over his bright and cloudless happiness.

A KISS ON DEMAND.

It was a very peculiar sound, something like the popping of a champagne cork, something like the report of a small pocket pistol, but exactly like nothing but itself. It was a kiss.

A kiss implies two parties—unless it be one of those symbolical kisses produced by one pair of lips, and wafted through the air in token of affection or admiration. But this particular kiss was genuine. The parties in the case were Mrs. Phebe Mayflower, the newly-married wife of honest Tom Mayflower, gardener to Mr. Augustus Scatterly, and that young gentleman himself. Augustus was a good-hearted, rattle-brained spendthrift, who had employed the two or three years which had elapsed since his majority in "making ducks and drakes" of the pretty little fortune left him by his defunct sire. There was nothing very bad about him, excepting his prodigal habits, and by these he was himself the severest sufferer. Tom, his gardener, had been married a few weeks, and Gus, who had failed to be at the wedding, and missed the opportunity of "saluting the bride," took it into his head that it was both proper and polite that he should do so on the first occasion of his meeting her subsequently to that interesting ceremony. Mrs. Mayflower, the other party interested in the case, differed from him in opinion, and the young landlord kissed her in spite of herself. But she was not without a champion, for at the precise moment when Scatterly placed his audacious lips in contact with the blooming cheek of Mrs. M., Tom entered the garden and beheld the outrage.

"What are you doing of, Mr. Scatterly?" he roared.

"O, nothing, Tom, but asserting my rights! I was only saluting the bride."

"Against my will, Tommy," said the poor bride, blushing like a peony, and wiping the offended cheek with her checked apron.

"And I'll make you pay dear for it, if there's law in the land," said Tom.

"Poh, poh! don't make a fool of yourself," said Scatterly.

"I don't mean to," answered the gardener, dryly.

"You're not seriously offended at the innocent liberty I took?"

"Yes I be," said Tom.

"Well, if you view it in that light," answered Scatterly, "I shall feel bound to make you reparation. You shall have a kiss from my bride, when I'm married."

"That you never will be."

"I must confess," said Scatterly, laughing, "the prospect of repayment seems rather distant. But who knows what will happen? I may not die a bachelor, after all. And if I marry—I repeat it, my dear fellow—you shall have a kiss from my wife."

"No he shan't," said Phebe. "He shall kiss nobody but me."

"Yes he shall," said Scatterly. "Have you got pen, ink, and paper, Tom?"

"To be sure," answered the gardener. "Here they be, all handy."

Scatterly sat down and wrote as follows:—

"THE WILLOWS, August —, 18—.

"Value received, I promise to pay Thomas Mayflower or order, one kiss on demand.

"AUGUSTUS SCATTERLY."

"There you have a legal document," said the young man, as he handed the paper to the grinning gardener. "And now, good folks, good by."

"Mistakes will happen in the best regulated families," and so it chanced that, in the autumn of the same year, our bachelor met at the Springs a charming belle of Baltimore, to whom he lost his heart incontinently. His person and address were attractive, and though his prodigality had impaired his fortune, still a rich old maiden aunt, who doted on him, Miss Persimmon Verjuice, promised to do the handsome thing by him on condition of his marrying and settling quietly to the management of his estate. So, under these circumstances, he proposed, was accepted, and married, and brought home his beautiful young bride to reside with Miss Verjuice at the Willows.

In the early days of the honeymoon, one fine morning, when Mr. and Mrs. Scatterly and the maiden aunt were walking together in the garden, Tom Mayflower, dressed in his best, made his appearance, wearing a smile of most peculiar meaning.

"Julia," said Augustus, carelessly, to his young bride, "this is my gardener, come to pay his respects to you—honest Tom Mayflower, a very worthy fellow, I assure you."

Mrs. Scatterly nodded condescendingly to the gardener who gazed upon her with the open eyes of admiration. She spoke a few words to him, inquired about his wife, his flowers, &c., and then turned away with the aunt, as if to terminate the interview.

But Tom could not take his eyes off her, and he stood, gaping and admiring, and every now and then passing the back of his hand across his lips.

"What do you think of my choice, Tom?" asked Scatterly, confidentially.

"O, splendiferous!" said the gardener.

"Roses and lilies in her cheeks—eh?" said Scatterly.

"Her lips are as red as carnations, and her eyes as blue as larkspurs," said the gardener.

"I'm glad you like your new mistress; now go to work, Tom."

"I beg pardon, Mr. Scatterly; but I called to see you on business."

"Well—out with it."

"Do you remember any thing about saluting the bride?"

"I remember I paid the customary homage to Mrs. Mayflower."

"Well, don't you remember what you promised in case of your marriage?"

"No!"

Tom produced the promissory note with a grin of triumph. "It's my turn now, Mr. Scatterly."

"What do you mean?"

"I mean to kiss Mrs. Scatterly."

"Go to the deuse, you rascal!"

"O, what is the matter?" exclaimed both the ladies, startled by Scatterly's exclamation, and turning back to learn the cause.

"This fellow has preferred a demand against me," said Scatterly.

"A legal demand," said the gardener, sturdily; "and here's the dokiment."

"Give it to me," said the old maid aunt. Tom handed her the paper with an air of triumph.

"Am I right?" said he.

"Perfectly, young man," replied Miss Verjuice; "only, when my nephew married, I assumed all his debts; and I am now ready myself to pay your claim."

"Fairly trapped, by Jupiter!" exclaimed Scatterly, in an ecstasy of delight.

"Stop, stop!" cried the unhappy gardener, recoiling from the withered face, bearded lip, and sharp nose of the ancient spinster; "I relinquish my claim— I'll write a receipt in full."

"No, sir," said Scatterly; "you pressed me for payment this moment—and you shall take your pay, or I discharge you from my employ."

"I am ready," said the spinster, meekly.

Tom shuddered—crawled up to the old lady—shut his eyes—made up a horrible face, and kissed her, while Mr. and Mrs. S. stood by, convulsed with laughter.

Five minutes afterwards, Tom entered the gardener's lodge, pale, weak, and trembling, and sank into a chair.

"Give me a glass of water, Phebe!" he gasped.

"Dear, what has happened?" asked the little woman.

"Happened! why that cussed Miss Verjuice is paying Mr. Scatterly's debts."

"Well?"

"Well, I presented my promissory note—he handed it to her—and—and— O murder!—*I've been kissing the old woman!*"

Phebe threw her arms about his neck, and pressed her lips to his, and Thomas Mayflower then and there solemnly promised that he would nevermore have any thing to do with KISSES ON DEMAND!

THE RIFLE SHOT.

A MADMAN'S CONFESSION.

It is midnight. The stealthy step of the restless maniac is no longer heard in the long, cheerless corridors; the ravings of the incurable cannot penetrate the deep walls of the cells in which their despair is immured; even the guardians of the establishment are asleep. Without, what silence! The branches of the immemorial trees hang pendulous and motionless; the last railway train, with its monster eyes of light, has thundered by. The neighboring city seems like one vast mausoleum, over which the silent stars are keeping watch and ward, and weeping silvery dew like angels' tears. Only crime and despair are sleepless.

To my task. They allow me a lamp. They are not afraid that the *madman* will fire his living tomb and perish in the ruins. Wise men of science! Cunning readers of the human heart, your decrees are infallible. I am mad. But perhaps some eager individual whose eyes shall rest upon these pages will pronounce a different sentence; perhaps he may know how to distinguish *crime* from *madness.*

A vision of my youth comes over me—a happy boyhood—a tree-embowered home, babbling brooks, fertile lawns—a father's blessing—a mother's kiss that was both joy and blessing—a brother's brave and tender friendship—and first love, that dearest, sweetest, holiest charm of all. O God! that those things were and are not! It is agony to recall them.

Pass, too, the brief Elysian period of wedded love. Julia sleeps well in her woodland grave. I was false to her memory.

If my boyhood were happy, my manhood was a melancholy one. A morbid temperament, fostered by indulgence, dropped poison even in the cup of bliss. I loved and I hated with intensity.

To my widowed home came, after the death of my wife, my fair cousin Amy, and my young brother Norman. Both were orphans like myself. Amy was a glorious young creature—my antithesis in every respect. She was light hearted, I was melancholy; she was beautiful, I ill favored; she was young, I past the middle age of life, arrived at that period when philosophers falsely tell us that the pulses beat moderately, the blood flows temperately, and the heart is tranquil. Fools! the fierce passions of the soul belong not to the period of youth or early manhood. But let my story illustrate my position.

Amy filled my lonely home with mirth and music. She rose with the lark, and carolled as wildly and gayly the livelong day, till, like a child tired of play, she sank from very exhaustion on her pure and peaceful couch. Norman was her playmate. In early manhood he retained the buoyant and elastic spirit of his youth. His was one of those natures which never grow old. Have you ever noticed one of those aged men, whose fresh cheeks and bright eyes, and ardent sympathy with all that is youthful and animated, belie the chronicle of Time? Such might have been the age of Norman, had not——But I am anticipating.

Between my cold and exhausted nature and Amy's warm, fresh heart, you might have supposed that there could have been no union. Yet she loved me warmly and well—loved me as a friend and father. I returned her pure and innocent affection with a fierce passion. I longed to possess her. The memory of her I had loved and lost was but as the breath on the surface of a steel mirror, which heat displaces and obliterates.

I was not long in perceiving the exact state of her feelings towards me, and with that knowledge came the instantaneous conviction of her fondness for my brother, so well calculated to inspire a young girl's love. I watched them with the keen and angry eyes of jealousy. I followed them in their walks; I played the eavesdropper, and caught up the words of their innocent conversation, endeavoring to turn them to their disadvantage. By degrees I came to hate Norman; and what equals in intensity a brother's hate? It surpasses the hate of woman.

In the insanity of my passion—then I was insane indeed—I sought to rival my brother in all those things in which he was my superior. He was fond of field sports, and a master of all athletic exercises; he was fond of bringing home the trophies of his manly skill and displaying them in the eyes of his mistress. He could bring down the hawk from the clouds, or arrest the career of the deer in full spring. I practised shooting, and failed miserably. His good-natured smile at my maladroitness I treasured up as a deadly wrong. While he rode fearlessly, I trembled at the thought of a leap. He danced gracefully and lightly; my awkward attempts at waltzing made both Amy and her lover smile.

But in mental accomplishments I was the superior of Norman; and in my capacity of teacher both to Amy and my brother, I had ample opportunity of displaying the powers of my mind.

Amy was gifted with quick intelligence; Norman was a dull scholar. What pleasure I took in humbling him in the eyes of his mistress! what asperity and scorn I threw into my pedantic rebukes! Norman was astonished and wounded at my manner. As he was in a good degree dependent on me, as he owed to me his nurture, sustenance, and training, I took full advantage of our relative position. With well-feigned earnestness and sorrow, I exaggerated my pecuniary embarrassments, and pointed out to him the necessity of his providing for himself, suggesting, with tears in my eyes, that he must adopt some servile trade or calling, as his melancholy deficiencies precluded the possibility of his success in any other line.

Norman had little care for money. Before the fatal advent of Amy, I had supplied him freely with the means of gratifying his tastes; but when I found that he expended his allowance in presents for his fair cousin, on the plea of hard necessity I restricted his supplies, and finally limited him to a pittance, which only a feeble regard for the memory of our indulgent mother forced me to grant.

One day—I remember it well—he came to me with joy depicted in his countenance, and displayed a recent purchase, the fruits of his forced economy. It was a fine rifle; and he urged me and Amy to come and see him make a trial of the weapon. I rebuked him for his extravagance with a sharpness which brought tears into his eyes—but I consented to witness the trial. His first shot centered the target. He loaded again, and handed the weapon to me. My bullet was nowhere to be found. Norman's second shot lapped his first. Mine was again wide of the mark. Norman laughed thoughtlessly. Amy looked grave, for with a woman's quickness she had guessed at the truth of my feelings. I cut the scene short by summoning both to their studies. That morning Norman, whose thoughts were with his rifle, blundered sadly in his mathematics, and I rebuked him with more than my usual asperity.

Be it understood that my character stood high with the world. I was not undistinguished in public life, and had the rare good fortune to conciliate both parties. I was a working man in many charitable and philanthropic societies. I was a member of a church, and looked up to as a model of piety. As a husband and brother, I was held up as an example. I had so large a capital of character, I could deal in crime to an unlimited amount.

Some days after the occurrence just related, I was alone with my brother in the library.

"Come, Norman," said I, "leave those stupid books. Study is a poor business for a young free heart like yours. Leave books for old age and the rheumatism."

Norman sprang up joyously. "With all my heart, brother; I'm with you for a gallop or a ramble."

"I'm but a poor horseman, and an indifferent walker," I answered. "What do you say to a little rifle practice? I should like to try to mend my luck."

Norman's rifle was in his hand in a moment, and whistling his favorite spaniel, he sallied forth with me into the bright, sunshiny autumnal day. We hied to a hollow in the woods where he had set up a target. He made the first shot—a splendid one—and then reloaded the rifle.

"Take care," said he, "how you handle the trigger; you know the lock is an easy one—I am going to have it altered." And he went forward to set the target firmer in the ground, as his shot had shaken it.

He was twenty paces off—his back turned towards me. I lifted the rifle, and covered him with both sights. It was the work of a moment. My hand touched the trigger. A sharp report followed—the puff of blue smoke swirled upward—and my brother fell headlong to the ground. The bullet had gone crashing through his skull. He never moved.

A revulsion of feeling instantly followed. All the love of former years—all the tender passages of our boyhood—rushed through my brain in an instant. I flew to him and raised him from the earth. At sight of his pale face, beautiful in death, of his long bright locks dabbled in warm blood, I shrieked in despair. A mother bewailing her first born could not have felt her loss more keenly, or mourned it more wildly. Two or three woodmen rushed to the spot. They saw, as they supposed, the story at a glance. One of those accidents so common to the careless use of firearms—and I was proverbially unacquainted with their use—had produced the catastrophe. We were borne home, for I had fainted, and was as cold and lifeless as my victim. What passed during a day or two I scarcely remember. Something of strange people in the house—of disconnected words of sympathy—of a coffin—a funeral—a pilgrimage to the woodland cemetery, where my parents and my wife slept—are all the memory records of those days.

Then I resumed the full possession of my senses. Amy's pale face and shadowy form were all that were left of *her*—my brother's seat at the table and the fireside were empty. But his clothes, his picture, his riding cap and spurs, a thousand trifles scattered round, called up his dread image every day to the fratricide. His dog left the house every morning, and came not back till evening. One day he was found dead in the graveyard where his master had been laid.

Amy clung to me with despairing love. She *would* talk of the lost one. She *would* find every day in me some resemblance to him. Perhaps she would even have wedded in me the memory of the departed. But that thought was too horrible. I loved her no longer.

Friends came to condole with me. Every word of sympathy was a barbed arrow. I could bear it no longer. Conscience stung me not to madness, but confession. I repelled sympathy—I solicited denunciation. I told them I was my brother's murderer. I forced my confession on every one who would hear it. Then it became rumored about that my "fine mind," so they phrased it, had given way beneath the weight of sorrow. I was regarded with fear. A physician of my acquaintance made me a friendly visit, and shook his head when he heard my story. One day this gentleman invited me to ride in his carriage. He left me here. Society believes me mad—that I am not, is to me a miracle.

O ye wise ones of the earth,—legislators of the land,—would ye avenge the blood that has been spilt by violence on the ruthless murderer, would ye inflict punishment upon him, spare and slay him not. Take down the gallows, and in its place erect your prisons doubly strong, for there, within their ever-during walls of granite, lies the hell of the villain who has robbed his brother of his life.

THE WATER CURE.

Since the introduction of the limpid waters of Lake Cochituate into the goodly city of Boston, the water commissioners have had their hands full of business, for the various accidents incidental to the commencement of the service, the bursting of pipes, the demands for payments of damages, applications for accommodations, &c., have rendered the offices no sinecures.

The other day, a poorly but decently-dressed Irish woman entered the office of the commissioners on Washington Street, and walked up to the head clerk.

"Well, my good woman, what do you want?"

"I want to see the dochthor."

"The doctor! what doctor?"

"How should I know his name, and me niver seeing him?"

"This is the water commissioner's office, my good woman."

"Ah! and sure I've hard of the wonderful cures you've made. If my poor Teddy had been alive at this moment, he wouldn't have been dead the day."

"O, you want the water brought into your house."

"Sure and I'd like that same."

"Well, where do you live?"

"Broad Strate—near Purchase Strate—it's a small cellar I have to myself. I used to take boarders; but it's poorly I am, and I can't work as I used to, dochthor."

"Well, haven't you got any water?"

"Divil a bit. I have to take my pail and go to Bread Strate for it."

"And the water doesn't come into your cellar?"

"Sure it comes into me cellar sometimes—but it's as salt as brine; it's the say water. I've tried to drink it, but it made me sick. O, I'm bad, dochthor, dear; if you think the water'll cure me, tell me where I can get it."

"You've got the pipes down your way?"

"I've got the pipes, dochthor, dear—but sorrow a bit of tibaccy. Do you think smoking is good for the rheumatiz?"

"There's some mistake here," said the clerk; "what's that you've got in your hand?"

"They tould me to bring this bit ov pasteboord here, sure."

The clerk took it. It was a dispensary ticket. He explained the mistake, and told the applicant where she should go to obtain medicine and advice.

"No, dochthor, dear—it's no mistake—it's the water cure I'm after. Sure it's the blissid wather that saves us. There was Pat Murphy that brak his leg when he fell with a hod of bricks aff the ladder in Say Strate, and they put a bit of wet rag round it, and the next wake he was dancing a jig to the chune of Paddy Rafferty, at the ball given by the Social Burial Society. And there was my sister Molly's old man, Phelim, that was took bad wid the fever—and he drank walth of whiskey, but it never did him a bit of good—but when he lift off the whiskey, and drank nothin' but wather, he came round in a wake. O, dochthor, let me have the blissid water."

"You must see your landlord about that."

"You wouldn't sind me to him, dochthor."

"I'm no doctor, good woman," said the clerk, now thoroughly annoyed, "and you've come to the wrong shop, as I told you."

"How do you use the water?" inquired the woman.

"Why, you turn the cock and let it on—in this way," said the clerk, letting a little Cochituate into a basin. "There, go along now, and go to the doctor's, as I have directed you."

"Sorrow a dochthor I go to but the water dochthor, this blissid day," said the woman, and she left the office.

She repaired to her cellar in no enviable frame of mind. She was sick and discouraged, and labored under the impression that she had been to the right place, but they had imposed upon her, from an unwillingness to aid her. In the mean while, however, during her absence, a service pipe had been admitted into her premises by the landlord, though she was not aware of the fact. She became acquainted with it soon enough, however. The next morning, about four o'clock, as she lay on the floor, bemoaning her hard fate and the neglect of the "dochthor," she heard a rushing noise. The water pipe had burst, and a stream, like a fountain, was now steadily falling into the cellar.

"Bless their hearts!" exclaimed the old woman, "they haven't forgotten the poor. The dochthor's sent the water at last—and I must lie still and take it."

The first shock of the invading flood was a severe one.

"Millia murther!" she exclaimed, "how could it is! Dochthor, dear, couldn't ye have let me had it a thrifle warmer?"

The water continued to pour in, and she was thoroughly soaked. Under the belief that the doctor must be somewhere about, superintending the operation, but keeping himself out of sight from motives of delicacy, she continued to address him.

"There! dochthor, dear. Blessings on ye! That'll do for this time. It's could I am! Stop it, dochthor! I've had enough! It's too good for the likes of me. I fale betther, dochthor; I won't throuble ye more, dochthor; many thanks to ye, dochthor! do ye hear? It's drowning I am!"

By this time she had risen, and was standing ankle deep in water. As the element was still rising, and the "dochthor" failed to make his appearance, the poor woman climbed upon a stool, which was soon insulated by the tide. From this she managed to escape in a large bread trough, and ferried herself over to a shelf, where she lay in comparative safety, watching the rising of the waters.

What would have been her fate, if she had remained alone, it is impossible to say. After some time the noise of waters alarmed the neighbors; they came to see what was the matter, and finally succeeded in rescuing the tenant of the cellar from the threatened deluge. She was comfortably cared for by a fellow-countrywoman, and a regular dispensary physician sent for. Wonderful to relate, the shock of the cold bath had accomplished one of those accidental cures, of which many are recorded in the history of rheumatic disorders; and in a few days, the sufferer was on her legs again. Furthermore, her sickness had proved the means of interesting several benevolent individuals in her fate, and by their assistance she was established in a little shop, where she is making an honest penny, and laying by something against a rainy day. This she all attributes to the "blissid wather," and, in her veneration for the element, has totally abjured whiskey, and signed the pledge, an act which gives assurance of her future fortune.

THE COSSACK.

CHAPTER I.

I'd give
The Ukraine back again to live
It o'er once more, and be a page,
The happy page, who was the lord
Of one soft heart and his own sword.

MAZEPPA.

Count Willnitz was striding to and fro in the old hall of his ancestral castle, in the heart of Lithuania. Through the high and narrow Gothic windows the light fell dimly into the cold apartment, just glancing on the massive pillars, and bringing into faint relief the dusty banners and old trophies of arms that hung along the walls, for the wintry day was near its close. The count was a dark-browed, stern-featured man. His cold, gray eyes were sunken in their orbits; and deep lines were drawn about his mouth, as if some secret grief were gnawing at his vitals. And, indeed, good cause existed for his sorrow; for, but a few days previously, he had lost his wife. They had buried the countess at midnight, as was the custom of the family, in the old, ancestral vault of the castle. Vassal and serf had waved their torches over the black throat of the grave, and the wail of women had gone up through the rocky arches. Still the count had been seen to shed no tear. An old warrior, schooled in the stern academy of military life, he had early learned to conquer his emotions; indeed, there were those who said that nature, in moulding his aristocratic form, had forgotten to provide it with a heart; and this legend found facile credence with the cowering serfs who owned his sway, and the ill-paid soldiers who followed his banner. The last male descendant of a long and noble line, he was ill able to maintain the splendor of his family name; for his dominions had been "curtailed of their fair proportion," and his finances were in a disordered state.

As, like Hardicanute in the old ballad,

"Stately strode he east the wa',
And stately strode he west,"

there entered a figure almost as grim and stern as himself. This was an old woman who now filled the office of housekeeper, having succeeded to full sway on the death of the countess, the young daughter of the count being unable or unwilling to assume any care in the household.

"Well, dame," said the count, pausing in his walk, and confronting the old woman, "how goes it with you, and how with Alvina? Still sorrowing over her mother's death?"

"The tears of a maiden are like the dews in the morning, count," replied the old woman. "The first sunbeam dries them up."

"And what ray of joy can penetrate the dismal hole?" asked the count.

"Do you remember the golden bracelet you gave your lady daughter on her wedding day?" inquired the old woman, fixing her keen, gray eye on her master's face as she spoke.

"Ay, well," replied the count; "golden gifts are not so easily obtained, of late, that I should forget their bestowal But what of the bawble?"

"I saw it in the hands of the page Alexis, when he thought himself unobserved."

"How!" cried the count, his cheek first reddening, and then becoming deadly pale with anger; "is the blood of the gitano asserting its claim? Has he begun to pilfer? The dog shall hang from the highest battlement of the castle!"

"May it not have been a free gift, sir count?" suggested the hideous hag.

"A free gift! What mean you? A love token? Ha! dare you insinuate? And yet her blood is——"

"Hush! walls have sometimes ears," said the old woman, looking cautiously around. "The gypsy child you picked up in the forest is now almost a man; your daughter is a woman. The page is beautiful; they have been thrown much together. Alvina is lonely, romantic——"

"Enough, enough!" said the count, stamping his foot. "I will watch him. If your suspicions be correct——" He paused, and added between his clinched teeth, "I shall know how to punish the daring of the dog. Away!"

The old woman hobbled away, rubbing her skinny hands together, and chuckling at the prospect of having her hatred of the young countess and the page, both of whom had excited her malevolence, speedily gratified.

Count Willnitz was on the eve of a journey to Paris with his daughter. They were to start in a day or two. This circumstance brought on the adventure we shall speedily relate.

Between Alexis, the beautiful page whom the late countess had found and fancied among a wandering Bohemian horde, and the high-born daughter of the feudal house, an attachment had sprung up, nurtured by the isolation in which they lived, and the romantic character and youth of the parties. About to be separated from his mistress for a long time, the page had implored her to grant him an interview, and the lovers met in an apartment joining the suite of rooms appropriated to the countess, and where they were little likely to be intruded upon. In the innocence of their hearts, they had not dreamed that their looks and movements had been watched, and they gave themselves up to the happiness of unrestrained converse. But at the moment when the joy of Alexis seemed purest and brightest, the gathering thunder cloud was overhanging him. At the moment when, sealing his pledge of eternal fidelity and memory in absence, he tremblingly printed a first and holy kiss upon the blushing cheek of Alvina, an iron hand was laid upon his shoulder, and, torn ruthlessly from the spot, he was dashed against the wall, while a terrible voice exclaimed,—

"Dog, you shall reckon with me for this!"

Alvina threw herself at her father's feet.

"Pardon—pardon for Alexis, father! I alone am to blame."

"Rise! rise!" thundered the count. "Art thou not sufficiently humiliated? Dare to breathe a word in his favor, and it shall go hard with thy minion. Punishment thou canst not avert; say but a word, and that punishment becomes death; for he is mine, soul and body, to have and to hold, to head or to hang—my vassal, my slave! What ho, there!"

As he stamped his foot, a throng of attendants poured into the room.

"Search me that fellow!" cried the count, pointing with his finger to Alexis.

A dozen officers' hands examined the person of Alexis, one of them, more eager than the rest, discovered a golden bracelet, and brought it to the count.

"Ha!" cried the count, as he gazed upon the trinket; "truly do I recognize this bawble. Speak, dog! when got'st thou this?"

Alvina was about to speak, and acknowledge that she had bestowed it; but before she could utter a syllable, the page exclaimed,—

"I confess all—I stole it."

"Enough!" cried the count. "Daughter, retire to your apartment."

"Father!" cried the wretched girl, wringing her hands.

"Silence, countess!" cried the count, with terrific emphasis. "Remember that I wield the power of life and *death!*"

Casting one look of mute agony at the undaunted page, the hapless lady retired from the room.

"Zabitzki," said the count, addressing the foremost of his attendants, "take me this thieving dog into the court yard, and lay fifty stripes upon his back.

- 163 -

Then bear him to the dungeon in the eastern turret that overlooks the moat; there keep him till you learn my further pleasure."

The page was brave as steel. His cheek did not blanch, nor did his heart quail, as he heard the dreadful sentence. His lips uttered no unmanly entreaty for forgiveness; but, folding his arms, and drawing up his elegant figure to its full height, he fixed his eagle eye upon the count, with a glance full of bitter hatred and mortal defiance. And afterwards, when submitting to the ignominious punishment, with his flesh lacerated by the scourge, no groan escaped his lips that might reach the listening ear of Alvina. He bore it all with Spartan firmness.

Midnight had struck when the young countess, shrouded in a cloak, and bearing a key which she had purchased by its weight in gold, ascended to the eastern turret, resolved to liberate the prisoner. The door swung heavily back on its rusted hinges as she cautiously entered the dungeon. Drawing back the slide from a lantern she carried in her left hand, she threw its blaze before her, calling out at the same time, "Alexis!"

No voice responded.

"They have murdered him!" she murmured, as she rushed forward and glanced wildly around her.

The cell was empty. She sprang to the grated window. The bars had been sawn through and wrenched apart, with the exception of one, from which dangled a rope made of fragments of linen and blanket twisted and knotted together. Had Alexis escaped, or perished in the attempt? The moat was deep and broad; but the page was a good swimmer and a good climber, and his heart was above all proof. There was little doubt in the mind of his mistress that fortune had favored him. Sinking on her knees, she gave utterance to a fervent thanksgiving to the almighty Power which had protected the hapless boy, and then retired to her couch to weep in secret. The next day the castle rang with the escape of Alexis. Messengers were sent out in pursuit of him in every direction; but a fall of snow in the latter part of the night prevented the possibility of tracking him, and even the dogs that the count put upon the scent were completely baffled. The next day the count and his daughter started on their journey.

CHAPTER II.

For time at last sets all things even;
And if we do but watch the hour,
There never yet was human power
Which could evade, if unforgiven,

The patient search and vigil long
Of him who treasures up a wrong.

BYRON.

Years had passed away. The storm of war had rolled over the country, and the white eagle of Poland had ceased to wave over an independent land. Count Willnitz and his daughter had returned to the old castle; the former stern and harsh as ever, the latter completely in the power of an inexorable master. She had received no tidings of Alexis, and had given him up as lost to her forever. Her father, straightened in his circumstances and menaced with ruin, had secured relief and safety by pledging his daughter's hand to a wealthy nobleman, Count Radetsky, who was now in the castle awaiting the fulfilment of the bargain.

"Go, my child," said the count, with more gentleness than he usually manifested in his manner. "You must prepare yourself for the altar."

"Father," said the young girl, earnestly, "does he know that I love him not?"

"I have told him all, Alvina."

"And yet he is willing to wed me!" She raised her eyes to heaven, rose, and slowly retired to her room.

Louisa, the old woman presented in the first scene of our tale, decked the unfortunate girl in her bridal robes, and went with her to the chapel, where her father and Radetsky awaited her. An old priest mumbled over the ceremony, and joined the hands of the bride and bridegroom. The witnesses were few—only the vassals of the count; and no attempt at festivity preceded or followed the dismal ceremony.

Alvina retired to her chamber when it was over, promising to join her bridegroom at the table in a few moments. The housekeeper accompanied her.

"I give you joy, Countess Radetsky," said the old woman.

"I sorely need it," was the bitter answer. "I have sacrificed myself to the duty I owe my sole surviving parent."

The old woman rubbed her hands and chuckled as she noted the tone of anguish in which these words were uttered.

"I can now speak out," she said. "After long years of silence, the seal is removed from my lips. I can now repay your childish scorn, and bitter jests, by a bitterer jest than any you have yet dreamed of. Countess Radetsky——"

"Spare me that name," said the countess.

"Nay, sweet, it is one you will bear through life," said the hag, "and you had better accustom yourself early to its sound. Know, then, my sweet lady, that the count, my master, had no claims on your obedience."

"How?"

"He is a childless man. He found you an abandoned orphan. Struck with your beauty, he brought you to his lady, and, though they loved you not, they adopted you, with a view to making your charms useful to them when you should have grown up. The count has amply paid himself to-day for all the expense and trouble you have put him to. He has sold you to an eager suitor for a good round price. Ha, ha!"

"And you knew this, and never told me!" cried the hapless girl.

"I was bound by an oath not to reveal the secret till you were married. And I did not love you enough to perjure myself."

"Wretch—miserable wretch!" cried Alvina. "Alas! to what a fate have I been doomed! Ah! why did they not let me rather perish than rear me to this doom? My heart is given to Alexis—my hand to Radetsky!"

"Go down, sweet, to your bridegroom," said the old woman, who was totally deaf to her complaints, "or he will seek you here."

Alvina descended to the banquet hall, uncertain what course to pursue. Escape appeared impossible, and what little she knew of Radetsky convinced her that he was as pitiless and base as her reputed father. She sank into a seat, pale, inanimate, and despairing.

At that moment, ere any one present could say a word, a man, white with terror, rushed into the hall, and stammered out,—

"My lord count!"

"What is it, fellow? Speak!"

"The Cossacks!" cried the man. And his information was confirmed by a loud hurrah, or rather yell, that rose without.

"Raise the drawbridge!" cried the count. "Curses on it!" he added, "I had forgotten that drawbridge and portcullis, every means of defence, were gone long ago."

"The Cossacks are in the court yard!" cried a second servant, rushing in.

"A thousand curses on the dogs!" cried Radetsky, drawing his sword. "Count, look to your child; I will to the court yard with your fellows, to do what we may."

By this time the court yard of the castle was filled with uproar and turmoil. The clashing of swords was mingled with pistol shots and groans, the shouts of triumph and the shrieks of despair. Alvina, left alone by her father and Radetsky, trembled not at the prospect of approaching death; she felt only joy at her deliverance from the arms of a hated bridegroom. But when the crackling of flames was heard, when a lurid light streamed up against the window, when wreaths of smoke began to pour in from the corridors, the instinct of self-preservation awakened in her breast, and almost unconsciously she shrieked aloud for help.

Her appeal was answered unexpectedly. A tall, plumed figure dashed into the room; a vigorous arm was thrown around her waist, and she was lifted from her feet. Her unknown preserver, unimpeded by her light weight, passed into the corridor with a fleet step. The grand staircase was already on fire, but, drawing his furred cloak closely around her, the stranger dashed through the flames, and bore her out into the court yard. Almost before she knew it, she was sitting behind him on a fiery steed. The rider gave the animal the spur, and he dashed through the gate, followed by a hundred wild Cossacks, shouting and yelling in the frenzy of their triumph.

Gratitude for an escape from a dreadful death was now banished from Alvina's mind by the fear of a worse fate at the hands of these wild men.

"You have saved my life," she said to her unknown companion; "do not make that life a curse. Take pity on an unfortunate and sorely persecuted girl. I have no ransom to pay you; but free me, and you will earn my daily prayers and blessings."

"Fear nothing," answered a deep and manly voice. "No harm is intended thee; no harm shall befall thee. I swear it on the word of a Cossack chieftain."

Alvina was tranquillized at once by the evident sincerity of the assurance.

"You are alone now in the world," pursued the stranger "I strove to save your bridegroom, but he fell before I reached him."

"I loved him not," answered Alvina, coldly; "I mourn him not."

"You may hate me for the deed," said the stranger, "and I would fain escape that woe; but here I vouch it in the face of heaven, Count Willnitz fell by my hand. My sabre clove him to the teeth. Years had passed, but I could not forget that he once laid the bloody scourge upon my back."

"Alexis!" cried Alvina, now recognizing her preserver.

"Yes, dear but unfortunate girl," cried the Cossack leader, turning and gazing on the young girl, "I feel that thou art lost to me forever. I have slain thy father. Love for thee should have stayed my hand; but I had sworn an oath of vengeance, and I kept my vow."

"Alexis," whispered Alvina, "he was not my father. He was my bitterest enemy. Nor am I nobly born. Like you, I am an orphan."

"Say you so?" shouted the Cossack. "Then thou art mine—mine and forever—joy of my youth—blessing of my manhood!"

"Yes, thine—thine only."

"But bethink thee, sweetest," said the Cossack; "I lead a strange wild life."

"I will share it with thee," said Alvina, firmly.

"My companions are rude men."

"I shall see only thee."

"My home is the saddle, my palace the wide steppe."

"With thee, Alexis, I could be happy any where."

"Then be it so," said the Cossack, joyously. "What ho!" he shouted, at the top of his ringing, trumpet-like voice. "Comrades, behold your hetman's bride!"

From mouth to mouth the words of the Cossack chieftain were repeated, and oft as they were uttered wild shouts of joy rose from the bearded warriors; for they had loved the gallant Alexis from the moment when, a wayworn, famished, and bleeding fugitive, he came among them. They galloped round and round the hetman and his fair companion in dizzying circles, like the whirling leaves of autumn, firing their pistols, brandishing their lances and sabres, and making the welkin ring with their terrific shouts. Alvina clung, terrified, to the waist of her lover, and he finally silenced the noisy demonstrations by a wave of his hand. Then, under his leadership, and in more regular order, the formidable band of horsemen pursued their march to those distant solitudes where happiness awaited their chieftain and his bride.

MARRIED FOR MONEY.

"Jack Cleveland!" exclaimed a fast young man in a drab driving coat with innumerable capes, (it was twenty years ago, reader, in the palmy days of Tom and Jerry and tandem teams,) as he encountered an equally fast young man in Cornhill; "what's the matter with you?"

"It's all over, Frank; I've gone and done it."

"Gone and done what, you spooney?"

"Proposed."

"Proposed what?—a match at billiards, a trot on the milldam, or a main of cocks?"

"Pooh!—something more serious," said Cleveland, gravely; "I've offered myself."

"Offered yourself? To whom?"

"Widow—Waffles—shy name—never mind—soon changed—one hundred and fifty thousand—cool, eh?—age forty—good looks—married for money—sheriff would have it—no friends—pockets to let—pays my debts—sets me up—house in Beacon Street—carriage—can't help it."

"You're a candidate for Bedlam," said Frank; "I've a great mind to order you a strait jacket."

"Be my bridesman—see me off—eh?" asked Cleveland.

"Yes, yes, of course—it will be great fun."

And so it was. Jack Cleveland was united to the widow Waffles in Trinity Church, and a smashing wedding it was. The party that followed it was, to use Cleveland's own expressions, "a crusher—all Boston invited—all Africa waiting—wax lights—champagne—music—ices—pretty girls—a bang-up execution."

During the honeymoon Jack Cleveland was all attention to his bride, (*il faut soigner les anciennes,*) but he promised to indemnify himself by taking full and complete liberty so soon as that interesting period of time had been brought to a close. Besides, his chains sat lightly at first; for the widow was one of those splendid Lady Blessington kind of women, who at forty have just arrived at the imperial maturity of their charms, and she was deeply enamoured of the young gentleman whom she had chosen for her second partner in the matrimonial speculation. Moreover, she paid the debts of the fast young man with an exemplary cheerfulness. The only drawback to this gush of felicity was that her property was "tied up;" not a cent could

Cleveland handle except by permission of his lady. Then she kept him as close to her apron strings as she did her Blenheim spaniel; she required him to obey her call as promptly as her coachman. Galling to his pride though it was, he was even forced to go a shopping with her; and the elegant Cleveland, who once thought it degrading to carry an umbrella, might be seen loaded with bandboxes, or nonchalantly lilting bundles of cashmere shawls. The only difference between Mrs. Cleveland's husband and her footman was that he received wages; but then the footman could leave when he chose, and there the parallel ended. Jack's habits had to submit to a rigid and inexorable censorship. "Those odious cigars" were prohibited, and then "his list of friends" was challenged. Frank Aikin, the bridesman, was tolerated the longest of all, and then he was "bluffed off" by Mrs. Cleveland, who determined to make her husband a domestic man. It was the old story of Hercules and Omphale modernized to suit the times.

Jack began to think the happiest day of his life had made him the most miserable dog alive, and, like Sir Peter Teazle, "had lost all comfort in the world before his friends had done wishing him joy." But his debts were paid—that was a great consolation. Several streets in Boston, which were blocked up by creditors, as those of London were to the respected Mr. Richard Swiveller, were now opened by the magic wand of matrimony. He could exhibit his "Hyperion curls" in Washington Street, without any fear of a gentle "reminder" in the shape of a tap upon the shoulder.

One morning, however, a lady was ushered up into the splendid drawing room in Beacon Street, being announced as Madame St. Germain. She was a showy French woman, about the same age as Mrs. Cleveland, and the latter waited with some curiosity to learn the object of her visit.

"You are Mrs. Cleveland, I believe," said the French woman.

Mrs. Cleveland bowed in her stateliest manner.

"You have undertaken, I learn, to pay the debts of Monsieur Cleveland, contracted before your marriage."

Mrs. Cleveland bowed again.

"I hold a note of his drawn in my favor for a thousand dollars, payable at sight, with interest, dated two years back."

"What was it given for?" asked Mrs. Cleveland, with some asperity.

"Pardon me, madam—I cannot state that without the permission of your husband."

Mrs. Cleveland applied her hand vigorously to a bell-pull communicating with her husband's dressing room.

He made his presence in a splendid *robe de chambre* and a Turkish cap with a gold tassel.

"This woman," said his better half, "says you owe her a thousand dollars."

"Monsieur cannot deny it," said the French woman, fixing her keen black eyes on the thunder-struck Cleveland.

"It's all right—pay her up!" said Mr. Cleveland.

"Not till I know what the debt was incurred for."

"I can't tell you," said Mr. Cleveland.

"I insist," said Mrs. Cleveland, stamping her foot.

"Then I won't tell—if you die!" said the rebellious Cleveland.

"I shall trouble you, ma'am, to leave my house," said the irritated mistress of the mansion. "Not one farthing on that note do you get out of me."

"Then I shall be under the unpleasant necessity of taking legal measures to obtain the debt," said the French woman, rising. "Mr. Cleveland, I wish you very much happiness with your amiable lady."

There was a storm—a regular equinoctial gale—after the departure of Madame St. Germain. Mrs. Cleveland was very provoking, and Mr. Cleveland indulged in epithets unbecoming a scholar and a gentleman. That night the "happy couple" luxuriated in separate apartments. The next day came a lawyer's letter, then a civil process, and finally Mr. John Cleveland was marched off to Leverett Street jail, where, after giving due notice to his creditor and obtaining bail, he was allowed the benefit of the "limits," with the privilege of "swearing out," at the expiration of thirty days.

Jack engaged lodging at a little tavern, on the limits, where he found Frank Aikin, who had run through *his* "pile," and a few kindred spirits of the fast young men school enacting the part of "gentlemen in difficulties." Cigars, champagne, and cards were ordered, and Jack became a fast young man once more. Towards the small hours of the morning, he forgot having married a widow, and thinking himself a bachelor, he proposed the health of a certain Miss Julia Vining, which was drank with three times three. The next morning, he sat down to a capital breakfast, with more fast young men, and for a whole week he enjoyed himself *en garçon*, without once thinking of the forsaken Dido in Beacon Street.

One day, however, when he had exhausted his cash and credit, and a racking headache induced him to regret the speed of his late life, a carriage rattled up to the door of the tavern, his own door was shortly after thrown open, and a lady flung herself into his arms. Mrs. Cleveland looked really fascinating.

"Come home, my dear Jack," said she, bursting into tears; "I've been so lonely without you."

"Not so fast, Mrs. Cleveland," said the young gentleman, as he perceived his power. "I'm very happy where I am. I can't go back except on certain conditions."

"Name them, dearest."

"I'm to smoke as many cigars as I please."

"Granted."

"Not to carry any more bandboxes or tomcats."

"Granted."

"To give a dinner party to the 'boys' once in a while."

"Granted—granted. And I've paid your note, and opened a cash account for you at the bank."

"You are an angel," said Cleveland; "and now it's all over—that note was given Madame St. Germain for tuition of a young girl, Miss Julia Vining, whom I educated with the romantic notion of making her my wife, when she should arrive at a suitable age, at which period she ran off with a one-eyed French fiddler, and is now taking in sewing at 191st Street, New York."

The happy pair went home in their carriage, and we never heard of any differences between them. Mrs. Cleveland wears very well, and Mr. Cleveland is now an alderman, remarkable chiefly for the ponderosity of his person, and the heaviness of his municipal harangues. "Sich is life."

THE EMIGRANT SHIP.

On a summer's day, some years ago, business brought me to one of the wharves of this city, at the moment when a ship from Liverpool had just arrived, with some two hundred and fifty emigrants, men, women, and children, chiefly Irish. Much as I had heard and read of the condition of many of the poor passengers, I never fully realized their distresses until I personally witnessed them.

Under the most favorable circumstances, the removal of families from the land of their birth is attended by many painful incidents. About to embark upon a long and perilous voyage, to seek the untried hospitalities of a stranger soil, the old landmarks and associations which the heartstrings grasp with a cruel tenacity are viewed through the mist of tears and agony.

The old church—the weather-worn homestead—the ancient school house, the familiar play ground, and more sadly dear than all, the green graveyard, offer a mute appeal "more eloquent than words." But when to these afflictions of the heart are added the pangs of physical suffering and privation; when emigrants, in embarking, embark their all in the expenses of the voyage, and have no hope, even for existence, but in a happy combination of possible chances; when near and dear ones must be left behind, certainly to suffer, and probably to die,—the pangs of separation embrace all that can be conceived of agony and distress.

The emigrant ship whose arrival we witnessed had been seventy odd days from port to port. Her passengers were of the poorest class. Their means had been nearly exhausted in going from Dublin to Liverpool, and in endeavors to obtain work in the latter city, previous to bidding a reluctant but eternal farewell to the old country. They came on board worn out— wan—the very life of many dependent on a speedy passage over the Atlantic. In this they were disappointed. The ship had encountered a succession of terrific gales; it had leaked badly, and they had been confined, a great part of the voyage, to their narrow quarters between decks, herded together in a noisome and pestilential atmosphere, littered with damp straw, and full of filth.

What marvel that disease and death invaded their ranks? One after another, many died and were launched into the deep sea. The ship entered Fayal to refit, and there that clime of endless summer proved to the emigrants more fatal than the blast of the upas-poisoned valley of Java. The delicious oranges, and the mild Pico wine, used liberally by the passengers, sowed the seeds of death yet more freely among their ranks. On the passage from Fayal, the mortality was dreadful, but at length, decimated and diseased, the band of emigrants arrived at Boston.

It was a summer's day—but no cheering ray of light fell upon the spires of the city. The sky was dark and gloomy; the bay spread out before the eye like a huge sheet of lead, and the clouds swept low and heavily over the hills and house tops.

After the vessel was moored, all the passengers who were capable of moving, or of being moved, came up or were brought up on deck. We scanned their wan and haggard features with curiosity and pity.

Here was the wreck of an athletic man. His eyes, deep-sunken in their orbits, were nearly as glassy as those of a corpse; his poor attire hung loosely on his square shoulders. His matted beard rendered his sickly, greenish countenance yet more wan and livid. He crawled about the deck *alone*—his wife and five children, they for whom he had lived and struggled, for whose sake he was making a last desperate exertion, had all been taken from him on the voyage. We addressed him some questions touching his family.

"They are all gone," said he, "the wife and the childer. The last one—the babby—died this mornin'—she lies below. They're best off where they are."

In another place sat a shivering, ragged man, the picture of despair. A few of his countrymen, who had gathered round him, offered him some food. He might have taken it eagerly some days before. *Now* he gazed on vacancy, without noticing their efforts to induce him to take some nourishment. Still they persevered, and one held a cooling glass of lemonade to his parched lips.

Seated on the after hatchway was a little boy who had that morning lost both his parents. He shed no tear. Familiarity with misery had deprived him of that sad consolation.

We passed on to a group of Irishmen gathered round an old gray-haired man lying at length upon the forward deck. One of them was kneeling beside him.

"Father, father!" said he, earnestly, "rouse up, for the love of Heaven. See here—I've brought ye some porridge—tak a sup ov it—it will give ye heart and life."

"Sorrow a bit of life's left in the old man any how. Lave him alone, Jamie."

"Lift him ashore," said the mate—"he wants air."

The dying man was carefully lifted on the wharf, and laid down upon a plank. His features changed rapidly during the transit. His head now fell back—the pallid hue of death invaded his lips—his lower jaw relaxed—the staring eyeballs had no speculation in them—a slight shudder convulsed his frame. The son kneeled beside him; closed his eyes—it was all over. And there, in the open air, with no covering to shield his reverend locks from the falling rain, passed away the soul of the old man from its earthly tabernacle.

The hospital cart arrived. Busy agents lifted into it, with professional *sang froid*, crippled age and tottering childhood. But all the spectators of this harrowing scene testified, by their expressions, sympathy and sorrow, one low-browed ruffian alone excepted.

"Serves 'em right d—— n—— 'em!" said he, savagely. "Why don't they stay at home in their own country, and not come here to take the bread out of honest people's mouths?"

Honest, quotha? If ever "flat burglary" and "treason dire" were written on a man's face, it stood out in staring capitals upon that Cain-like brow.

But there were lights as well as shadows to the picture. Out of that grim den of death, out of that floating lazar house, there came a few blooming maidens and stalwart youths, like fair flowers springing from the rankness of a charnel. Their sorrows were but for the misfortunes of others; and even these were a while forgotten in the joy of meeting near and dear relatives, and old friends upon the shore of the promised land. They went their way rejoicing, and with them passed the solitary ray of sunshine that streamed athwart the dark horrors of the emigrant ship, like the wandering pencil of light that sometimes visits the condemned cell of a prison.

———

THE LAST OF THE STAGE COACHES.

A FRAGMENT OF A CLUB-ROOM CONVERSATION.

"Did you ever," said the one-eyed gentleman, fixing his single sound optic upon us with an intensity which made it glow like one of the coals in the grate before us, "did you ever hear how I met with this misfortune?"

"What misfortune, sir?"

"The misfortune which made a Cyclops of me—the loss of my left eye."

"Never, sir. Pray how was it?"

"Put out by the cinder of a locomotive," growled the one-eyed gentleman, seizing the poker and stirring up the fire viciously. "Bad things these railroads, sir," he added, when he had demolished a huge fragment of sea coal. "Only last week—little boy playing on bank in his father's garden—little dog ran on the track—boy went down to call him off—express train came along—forty-five miles an hour and no stoppages—ran over boy and dog—agonized parents sought for the remains—nothing found except one shoe, the buckle of his hatband, and brass collar of the dog."

"Extraordinary!"

"No, sir; not extraordinary," said the one-eyed gentleman. "I maintain it's a common occurrence. Sir, I keep a railroad journal at home, as large as a family Bible. It is filled with brief accounts—*brief*, mind you—of railroad accidents. Next year I shall have to buy another book."

"Then you are a decided enemy of railroads?"

"Decided!" said the one-eyed gentleman. "Their prevalence and extent is a proof that the age is lapsing into barbarism. Ah! you remember the stage coaches?"

"Certainly."

"Well, sir," said the one-eyed gentleman, warmly, "travelling was travelling in those days; sir, it was a pleasure. The coaches were fast enough for any reasonable man; ten miles an hour, including stoppages. Ah!" he added, smacking his lips, "what a fine thing it was to start on a journey of a glorious October morning, when every thing looked bright and smiling! You mounted to the box or the roof, well wrapped up in your greatcoat and shawl, with your trunk safely strapped upon the rack behind. The driver was a man of substance—solid, of a gravity tempered with humor, a giant in a brown box-coat, with gray hat and mittens. How he handled the ribbons and took his cattle through Elm Street! How the long bridges rumbled and thundered as we bowled along away, away into the country! The country! it *was* the country then; inhabited by country people, not peopled with a mixed society of farmers and cits, six o' one and half a dozen of t'other. How nicely we glided along! There were birds, in those days, singing by the roadside; now the confounded locomotives have scared them all off. By and by we came to a tavern. Out rushed a troop of hostlers and keepers skilled in horse flesh. The cattle were just allowed to wet their lips, water was dashed on their legs and feet, and then, after the parcels and papers had been tossed off, away we went again. Five miles farther on, we pulled up to change. The fresh team was led out, bright, shining, and glittering, in tip-top condition. The driver descended to stretch his legs and personally superintend the putting to of the fresh horses. When he mounted the box again, his experienced eye glanced rapidly at the team, and then, with an 'all right—let 'em go!' we were on the road once more."

The one-eyed gentleman paused, after this flow of eloquence, and gazed pensively into the midst of the glowing coals. After a few moments' silence, he resumed:—

"Rather a singular occurrence happened to me last year on the 14th of October, about half past twelve, P.M. I am thus particular about dates, because this event is one that forms an era in my life. I had been driving across the country in my gig, to visit a friend who had recently moved upon a farm. The localities were new to me, and the roads blind. Guideboards were few, and human beings fewer. In short, I got astray, and hadn't the remotest conception of what part of the country I was in. It was a cold, cloudy day, with a sort of drizzling Scotch mist that wet one to the bone. I plodded along in hopes of soon reaching some tavern, where I could bait my horse and get some dinner for myself. All at once, at a turn of the road, just after having crossed the Concord River, I perceived a stage coach coming towards me. I had heard no noise of wheels or horses' feet; but there it was. The road was narrow, and the coachman pulled up to let me work my way past. The vehicle was a queer old affair, that looked as if it had been dug out of some antediluvian stable yard. The curtains were brown with age and dust, and riddled with holes; the body was bare and worm-eaten, and the springs perfectly green with mould. The horses were thin and lank, and the harness in as sorry a condition as the coach. The driver's clothes, which were very old fashioned, hung about him in loose folds, and he gazed upon me with a strange, stony stare that was absolutely appalling; yet his lips unclosed as I worked past him, and he exclaimed in a harsh, croaking voice, 'One eye!' Thereupon two or three queer people poked their heads out of the coach window. There was one old woman with false teeth, in an unpleasant state of decay, and a voice like a parrot. 'One eye!' she shrieked, as she gazed on me with an eye as stony as the coachman. A pale, simpering miss smirked in my face, and cried, 'One eye!' and a military gentleman, with a ghastly frown, hissed forth the same words. I should have scrutinized the queer coach and the queer people closer, had not my horse—my good, old, quiet, steady horse—seized the bit in his mouth and started off at a dead run. I tried to saw him up, but it was no use; he ran for a couple of miles, and did not slacken till he had brought me to the door of an old, decayed tavern, where I resigned him to the charge of a lame hostler, and made my way into the house in search of the landlord. I found him at last—a poor, poverty-pinched man, who had been ruined by the railroad. He complained bitterly of the hard times. 'But,' said I, 'you must have some custom; the stage coaches——' 'Bless your soul,' replied he, 'there hasn't been a coach on this road for fifteen years.' 'What do you, mean?' said I; 'I met a coach and passengers two miles back, near the river.' The landlord turned pale. 'What day is this?' he asked. 'The 14th of October.' 'The 14th of October!' cried the landlord; 'I remember that date well. That day, fifteen years since, was the last trip of the old mail coach. It left here, with Bill Snaffle, the driver, and three insides, a military man, an old woman, and a young lady. They were never heard of after they left here. Their trail was followed as far as the bridge. It is supposed that the horses got frightened at something, and backed off into the Concord River. But I have heard,' added the landlord, in a hollow whisper, 'that on this anniversary the ghost of that coach and company may be seen upon the turnpike. More, I will tell you, in confidence, that I have seen them myself.' After this I was convinced that I had been favored—if favor it may be called—with a spiritual visitation."

The one-eyed gentleman looked me full in the face, as if to say, "What do you think of it?" It was useless to argue with him; so I only shook my head. He nodded his in a very mysterious manner, and fell to poking the fire with redoubled activity; and I bade him good night, and left him to pursue his occupation.

THE SEXTON OF ST. HUBERT'S.

A STORY OF OLD ENGLAND.

CHAPTER I.

THE QUEEN OF THE MAY.

In a remote region in the northern part of England, the people still cherish an attachment to old usages and sports, and hold the observance of Christmas, May-day, and other time-honored festivals, a sacred obligation. One village, in particular, is famous for its May-day sports, which, as the curate is a little withered antiquary, are conducted with great ceremony and fidelity to old authorities. The May-pole is brought home, garlanded, and decked with ribbons, to the sound of pipe and tabor, surrounded by a laughing throng of sturdy yeomen and buxom maidens. It is erected on the great green, in the centre of the village, to the universal delight of old and young, and the dancing commences round it with high glee. The scene presented is like that described by Goldsmith,—

"Where all the village train, from labor free,
Led up their sports beneath the spreading tree;
While many a pastime circled in the shade,
The young contending as the old surveyed;
And many a gambol frolicked o'er the ground,
And sleights of art and feats of strength went round."

It was a delightful spring, that of 17—, and a softer sky never before smiled upon the village-green of Redwood, upon the 1st of May; and among the merry damsels dancing round the May-pole, no heart was happier, and no step was lighter, than that of Margaret Ellis, who, for the first time, joined in the sports of the day. She was a child of May, and this was the sixteenth anniversary of her birthday. A gay brunette, her sparkling eyes had all the fire and the mirth of the sunny and passionate south, while no lighter or more delicate foot than hers could have been found upon the merry green. A rich bloom mantled on her cheek, her lips were fresh and red, and her regular teeth, displayed as she panted in the dance, were white as unsullied snow. A tight little bodice, and a milk-white frock, set off the charms of her person in the best manner. Then there was an air of gayety and innocence about her which delighted every good-natured observer; and all the villagers allowed that Margaret Ellis deserved the tiara of flowers that crowned her Queen of the May. She blushed at the tokens of good will and approbation, as she placed her hand in that of a young and rustic stranger, who led her off triumphantly at the head of the dancers. The youth was fair-haired, ruddy, athletic, and active; and those who saw them in the dance could not help acknowledging that they were a lovely pair.

There was one who regarded them with eyes of jealous displeasure. This was a man of forty, of a handsome face and figure, but swarthy, dark-haired, and melancholy. He bent over the seat upon which old Farmer Ellis and his dame were seated, and whispered, "Do you know the young man who is dancing with your daughter?"

"Ah! he be a right good young mon, I warrant me," said the dame. "He do come fra the next county. William Evans, he calls himself."

"He calls himself!—umph!" muttered the person who had first spoken. "But what do others call him? Who knows any thing about him? Who can vouch for his character? I would not suffer a daughter of mine to be gadding about, and dancing with a stranger."

"Whoy, for the matter o' that," said Farmer Ellis, "you were nought but a stranger yourself, when you first did come to see us, Maister Pembroke. We didn't know you were the sexton of St. Hubert's. And yet you turned out a right good friend to me, mon; for when ye first knew me, things were deadly cross wi' me. What wi' the rot among my sheep, and the murrain among my cattle, I were all but ruined. Short crops and a hard landlord are bitter bad things. But you were the salvation of me, and I'll work my fingers to the bone, but what you shall have your own again, John Pembroke."

"There is one way in which you can liquidate your debt."

"Name it, Maister Pembroke," said the farmer, eagerly.

"No matter," muttered the sexton, and a hollow sigh escaped his lips. "I had an idea, but it is gone. Touching the stranger, in whom you both repose such confidence. In what manner does he earn his daily bread?"

"Whoy," said the farmer, "in the way that Adam did, mon. He do say he is a gardener."

"A likely tale!" ejaculated the sexton. "Look at his hands. Why, his fingers are delicate and white. Your gardener has horny fingers, and a palm of iron."

"Dang it! so they be!" cried Ellis. "Well, I never noticed that afore. Whoy, dame, he may be an impostor And though he be so cruel koind, and deadly fond of the girl, now, he may forsake—may——"

"Look at, them, now," said the sexton of St. Hubert's. "See how he grasps her hand; and how, as he whispers his soft, insinuating flattery in her ear, she blushes and smiles upon him. Damnation!"

"Whoy, John!" exclaimed Dame Ellis; "what would the rector say to hear thee? Thou art surely distraught."

And now, as Margaret, flushed and panting with exercise, was suffering her partner to lead her towards her seat, her father beckoned her to approach.

"Come hither, girl," said he. The smiling maiden obeyed. "Margaret," said the old man, "thou knowest I love thee. I ha' always been cruel koind to thee, and so has thy mother, girl. If any harm was to happen to thee, I should take it desperately to heart. I should, indeed. It would kill thy father, Margaret. Now, William Evans may be a good young man, and he may not; but we must beware of strangers. Wait till we have tried him a bit. Many a handsome nag turns out a vicious one. So it be my pleasure, and the dame's, that thou dost not dance any more to-day wi' William Evans; and even if he speaks to thee, be a little offish loike to him."

The poor girl sighed. "I hope, sir," said she, glancing at the sexton, "that no person possessed of an unhappy and suspicious temper has been prejudicing you against poor William. I hope Mr. Pembroke——"

"Hush, girl—hush!" cried Ellis. "Doant thee say a word against that man. But for him we mought all ha' been beggars. Do as I bid thee, girl, and doan't thee ask no questions; for you know I've got no head to argury."

Margaret slowly sank into a seat. The sexton leaned over her, and addressed to her some commonplace remarks, to all of which she returned answer in monosyllables. When the music recommenced a lively air, William advanced, and solicited her hand for the next dance. Poor Margaret bent her eyes upon the ground, and falteringly refused. Thinking he could not have heard her rightly, Evans again asked the question, and received, a second time, the same answer. For a moment his countenance expressed astonishment; the next there was a look of grief, and then his lip curled, and drawing himself up proudly, he stalked away. He was followed by the sexton of St. Hubert's, who overtook him, and laid his hand upon his shoulder. William turned fiercely, and endeavored to shake off the grasp.

"Young man," said the sexton, "you are discovered!"

"Discovered!" exclaimed William. "What do you mean?"

"You understand me," said the sexton; "your manners, your language, your figure, contradict the story you have fabricated. Margaret shall never be your victim. With her your boasted arts are valueless!"

"If you were a gentleman——" said William.

"Ha, ha!" laughed the sexton of St. Hubert's. "Is this the resentment of a rustic? Go, young man; you have exposed yourself."

"Remove your hand!" said the young man; "and think it unusual forbearance on my part, that I do not chastise you as you deserve. We shall meet again, and with a sterner greeting." So they parted.

CHAPTER II.

THE GYPSY CAMP.

The clear, unshadowed sun, as it declined towards the western verge of the horizon, shone brightly upon the gypsy encampment, a few miles from Redwood. The wandering tribe had displayed their proverbial taste, in their selection of a spot wherein to pitch their tents. A green and glossy pasture was partly surrounded by a luxuriant forest of ancient oaks, which supplied the crew with firewood; while a beautiful and clear stream, the pride and boast of the county, curved into the waving grass land, and kept it ever fresh and verdant. Here and there its silvery bosom reflected a small tent, or the figure of an idler, bending over the bank, with fishing rod in hand, a perfect picture of patience and philosophy. Half a dozen tents served to accommodate the gregarious fraternity; and though the sail cloths which composed them were worn and weather-beaten, yet their brown hues harmonized well with the rich tints of the landscape, and showed distinct enough against the dark background of the forest. As the shades of the evening darkened the ancestral trees, a line of fire was lit up, the flames of which glared ruddily against the huge trunks of the woodland, and played and flickered in the rippling stream. Huge kettles, suspended on forked sticks, were beginning to send up a savory steam; and several swarthy beings, lounging round the fires, occasionally fed them, or basking in the blaze, watched the bubbling of the caldrons with intense anxiety. Even the king of the gypsies observed the preparations for supper with an eager air, which ill assorted with his lofty forehead and reverend white beard. Every moment some stroller would come in with a pilfered fowl, or a basket of eggs; and each addition to the feast was hailed with shouts of applause by the swarthy crew.

Somewhat remote from this scene of bustle and noise, at the door of a small tent, sat two female gypsies. One of these was the queen, an aged crone, who, though bent with age and care, and wrinkled by time and the indulgence of vehement passions, yet prided herself upon the unfrosted darkness of her raven tresses, which fell over her shoulders in profusion. A turban of rich crimson cloth crowned her head, and a shawl of the same color and material was wrapped around her shoulders. Her skinny hands were supported by a silver-headed staff, which was covered with quaint carvings. Her gown was of dark serge, and her shoes were pointed, and turned up in the Oriental fashion, and garnished with broad silver buckles. She sat apart, and the rising moon shone down upon her dusky figure, and threw her wild features into bold relief. At her feet sat a beautiful girl, with dark Grecian features, and a full, voluptuous form. She, too, had long, flowing, raven tresses, into which were twisted strings of pearl. From a necklace of topaz hung a little silver crucifix, resting upon a full and heaving bust, to which was fitted a close jacket, made of deep-blue cloth, and fastened together with loops and silver buttons. Her soft and round arms were naked, save at the shoulders, and her wrists were encircled with tarnished gold bracelets. Her white petticoat was short enough to display a well-turned ankle, and a small foot, encased in neat black slippers. Her features, dark and sun-browned, showed to more advantage in the pale moonlight than they would have done in the broad blaze of day. The gypsy girl sat at the feet of the queen, and looking up in her face, listened attentively to her discourse.

"Myra," said the queen of the gypsies, "do you love him yet?"

"Love him!" repeated the girl. "Yes, mother—passionately. To obtain his hand—his heart, I would peril every thing!"

"Strange and mysterious passion!" said the crone, "which defies reason and law. Many years agone I loved with the same intense devotion. The same fiery blood courses in your veins; the same contempt of obstacles. Yet the man I loved was nobler and prouder than the sexton of St. Hubert's. We lived among the Gitanos of Spain, when we were wedded. Five sons I bore to the partner of my cares. Where are they? One followed his father to the gibbet; a second hurled defiance at his enemies, as he perished in the flames of an *auto da fe*; the third and fourth died in the galleys; the fifth—the fifth, Myra—my best beloved, my brave, my beautiful, received his death wound in defending me from outrage. *You are his child!* Judge, then, how I love you, my daughter. You love the sexton of St. Hubert's—he shall marry you."

"Ah, mother!" said the gypsy girl, "I fear me he is lost. He is the accepted lover of Margaret Ellis. She did love a young stranger; but the sexton of St. Hubert's has Farmer Ellis in his debt, and threatened to throw him in jail, if the latter did not grant him the hand of his daughter. He has done so, and the wedding day is fixed. Alas! before he saw his May-day queen, he loved me, and promised to marry me. Often beneath that very moon, mother, has he sat and told me his love. When I smiled at his protestations, he would speak of his wealth, and tell me of hidden stores of gold, for a thrifty and a rich man is the sexton of St. Hubert's. I do not love him less because he does not frown upon our wandering tribe, but has lax principles that suit the fiery passions of our race. I know not in what consists the art by which he won me; it is enough for me to know that I am devoted to him. Alas! that knowledge is too much, since he has owned the fascination of the Queen of the May."

"Enough said, daughter!" cried the crone. "Before the altar he shall marry you. He shall love you better than he loves the May queen. What are her attractions when compared to yours? Praise from the old is little to the young; yet let me say that I have wandered east and west, north and south; have seen the Georgian and Sicilian maids, have seen the dark-haired girls of Naples, and the donnas of Madrid; yet never did these aged eyes rest on a finer form or face than yours, my daughter."

The gypsy girl smiled.

"Ay," said the old woman, "now you look lovelier than ever. That smile is like a sunbeam to my heart; it thaws the frost of age. Believe me, Myra, the sexton of St. Hubert's shall adore you."

"Then you must have love charms," said the gypsy girl, blushing.

"Love charms I have," said the old woman, "and those of wondrous potency. We are a favored race, Myra. Descended from the old Egyptians, we inherit their mysterious learning. To a few among us, the queens and magi of our tribes, there has come down a knowledge of charms and medicine, and some of the secrets of astrology. Go, Myra; leave me. I will provide for your peace. Yes, yes, I have love charms. I have them!"

The gypsy girl smiled, rose, kissed the hand of her grandmother, and then bounded away like a fawn.

"Poor child!" muttered the old woman, when alone; "she must not die of a broken heart. Love charms, did she say! Yes—I have them for fools; but the love charm I shall use to give her joy is poison. The betrothed bride of the sexton of St. Hubert's lies ill of an unknown malady. The physicians cannot do her good, for she is sick of a wounded heart. To-night the sexton of St. Hubert's, who has faith in my skill, comes to seek a remedy. He shall have one. Does he think to spurn the poor gypsy girl? He is mistaken. He plighted his troth to her in the silence of the forest; they broke a piece of gold across a running brook; they swore truth and fidelity! One has broken the oath, but it shall be sworn anew. None but Myra shall wed the sexton of St. Hubert's!"

CHAPTER III.

RETRIBUTION.

It was a fierce and stormy night. The wind howled around the houses of Redwood, and wherever a shutter had lost its fastening, it flapped to and fro with a frequent and alarming sound. The rain, too, descended in torrents, and flooded the streets of the village, while ever and anon heavy peals of thunder and vivid flashes of lightning increased the terror of the night. In the house of Farmer Ellis a few persons were assembled to witness the bridal of the sexton of St. Hubert's. The bridegroom was as one excited by wine, for there was a wild radiance in his eyes and an unwonted smile upon his lips, and he occasionally gave utterance to some jest, and when it failed of producing the expected mirth, his own laugh sounded hollow and strange. The bride, too, so pearly pale, in her white dress, with white roses in her hair, seemed like the bride of Corinth in the German tale. A few of the guests, huddled anxiously together, whispered among themselves, "It is a churchyard bridal."

Still the cake and wine went round, and the strange laugh of the bridegroom was more frequent. The night wore on, and the arrival of the clergyman was prolonged far beyond the expected time. At length he came, and the ceremony was about to take place, when the bride suddenly sank in the arms of her companions. They raised her, and applied the usual remedies resorted to in cases of fainting, but the vital spark itself had fled.

In the depth of a stormy night, the sexton of St. Hubert's sought the queen of the gypsies. He was mounted on an active horse, and accompanied by the sheriff of the county and a few resolute men, well mounted and armed to the teeth. As he approached the river which bounded the gypsy camp upon one side, the sexton looked in vain for a guiding light—no fires blazed upon the green, no hidden glare was reflected in the mirror of the stream. Still he spurred on his horse, and followed hard by his companions, gallantly forded the stream and crossed the open meadows. The tents had all been struck, and no sound was heard in that deserted place, except the rushing of the boisterous wind and the tinkling of the raindrops as they fell upon the river. The parties reined up their horses, and the sexton and the sheriff held a brief conference together. While they were yet conversing, a broad and brilliant blaze shot up from the centre of the forest, illuminating a wide and well-trodden path which led directly to the light. The first flash of radiance dazzled the eyes of the horsemen, but when they became accustomed to the glare, they beheld distinctly several wild forms lounging around the fire, evidently unconscious of the approach of danger.

"Now is our time, my lads," said the sheriff, in a low tone. "Forward, and we shall have them all."

Every rowel was instantly employed, and the party pushed forward at a gallop. Bowing their heads to avoid the swaying branches, they bent over their horses' necks in the intense ardor of pursuit. The sheriff and the sexton rode side by side, and had nearly attained their object, when their horses fell suddenly, and threw them to the ground with violence. In fine, the whole party had stumbled upon pitfalls dug for them, and not a horseman of the troop escaped an overthrow. While they were rolling on the ground, entangled in the stirrups, and receiving severe injuries from the struggling horses, a shrill cry arose from the depth of the woods, and a dozen stout ruffians set upon them, seized, and pinioned them. The sexton and the sheriff were conducted by two of the gang to the presence of the gypsy queen, who sat upon a rude form raised upon the trunk of a huge oak, and sheltered by an ample awning of oiled cloth. The sheriff's followers were borne away in another direction. The wild woman and her wilder attendants were perfectly distinct in the ruddy firelight, though the whole scene had, to the eyes of the victims, the appearance of a vision of night.

"Well, sirs," said the queen, "you came to see us, and you have found us. Have you not some message for us? You myrmidon of the law, have you no greeting for the queen of the gypsies?"

The sheriff looked at the queen and then at her attendants. They were fierce-looking, unshorn fellows, with butchers' knives stuck in their rope girdles, and seemed but to await a nod from her tawny majesty to employ their formidable weapons.

"Have you nothing for us?" asked the dark lady.

"Nothing," said the sheriff, faintly.

"Ho, ho!" laughed the wrinkled crone. "The man of law is forgetful. You, *Dommerar*, search him, and see if he speaks the truth."

A sandy-haired little fellow advanced at the summons, and rifled the pockets of the sheriff with a dexterity which proved him an adept in the business. A teacher of music would have envied his fingering. Having caused the pockets of the sheriff to disgorge, he thus, in the canting language, enumerated their contents:—

"The *moabite's ribbin runs thin*, (the sheriff's cash runs low.) He has no *mint*, (gold,) and only a *mopus* or two."

"Fool!" said the queen, "has he no paper?"

"Ay, ay, missus, here's his *fiddle*," (writ,) was the answer.

"Give it me," cried the queen. "Here, you *patrico*, our eyes are bad. Read this scrawl, and acquaint us with the contents."

The *patrico*, or hedge priest, a fellow in a rusty, black suit, with a beard of three weeks' growth, bleared eyes, and a red, Bardolph nose, took the writ, which he had more difficulty in reading than Tony Lumpkin, when he received the letter of Hastings. At first, he held it upside down, then reversed it, looking at it at arm's length, and then gave it a closer scrutiny. He finally gave it as his opinion, that it empowered the *queer-cuffin* (so he termed the sheriff) to seize upon the so called queen of the gypsies, accused of the crime of murder, and also to apprehend her followers. When he had concluded, the old crone snatched the writ from his hand, and, tearing it to pieces, flung the fragments into the face of the sheriff.

"Take him away," said she, "and leave us alone with the sexton of St. Hubert's. Guard him well, for we wish to show him how we administer justice among us. We will be judge and jury, and our *upright man* shall be the executioner."

She waved her tawny hand with the air of a princess dismissing her courtiers, and her mandate was obeyed. She was left alone with the sexton of St. Hubert's. Looking him steadily in the face, she said,—

"John Pembroke, I give you joy of your marriage."

"Wretched woman!" said the sexton, "you poisoned her. By your hand she died."

"You are mistaken," answered the old woman, with a bitter smile. "She is not dead, but sleepeth. You see the devil can quote Scripture. It was my first intention to have poisoned her; but my second thoughts were better. So, instead of the medicine you sought, I gave you a powerful narcotic, which has thrown her into a deep sleep. She lies, at this moment, you know, in the chapel of St. Hubert's. There are flowers on her coffin, and there is a shroud around her. If I am not very much mistaken, about this hour she awakes."

"And perishes! Fiend in human shape, how you have deceived me! At this hour, remote from help, my Margaret is dying."

"She is not your Margaret, neither is she dying," said the crone. "Listen to me. I sent a trusty messenger to him that Margaret loves—to him who loves her fondly and faithfully—and if all things have gone as well as I anticipate, by this time she is in his arms. The draught she drank is harmless."

"Cursed deceiver!" cried the sexton, struggling frantically to free himself from the ligatures which bound him. "You have done an accursed deed. You have deprived me of my betrothed bride."

"Your betrothed bride!" said the queen of the gypsies. "Behold her!" She waved her hand, and Myra stood before the sexton of St. Hubert's. "There she stands," said the gypsy. "Have you forgotten that your troth is plighted to her? The bride and the priest are ready. Man of guilt and passion, wed her you may, wed her you must!"

"Never!" cried the sexton. "When I sought your lawless crew to indulge my love of revelling and pleasure, the person of Myra lighted a fire in my breast. But it was an unholy flame. I will never marry her. Let her live—live to be branded with infamy and disgrace!"

"Ha!" cried the crone, rising from her seat. "Is it so? Speak, Myra! child of my heart, is it so?"

The gypsy girl clasped her hands together, and hung her head in shame. Her cheeks were suffused with crimson; then they became deadly pale, and she sank lifeless on the ground.

"You have killed her!" shrieked the gypsy queen, "and dearly shall you rue it."

She placed a whistle to her lips, and blew a shrill blast. But she received a far different answer than she had anticipated; for one of the sheriff's men had succeeded in escaping from the hands of the gypsy crew, and galloped to the neighboring town, where a troop of horse was quartered. The commanding officer instantly repaired to the gypsy camp, where he arrived in time to apprehend the crew before they had committed any act of violence. The sexton of St. Hubert's did not long survive this night, and Myra became a maniac. The fate of the lovers we shall next describe.

When the lover of Margaret received the message of the queen of the gypsies, he repaired to the spot where his mistress lay, to all appearance, in the arms of death. But life had not departed; and even as he hung gazing over her, a faint color mounted to her cheek, and her bosom began to heave beneath her white garment. He raised her in his arms, bore her to the air, and she revived. When her senses were fully restored, she consented to guard against another separation by marrying her lover and savior. William had provided a humble post-chaise to convey his bride far from the scene of her past perils and temptations. They journeyed by slow stages to the north, and at the close of a few days entered a romantic village. The lover bridegroom pointed out a gray and noble old pile, the turrets of which rose lofty above the waving trees of an ancient park. He asked if she should like to visit it. She replied in the affirmative, and they drove, unchallenged, through the gateway and along a noble avenue shaded by huge oaks. When they reached the portals of the building, the post-boy stopped the horses, dismounted, threw open the door of the chaise, and let down the steps. William lifted his companion from her seat in his arms.

"Margaret," said he, "look up. This is Woodley Castle, and you are Lady Armitage."

JACK WITHERS.

Every body liked Jack Withers. He was a handsome, active young fellow of five-and-twenty, of a good family, an orphan, who came into possession of thirty thousand dollars when he came of age. In this age of California gold, when fortunes are made by shovelling dust, and the wonders of Aladdin's treasure house are realized by men of no capital but pickaxes and muscles, thirty thousand dollars does not seem a prodigious sum. Yet our great-grandfathers retired from business on that amount, and were thought, at least, comfortably well off; and even nowadays, thirty thousand dollars, judiciously managed, will keep a man out of the poorhouse, and give him a clean shirt and a leg of mutton for his lifetime. But poor Jack was not a judicious manager, and a tandem team and champagne suppers, with a shooting-box and turf speculations, soon made ducks and drakes of a little fortune. Thus at twenty-five, our friend Jack was *minus*; or, in the elegant phraseology of the day, "a gentleman at large with pockets to let."

When a man's riches have taken wings and *vamosed*, when all his old uncles are used up, and he has no prospective legacy to fall back upon, he is generally cut by the acquaintances of his prosperous days. The memory of "what he used to was" is seldom cherished, and the unhappy victim of prodigality discovers to his sorrow, that

"'Tis a very good world that we live in,
To lend, or to spend, or to give in;
But to beg, or to borrow, or get a man's own,
'Tis the very worst world, sir, that ever was known."

Jack, however, was not destined to drink the cup of this bitter experience. He was just as popular and just as much courted without a penny in his pocket, as he was when he possessed the means to be extravagant, when he

"Spread to the liberal air his silken sails,And lavished guineas like a Prince of Wales."

The secret of his prodigious popularity was his obliging disposition. His time and talents—and he had plenty of the former, and no lack of the latter—were always at the service of his friends; and though the idlest dog in the world when his own affairs were in question, in the cause of his friends he was the busiest man alive. Thus he fairly won his dinners, his rides, his drives, and his opera tickets—they were trifling commissions on his benevolent transactions.

"Jack," one fellow would say, "my horse is too confoundedly high strung, and only half broke. He threw me yesterday."

"I'll ride him for you, Bill," would be the ready reply; "give me your spurs, and I'll give him a lesson."

And away he would go, without a thought of his neck, to mount a restive rascal that had half killed the rough rider of a cavalry regiment.

"Jack," another would say, "I've got an awkward affair on hand with Lieutenant ——; he fancies I've insulted him, and has thrown out dark hints about coffee and pistols."

"Make yourself perfectly easy, my boy; I'll bring him to reason or fight him myself."

So Jack had his hands full of business. Well, one dreary, desolate afternoon in March, when the barbs of all the vanes in the city were looking pertinaciously eastward, and people were shivering over anthracite grates, Jack Withers "might have been seen," as James would say, seated in the little back parlor of the coffee room in School Street, sipping Mocha with his particular friend Bill Bliffins, who had an especial claim upon his kindness, from the fact that he had already extricated Bill from scrapes innumerable.

Mocha is a great prompter of social and kindly feelings, and prompts, in *tête-à-têtes*, to that unreserved confidence on one part, and that obliging interest on the other, which unite two congenial and kindred spirits in adamantine bonds.

"Jack," said Bill, smiting the marble table emphatically, "you are my best friend."

"Pooh, pooh! you flatter me," said Jack, blushing like a peony; "I've never done any thing for you."

"Yes, you have, and you know it," persisted Bliffins. "Didn't you fight Lieutenant Jenkins, of the Salamander, when I ought to have fought him myself? Haven't you endorsed my notes when nobody else would back my paper?"

"I'll do it again, my boy," said Jack, with a gush of enthusiastic feeling.

"Ahem! your name on short or long paper isn't exactly what it used to be," said Bill, rather unfeelingly, perhaps.

"True, true," returned Jack, in a more subdued tone; "I haven't got many friends left in the synagogues."

"But what you have done, Jack," continued Bliffins, with enthusiasm, "emboldens me to trespass yet further on your patience."

"With all my heart," said Jack; and there was no reservation implied in the hearty tone in which the words were uttered.

"Then listen to my story, as the postilion of Longjumeau sings. Hear me for my cause, and be silent that you may hear."

"I'll be mute as the codfish in the House of Representatives."

"Well, then," said Bill, in a solemn tone, "I'm dead broke."

"Dead broke?"

"Yes; I'm running on my last hundred."

"Impossible!"

"True, though, for all that. Yet my circumstances are not so desperate, either. There's a vacant clerkship in the secretary of state's office; and the governor has been sounded, and I think he might be disposed to give it to me."

"Go to him at once, then, my dear boy. If he wants any reference, send him to me. I'll endorse your character, as I used to your paper when my name was worth something on 'change. Go to him at once."

"It's easy to say it, Jack; but the fact is, that I have such a confounded hesitating address that I fear I should make an unfavorable impression, and ruin my cause; whereas, if a plausible, voluble fellow like yourself could get his ear and plead for me, my appointment would be certain. Now will you——"

"Call on the governor? With all my heart—consider the thing settled."

"That's not all; you must be my advocate in another quarter. I'm over head and ears in love with Juliet Trevor—Trapp & Trevor—W. I. Goods, wholesale. You know the firm?"

"Like a book."

"I want you to see the girl and the old people; I haven't confidence to propose in person. You can do it for me?"

"With all my heart. I give you joy of the clerkship and the girl—they're yours."

"I'm eternally obliged, Jack."

"Not the least, my boy—always ready to serve my friends. By the way, have you got any money about your clothes? I invited you to take coffee, but I forgot my purse in my other trousers—no change, you know."

"There, get this V changed," said Bliffins, handing him a bank note.

Jack took the note and walked up to the counter.

"Coffee and pie for two, my dear" said he to the attendant. "It's all right—you know me—pay next time—Withers and friend. Come, Bill, I've fixed it."

"But the change!" said Bill.

"Never mind the change—morrow do as well. By, by,—*au revoir*."

"Remember the governor!"

"All right, my boy."

"And Juliet!"

"Make yourself easy."

So they parted. The next day, Jack sent in his card to the governor at the Adams House, and followed the pasteboard before the message could be returned. The governor received his visitor with his usual urbanity.

"Good quarters, governor!" said Jack, looking round him as he dropped into a rocking chair, and tapped his boot with his walking stick. "Chief magistrate of the commonwealth—well lodged—people pay—all right."

The governor was much amused at the coolness of his guest, and waited patiently to learn his business. He was not kept long in suspense.

"Governor," said Jack, "I come to solicit your favor not on my behalf, but in the cause of friendship—sacred friendship—holy bond of two congenial hearts, &c.—but you know all that. My friend, sir, William Bliffins—unfortunate young man—reduced in circumstances—good family—good blood—grandfather in the revolution—soil of Bunker Hill irrigated with the blood of Bliffins—but you know all that—run through his fortune—on the town—not a penny—hard case."

"Do you solicit charity, sir, for your friend?"

"Not exactly—official favor—vacant clerkship—secretary's office—make him comfortable—but you know all that."

"Really, sir, you run on at such a rate——"

"Way I've got—few leading points all you want—time precious—money (old saw)—Bliffins—clerkship—don't you take?"

"I think I recollect the name, now. But I must inquire into the character of the applicant. How did he lose his fortune?"

"Unbounded benevolence—heart like an ox—bigger—endorsing notes for friends—founding hospitals for indigent Africans—temperance movement—philanthropy expensive—but you know all that."

"The office in question requires a good penman. Can your friend write well?"

"Splendid hand—copperplate—*currente calamo*—shine in your eyes."

"Have you a specimen of his penmanship?"

"Cords at home—some in pocket. Here you have it! no, that's my washerwoman's bill. Ah, here it is!" and Jack pulled out a crumpled note, and placed it before the governor.

The governor scanned the document curiously, and with great difficulty deciphered the following words, which he read silently:—

"Dear Jack,—Fashion has been beaten, and I lost on the mare. I shall back Tom Hyer to the extent of my pile. He is training finely. Bricks has a couple of Santa Anna's game cocks for me, on board the Raritan, at Lewis's wharf. Can you run down and get 'em from the steward? Yrs, &c."

The governor smiled as he handed back the note, but made no remark.

"Where can I communicate with you, sir?" he asked.

"Dog and Thistle, Blackstone Street. I'll write my address."

So Jack wrote his address card, (by the way, he wrote a splendid hand,) and took his leave of the governor.

From the Adams House he posted to Louisburg Square, where the Trevors were living in great style. Slightly acquainted with Miss Trevor, he found no difficulty in being admitted to her presence. After rattling over a few commonplace topics, he came to the object of his mission.

"Have you seen Bliffins lately?"

"Not very," replied the fair one, languidly.

"Dying, ma'am, dying."

"Is it possible? What's the matter, sir?"

"Love—desperation—patience on a monument couldn't sit there forever—heart ache—only one thing to save him."

"Indeed! and what is that?"

"He loves you, madam, passionately, devotedly, enormously—Petrarch, Abelard, lukewarm lovers in comparison. Throws himself at your feet—save him!—marry him quick! or you'll lose him!—say yes."

"Sir, my father will communicate with you," said the lady, rising to terminate the interview.

"Dog and Thistle, Blackstone Street," said Jack, and bowed himself away.

The next day Jack and Bill were again seated together in a small room at the Dog and Thistle, waiting the result of the obliging operations of the former. In a few moments a waiter brought in a note, superscribed John Withers, Esq. Jack tore it open, and read as follows:—

"Sir,—In answer to your application yesterday, I am sorry to return you an unfavorable reply; but the chirography of the person you recommended, to say nothing of other considerations, unfits him for the vacancy in question. Having made inquiries with regard to yourself, and finding that you are in circumstances which might render employment acceptable, while your conduct proves that you have sincerely repented of the follies of your early years, I have concluded to request your acceptance of the office yourself. If you accept the offer, please report yourself to-morrow.

"Yours, respectfully,

—— ——,

"Governor of the Commonwealth of Massachusetts."

"You're an impostor!" shouted Bliffins. "Is this your friendship?"

"I can't help it," said Jack, ruefully. "I'm innocent—I did the best I could for you."

"How did he know any thing about my penmanship?"

"I showed him this note," said the unhappy Jack, producing the document.

"That note? You've ruined me! Do you know what it was about?"

"I'd forgotten."

"Why, it was all about horseracing, pugilism, and cock fighting, you jackass!"

"Letter for Mr. Bliffins!" said the waiter, entering with another epistle. Bliffins read it aloud.

"Mr. William Bliffins.

"Sir: In answer to application of your friend, yesterday, for daughter's hand, have to reply for daughter, and say that the honor is respectfully declined. Had you obtained the office you applied for, might have treated with you. Daughter requests me to say that she could not have done so in any case.

"Your ob't servant,

J. TREVOR."

"P.S. Please hand the enclosed to Mr. Withers."

The "enclosed" was an invitation to a grand ball given by the Trevors on the ensuing night.

After overwhelming his friend with anathemas, Bliffins rushed wildly from the Dog and Thistle, and enlisted in the second dragoons.

Jack Withers, who had never before looked out for number one, now became so "obliging" as to take care of that neglected personage. He became a praiseworthy clerk, and a steady man of business. He went to the ball and polked himself into the good graces of Miss Juliet Trevor. The old gentleman and lady smiled upon their loves, and in due time he was united to the object of his affections, securing thereby a handsome and amiable wife, and an independent fortune, which she insisted on settling upon her husband on the wedding day. There is no fear of Jack's relapsing into his old habits of extravagance; and while he is still as popular as ever, he never neglects his own affairs for those of other people.

THE SILVER HAMMER.

The sun was sinking in the west, and gilding with its slant beams a pastoral landscape, as a young soldier, weary and footsore, slowly toiled along a lonely road that ran parallel with the course of the bright and winding Seine. A dusty foraging cap rested on his dark locks, and his youthful form bent beneath the weight of a well-filled knapsack. Pierre Lacour had served with honor in that glorious little band of heroes, which, under the leadership of the youthful Bonaparte, had crossed the snow-clad Alps, and fallen like an avalanche upon the plains of Lombardy, sweeping before it the veteran troops of Austria, and astonishing all Europe by unparalleled audacity and unexampled success. Pierre had marched farther on that day than he had ever done while following the colors of his regiment—but he was on his way home, and he longed to see his mother, his fair young sister Maria, and a lovely maiden, named Estelle, dearer to his heart than all beside. They had news of his coming,— at least, Maria and his mother had,—and he had sent them in advance, by a sure hand, a large amount of money, his share of the spoils of battle honorably won—enough, in short, to give a dowry to his sister, and enable him to demand the reward of all his toils and dangers—the hand of his betrothed.

His heart beat quick as he climbed the last vine-clad hill which separated him from his native valley. A few steps more would bring him to the summit, whence his eye would rest on the neat whitewashed cottage, with its surrounding palings, and trim garden; and there, perhaps, at the rustic gate, he should see the well-known figures of his mother and sister. Far as he had travelled, he sprang up the ascent with a buoyant step, and soon gained the eminence. The cottage lay full in view, but though it was the usual hour for preparing the evening meal, no blue smoke wreath curled upward from the chimney. A vague presentiment of evil weighed upon his heart. Hastening to dispel the dark and chilling fears that came thick upon him, he hurried down the slope, and soon passed through the garden and stood within the cottage. He called aloud—no voice responded to his cry. He rushed into the little room, which served at once for kitchen and parlor. It was empty—no fire burned upon the hearth. The humble furniture was in strange disarray. The casement, which looked out upon the garden was shattered. The walls and floor were charred and blackened with smoke, as if the house had taken fire and been saved with difficulty. Pierre sprang up stairs. In neither of the chambers could he find the loved ones whom he sought—only the same scene of confusion and desolation. Turning in dismay from the spectacle, he rushed out of the cottage to make his way to the nearest neighbors, and inquire into this appalling mystery. As he hurried along—his brain whirling, his footsteps uncertain and unsteady—he stumbled against an aged man of venerable appearance, who was coming in the opposite direction. The young soldier halted, and touching his cap, begged pardon for his involuntary rudeness.

"My poor Pierre," said the old man, "I know too well the cause of your forgetfulness."

The soldier looked up and recognized the familiar and benevolent features of the good priest of the village, his old tutor and pastor.

"Father," he said, pointing to the cottage, "you have been there—you know all—tell me—where are they?"

The old man's eyes filled with tears, as he shook his head, and laid his hand kindly on the young man's shoulder.

"Pierre," said he, "you have read 'whom the Lord loveth he chasteneth?'"

The soldier bowed his head.

"Pierre," exclaimed the good priest, "let us sit down on this bank. You are a good and brave boy. You can face danger, and I have sought to furnish you weapons to wage war against sorrow and trial."

"You have been a father to me, sir," replied the young soldier, complying with the invitation of his pastor, and taking a seat beside him. "I will endeavor to listen calmly to all you have to communicate. Where are my mother and sister?"

"Pierre," said the old man, "arm yourself with all your fortitude. You will never see your mother more till you meet her in that happier world, where the wicked cease from troubling and the weary are at rest."

Pierre groaned deeply, and covering his face with his hands, rocked his body to and fro as he burst into an agony of tears. The priest sought not to interrupt him, but turned away his own weeping countenance, for the anguish of the youth was too painful to contemplate.

At last the poor soldier looked up and spoke again: "What of my poor sister?"

"I know nothing," replied the priest; "she is gone whither, none can tell. A great crime has been committed. By whom, none knows, save God and the perpetrator thereof. You sent home a large sum of money to your mother. She was so overjoyed at your good fortune, that she made no secret of its reception, though I cautioned her against speaking of it. A fortnight ago, the village was alarmed by the cry of fire. Your cottage was seen to be in flames. The neighbors hastened thither and extinguished the blaze. In the smoke and confusion it was not perceived at first that murder, as well as incendiarism, had done its foul work." The priest paused, overcome with agitation.

"On! on!" shouted Pierre, "I can bear it all now!"

"Your poor mother was the victim," continued the priest; "she lay on the hearthstone dead and bleeding. Her bureau had been broken open and rifled of its contents."

"My sister! my sister!" cried the soldier.

"She was gone. The whole surrounding country was searched, but nothing was discovered."

"Maria! Maria! could gold have tempted *you*? No! no!—dog that I am, to suspect you! Misery has driven me mad!" cried the soldier, dashing his hand against his forehead.

"The whole dreadful crime," said the old priest, "is shrouded in a mystery as appalling as death itself. But God does not permit such deeds to slumber undetected or unavenged. Sooner or later they are brought to light."

"May I prove the instrument of detection!" said the soldier. "Some of the coins that I sent my poor murdered mother were marked—I could recognize them again. Father, you shall take me to my mother's grave. One prayer there—one word with Estelle—and then I will go to Paris; it is the resort of every criminal, and thence it sends forth its crime-blackened ruffians to desecrate this fair earth with horror. Come, father, come—my mother's grave—lead me there at once!"

Years passed away. Save by two or three persons, the crime which had desecrated the hearthstone of a humble village home was forgotten in those great historical events, of which Europe and France were then the theatres. In those days of bloodshed and battle, of victory and triumph, Pierre Lacour, who had commenced his military career as a brave young soldier, might have risen to the highest honors, had he followed the victorious eagles of his emperor. Why might not he rise as well as Murat, Ney, Lannes, or a hundred others? The epaulets of a colonel, nay, the baton of a marshal of France, were prizes within the reach of the lowliest, provided he had the head to plan and the heart to execute daring and chivalric deeds. But his heart no longer bounded like a war horse to the charge of the trumpet and the roll of the drum. He lived for one purpose—to discover the assassin of his mother and the sister, of whom nothing had been heard since the dreadful night of murder and conflagration. To facilitate his purposes, he had procured himself to be enrolled in the unrivalled police force of Fouché. That wily minister had no more able assistant under his command, and none in that fraternity (of which many were miscreants, who had purchased impunity for crime by selling the lives and liberties of former accomplices and comrades) who could compare with him for purity of life and elevation of motive. To punish evil for the sake of society, was the aim of the young police officer. None more untiring or intelligent than he in ferreting out the perpetrators of deeds of violence. In the criminals whose arrest he effected, and whose conviction he secured, he expected, constantly, to find some cognizant of the offence which had thrown so black a shadow over his life. He read with eager avidity the dying confessions of the condemned. He caught eagerly every syllable that fell from the lips of men, who, standing on the brink of eternity, seemed to be impressed with the necessity of revealing truth. But for years his expectations were baffled.

At last, all Paris was thrown into commotion by the murder of a Colonel Belleville, an officer who had served with distinction in the grand army, and who was found dead, one morning, in a room at house number 96 Rue La Harpe. The only mark of violence discovered by the surgeons was a dark, purple spot, about the size of a five-franc piece, on the left temple. The police were apprised that, on the morning of the day before, a slight young man, with fair hair and polished address, giving his name as Adolph Belmont, had hired the room at number 96 Rue La Harpe, and paid a week's rent in advance. It further appeared that, in the evening, just after the close of the performances at the opera, this young man had come home in company with an officer of the army. After the lapse of about an hour, the young man, Belmont, left the house, telling the porter he should return in a few minutes. But he never reappeared. About ten o'clock in the morning, the porter went up to his room, and found the door locked. He knocked and called, without receiving any answer. Looking through the keyhole, he saw the feet and legs of a man, in military boots and pantaloons, lying on the floor. Much alarmed and disturbed, he sought out a commissary of police, and that functionary, breaking open the door, discovered the body of Colonel Belleville. This tragedy excited an unusual sensation. Even the emperor heard of it, and, from his private purse provided a large sum of money to be paid as a reward to the discoverer of the perpetrator of this fearful crime.

Not many days after this occurrence, and while it yet remained shrouded in mystery, another murder roused the excitable population of Paris to a frenzy of anxiety and horror. An army commissary, named Captain Eugene Descartes, was found dead in his lodgings, in the Rue Richelieu, with the same fatal purple mark on the left temple.

Yet a third murder was perpetrated in the Boulevard des Italiens. A banker, named Monval, was, in this instance, the victim. His left temple bore the fatal discoloration of the size of a five-franc piece; but, although he had a large sum of money on his person, and wore a costly watch and many valuable trinkets, and though articles of high price abounded in his sumptuously-furnished apartment, not an article, as his steward testified, was missing.

On the morning of the announcement of this last crime in the Moniteur, the minister of police received a summons from the emperor to attend him. He found him in his private cabinet, pacing to and fro in high excitement. His face was more colorless than ever, except that an angry hectic spot burned upon each cheek. As the minister entered, the emperor turned upon him, and exclaimed,—

"Fouché, what is the meaning of all this? Is this Paris, and are we living in the nineteenth century? It appears that there is no security for life in our capital. Mr. Fouché, if such crimes can be committed with impunity, there is an end of all things; and if you cannot ferret out the perpetrators of such atrocities as these, it is time for you to vacate your position. I must appoint a new minister of police."

"Sire," replied the minister, "how much time will you give me to discover the assassin?"

"One week," replied the emperor.

"I thank your majesty," replied the minister, bowing. "In one week, you shall have the assassin's head, or my resignation."

"Good," said the emperor; "and to stimulate the activity of your people, I hereby authorize you to offer a reward of twenty thousand francs, for the detection of the assassin of the Rue La Harpe, the Rue Richelieu, and the Boulevard, if it prove, as I imagine, that one individual perpetrated these crimes, or five thousand francs each, if there were three criminals. Good day, Mr. Fouché; let me have a report of your doings without delay."

The secret of Mr. Fouché's confident promise to detect the assassin was the reliance he placed in the activity, daring, and intelligence of Pierre Lacour. He sent for him, and related his conversation with the emperor, enlarging on the munificent reward promised by Napoleon.

"I am poor," said Lacour, "but higher motives than hopes of reward stimulate me to perform this duty. Yet, should I be successful, a sum of money like this would enable me to wed one, who, though I voluntarily offered to release her from her engagement has loved me as well in my misfortunes as in happier times. In one week, therefore, Mr. Fouché, I will enable you to redeem your pledge to the emperor."

Four days passed away, and yet the minister of police heard nothing from Lacour. But the young man had not been inactive; and once or twice he had obtained, what he considered, traces of the person calling himself Belmont, the supposed assassin of the Rue la Harpe, and, by presumption, of the other murders; but these traces led to no result.

Whether in search of diversion, or that a vague hope whispered to him that he might obtain some intelligence by so doing, Lacour, on the fifth night after his interview with the minister, went to a masked ball at the grand opera house, in the costume of an officer of the Fusilier Guard, which chance led him to select. Weary of the noise and confusion, sad and discouraged, he had withdrawn from the crowded circle of dancers, when some one touched him on the shoulder.

"Captain Lassalle," said a sweet musical voice, "you are known, though the uniform you wear is not that of your own corps."

Lacour turned with the intention of correcting the mistake, when a secret impulse restrained the disavowal. The person who addressed him was a slight young man, fashionably dressed, with no other disguise than a half-mask of black velvet, which did not conceal his light hair.

"I perceive you know me," said Lacour, favoring the mistake; "though you have the advantage of me. I cannot possibly conjecture whom I am addressing."

The masked laughed lightly.

"Perhaps it would be of no use for me to unmask," was the reply; "but if I tell you I have something of importance to communicate to you—something in reference to your application to the emperor for preferment, you may be disposed to listen to me."

"With all my heart."

"I see you are tired of this noisy scene," said the mask, "and so in faith am I. Besides, this is no place to talk of business. What say you to a moonlight walk to my lodgings, in the Rue Montmartre? There we can discuss our affairs over a glass of champagne."

"I will willingly accompany you," said Lacour, "if you will give me a few minutes to speak to a friend, with whom I had a previous appointment."

"Make haste, then," said the mask; "you will find me here for fifteen minutes."

Lacour hastened to the nearest post, and made himself known to the commandant.

"Quick!" said he, "I want a sergeant and a dozen *gens d'armes*. In fifteen minutes I shall leave the opera house, in company with a young man, for the Rue Montmartre. Let the squad follow us without appearing to do so. Keep in the shadow of the houses. We shall enter a house. As soon as the door has closed, demand instant admittance of the porter. Let the sergeant follow hard upon my heels, and wait outside the door of whatever room I enter. At a call from me, let him be ready to burst in and secure the person with whom I am in company."

As soon as he had given these directions, the police officer hastened back to the opera house, where the mask was still awaiting him. Arm in arm they left the hall, and chatting familiarly, entered the Rue Montmartre, and soon arrived at an old house of seven stories, to which they were admitted by the porter. Lacour's heart beat as he accompanied his guide, in the dark, up three pairs of stairs—but before he had reached the head of the third flight, he heard the street door open and shut below, and knew that the sergeant had obeyed his directions, and that help was at hand in case his suspicions proved true.

The mask opened the door of a room, and ushered in his guest. It was a small, boudoir-like apartment, and exquisitely furnished. Silken hangings fell over gold arrows, from the ceiling to the floor. Tapestry carpets, soft as velvet, covered the floor. Rich ottomans, superb mirrors, marble tables, and pictures, were crowded together. A soft light was diffused through the apartment by an alabaster shade-lamp. An intoxicating perfume loaded the atmosphere, and even oppressed the senses. Lacour, as he sank upon the sofa, felt overcome by a strange languor. The mask sat close beside him.

"Captain," said the mask, in a musical, insinuating voice, "have you ever loved?"

"Before I answer this question," replied Lacour, "I must first know what prompts you thus to catechize me."

"Because," replied the unknown, "I have deceived you—because I am a woman—one who has long known and loved you, till an uncontrollable desire to make this confession has compelled her to a step that you will blame, and, perhaps, despise her for."

Lacour was puzzled, and remained silent for a few moments.

"I see," said the mask, with a sigh, "you despise me for my very boldness. Yet, I am a lady of rank and reputation, and my affection for you is as pure as that of maiden can be."

"Fair lady," said Lacour, "if such you be indeed, you must permit me to request you to remove that envious mask."

"It may not be," replied the stranger, with a laugh. "Ask that, or presume to remove this shield, and I vanish like a fairy or a phantom. But if you promise to be very obedient, I may give you hopes of disclosing my face—perhaps my name—at our next interview. But in reward for your submission to my behest, I will allow you, like a benignant sovereign, to do homage to my ungloved hand."

She withdrew her kid glove, and presented, playfully, a hand so white, so delicately veined, and small, that Lacour could no longer doubt that he was addressing a lady. He raised the hand respectfully to his lips. But he felt now that his suspicions were groundless, and that he did wrong in deceiving a person, who, however romantic and unjustifiable her behavior might seem, was still one entitled to respect and honor. But as he was framing an apology for taking advantage of her mistaking him, the stranger suddenly sprang upon him like a tigress. The delicate hand he had just kissed now compressed his throat like an iron vice; the other suddenly brandished in the air a small *silver hammer*, while a fierce voice hissed in his ear, "Lassalle! your hour has come! Belleville, Descartes, and Monval, have gone before you to answer for their crimes. You are the fourth, and last. Die, villain!"

But Lacour struggled free, and shouted for help. The door fell with a crash; the soldiers poured in, and the female assassin was secured and disarmed. Eager to unravel the mystery, the police officer tore the mask from the face of the unknown, and recognized in the wild and inflamed features of the assassin of the Rue La Harpe, the Rue Richelieu, and the Boulevard des Italiens, his sister, Maria Lacour!

But Maria Lacour died not on the scaffold. She was saved from that doom by unquestionable proofs of insanity. Her sad story was learned afterwards from various sources, and corroborated, in the most important particulars, by Captain Lassalle, who was arrested for a criminal offence shortly after the above incident, and made a full confession of his guilt. It appeared, then, that the house of the widow Lacour, a short time before the opening of our story, had been broken into by four villains, named Belleville, Descartes, Monval, and Lassalle. They were all men of bad habits, and urgently necessitous, but yet of decent education and family. Hearing a noise in the kitchen, Maria descended only in time to witness the death pangs of the mother. The three first-named ruffians, demons who had murdered to rob, wished to destroy this witness of their guilt, but the fourth interceded, and her life was spared. But the horror of the deed overthrew her reason. She fled from the house that night a maniac; whither she wandered, how she was cared for, for a long time was and must ever remain a mystery. She finally, it seems, became in a degree tranquillized, found her way to Paris, and there she supported herself by her extraordinary skill as an embroideress.

But it was conjectured that her memory of early events had gone. The casual sight of one of the assassins, all of whom had prospered and risen in the world, revived the recollection of that one fearful night of horror, and with it came to her disordered brain the thirst of vengeance. It did not appear that for a moment she had dreamed of appealing to the interposition of the law.

To execute a summary vengeance, personally, was her terrible resolve. With a cunning that often supplies the loss of reason with the insane, she contrived snares, into which three of the assassins fell, and, with the singular implement her fancy had suggested, was the means of their death. Chance led to the failure of her plan for punishing the last of the assassins, Lassalle, and to her discovery by her brother.

Immediately after her arrest and examination, on proof of the condition of her mind, she was conveyed to a private asylum, and carefully attended to. Fortunately, her madness here assumed a happier phase. She took great pleasure in seeing her brother, and appeared to have forgotten that her mother was no more, asking him every day how soon their mother would come and take her back to the country. But the trials she had undergone had undermined her health. She sank very rapidly, and soon breathed her last.

Lacour only remained long enough in the service of the police to effect the arrest, and witness the condemnation of Lassalle, the last of the four assassins, who escaped the silver hammer of the maniac girl, to die by the hand of the executioner.

The sorrows he had experienced would have blighted the heart and sapped the life of Pierre Lacour, but for the love of one who had proved true to him through all his trials. Some months after the death of his sister, he married his faithful Estelle, and retired to a small and well-stocked farm, for which he was indebted to the generosity of the emperor; and he lived long enough, if not to forget his sorrows, at least to find consolation in the bosom of his family.

THE CHRIST CHURCH CHIMES.

It was a cold winter evening. The chill blast came sweeping from the chain of hills that guard our city on the north, laden with the cold breath of a thousand leagues of ice and snow. There was a sharp, polar glitter in the myriad stars that wheeled on their appointed course through the dark blue heaven, in whose expanse no single cloud was visible. Howling through the icy streets came the strong, wild north wind, tearing in its fierce frenzy the sailcloth awnings into tatters, swinging the public-house signs, and shaking the window shutters, like a bold burglar bent on the perpetration of crime. Then onward, onward it sped over the dark steel-colored bay, and out to the wild, wide, open sea, to do battle with the sails of the stanch barks that were struggling towards a haven.

But within, the good people of Boston were stoutly waging battle against the common enemy on this bitter Christmas eve. In some of the old-fashioned houses at the North End, inhabited by old-fashioned people, the ruddy light that streamed through the parlor windows on the street announced that huge fires of oak and hickory were blazing on the ample hearths. But in far the greater number of dwellings, the less genial, but more powerful anthracite was contending with the wintry elements.

In an upper room of an old, crazy, wooden house, a poor woman, thinly clad, sat sewing beside a rusty, sheet-iron stove, poorly supplied with chips. She had been once eminently handsome, and but for the wanness and hollowness of her face, would have appeared so still.

Two little boys, of eight and nine years of age, were warming themselves, or seeking to warm themselves, at the stove, before retiring to their little bed in a small room adjoining.

"Isn't this nice, mother?" said the younger, a bright, black-eyed boy. "Didn't I get a nice lot of chips to-day?"

"Yes, dearest, you are always a good and industrious boy," said the mother, snatching a moment from her work to imprint a kiss upon his forehead.

"Poor pa' will have a nice fire to warm him when he comes home," said the elder boy.

At this allusion to the child's father, the mother burst into tears. The countenances of both the children fell. They knew too well the cause of their mother's bitter sorrow—the same cause had blighted their own young hearts and clouded their innocent lives—their father was a drunkard! Hence it was that, bright and intelligent as they were, they could not go to school—they were too ragged for that—and their time was required on the wharves to pick up fuel and such scraps of provision as are scattered from the sheaves of the

- 205 -

prosperous and prodigal. For this reason, too, the mother had carefully forborne to remind the children that this was Christmas eve. But they knew it too well, and they contrasted its gloominess and sorrow with the well-remembered anniversaries when this was a season of delight—the eve of promised pleasures, of feasts, of dances, and of presents. With this thought in their hearts they silently kissed their mother, and retired to their little bed, committing themselves to "Our Father who art in heaven," while the poor mother toiled on, listening with dread for the returning footsteps of her husband.

The husband and father, whose return was thus dreaded, had worked late at night in the shop of the carpenter who had given him temporary employment, and who was to pay him this evening. Five or six dollars were coming to him, more than he had earned honestly for a long while, and his hand shook with eagerness as his employer counted out his wages. As he put on his hat to leave the shop, he observed his fellow-workmen, who were all sober and steady men, eying him with sad, inquiring looks; he almost ran out of the shop.

"I know what they mean," he said to himself. "But what is it to them how I spend my money—the prying busy-bodies! I'm not a slave—I have a right to do what I please with my own. Whew! how cutting the wind is! A glass or two of hot whiskey toddy will be just the thing!"

Without one thought of his toiling wife and neglected children, the poor, infatuated man hastened towards a grocery with the intention of slaking his morbid thirst. At the moment his foot was on the threshold, out from the belfry of Christ Church, ringing clear in the frosty air, streamed a tide of sweet and solemn music. Simple, yet touching, was the melody of those sacred bells, chiming forth the advent of the blessed Christmas time. And as the song of the bells fell upon his ear, it awakened in the drunkard a thousand memories of happier, because better days. The comfortable dwelling, the quiet, neat parlor, with its Christmas dressings, the sweet face of his wife, the merry laugh of his bright-eyed children—all flashed back vividly upon his mind. He recked not of the bitter blast—he forgot his late purpose—he could wish those sweet bells to play on forever. But they ceased.

"It was a voice from heaven!" said the man, as the tears rolled down his cheeks. "Surely God has blessed those Christ Church chimes. I'll never more drink one drop. This money shall go to my family, every cent of it. It is not too late yet to buy provision for to-morrow, and some comfortable things for the children."

It was late that night when the watching wife heard the step of her husband on the staircase. It was as slow and heavy as usual; but how relieved, how astonished, how grateful she felt, when the door opened, and he came in, happy, sober, bearing a huge basket filled with provisions, and threw down a parcel containing stockings, comforters, and mittens for the children, not forgetting some simple Christmas wreaths, and some of those condiments which children love.

The next day was a happy one indeed for the mother and the little boys—a merry Christmas that reminded them of old times, and gave them assurance of a happy future. May we not hope that the effect we have attributed to the Christ Church chimes is not a solitary instance of the power of music?

THE POLISH SLAVE.

Gayly opened the bright summer morning on the gray feudal turrets of Castle Tekeli, the residence of the old Count Alexis Tekeli, that crowned a rocky eminence, and was embosomed in the deep secular forests of Lithuania. The court yard was a scene of joyous noise and gay confusion; for the whole household was mustering for the chase. Half a dozen horses, gaily caparisoned, were neighing, snorting, and pawing the ground with hot impatience; a pack of stanch hounds, with difficulty restrained by the huntsmen, mingled their voices with the neighing of the steeds, while the slaves and relatives of the family were all busy in preparation for the day's sport.

Count Alexis was the first in the saddle; aged, but hale and vigorous, he was alert and active as a young man of five-and-twenty.

"Where are my daughters?" he exclaimed, impatiently, as he drew on his buff gantlets. "The sun is mounting apace, and we should not lose the best portion of the day."

As if in reply to his question, a tall, dark-haired girl, of elegant figure and stately bearing, appeared by his side, and with the assistance of a groom, mounted her prancing gray palfrey.

"This is well, Anna," said the count. "But where is Eudocia? She must not keep us waiting."

"Eudocia declines to be of our party, father," replied the girl.

"Pshaw!" said the old man; "she will never have your color in her cheeks, if she persist in moping in her chamber, reading old legends and missals, and the rhymes of worthless minnesingers. But let her go; I have one daughter who can live with the hunt, and see the boar at bay without flinching. Sound, bugle, and forward!"

Amid the ringing of silver curb chains, the baying of hounds, and the enlivening of the bugle, the cavalcade and the train of footmen swept out of the court yard, and descending the winding path, plunged into the heart of the primeval forest. The dogs and the beaters darted into the thick copsewood, and soon the shouts of the huntsmen and the fierce bay of the dogs announced that a wild boar had been found and started. On dashed the merry company, Count Alexis leading on the spur. The lady Anna soon found herself alone, but she pressed her palfrey in the direction of the sounds of the chase as they receded in the distance. Suddenly she found herself in a small clearing, and drew her rein to rest her panting steed. She had not remained long in her position, when she heard, opposite to her, a crashing among the branches, and the next moment a huge wild boar, maddened with pursuit, and foaming with rage, broke into the opening and sprang directly towards her. Her horse, terrified at the apparition, reared so suddenly that he fell backwards, throwing his rider heavily, and narrowly missing crushing her. Springing to his feet, he dashed wildly away with flying mane and rein, while the lady lay at the mercy of the infuriated animal, faint and incapable of exertion.

At that critical moment, a young man, in the livery of the count, dashed before the prostrate form of the lady, and dropping on one knee, levelled his short spear, and sternly received the charge of the boar. Though the weapon was well directed, it shivered in the grasp of the young huntsman; and though he drew his short sword with the rapidity of thought, the boar was upon him. The struggle was short and fierce, and the young huntsman succeeded in slaying the monster, but not until he had received a severe wound in the arm from the tusks of the boar. Heedless of his sufferings, however, he ran to a neighboring rivulet, and filling his cap with water, returned and sprinkled the face of the fainting girl. In a few moments she revived.

Her first words, uttered with a trembling voice, were,—

"Where—where is the wild boar?"

"There, lady," said the huntsman, pointing to the grizzly monster. "His career is ended."

"And it is you who have saved my life," exclaimed Anna, with a grateful smile.

"I did my duty, lady," answered the huntsman.

"But who are you, sir? Let me, at least, know your name that I may remember you in my prayers."

"My name is Michael Erlitz; though your eyes, lady, may never have dwelt on one so lowly as myself, I am ever in your father's train when he goes to the chase. I am Count Tekeli's *slave*," he added, casting his eyes on the ground.

"A slave? and so brave—so handsome!" thought the lady Anna; but she gave no utterance to the thought.

At this moment the count rode up, followed by two or three of his retainers, and throwing himself from his horse, clasped his daughter in his arms.

"My child, my child!" he exclaimed; "thank God, you are alive! I saw your horse dash past me riderless, and flew to your assistance. But there is blood upon your dress."

"It is my blood!" said the slave, calmly.

"Yours, Michael?" cried the count, looking round him. "Now I see it all—the dead boar, the broken spear, your bleeding arm. You saved my daughter's life at the risk of your own!"

"The life of a slave belongs to his master and his master's family," answered Michael, calmly. "Of what value is the existence of a serf? He belongs not to himself. He is of no more account than a horse or a hound."

"Say not so," said Count Alexis, warmly. "Michael, you are a slave no longer. I will directly make out your manumission papers. In the mean time you shall do no menial service; you shall sit at my board, if you will; and be my friend, if you will accept my friendship."

The eagle eye of the young huntsman kindled with rapture. He essayed to speak, but the words died upon his tongue. Falling on his knees, he seized the count's hand, and pressed it to his lips and heart. Tekeli raised him from his humble posture.

"Michael," said he, "henceforth kneel only to your Maker. And now to the castle; your hurt needs care."

"Willingly," said the young man, "would I shed the best blood in my body to obtain my freedom."

"Ho, there!" said the count to his squire; "dismount, and let Michael have your horse; and bring after us Michael's dearly-earned hunting trophy. He has eclipsed us all to-day."

Michael was soon in the saddle, riding next to the lady Anna, who, from time to time, turned her countenance, beaming with gratitude, upon him, and addressed him words of encouragement and kindness; for her proud and imperious nature was entirely subdued and changed, for the time, by the service he had rendered her.

When the cavalcade reached the castle, they found the lady Eudocia, the count's eldest daughter, waiting to receive them. She heard the recital of the morning's adventure with deep interest; but a keen observer would have noticed that she seemed less moved by the recollection of her sister's danger, than by the present condition of the wounded huntsman. It was to her care that he was committed, as she was skilled in the healing art, having inherited the knowledge from her mother. She compelled Michael to give up all active employment, and, in the course of a few weeks, succeeded in effecting a complete restoration of the wounded arm.

Count Tekeli treated the young man with the kindness of a father, losing all his aristocratic prejudices in a generous sense of gratitude. Splendidly attired, promised an honorable career in arms, if he chose to adopt the military profession, his whole future changed by a fortunate accident, Michael was happy in the intimacy of the two sisters. He now dared to aspire to the hand of her whom he had saved, and whom he loved with all the intensity of a passionate nature. Thus weeks and months rolled on like minutes, and he only awaited the delivery of his manumission papers to join the banner of his sovereign.

One day—an eventful day, indeed, for him—he received from Eudocia, the elder sister, a message, inviting him to meet her in a summer house that stood in a small garden connected with the castle. Punctual to the hour named, he presented himself before her.

"Michael," said she, extending her hand to him, "I sent for you to tell you a secret."

Her voice was so tremulous and broken, that the young man gazed earnestly into her face, and saw that she had been weeping, and now with difficulty suppressed her tears.

"Nay," said she, smiling feebly; "it will not be a secret long, for I must tell it to my father as soon as he returns from court with the royal endorsement to your manumission. I am going to leave you all."

"To leave us, lady?"

"Yes; I am going to take the veil."

"You, so beautiful, so young! It cannot be."

"Alas! youth, beauty, are insufficient to secure happiness. The world may be a lonely place, even to the young and beautiful; the cloister is a still and sacred haven on the road to a better world."

"And what has induced you to take this step? I have not noticed hitherto any trace of sorrow or weariness in your countenance."

"You were studying a brighter page—the fair face of my sister. Start not, Michael; I have divined your secret. She loves you, Michael; she loves you with her whole soul. You will wed her and be happy; while I——" She turned away her face to conceal her tears.

The young man heard only the blissful prediction that concerned himself; he noted not the pangs of her who uttered it.

"Dearest lady!" he exclaimed, "you have rendered me the happiest of men;" and dropping on his knees, he seized her hand and covered it with kisses.

"Hark!" said Eudocia, in alarm; "footsteps! We are surprised; I must not be seen here!" and with these words she fled.

Michael sprang to his feet. Before him stood the younger daughter of Count Alexis, her eyes flashing fire, her whole frame quivering with passion. He advanced and took her hand, but she flung it from him fiercely.

"Slave!" she exclaimed, "dare you pollute with your vile touch the hand of a high-born dame—the daughter of your master?"

"Anna, what means this passion?" cried Michael, in astonishment.

"Silence, slave!" cried the imperious woman. "What ho, there!" she added, stamping her foot; "who waits?"

Half a dozen menials sprang to her call.

"Take me this slave to the court yard!" she cried vehemently; "he has been guilty of misbehavior. Let him taste the knout; and woe be to you if you spare him. Away with him! Rid me of his hateful presence!"

While Michael was subjected to this hateful punishment, the vindictive girl, still burning with passion, sought her sister. What passed between them may be conjectured from what follows.

Michael, released from the hands of the menials, stood, with swelling heart and burning brow, in one of the lofty apartments of the castle. He had felt no pain from the lash, but the ignominy of the punishment burned in his very soul, consuming the image that had been in his inner heart for years. The scales had fallen from his eyes, and he now beheld the younger daughter of the count in all the deformity of her moral nature—proud, imperious, passionate, and cruel.

A door opened—a female, with dishevelled hair, and a countenance of agony, rushed forward and threw herself at his feet, embracing his knees convulsively. It was Anna!

"O Michael!" she cried, "forgive me, forgive me! I shall never forgive myself for the pain I inflicted upon you."

"I have suffered no pain," replied Michael, coldly. "Or if I did, it is the duty of a slave to suffer pain. You reminded me this morning that I was still a slave."

"No, no! It is *I* that am *your* slave!" cried the lady. "Your slave—body and soul. Behold! I kiss your feet in token of submission, my lord and master! Michael, I love you—I adore you! I would follow you barefoot to the end of the world. Let me kiss your burning wounds; and O, forgive—forgive me!"

Michael raised her to her feet, and gazed steadily in her countenance.

"Lady," said he, "I loved you years ago, when, as a boy, I was only permitted to gaze on you, as we gaze upon the stars, that we may worship, but never possess. It was this high adoration that refined and ennobled my nature; that, in the mire of thraldom, taught me to aspire—taught me that, though a slave, I was yet a man. Through your silent influence, I was enabled to refine my manners, to cultivate my mind, and to fit myself for the freedom which bounteous Heaven had in store for me."

"Yes, yes!" replied Anna. "You have made yourself all that can render a woman happy. There is not a noble in the land who can boast of accomplishments like yours; and you are beautiful as a virgin's dream of angels."

"These are flattering *words*, lady."

"They come from the heart, Michael."

"You have told me what I am, lady. Now hear what I require in the woman I would wed. She must be beautiful, for beauty should ever mate with beauty; high born, for the lowly of birth are aspiring, and never wed their equals; yet above all, gentle, womanly, kind, forgiving, affectionate. No unsexed Semiramis or Zenobia for me."

"I will make myself all that you desire, Michael."

"We cannot change our natures," replied Michael, coldly.

"But you will forgive me?"

"I am not now in a condition to answer you. Smarting with indignation I can ill suppress, I cannot command the calmness requisite to reply in fit terms to the generous confidence of a high-born lady. Retire to your apartment, lady, for your father is expected momently, and I must see him first alone."

Anna kissed the hand of the slave, and retired slowly. A few moments afterwards the gallop of a horse was heard entering the court yard, and this sound was followed by the appearance of Count Alexis, who threw himself into the arms of Michael, and pressed him to his heart.

"Joy, joy, Michael!" he exclaimed. "You are now free—as free as air! Here are the documents; my slave no longer—my friend always. And as soon as you choose to join the service, you can lead a troop of the royal cavaliers."

Michael poured out his thanks to his generous master.

"And now," said the count, "to touch upon a matter nearer still to my heart. Since the adventure in the forest, I have loved you as a son. To make you such in reality would be to crown my old age with happiness. My daughters are acknowledged to be beautiful, fitting mates for the proudest of the land. I offer you the hand of her you can love the best; make your election, and I doubt not her heart will second my wishes and yours."

"My noble friend," said Michael, "I accept your offer gratefully. You have made me the happiest of men. You will pardon me, I know, when I confess that I have dared to raise my eyes to one of your daughters. Without your consent the secret should have been hidden forever in my own heart, even had it consumed it."

Count Tekeli shook the hand of the young man warmly, and then summoned his two daughters. They obeyed promptly. Both were agitated, and bent their eyes upon the floor.

"Count Tekeli," said Michael, speaking in a calm, clear voice, "I have a word to say to this your younger daughter, the lady Anna."

As her name was uttered, the young girl raised her eyes, inquiringly, to the face of the speaker.

"Lady, but now," said Michael, "you solicited my forgiveness on your knees."

"What!" cried the count, the blood mounting to his temples; "a daughter of mine solicit on her knees forgiveness of one so late my more than vassal— my slave! What is the meaning of this?"

"It means," cried Michael, kindling as he spoke, "that this morning, during your absence, count,—nay, a half hour before your return, this, your younger daughter, in a moment of ill-founded jealousy and rage, usurping your virtual rights,—rights you had yourself annulled,—doomed me to the knout!—yea, had me scourged by menials in the court yard of your castle!"

"How," cried the count, addressing his daughter, "dared you commit this infamy on the person of my friend—the savior of your life?"

"I did, I did!" cried Anna, wringing her hands.

"And you asked me to forgive you," said Michael. "You offered me your hand, and begged me to accept it. My answer is, Never, never, never! The moment you laid the bloody scourge upon my back, you lost your hold upon my heart forever! I were less than a man could I forgive this outrage on my manhood. I saved your life—you repaid it with the lash. It is not the lash that wounds, it is the shame. The one eats into the living flesh, the other into the living heart. Were you ten times more lovely than you are, you would ever be a monster in my eyes."

The tears that coursed freely down the cheeks of the lady Anna ceased to fall as Michael ceased to speak. A deep red flush mounted to her temples, and her eyes, so lately humid, shot forth glances like those of an angry tigress. She turned to the count.

"Father," said she, "will you permit a base-born slave to use such language to your daughter?"

"Silence!" said the old man. "His heart is nobler than yours. More measured terms could not have passed his lips. I should have despised him had he felt and said less. Get thee to thy chamber, and in penitence and prayer relieve thy conscience of the sin thou hast committed."

The lady Anna retired from the apartment with a haughty air and measured step.

"Lady," said Michael, approaching Eudocia, "between your sister and myself there is a gulf impassable. If ever I can forgive her, it must be when those sweet and tender eyes, that speak a heart all steeped in gentleness and love, have smiled upon my hopes, and made me at peace with all the world. Dearest Eudocia, will you accept the devotion of my heart and life?"

He took her hand; it trembled in his grasp, but was not withdrawn. She struggled for composure a moment, and then, resting her head upon his shoulder, wept for joy.

The nuptials of Michael and Eudocia were soon celebrated. A brilliant assemblage graced the old castle on the occasion; but long before the solemnization, the count's younger daughter had fled to a convent to conceal her anger and despair.

OBEYING ORDERS.

The "oldest inhabitant" perfectly remembers the Widow Trotter, who used, many years ago, to inhabit a small wooden house away down in Hanover Street, in somewhat close proximity to Salutation Alley. Well, this widow was blessed with a son, who, like Goldsmith, and many other men distinguished in after life, was the dunce of his class. Numerous were the floggings which his stupidity brought upon him, and the road to knowledge was with him truly a "wale of tears."

One day he came home, as usual, with red eyes and hands.

"O, you blockhead!" screamed his mother,—she was a bit of a virago, Mrs. Trotter was,—"you've ben gettin' another lickin', I know."

"O, yes," replied young Mr. Trotter; "that's one uv the reg'lar exercises—lickin' me. 'Arter I've licked Trotter,' sez the master, 'I'll hear the 'rithmetic class.' But, mother, to change the subject, as the criminal said, when he found the judge was getting personal, is there enny arrand I can do for you?"

"Yes," grumbled the widow; "only you're so eternal slow about every thing you undertake—go get a pitcher of water, and be four years about it, will ye?"

Bob Trotter took the pitcher, and wended his way in the direction of the street pump; but he hadn't got far when he encountered his friend, Joe Buffer, the mate of a vessel, issuing from his house, dragging a heavy sea chest after him.

"Come Bob," said Joe, "bear a hand, and help us down to Long Wharf with this."

"Well, so I would," answered Bob, "only you see mother sent me arter a pitcher o' water."

"What do you care about your mother—she don't care for you? Come along."

"Well," said Bob, "first let me hide the pitcher where I can find it again."

With these words he stowed away his earthenware under a flight of stone steps, and accompanied his friend aboard his ship. The pilot was urging the captain to cast off, and take advantage of the tide and wind, but the latter was awaiting the arrival of a boy who had shipped the day before, wishing no good to his eyes for the delay he had occasioned.

At last he turned to Bob, and said,—

"What do you say, youngster, to shipping with me? I'll treat you well, and give you ten dollars a month."

"I should like to go," said Bob, hesitatingly. "But my mother——"

"Hang your mother!" interrupted the captain. "She'll be glad to get rid of you. Come—will you go?"

"I hain't got no clothes."

"Here's a chestfull. That other chap was just your size; they'll fit you to a T."

"I'll go."

"Cast off that line there!" shouted the captain; and the ship fell off with the tide, and was soon standing down the bay with a fair wind, and every stitch of canvas set. She was bound for the northwest coast, *via* Canton, and back again, which was then called the "double voyage," and usually occupied about four years.

In the mean while, the non-appearance of Bob seriously alarmed his mother. A night passed, and the town crier was called into requisition a week, when she gave him up, had a note read for her in meeting, and went into mourning.

Just four years after these occurrences the ship returned to port, and Bob and his friend were paid off. The wages of the widow's son amounted to just four hundred and eighty dollars, and he found, on squaring his accounts with the captain, that his advances had amounted to the odd tens, and four hundred dollars clear were the fruits of his long cruise.

As he walked in the direction of his mother's house, in company with Joe, he scanned with a curious eye the houses, the shops, and the people that he passed. Nothing appeared changed; the same signs indicated an unchanging hospitality on the part of the same landlords, the same lumpers were standing at the same corners—it seemed as if he had been gone only a day. With the old sights and sounds, Bob's old feelings revived, and he almost dreaded to see, debouching from some alley, a detachment of boys sent by his ancient enemy, the schoolmaster, to know why he had been playing truant, and to carry him back to receive the customary walloping.

When he was quite near home, he said,—

"Joe, I wonder if any body's found that old pitcher."

He stooped down, thrust his arm under the stone steps, and withdrew the identical piece of earthenware he had deposited there just four years ago.

Having rinsed and filled it at the pump, he walked into his mother's house, and found her seated in her accustomed arm chair. She looked at him for a minute, recognized him, screamed, and exclaimed,—

"Why, Bob! where *have* you been? What have you been doing?"

"Gettin' that pitcher o' water," answered Bob, setting it upon the table. "I always obey orders—you told me to be four years about it, and I was."

THE DEACON'S HORSE.

As you turn a corner of the road, passing the base of a huge hill of granite all overgrown with ivy and scrub oak, the deacon's house comes full in sight. It is a quaint old edifice of wood, whose architecture proclaims it as belonging to the ante-revolutionary period. Innocent of paint, its dingy shingles and moss-grown roof assimilated with the gray tint of the old stone fences and the granite boulders that rise from the surrounding pasture land. The upper story projects over the lower one, and in the huge double door that gives entrance to the hall there are traces of Indian bullets and tomahawks, reminiscences of that period when it was used as a blockhouse and served as a fortalice to protect the inhabitants of the surrounding district, who fled hither for protection from the vengeful steel and lead of the aborigines. On one side of the mansion is an extensive apple orchard of great antiquity, through which runs a living stream, whose babble in the summer solstice, mingled with the hum of insects, is the most refreshing sound to which the ear can listen. On the other side is one of those old-fashioned wells, whose "old oaken bucket" rises to the action of a "sweep." Two immemorial elm trees, in a green old age, shadow the trim shaven lawn in front. Opposite the house, on the other side of the road, is a vast barn, whose open doors, in the latter part of July, afford a glimpse of a compact mass of English hay, destined for the sustenance of the cattle in the dreary months of winter. We must not forget the huge wood pile, suggestive of a cheerful fireside in the long winter evenings.

But where is the deacon's horse? Last year, and for the past twenty years preceding, you could hardly pass of a summer evening, without noticing an old gray quietly feeding by the roadside, lazily brushing off, with his long switch tail, the hungry flies that fastened on his flanks. The landscape is nothing without the old horse. The deacon reared him on the homestead. When a yearling he used to come regularly to the back door and there receive crusts of bread, crumbs of cake, and other delicacies, the free gifts of the children to their pet. He was the most wonderful colt that ever was—as docile as the house dog. When stray poultry trespassed on the grounds, he would lay his little ears back, and putting his nose close to the ground, curling up his lips and showing his white teeth, drive the marauders from the premises with such a "scare," that they would refrain from their incursions for a week to come. But he was incapable of injuring a living thing.

When old enough for use, he submitted to the discipline of bit and bridle without a single opposing effort. And what a fine figure he made in harness! How smartly he trotted off to church carrying the whole family behind him in a Dearborn wagon! How proud was his carriage when he bore the deacon on his back!

The old man once made a long journey on horseback, to visit a brother who lived in the northern part of New England. A great portion of the way there was only a bridle path to follow through the woods, and this was frequently obstructed by fallen trees. When the impediment was merely a bare trunk, the gallant gray cleared it gayly at a flying leap; when the tree was encumbered with branches, he clambered over it like a wild cat. Once the deacon was obliged to dismount, and crawl on his hands and knees through the dense branches; the sagacious horse imitated his example, and worked his way through like a panther.

But age came upon the good gray. His sight began to fail—his knees to falter. His teeth were entirely worn away.

After a bitter struggle the deacon concluded to replace him by a younger horse. Life had become a burden to the old family servant, of which it was a mercy to relieve him. Yet, even then, the deacon was reluctant to give a positive order for his execution.

One day he called his eldest son to him.

"Abijah," said he, "I'm going over to W., to get that colt I was speaking about. While I am gone I want you to *dispose* of the poor old gray. I shouldn't like to sell him to any body that would abuse him."

He could say no more—but Abijah understood him. When his father had gone, he went into the meadow, and dug a deep pit, beside which he placed the sods at first removed by the spade. He then carefully loaded his rifle and called to the old gray. The poor animal, who was accustomed to obey the voice of every member of the family, feebly neighed and tottered to the brink of the pit. The young man threw a handkerchief over the horse's eyes, and placing the muzzle of the rifle to his ear, fired. The poor old horse fell, without a groan, into the grave which had been prepared for him. With streaming eyes, Abijah threw the earth over the remains of his playmate, and then carefully replaced the sod.

When the deacon returned with his fine new horse, he manifested no elation at his purchase, nor, though he perceived that the stall was empty, did he trust himself to make any inquiries respecting the old gray. Only the family noticed, that in the course of the afternoon, in wandering through the meadow, he came upon the new-made grave, and though the sods had been carefully replaced, he evidently noticed traces of the spade, and suspected the cause, for he tried the soil with his foot, and was also observed to pass the back of his hand across his eyes. But he never alluded to his old servant.

If there be men who can smile at the grief of a family for the loss of an animal who has been long endeared to them by service and association, be assured that their hearts are not in the right place; and that they are individuals who would exhibit a like callousness to the loss of human friends.

THE CONTRABANDISTA.

A TALE OF THE PACIFIC COAST.

Night was setting in—a clear, starlight night—as a small armed brig was working her way into a little bay upon the western coast of Mexico. She was a trim-built craft, and not too deeply laden to conceal the symmetry of her dark and exquisitely-modelled hull. The cleanness of her run, the elegance of her lines, the rake of her slender masts, and the cut of her sails, showed her, at a glance, to be a Baltimore-built clipper—at the time of which we speak— some years ago—the fastest thing upon the ocean. She was working to windward against a light breeze, and hence was unable to exhibit any thing of her qualities, though a seaman's eye would have decided at a glance that she could sail like a witch. The Zanthe, for that was the name inscribed in gilt letters on her stern and sideboards, might have been a dangerous customer in a brush, for her armament consisted of ten brass eighteens, and her crew of sixty picked seamen—an abundance of men to work the brig, and serve her batteries with satisfaction and credit.

Not to keep the reader any longer in suspense with regard to her character and purpose, we will inform him that the Zanthe was a smuggler, and for some years had been engaged in the illegal game of defrauding the revenue of the Mexican republic. She was commanded by a Scotchman named Morris, and her first mate was a Yankee, answering to the hail of Pardon G. Simpkins, as gallant a fellow and as good a seaman as ever trod a plank. It was her custom to land contraband goods at different points upon the coast where lighters were kept concealed, and where the merchandise was taken charge of by the shore-gang, a numerous and well-appointed body of picked men, mounted and armed to the teeth, and provided with a large number of mules for transporting the goods into the interior. The merchandise, lightered off from the brig, was hidden in the *chaparral*, if it came on shore before the mule trains were ready, and it was piled up with combustibles, in such a manner that, should the *vigilantes* surprise them in sufficient numbers to effect a seizure, and overcome resistance, a match thrown among the booty secured its destruction in a few moments. A smoke by day and a fire by night, upon the shore, was the signal for the brig to approach and come to anchor.

The Zanthe, as we before said, slowly worked her way to her anchorage. One by one, her white sails, on which the last flush of the sunset fires had just faded, were all furled, and, her anchors dropped, she swung round with the tide, and rode in safety. A Bengola light was displayed for a moment from the foretop, and answered by another from the shore.

"All right, cap'n," said the mate, walking aft to where Morris was standing, near the wheel. "The critters have seen us, and that are firework means that there aint no vigilantes round abeout. I spose we shall hev the lighters along side airly in the mornin'."

"Yes," said the captain. "I wonder whether Don Martinez is with the shore gang."

"Not knowin', can't say," replied the mate. "Most likely he is, howsomdever—'cause our cargo is vallable, and he'd be likely to look after it."

"You know, Pardon," said the captain, "this is to be our last voyage."

"Edxactly," answered the mate.

"And I hope it will turn out well for the owners. For my part, I'm tired of this life. Circumstances induced me to adopt it; but I can't say that in my conscience I have ever approved it."

"Why, cap'n, you astonish me!" exclaimed the mate. "You don't mean to say that you think it's any harm to cheat the greasers."

"Yes I do," replied the captain, shaking his head. "And I think the aggravation of the offence is, that I am an adopted citizen of the republic of the stars and stripes. I am engaged in defrauding the government of a sister republic."

"A pretty sort er sister republic," replied the mate, disdainfully. "A poor, miserable set of thievin', throat-cuttin', monte-playin', cattle-stealin', bean-eatin' griffins. If our government had had any spunk, we'd have pitched into 'em long ago. And it was only because they're weaker than we be, that we haven't licked 'em into spun yarn."

"But suppose, Pardon, we should be (a chance that, thank Heaven, has never yet occurred) overhauled by one of their revenue cutters."

"The little Zanthe could walk away from her like a racer from a plough horse."

"But, supposing we were surprised, and lay where we couldn't run."

"Cap'n," said Pardon, glancing along the grim batteries of the Zanthe, "do you see them are lovely bull dogs? And them are sturdy Jacks what's a sittin' on the breeches of the guns? What on airth was they made for? A couple of broadsides, starboard and larboard, would settle the hash of the smartest revenue cutter that ever dipped her fore foot in the water."

"And the after thought would never trouble you, Pardon?"

"Never! 'shelp me, Bob," replied the mate, energetically. "Greasers isn't human bein's. Besides, it's all fair play, life for life, and the gentleman with the single fluke tail take the loser. Haint they set a price on our heads? Eight thousand dollars on your'n, and five thousand on mine? I never was worth five thousand down at Portland; but if they've marked me up too high, it's their own look out. They'll never be called upon to pay it. But this sellin' a fellur's head standin', like a lot of firewood, is excessively aggravatin', and gets a fellur's mad up. But, hallo, cap'n, here comes a shore boat. I'll bet it's Don Martinez."

A row boat, manned by eight Mexicans, with a muffled figure in the stern sheets, now pulled out for the brig, and soon lay alongside. On being challenged, a preconcerted watchword was given in reply, and the oars being shipped, a couple of boat hooks held the boat fast at the foot of the starboard side-ladder. This done, the person in the stern sheets arose and prepared to ascend the brig's side.

"Petticoats, by thunder!" muttered the mate. "What does this mean, cap'n?"

Captain Morris was evidently surprised at the sex of his visitor, but he assisted and welcomed her on board with the frank courtesy of a seaman. The light of a battle lantern that stood upon the harness cask, displayed the dark but handsome features of a young Mexican señorita, whose small and graceful hand, sparkling with rings, gathered her silken *rebosa* around her symmetrical figure, in folds that would have enchanted an artist.

"Señor captain," said she, "I bear you a message from Martinez. He bade me tell you to land half your cargo here to-morrow, as before agreed upon. The remainder goes to Santa Rosara, fifty miles to the northward, where he awaits you with a chosen band."

"Señorita," replied the captain, with hesitation, "it were ungallant to express a doubt. But ours is a perilous business, and on the mere word of a stranger— though that stranger be an accomplished lady——"

"O, I come furnished with credentials, señor," interrupted the lady, with a smile; "there is a letter from Martinez."

Captain Morris hastily perused the letter which the lady handed him. Its contents vouched for her fidelity, and, intimating that the lady was a dear friend of his, and likely to be soon intimately connected with him, committed her to the charge of the captain, and requested him to bring her on to Santa Rosara on board the brig.

Morris immediately expressed his sense of the honor done him, and escorted the señorita below, where he abandoned his state room and cabin to her use.

Pardon G. Simpkins walked his watch in great ill humor, muttering to himself incessantly.

"What in the blazes keeps these here women folks continually emergin' from their aliment and mixin' into other spheres? They're well enough ashore, but on soundin's and blue water they beat old Nick. And aboard a *contrabandista*, too! It's enough to make a Quaker kick his grandmother. Howsomdever, Morris is just soft-headed fool enough to like it, and think it all fine fun. I shouldn't wonder if he was ass enough to get spliced one of these days, and take his wife to sea. I think I see a doggarytype of myself took as mate of a vessel that sails with a cap'n's wife aboard."

And, chuckling at this idea, he put an extra quid in his mouth, and ruminated in a better frame of mind.

In the morning, Mr. Simpkins turned out betimes to prepare for the landing of a portion of the cargo; and he was busied in this duty, when an incident occurred that might well have startled a less ready and self-possessed man than the mate of the Zanthe.

Suddenly rounding the headland on the north, a cutter, with the Mexican flag flying at her mizzen peak, and the muzzles of her guns gleaming through the port holes, came in view of the astonished mate. She stood into the bay, till within rifle shot of the bow of the Zanthe, when she dropped her sails and came to anchor.

As she accomplished this manœuvre, the mate mustered the crew, run out his guns, which were all shotted, and then quietly roused the captain and brought him on deck.

"That looks a little wicked, cap'n," said the mate, pointing at the revenue cutter.

The captain shook his head.

"Now, cap'n," said the mate, briskly, "just speak the word, and I'll give him my starboard battery before the slow-motioned critter fires a gun."

"No, no," said the captain; "wait!"

Mr. Simpkins looked fixedly at the captain, thrust his hands deep into the pockets of his pea jacket, and sitting down on the breech of a gun, whistled Yankee Doodle in such slow time that it sounded like a dead march.

In another minute, a barge was lowered from the side of the Mexican cutter, and manned with armed sailors, while an officer in uniform took his seat in the stern sheets.

The barge pulled alongside, Captain Morris neither hailing nor offering to take any action in the premises. Leaving only a boatkeeper in the barge, the Mexican officer, followed by his crew, sprang up the ladder, and bounding on deck, struck his drawn sword on the capstan, and announced the Zanthe as his prize.

"To whom shall I have the honor of surrendering?" asked Captain Morris, touching his hat.

"My name," said the officer, glancing from a paper he held in his hand, as he spoke, "is Captain Ramon Morena, of the Vengador cutter. You, I presume, are Captain Morris, of the Zanthe."

Morris bowed.

"And you are Pardon G. Simpkins, I suppose," said the Mexican, addressing the mate.

"Pardon G. Simpkins—five thousand dollars," replied that gentleman.

"Captain Morena," said Morris, "before we proceed to business, do me the favor to walk into my cabin. While we are below," he added, "I trust your men will be ordered not to maltreat my poor fellows."

The Mexican captain glanced, with some surprise, at the formidable array of men upon the deck of the Zanthe, and then, after a few words in Spanish to his boat's crew, followed the captain and mate into the cabin.

Captain Morena was a very fine looking man of thirty, with magnificent hair and mustaches, and wore a very showy uniform. He threw himself carelessly upon the transom, and laid his sword upon the cabin table, while Morris and the mate seated themselves on camp stools.

"Señor capitan," said Morris, "I trust, though it be early in the day, that you have no objection to take a glass of wine with me."

The Mexican assented to the proposition, and the steward produced a bottle, glasses, and cigars.

"Your health, capitan," said Morris, with a courteous smile; "and may you ever be as successful as on the present occasion."

"Muchas gracias señor," replied the Mexican; "you bear the loss of your brig very good humoredly. What may she be worth?"

"She cost thirty thousand dollars in Baltimore," replied Morris.

"You must regret to lose her."

"That admits no question, señor."

"But that is of minor importance, compared with your other loss."

"What loss?"

"The loss of your life. I fear nothing can save you or your friend here. Yet, perhaps, intercession may do something. I suppose you would prefer being shot to hanging from the yard-arm."

"Decidedly," answered Morris.

"Or working for life on the highway, with a ball and chain, you would think preferable to both."

"Cap'n Morris," said the mate, speaking in English, "it strikes me that our friend in the hairy face is a leetle grain out in his reckoning; 'pears to me, that instead of our bein' in his power, he's in ourn. Just say the word, and I'll gin the Vengador a broadside that'll sink her in the shiver of a main topsail."

"You are right, Pardon," said the captain, smiling; "the gentleman has missed a figure, certainly. Captain Morena," he added, speaking in Spanish, "you have made a small mistake; you are *my* prisoner, sir. Nay, start not; you are completely in my power. Dare but to breathe another word of menace, or offer to resist me, and the Vengador shall go to Davy Jones. Pass me that sword."

Morena, taken by surprise, obeyed.

"Gi' me his toastin' fork, cap'n," said the mate, "and I'll lock it up in my state room;" which was done almost as soon as said.

"And now, Captain Morena," said Morris, "just walk on deck and explain matters to your people, and then I'll show you how fast a Yankee crew and Mexican lightermen can unload a contrabandista."

They adjourned to the deck, and the Mexican captain was compelled to remain an inactive witness, while boat load after boat load of contraband goods was landed under his own eyes, and the very guns of his cutter. When the work was finished, Captain Morris approached Morena, and said,—

"Captain, I have a word to say to you. I am going up the coast fifty miles, to land the remainder of my cargo at Santa Rosara. Give me your word that you will not follow and molest me, that you will not breathe a word of what you have seen and heard, and I will restore your sword and release you on *parole*."

The revenue captain gave the required pledge, and his sword was restored; after which his men were permitted to man the barge.

"And now, captain, one bumper at parting," said the hospitable Morris. "The steward has just opened a fresh bottle, and besides I have a pleasant surprise for you."

As they entered the cabin, Morena started back and uttered an exclamation as his eyes fell on the beautiful face and graceful figure of the Mexican señorita, who had taken her seat at the table.

"Maria!" he exclaimed.

"Yes," replied the lady, with sparkling eyes and heightened color. "I have escaped your power. The man who basely sought to coerce my inclinations has been baffled, and ere another sun has set, I shall be the bride of the smuggler Martinez."

"Malediction!" cried the Mexican.

"Come, come, cap'n," said the mate, "take a horn, and settle your proud stomach."

"Never," said the Mexican. "A curse on all of ye!" and he sprang to the deck, threw himself into his barge, and was soon aboard of the cutter.

As the clipper brig, with all her canvas set, and her larboard tacks aboard, bowed gracefully to the freshening breeze, and bowled away under the stern of the Mexican cutter, the mate said to the captain,—

"Cap'n, I wish you'd just let me give that fellur a broadside, if it was only just to clean the guns, afore I run 'em in."

"No, no," replied the captain, smiling, "honor bright, my boy. We'll keep our word to him."

"That's more than he'll do to us," answered the mate, "or I don't know the natur of a greaser. One broadside from our starboard battery would settle him, and save all future trouble, and make every thing pleasant and comfortable on all sides."

But Captain Morris would not listen to reason, and so the guns were secured, and the ports closed, and the little Zanthe went bounding on her course to Santa Rosara.

She came to anchor in a deep bay which she entered at nightfall, and almost immediately a shore boat, under the command of Martinez, boarded the brig. The meeting between the smuggler and his bride was so affectionate, as to call a tear even into the eye of Mr. Pardon G. Simpkins. The smuggler laughed loudly when he heard of the discomfiture of Captain Morena, the discarded suitor of the señorita Maria.

The next day all hands were employed in landing the remainder of the cargo, and at night a very worthy and accommodating priest came off from the shore, and united Martinez and Maria in the bonds of holy matrimony. The nuptials were celebrated with great rejoicings and revelry, and the fun was kept up till a late hour of the night, when the happy couple retired to the cabin.

The first faint streaks of dawn were beginning to appear in the east, when the ever vigilant ear of the mate, who never took a wink of sleep while the brig was lying on shore, detected the cautious plunge of oars, and soon he descried a barge pulling towards the brig.

"Catch a weazle asleep," said the Yankee to himself; "these greasers don't know as much as a farrer hen." And without arousing the captain, he quietly mustered the crew, and with as little noise as possible, the guns were run out upon the starboard side, which the boat was fast approaching.

A moment after he hailed. No answer was given, but the light of the lanterns flashed on the arms of a large body of men, and the mate recognized the figure of the captain of the Vengador in the stern sheets.

"Sheer off," shouted the mate, "or by the shade of Gin'ral Jackson, I'll blow you all to Davy Jones."

"Pull for your lives," shouted the voice of Morena; and the boat bounded towards the brig.

"Fire!" cried the mate.

Crash went the guns! The iron hurtled through the air, and the splintering of wood, as the metal struck the barge, was distinctly heard amid the groans and shrieks of the vigilantes.

In one moment it was all over. Morris and Martinez rushed to the deck.

"What's the matter, Pardon?" asked the former.

"Nothin', cap'n—cap'n, nothin'," answered the mate. "Only there aint quite so many greasers in the world at present, as there was five minutes since. Morena broke his parole, and tried to board us by surprise, and I gin' him my starboard battery—that's all."

"Then I'm off for blue water!" cried the captain.

"And I for the mountains!" said Martinez. "The mules are all packed and the horses saddled. The vigilantes must wear sharp spurs if they catch us."

It was a hurried parting—that of the smuggler and his bride with the captain and mate of the Zanthe. But they got safely on shore, and the whole band effected their escape.

The Zanthe spread her wings, and some days afterwards was crossing the equator. She was never known again as a free trader. The captain and mate had both "made their piles," and after arriving at the Atlantic states retired from sea. Pardon G. Simpkins took up his residence in Boston, and during the late war with Mexico, was very prominent in his denunciations of that republic, and very liberal in his donations to the Massachusetts regiment, to the members of which his parting admonition was, to "give them greasers fits."

THE STAGE-STRUCK GENTLEMAN.

Few amateurs of the drama have passed through their town lives, without having been, at some one period of their career, what is called stage struck, afflicted with a maniacal desire to make a "first appearance," to be designated in posters as a "YOUNG GENTLEMAN OF THIS CITY," in connection with one Mr. Shakspeare, the "author of certain plays." The stage-struck youth is easily recognized by certain symptoms which manifest themselves at an early stage of the disorder. He is apt to pass his hand frequently through his "horrent locks," to frown darkly without any possible reason, and to look daggers at his landlady when invited to help himself to brown-bread toast. His voice, in imitation of the "Boy," the "Great American tragedian," alternates between the deep bass of a veteran porker and the mellifluous tenor of a "pig's whisper." He is apt to roll his eyes quickly from side to side, to gasp and heave his chest most unaccountably. He reads nothing of the papers but the theatrical advertisements and critiques. He has an acquaintance with two or three fourth-rate stock actors and a scene shifter, and is consequently "up" in any amount of professional information and slang, which he retails to every one he meets, without regard to the taste or time of his auditors. Have you seen the new drama of the Parricidal Oysterman? If you have, you must agree with him it is the greatest affair old Pel. has ever brought out; if you have not, you must submit to his contemptuous pity for your ignorance. For a person who passes his evenings in the society of books and friends, or in the country, the stage-struck gentleman has the most profound contempt. How one can live without nightly inhaling the odor of gas and orange peel, is to him a mystery inexplicable. He is aided and abetted in his practices by the sympathy and example of other stage-struck youths, all "foredoomed their fathers' soul to cross," all loathing their daily avocations for the time being, all spending their earnings, or borrowings, or stealings, on bits of pasteboard that admit them to their nightly banquet. The stage struck always copy the traits of the leading actor of the hour, whoever he may be, and grunt and bluster in imitation of "Ned"—meaning Forrest—or quack and stutter *à la* "Bill"—that is, Macready—as the wind of popular favor veers and changes. It is curious, at a representation of the "Gladiator," to winnow these young gentlemen from the mass by the lens of an opera glass. There you may see the knit brows, the high shirt collars, the folded arms, the pursed-up lips, the hats drawn down over the eyes, that are the certain indications of the stage-struck Forrestians.

If, after the performance, fate and a designing oysterman place you in the next box to three or four of these geniuses, you will, unless very much of a philosopher, be disgusted, for the time being, with human nature. Their paltry imitations, their miserable brayings, their misquotations from

Shakspeare, their mendacious accounts of interviews with the "Boy," will be enough to drive you mad. Some such thing as the following will occur:—

Waiter. Here are your oysters, *gentlemen;* ("a slight shade of irony in the emphasis.")

Stage-struck Youth, No. 1, (in a deep guttural tone.) "Let em come in—we're armed!"

Stage-struck Youth, No. 2, (to waiter.) "Red ruffian, retire!"

Stage-struck Youth, No. 3, (to Stage-struck Youth, No. 4.) "How are you *now,* Dick?"

Stage-struck Youth, No. 4. "Richard's himself again!"

O, Dii immortales! can these things be? In other words, *can* such *animals* exist?

It has been calculated by a celebrated mathematician, that out of every fourteen dozen of these stage-struck young gentlemen, one actually makes a first appearance. This event causes an enormous flutter in the circle of aspirants from which the promotion takes place. As the eventful night approaches, the most active and enterprising among them besiege the newspapers with elaborate puffs of their *confrère,* a column long, and are astonished and enraged that editors exclude them entirely, or exscissorize them to a dozen lines. Of what importance is the foreign news, in comparison with the first appearance of Bill Smithy in the arduous character of Hamlet? Has Colonel Greene no sympathy with struggling genius? Or is it the result of an infernal plot of the actors to put down competition, and sustain a professional monopoly?

The stage-struck young gentleman has passed through the fiery ordeal of "rehearsals," has been duly pushed and shaken into his "suit of sables," glittering with steel bugles, his hands have been adorned with black kids, his plumed hat rests upon his brow, his rapier dangles at his side. The curtain goes up and he is pushed upon the stage. His first appearance is the signal for a thundering round of generous applause, in which his faithful fellow-Forrestians are leading *claquers.* But the audience soon discover that he is a "guy" escaped from the *surveillance* an anxious mother. The stage-struck young gentleman is "goosed." Storms of hisses or bursts of ironical applause greet every sentence that he utters, and the curtain finally falls on his disgrace. This generally cures the disease of which we have been speaking. A night of agony, a week of pain, and the young gentleman, disenchanted and disenthralled, looks back upon his temporary mania with feelings of humiliation and surprise, cuts his aiders and abettors, and betakes himself seriously to the rational business of life.

But there are some stage-struck gentlemen whom nothing can convince of their total unfitness for the stage. You may hiss them night after night, you may present them with bouquets of carrots, and wreaths of cabbage leaves and onions, and leather medals, and services of tin plate; and if you find them "insensible to kindness," you may try brickbats—but in vain. They will cling to the stage for life—living, or rather starving, as *attachés* to some theatre, the signal for disturbance whenever they present themselves; detected by the lynx eyes of the public, whether disguised as Roman citizens or Neapolitan brigands, and severely punished for incompetency by heaped-up insult and abuse. These men live and die miserably; yet, doubtless, their lives are checkered with rays of hope; they regard themselves as martyrs, and die with the secret consciousness that they have "acted well their parts."

THE DIAMOND STAR;

OR,

THE ENGLISHMAN'S ADVENTURE.

A STORY OF VALENCIA.

In a fine summer night in the latter half of the seventeenth century, (the day and year are immaterial,) Clarence Landon, a handsome and high-spirited young Englishman, who had been passing some time in the south of Spain, was standing on the banks of the Guadalquiver, in the environs of the ancient city of Valencia, watching with anxious eyes the fading sails of a small felucca, just visible in the golden rays of the rising moon, as, catching a breath of the freshening western breeze, they bore the light craft out upon the blue bosom of the Mediterranean. Though the scene was one of surpassing beauty, though the air was balmy, and came to his brow laden with the fragrance of the orange, the myrtle, and the rose, the expression of the young man's face was melancholy in the extreme.

"Too late!" he muttered to himself; "too late! It is hard, after having ventured so much for them, that I should have been baffled in my attempt to escape with them. However, they are safe and happy. If this breeze holds, they will soon pass Cape St. Martin. Dear Estella, how I value this pledge of your friendship and gratitude."

And the young man, after raising to his lips a small diamond star, attached to a golden chain, deposited the trinket in his bosom, and then, with a parting glance at the distant vessel, turned homewards in the direction of the city gates.

Absorbed in his own reflections, he did not notice that his footsteps were dogged by a tall figure, muffled in a black cloak, which pursued him in the moonlight, like his shadow, and left him only when he entered his *posada*.

Landon spent some time in his room in reading and arranging letters and papers; and when the clock of a neighboring cathedral sounded the hour of eleven, threw himself upon his bed without undressing, and was soon asleep. From a disturbed and unrefreshing slumber, crowded with vexatious visions, he was suddenly and rudely roused by a rough hand laid upon his shoulder. He started upright in bed, and gazed around him with astonishment. His chamber was filled by half a dozen sinister-looking men, robed entirely in black, in whom he recognized, not without a shudder, the dreaded familiars of the Holy Office, the officials of the Inquisitorial Tribune. His first impulse was to grope for his arms; but his sword and pistols had been removed. A rough voice bade him arise and follow, and he had no choice but to obey the mandate. Preceded and followed by the familiars, who were all armed, as he judged by the clash of steel that attended each footstep, though no weapons were apparent, he descended the staircase, came out upon the street, and was conducted through many a winding lane and passage to a low-browed arch, which opened into the basement story of a huge embattled building, that rose like a fortress before him. The conductor of the band halted here, and knocking thrice upon an oaken door, studded with huge iron nails, it was opened silently, and the party entered a dark, subterranean passage of stone, lighted only by a smoky cresset lamp swinging in a recess.

After passing through this corridor, Landon was conducted into a huge vaulted hall, dimly illuminated by the branches of an iron chandelier, by whose light he discovered in front of him a raised platform, on which were seated three men, robed in black, while before them, at a table, sat two others, similarly attired, with writing implements before them. On the platform was planted a huge banner, the blazon on the folds of which was a wooden cross, flanked by a branch of olive and a naked sword, the motto being, "*Exurge, Domine, et judica causam tuam.*" *Rise, Lord, and judge thy cause.* It wanted neither this formidable standard, nor the implements of torture scattered around, to convince the young Englishman that he stood in the halls of the Inquisition.

After being permitted to stand some time before the judges, that his mind might be impressed with the terrors of the place, the principal Inquisitor addressed him, demanding his name.

"Clarence Landon," was the reply.

"Your birthplace?"

"London, England."

"Your age?"

"Twenty-five years."

"Occupation?"

"I am a gentleman of fortune, with no pursuit but that of knowledge and pleasure."

"You are accused," said the judge, "of having aided and abetted a countryman of yours, named Walter Hamilton, in seducing and carrying off Estella Martinez, a lady of a noble house, and a sister of St. Ursula. How say you, guilty or not guilty?"

"I am not guilty—I am not capable of the infamy with which you charge me."

"He refuses to confess," said the judge, turning to a familiar, the sworn tormentor. "We must try the question. Sanchez, is the rack prepared?"

The man addressed was a brawny, muscular ruffian, with a livid and forbidding countenance, whose dark eyes sparkled with pleasure as he bowed assent to the interrogation.

"Hold!" cried Landon. "The truth can no longer harm any but myself; and though you may inflict death upon me, you shall not enjoy the fiendish satisfaction of mutilating my limbs with your horrid enginery. I did aid Hamilton, not indeed in ruining an injured maiden, but in rescuing from the thraldom she abhorred a lovely lady whom Providence formed to make the happiness of an honorable man. By this time Estella is a happy bride."

"Her joys will be shortened," said the inquisitor, frowning. "They cannot long elude the power of Rodrigo d'Almonte, at once judge of the Holy Office and governor of Valencia."

"Moderate your transports, governor," replied the Englishman, boldly; "the fugitives are beyond your reach. This very night a swift-winged felucca bore them away from these accursed shores, to a land of liberty and happiness."

The brow of Rodrigo grew black as night.

"Insolent!" he answered; "you have outraged and set at naught the authority of church and state; your life shall pay the forfeit."

"Be it so," replied Landon, folding his arms; "but let me tell you, that for every drop of blood shed, my country will demand a life. The cross of St. George protects the meanest subject of the English crown."

Rodrigo d'Almonte made no reply, but waving his hand, Landon was removed from the tribunal and thrown into a dungeon on the same floor with the hall of torture.

Towards the close of a sultry summer day, the narrow streets of Valencia wore an aspect of unusual activity and life, filled, as they were, with representatives of every class of citizens. The tide of human beings seemed to be setting in one direction, towards a plaza, or square, in the centre. The Alameda was deserted by its fashionable promenaders; and young and old— all, indeed, who were not bedridden—were at length congregated in the square. The attraction was soon explained; for in the centre of the plaza was seen a lofty platform of wood, on which was erected a stout stake or pillar, to which was affixed an iron chain and ring. Around this were heaped, to the height of several feet, huge fagots of dry wood, ready for the torch. A large body of men-at-arms kept the crowd back from a large open space around the platform. These preparations were made, so the popular rumor ran, for the punishment of a young Englishman, who had aided a Spanish nun in the violation of her vows.

The numerous bells of the city were tolling heavily; and at length, after the patience of the populace had been nearly exhausted, the head of a column of men, marching in slow time, was seen to enter upon the plaza. First came the governor's guard, their steel caps and cuirasses and halberds polished like silver. After these, walked the officials of the Inquisition, and some friars of the order of St. Dominic, surrounding the unfortunate Landon, who wore the *corazo*, or pointed cap, upon his head, and the *san benito*, a robe painted all over with flames and devils, typifying the awful fate which awaited him. He ascended the scaffold with a firm step, while the *cortége* ranged themselves around it; and the governor of Valencia, mounted on a splendid barbed charger, and wearing his inquisitorial robes over his military uniform, rode into the square, amid the *vivas* of the crowd and the presented arms of the troops, and made a sign for the ceremony to proceed.

As an officer, appointed for the purpose, was about to read the sentence, a great tumult arose in the square, and attracted the attention of all the spectators.

"What is the meaning of this, Alvarez?" asked the governor, addressing one of his lieutenants.

"The people, please your excellency, have got hold of Isaac, the rich Jew, and insist on his beholding the august spectacle of the *auto da fe.*"

"The unbelieving dog has never liked these brave shows," answered the governor, with a grim smile, "since his well-beloved brother, Issachar, expiated his heresy on this spot in the great auto, when we burned twenty of his tribe before the king. Beshrew my heart! he abuses my clemency in permitting him to hold house and gold here in Valencia. He shall behold the execution! Make room there, and drag him into the heart of the hollow square."

The cruel order was obeyed; and the old Jew, who was a mild and venerable-looking man, was forced into the centre of the plaza, whence he could have a full view of the horrid scene about to be enacted.

But the indignities to which he had been subjected aroused a latent spark of fire even in the soul of the aged Hebrew. He lifted up his voice and cried aloud:—

"Spaniards! Christians! are ye men, or are ye brutes? Fear ye not the vengeance of Heaven, when ye enact deeds that would make the savage blush? Think ye that Heaven will long withhold its vengeance from atrocities that cry aloud to it night and day—that the innocent blood ye have spilt will sink, unavenged, into the earth? Fear and tremble, for the hour of wrath and woe is at hand!"

The energy and eloquence with which he spoke sent a strange thrill of terror through the crowd. The governor, alone insensible to fear, shouted from his saddle:—

"Tremble for yourself, Isaac! for, by the rood! if you dare question the justice of the Holy Office, you shall share the fate of yonder prisoner."

"I fear not the wrath of man," replied the Jew; "fear you the wrath of Heaven!"

And at this moment, as if in vindication of his words, a heavy clap of thunder, that shook the city like the discharge of a park of artillery, broke upon the ear; and one of those sudden storms, so common in southerly latitudes, rolled up its dark masses of clouds, and the light of day was suddenly quenched, as in an eclipse. Vivid flashes of lightning lit the upturned and terror-stricken faces of the cowering multitude. At the same time, the wind howled fiercely through the streets that debouched upon the plaza, and tore the plumage that waved and tossed upon the helmets of the soldiery.

"Executioner!" roared the governor, whose high, stern tones of military command were heard above the roar of the sudden tornado, "do your duty! Set fire to the fagots!"

The order was obeyed; the torch was applied, and already a quivering, lurid flame shot up at the feet of the luckless Landon, when the storm burst forth with ungovernable fury. The scaffolding was blown down, the fragments scattered, and the rain, descending in torrents, instantly quenched both torch and fagot. The vast crowd was thrown into utter confusion; the terrified horses of the cavalry plunged madly among the footmen; hundreds fell and were trampled under foot; and prayers, shrieks, and imprecations filled the darkened air.

Landon was unhurt amid the wreck of the sacrificial pyre. A ray of hope shot up in his heart. Scrambling out of the ruins, unobserved and unpursued, he fled down the nearest lane with the utmost speed. Anxious to obtain shelter, he, without even a thought, climbed a garden wall; once within which he was safe, for a moment, from pursuit. Rushing through a shaded alley of the garden, he found himself at the door of a large and splendid house. Almost without a hope of finding it yield, he tried the handle, and the door opened. Silently and swiftly he ascended a large, stone staircase, and took refuge in the first apartment which he found before him. A beautiful young girl, the only occupant of the room, starting at the fearful apparition of a stranger flying for his life, in the robe of the *san benito*, fell upon her knees and crossed herself repeatedly, as her dark eyes were fixed in terror on the intruder.

"Lady!" cried Landon, "for the love of that Being whom we both worship, though in a different form, take pity on a wretched fellow-being. Save me! save me!"

"You are accursed and condemned," she answered, rising and recoiling.

"I am! I am!—but you know my offence. If you ever loved yourself, you know how to pardon it. Think of the horrid fate which awaits me, if you are pitiless."

The lady paused and reflected, Landon watching the expression of her countenance with the most intense anxiety. At length her brow cleared up; there was an expression of sweetness about her rosy lips that revived hope in the heart of the fugitive.

"I will save you if I can," she answered.

"Heaven's best blessing on you for the word!" exclaimed the Englishman.

"But you have come to a dangerous place for shelter and safety," she continued, sadly. "Do you know whose house this is? It is the dwelling of my father, Don Rodrigo d'Almonte, the governor of Valencia."

Landon started back in terror, but he instantly recovered from that feeling.

"You, then," he said, "are Donna Florinda, in praise of whose beauty and goodness all Valencia is eloquent. I feel that I am safe in your hands."

"I will never betray you," said the lady. "You are safe here. It is my bed chamber," she continued, blushing; "but I resign it to you—sure, from your countenance, that you are a cavalier of honor, who will never give me cause to repent of the step."

"Be sure of that."

"Swear it," she said, "upon this trinket, which my father took from your person in the hall of the Inquisition."

Landon took from Florinda's hand the diamond star given him by Estella, and thus mysteriously restored, and pressed it to his lips.

"By this talisman," he said, "by this token, which I prize so highly, I pledge myself not to abuse your confidence, but to repay the priceless service you render me by a life of gratitude."

"You may remain here, then, for the present," said Florinda, "till I can think what can be done for you."

"If I can only make my way to the house of the English ambassador," replied Landon, "I think I can count upon my safety."

Donna Florinda, after lighting a lamp, (for it was now nightfall,) and setting upon a table some wine and fruit, left the chamber, locking the door behind her.

Descending to the garden, she went directly to a secluded arbor, embowered in foliage, at no great distance from the house.

"Cesareo!" she whispered.

A young cavalier, who was concealed in the arbor, instantly advanced, and clasped her in his arms.

"Dear Florinda," he cried, "I feared that you would disappoint me. But we have yet some happy moments to pass together."

"Not a moment, Cesareo," replied the lady; "my father will soon return. I come to beg you to retire instantly, and await another opportunity of meeting."

"You are anxious to get rid of me!" replied the cavalier.

"Not so; my father will soon return, and he will be sure to inquire for me directly."

"Well, then," said the lover, "if it must be so, go you to the house, and leave me the solitary pleasure of watching the window of the room gladdened by your presence."

"No, no, Cesareo," cried Florinda, in terror, "that must not be."

As she said this, her eyes were instinctively turned to the window of her room, and Cesareo's followed the same direction. The shadow of Landon's figure, as it passed between the lamp and the window, was seen defined distinctly on the curtain.

"By Heaven!" cried Cesareo, "there is a man in your bed chamber!"

"My father!" said Florinda.

"You told me in your last breath that he had not returned. You are playing me false, Florinda. You have a lover, and a favored one."

"No, no!" cried the agonized girl. "It is nothing, believe me—trust not appearances. I will explain all."

But at this moment the distant clang of trumpets and kettledrums was heard, announcing the governor's return.

"I must begone!" cried Florinda; "believe me, I am faithful;" and with these words she fled into the house.

"The dream is over!" said Cesareo. "But I will have vengeance on my rival;" and he left the garden, muttering curses, and grasping the cross hilt of his sword.

Florinda flew to her chamber.

"Fly!" she cried to Landon. "I have sheltered you at the risk of my reputation—my father is returning, and you must leave this house. A jealous lover may denounce me, and both of us be ruined forever. Farewell; climb the wall at the back of the garden, and take refuge in the next house. I will still watch over you."

Landon obeyed, and made his escape from the governor's garden just as Don Rodrigo was entering his court yard. He crossed another small garden, and entered a small house at the extremity, the door of which was unbarred, and again found refuge in a room on the first floor, where he concealed himself behind a screen.

He had not been here long before he heard footsteps entering the room, and the voices of two persons in conversation, one of whom was evidently a female, and the other an old man.

"Dear father!" said the female, "I am rejoiced to see that you are returned. You never go forth in this city that you do not leave me trembling for your safety."

"I have passed through much peril, Miriam," replied the man. "Snares and violence have beset my path. I went to carry the gold and the silver I had promised to Jacob, the goldsmith, when, lo! I was beset by the ungodly rabble."

"Dear father!"

"Yea! and they dragged me to their place of skulls—even to their accursed Golgotha, where the blood of mine only brother was drunken by the ravening flames, and where thirty of our brethren perished because they believed in the God of Abraham, and of Isaac, and of Jacob."

"And did they force you to witness the *auto da fe*?"

"They brought me to the place, Miriam—but there the spirit of prophecy descended upon me, and I lifted up my voice and denounced their abominations, even as the prophet of old did the iniquities of the Egyptian king. And lo! Miriam, there was a miracle wrought. The voice of Heaven spake in thunder to rebuke their impious bloodthirstiness. The floodgates of heaven were opened, and the rain descended in mighty torrents, and quenched the Moloch fires kindled by the Christians. And a great wind arose, and the scaffold was destroyed, and the goodly youth that stood thereupon was saved from the death of fire as the multitude were scattered."

"And lives he, father?"

"I fear not," answered the old man, sadly. "For if he were not crushed by the falling scaffold, yet verily the cruel swords of the troopers and the men-at-arms must have sought out his young life."

At this moment, Landon stepped from his concealment.

"No, my friends," said he, "I yet live to thank Heaven for its providential care. I have even found a friend in the household of my bitter enemy, for Donna Florinda d'Almonte sheltered me, and commended me to your roof."

He now had time to scan the persons of his hosts. The elder, Isaac, the Jew, was, as we described him on his appearance in the plaza, a man of venerable appearance, with a mild and noble countenance, wearing the long beard and flowing robes of his race. His daughter, Miriam, had the commanding beauty, the dark eyes, the flowing hair, and the bold features of the daughters of Israel. She was richly clad in robes of silk, and many a jewel of price gleamed in the raven tresses of her hair.

"Thou art safe beneath this roof," said the Hebrew, "for Donna Florinda, though the daughter of the man of tiger blood, hath yet befriended us and ours, and for her sake as well as for thine, thou art welcome."

Landon thanked his new friends for their hospitable pledges.

"I would fain," said the old Hebrew, "give thee garments more fitting than the accursed robe that wraps thy youthful limbs. But of a truth I have none of Spanish fashion, and the Jewish gabardine is almost as fatal to the wearer as the robe of the *san benito*."

"Here comes Reuben," said Miriam. "Welcome home, dear brother."

A handsome youth of sixteen entered at this moment, and saluted his father, his sister, and the stranger. He bore a bundle in his arms.

"I was charged," he said, "by the lady Florinda, to bear this packet to the stranger I should find here. It contains a Spanish dress. She bid me say," he continued, addressing Landon, "that when you have put on these habiliments, you can repair with me to the governor's garden at midnight. The waiting maid and confidant will conduct you through the house to the street, and once there you can make your way to the English ambassador's."

After thanking the youthful messenger, Landon was shown to an apartment, where he was left alone to change his dress. Donna Florinda had supplied him with a plain but handsome cavalier's suit, including mantle, hat, and plume, and in addition to these, a good sword. Landon hailed this latter gift with joy, and buckled the belt with trembling eagerness. He drew the weapon, and found it to be a Toledo blade of the best temper. He kissed the sword with ecstasy.

"Welcome!" he cried, "old friend! With you I can cut through odds, and at least sell my life dearly, if I fall again into the hands of the Philistines."

Returning to his new friends, he sat down to a hearty meal which they had prepared for him, and to which he did an Englishman's justice. At the hour of twelve, his young friend Reuben signified his readiness to accompany him on his adventure.

"Farewell!" he cried; "I owe you a debt that nothing can repay. But believe me that your kindness will always dwell in the heart of Clarence Landon."

Reuben and the Englishman were soon in the governor's garden. It was pitch dark, and they advanced cautiously, groping their way. All at once Landon stumbled against some person.

"Is it you, Reuben?" said he, in a low tone.

But he was instantly grasped by the throat. Dealing his unknown assailant a blow with his clinched hand, which made him release his hold, the Englishman instantly drew his sword and threw himself on guard. His steel was crossed by another blade, and a fierce encounter ensued, the combatants being practised swordsmen, and guided, in the dark, by what swordsmen term the "perception of the blade." Reuben had made his escape, and gone to inform his father of this new disaster. The struggle was brief, for the antagonist of Landon, closing at the peril of his life, and being a man of herculean strength, wrested the sword from the Englishman's grasp, and held him at his mercy.

"Now, dog!" whispered the victor, "have you any thing to offer why I should not take your life as a minion of the tyrant Rodrigo?"

"I scorn to ask my life of an unknown assassin," replied Landon; "but I am no minion of Rodrigo's, and I was even now seeking to escape his clutches."

"If there was light here," said the stranger, "I could see whether you lied, friend, by your looks. You may be palming off a tale upon me. How did you propose to escape Rodrigo?"

"By making my way through his house," answered Landon.

"A likely tale. How are you to gain access to his house?"

"A waiting maid was to let me in."

"Well, I'll test your veracity. I have your life in my hands. You are unarmed; I have rapier and dagger. The experiment costs me nothing."

"It would be idle in me to interrogate you," said Landon; "it would be idle to ask who you are."

"I will answer you frankly," replied the stranger; "I am one of those freebooters whose fortunes are their swords. If I were in Rodrigo's power, my life would not be worth five minutes' purchase; and yet I am seeking him to-night."

"You speak in riddles."

"Perhaps; but be silent now, if you value your life, and follow me."

The stranger, still retaining a firm grasp upon the luckless Landon, approached a door which led into the governor's house, showing, in their progress, a perfect acquaintance with the labyrinthian alleys of the garden. They halted, and a female voice spoke in a whisper, saying, "Here's the key."

The stranger grasped it, and dragging Landon into the house, instantly locked the door behind him. A dark lantern was placed on the floor of the corridor; the stranger told Landon to take this up, and precede him up stairs. Landon obeyed, the stranger following close behind, and giving him whispered directions as to his course.

Having reached a certain door, the stranger took the light and entered a chamber, followed by the wondering Englishman. The walls of the room were heavily draped, and upon a huge bed the governor of Valencia was reclining, buried in a deep slumber.

"He sleeps!" whispered the stranger in the ear of Landon; "he sleeps, as if he had never shed blood—as if the head of my brother had never fallen on the block by the hand of his bloody executioner. He will soon sleep sounder."

"What mean you?" asked Landon.

"Wait and see," was the reply.

The stranger cautiously lifted the light in his left hand, bending over the sleeper, while with his right he drew a broad, sharp poniard from his belt, and raised it in the act to strike. But just as it was descending, Landon caught the assassin's arm, and shouted in his loudest tones,—

"Don Rodrigo, wake!"

"Baffled!" cried the ruffian, with an oath. "You shall pay with your life for interfering."

The governor sprang from his bed in time to witness the deadly struggle between Landon and the midnight assassin. It was short and decisive, for as the robber was aiming a blow at his antagonist, the latter changed the direction, and it was buried to the hilt in his own heart. He fell, and died without a groan. The noise of the struggle had aroused the household, and the servants came pouring into the room with lights, accompanied by Donna Florinda, who was agonized with terror.

"Dear father!" she cried, rushing into the governor's arms, "what does this mean?"

"It means," replied Don Rodrigo, "that this ruffian, who had sworn to take my life because I had condemned his brother to death for manifold misdeeds, has been slain in the attempt by this young man."

"And do you recognize your generous savior?" exclaimed the daughter. "Behold! it is the young Englishman you condemned to perish at the stake. O father!" And she explained the manner in which Landon had been enabled to save the governor's life.

"Young man," said the governor, addressing Landon with deep emotion, "a mightier Power than the hand of man is visible in this. For the life you have saved I will repay you in the same manner. I insure you a full and free pardon, and you shall not have it to say that Don Rodrigo d'Almonte, bad as he has been represented, was a monster of ingratitude."

And he kept his word. Landon soon after set sail for England, in company with the Hebrew family who had sheltered him, and there, in due time, was united to the lovely Miriam, with whose beauty he had been impressed on first sight. In England, he rejoined Hamilton and his Spanish bride, to secure whose happiness he had perilled his own life; and he always preserved Estella's diamond star as a memorial of his adventures in Valencia. Soon after his arrival he received a letter from Donna Florinda, announcing her marriage to Cesareo, whose jealousy had been so signally excited by Landon's shadow on the window curtain. When Don Rodrigo died, he was buried with all the honors due to a soldier, a governor, and an eminent member of that mild and benevolent institution, the Spanish Inquisition.

THE GAME OF CHANCE.

CHAPTER I.

At nightfall, on an autumnal evening, when the stars were just beginning to twinkle overhead like diamonds on a canopy of azure, two young men were standing together, engaged in conversation on the steps of the Black Eagle, a fashionable hotel in one of the principal streets of the gay and celebrated city of Vienna. One of them wore the rich uniform of an Austrian hussar; the other was clad in the civic costume of a gentleman.

"So, all is completed at the ministry of war, except the signature of the commission, and the payment of the purchase money?" said the soldier.

"Exactly so."

"And to-morrow, then," continued the hussar, "I am to congratulate you on the command of a company, and salute you as Captain Ernest Walstein."

The last speaker was Captain Christian Steinfort, an officer who had seen some two years' service.

"Ah! my boy!" continued he, twirling his jet black mustache, "your uniform will be a passport to the smiles of the fair. But you already seem to have made your way to the good graces of Madame Von Berlingen, the rich widow who resides at this hotel."

"Bah! she is forty," answered Ernest, carelessly.

"But in fine preservation, and a beauty for all that," said Captain Steinfort. "The Baron Von Dangerfeld was desperately in love with her; but within a few days, the widow seems rather to have cut him. You are the happy man, after all."

"Undeceive yourself, my dear Christian," said Ernest, blushing; "I have only flirted with the handsome widow. My hand is already engaged to a charming girl, Meena Altenburg, the playmate of my infancy, adopted and brought up by my good father. I am to marry her as soon as I get my company."

"And what is to support you, Captain Ernest?"

"My pay, of course, and the income of the moderate dowry my father, who is well enough off for a farmer, proposes to give his favorite. So, you see my lot in life is settled."

"Precisely so," replied the captain. "But since you are free this evening, I engage you to pass it with me. Have you got any money about you?"

"A good deal. Besides the price of my company, which is safely stowed away in bank notes in this breast pocket, I have a handful of ducats about me, with which I propose purchasing some trinkets for my bride. But I have a gold piece or two that I can spare, if——"

"Poh! poh! I'm well enough provided," answered the captain. "You know this is pay day. Come along."

"But whither?"

"You shall see."

With these words, the captain thrust his arm within that of his companion, and the pair walked off at a rapid rate. After passing through several streets, Steinfort halted, and rang at the door of a stately mansion. It was opened by a servant in handsome livery, and the young gentlemen entered and went up stairs.

Walstein soon found himself in a scene very different from any of which he had ever dreamed of in his rustic and simple life upon his father's farm. Around a large table, covered with cloth, were seated more than a dozen persons of different ages, all so intent upon what was going forward, that the captain and his friend took their seats unnoticed. At the head of the table sat a man in a gray wig, with a pair of green spectacles upon his nose, before whom lay a pile of gold, and who was busily engaged in paying and receiving money, and in giving an impetus to a small ivory ball, which spun at intervals its appointed course. Walstein soon learned that this was a *rouge-et-noir* table. The gentleman in the gray wig was the banker.

"Make your game, gentlemen," said this individual, "while the ball spins. Your luck's as good as mine. It's all luck, gentlemen, at rouge-et-noir. Rouge-et-noir, gentlemen, the finest in all the world. Black wins; it's yours, sir— twenty ducats, and you've doubled it. Make your game—black or red."

"Try your fortune, Ernest," said the captain. Ernest mechanically put down a few ducats on the red.

"Red wins," said the banker, in the same monotonous tone. "Make your game, gentlemen, while the ball rolls."

Why need we follow the fortunes of Ernest on this fatal evening, as he yielded, step by step, to the seduction to which he was now exposed for the first time in his life? Long after Steinfort left the gambling house, he continued to play. His luck turned. He had soon lost all his winnings, and the money set apart for his bridal presents. Still the ball rolled, and he continued to stake. He had broken the package of bank notes, the money he had received from his father for the purchase of his commission; and though he saw bill after bill swept away before his eyes, he continued to play, in the desperate hope of winning back his losses. At length his last ducat was gone. He rose and left the room, the last words ringing in his ears being,—

"Make your game, gentlemen, while the ball rolls."

Despairing and heart-stricken, the young man sought his hotel and his chamber. On the staircase he encountered Madame Von Berlingen, but he saw her not. His eyes were glazed. He did not notice or return her salutation. He threw himself upon his bed without undressing, and towards morning fell into an unrefreshing and dream-peopled slumber.

When he arose, late the next day, he looked at himself in the glass, but scarcely recognized his own face, so changed was he by the mental agonies he had undergone. When he had paid some little attention to his toilet, he received a message from Madame Von Berlingen, requesting the favor of an interview in her apartments. He mechanically obeyed the summons, though ill fitted to sustain a conversation with a lady.

The widow requested him to be seated.

"Mr. Walstein," said she, with a smile, "you are growing very ungallant. I met you last night upon the staircase; but though I spoke to you, you had not a word or a nod for me."

"Last night, madam," answered the unfortunate young man, "I was beside myself. O madam, if you knew all!"

"I do know all," replied the lady.

"What! that I had been gambling—that I had thrown away—yes, those are the words—every ducat of the money my poor father furnished me with to purchase my commission?"

"Yes, I know all that. But the loss is not irreparable."

"Pardon me, madam. My father, though reputed wealthy, is unable to furnish me with a similar sum, even if I were base enough to accept it at his hands."

"But if some friend were to step forward."

"Alas! I know none."

"Mr. Walstein," said the lady, "I am rich. A loan of the requisite amount would not affect me in the least."

"O madam!" cried the young man, "if you would indeed save me by such generosity, you would be an angel of mercy."

"What is the amount of your loss?" inquired the lady, calmly, as she unlocked her desk.

"Three thousand ducats," answered Ernest. "But I can give you no security for the payment."

"Your note of hand is sufficient," said the lady, handing the young man a package of notes. "Please to count those, and see if the sum is correct. Here are writing materials."

Ernest did as he was bid—counted the money, and then sat down at the desk.

"Write at my dictation," said the lady.

Ernest took up a pen and commenced.

"The date," said the lady.

Ernest wrote it.

"Received of Anna Von Berlingen the sum of three thousand ducats."

Ernest wrote and repeated, "three thousand ducats."

"In consideration whereof, I promise to marry the aforesaid Anna Von Berlingen."

"To marry you?" exclaimed Ernest.

"Ay—to marry me!" said the lady. "Am I deformed—am I ugly—am I poor?"

"I cannot do it—you know not the reason that induces me to refuse."

"Then go home to your father and confess your guilt."

Ernest reflected a few moments. He could not go home to his father with the frightful tale. It was a question between suicide and marriage—he signed the paper.

"Now then, baron," said the widow to herself, as she carefully secured the promise, "you cannot say that you broke the heart of Anna by your cruelty. Take the money, Ernest," she added aloud; "go and purchase your commission."

Ernest obeyed. His dreams of yesterday morning had all been dissipated by his own act; he felt a degraded and broken-spirited criminal. He had sold himself for gold.

CHAPTER II.

"Here comes Captain Ernest!" cried a youthful voice. And a beautiful, blue-eyed girl of nineteen stood at the garden gate of a pretty farm house, watching the approach of a horseman, who, gayly attired in a hussar uniform, was galloping up the road. At her shout of delight, a sturdy old gray-haired man came forth and stood beside her.

"Captain Ernest!" he repeated. "That sounds well. When I was of his age, I only carried a musket in the ranks. I never dreamed then that a son of mine could ever aspire to the epaulet."

Ernest, waving his hand to Meena Altenburg and his father, rode past them to the stable, where he left his horse. He then rushed into the farm house where his father met him.

"What is the meaning of this, boy?" he said. "How wild and haggard you look! And you have avoided Meena—and this, too, upon your wedding day."

"My wedding day—O Heavens! I shall die," said the young man, sinking into a seat.

As soon as he could collect himself, he told his father that he could not marry Meena, and the reason—he had pledged himself to another. The old man, who was the soul of honor, burst forth in violent imprecations, and drove him from his presence. As he left the house, the unfortunate young man encountered a person whom he at once recognized as the Baron Von Dangerfeld, the reputed suitor of Madame Von Berlingen.

"I have been looking for you, Captain Walstein," said the baron, sternly.

"And you have found me," answered the young man, shortly.

"Yes—and I thank Heaven you wear that uniform. It entitles you to meet a German noble, and answer for your conduct."

"I am answerable for my conduct to no living man," retorted Ernest.

"You wear a sword."

"Yes."

"Very well—if you refuse to give satisfaction for the injury you have done me, in robbing me of my mistress, I will proclaim you a coward in the presence of the regiment upon parade."

"O, make yourself easy on that score, baron," answered Ernest. "Life is of too little worth for me to think of shielding it. If you will step with me into the shadow of yonder grove, we can soon regulate our accounts."

The two men walked silently to the appointed spot, and without any preliminary, drew their swords and engaged in combat. The struggle was not of long duration, for Ernest wounded his adversary in the sword arm, and disarmed him.

"Are you satisfied?" he asked.

"I must be so for the present," replied the baron, sullenly. "When I recover, you shall hear from me again."

"As you please," said Ernest, coldly. "In the mean time, suffer me to bind up your arm."

The young man bandaged the wound of his adversary, and as he faltered from the loss of blood, led him towards the farm house. As they approached it, two ladies advanced to meet them—one of them was Meena, the other Madame Von Berlingen.

"Dangerfeld wounded!" cried the latter, bursting into tears—"O, I have been the cause of this: forgive me—forgive me, Dangerfeld, or you will kill me."

"You forget, madame, that you belong to another."

"I am yours only—I can never love another. Nor does the person you allude to," added the lady, turning to Ernest, "cherish any attachment to me."

"My only feeling for you, madame," said Ernest, with meaning, "would be gratitude, were a certain paper destroyed."

"What is the meaning of all this?" asked the father of Ernest, coming forward.

"It means," said Ernest, tearing to atoms the promissory note he received from the widow's hands, "that I had very ugly dreams last night—I dreamed that I played at rouge-et-noir, and lost all the money you gave me to purchase my commission with, and then that I made up the loss by promising——"

"Hush!" said the widow, laying her finger on her lips.

"Then it was all a dream," said the old man.

"Look at my uniform," replied the captain.

"And what did you mean in the story you told me just now?" asked the old man.

"Forget it, father," said Ernest. "Dear Meena, look up, my love. It is our wedding day; and if you do but smile, I'm the happiest dog that wears a sabre and a doliman."

That very day two weddings were celebrated in the farm house, those of Captain Ernest Walstein with the Fraulein Meena Altenburg, and Baron Von Dangerfeld with the yet beautiful and wealthy widow. The captain never tried his luck again at any GAME OF CHANCE.

THE SOLDIER'S SON.

Many, many years ago, at the close of a sultry summer's day, a man of middle age was slowly toiling up a hill in the environs of the pleasant village of Aumont, a small town in the south of France. The wayfarer was clad in the habiliments of a private of the infantry of the line; that is to say, he wore a long-skirted, blue coat, faced with red, much soiled and stained; kerseymere breeches that were once white, met at the knee by tattered gaiters of black cloth, an old battered chapeau, and a haversack, which he carried slung over his right shoulder, on a sheathed sabre. From time to time, he paused and wiped the heavy drops of perspiration that gathered constantly upon his forehead.

"Courage, François, courage," said the soldier to himself; "a few paces more, and you will reach home. Ah, this is sufficiently fatiguing, but nothing to the sands of Egypt. May Heaven preserve my eyesight long enough to see my home—my wife—my brave boy Victor, once more! Grant me but that, kind Heaven, and I think I will repine at nothing that may happen further."

It will be seen from the above, that François Bertrand belonged to the army which had recently covered itself with glory in the Egyptian campaign, under the command of General Bonaparte, a name already famous in military annals. He had fought like a hero in the battle of the Pyramids, when the squares of the French infantry repulsed the brilliant cavalry of Murad Bey, and destroyed the flower of the Mamelukes by the deadly fire of their musketry. Wounded in that memorable battle, he was afterwards attacked by the ophthalmia of the country; but his eyesight, though impaired, was not yet utterly destroyed. Honorably discharged, he had just arrived at Marseilles, from Egypt, and was now on his way home, eager to be folded in the arms of his beloved wife and his young son. So the soldier toiled bravely up the hill, for he knew that the white walls of his cottage and the foliage of his little vineyard would be visible in the valley commanded by the summit.

At length he reached the brow of the hill, and gazed eagerly in the direction of his humble home; but O, agony, it was gone! In its place, a heap of blackened ruins lay smouldering in the sunlight that seemed to mock its desolation. Fatigue—weakness—were instantly forgotten, and the soldier rushed down the brow of the hill to the scene of the disaster. At the gate of his vineyard, he was met by little Victor, a boy of ten.

"A soldier!" cried the boy, who did not recognize his father. "O sir, you come back from the wars, don't you? Perhaps you can tell me something about my poor papa?"

"Victor, my boy, my dear boy! don't you know me?" cried the poor soldier; and he strained his son convulsively in his arms.

"O, I know you now, my dear, dear papa," said the boy, sobbing. "I knew you by the voice—but how changed you are! Why, your mustaches are turned gray."

"Victor, Victor, where is your mother?" gasped the soldier.

"Poor mamma!" said the boy.

"Speak—I charge you, boy."

"She is dead."

"Dead!" François fell to the ground as if a bullet had passed through his brain. When he recovered his senses, he saw Victor kneeling beside him, and bathing his head with cold water, which he had brought in his hat from a neighboring spring. In a few words, the child told him their cottage had taken fire in the night, and been burned to the ground, and his mother had perished in the flames.

A kind cottager soon made his appearance, and conducted the unfortunate father and son to his humble cabin. Here they passed the night and one or two days following. During that time, François Bertrand neither ate nor slept, but wept over his misfortune with an agony that refused all consolation. On the third day only he regained his composure; but it was only to be conscious of a new and overwhelming misfortune. His eyesight was gone. The agony of mind he had suffered, and the tears he had shed, had completed the ravages of his disorder.

"Where are you, Victor?" said the soldier.

"Here, by your side, father; don't you see me?"

"Alas! no, my boy. I can see nothing. Give me your little hand. Your poor father is blind."

The agonizing sobs of the boy told him how keenly he appreciated his father's misfortune.

"Dry your eyes, Victor;" said the soldier. "Remember the instructions of your poor mother, how she taught you to submit with resignation to all the sufferings that Providence sees fit to inflict upon us in this world of sorrow. Henceforth you must see for both of us; you will be my eyes, my boy."

"Yes, father; and I will work for you and support you."

"You are too young and delicate, Victor. We must beg our bread."

"*Beg*, father?"

"Yes, you shall guide my footsteps. There are good people in the world who will pity my infirmities and your youth. When they see my ragged uniform, they will say, 'There is one of the braves who upheld the honor of France upon the burning sands of Egypt,' and they will not fail to drop a few sous into the old soldier's hat. Come, Victor, we must march. We have been too long a burden on our poor neighbor. *Courage, mon enfant, le bon temps viendra.*"

And so the boy and his father set forth upon their wanderings. Neither asked alms; but when seated by the roadside, under the shadow of an overhanging tree, the passer-by would halt, and bestow a small sum upon the worn and blind soldier. Victor was devoted to his father, and Heaven smiled upon his filial affection. Though denied the society and sports so dear to his youth, he was always cheerful and happy in the accomplishment of his task. Often did his innocent gayety beguile his father into a temporary forgetfulness of his sufferings. Then he would place his hand upon the boy's head, and stroking his soft, curling locks, smile sweetly as his sightless eyes were turned towards him, and commence some stirring narrative of military adventure.

In this way, days, weeks, months, and even years rolled by. They were every where well received and kindly treated; and all their physical wants were supplied. But the old soldier often sighed to think of the burden his misfortunes imposed upon his boy, and of his wearing out his young life without congenial companionship, without instruction, without a future beyond the life of a mendicant. He often prayed in secret that death might liberate, his little guide from his voluntary service.

One day, François was seated alone on a stone by the roadside, Victor having gone to the neighboring village on an errand, when he suddenly heard a carriage stop beside him. The occupant, a man of middle age, alighted, and approached the soldier.

"Your name," said the stranger, "is, I think, François Bertrand."

"The same."

"A soldier of the army of Egypt?"

"Yes."

"And that pretty boy who guides you is your son?"

"He is—Heaven bless him!"

"Amen! But has it never occurred to you, my friend, that you are doing him great injustice in keeping him by you at an age when he ought to be getting an education to enable him to push his way in the world?"

"Alas! sir, I have often thought of it. But what could supply his place? and then, who would befriend and educate him?"

"His place might be supplied by a dog—and for his protector, I, myself, who have no son, should be glad to adopt and educate him."

His son's place supplied by a dog! The thought was agony. And to part with Victor! The idea was as cruel as death itself. The old soldier was silent.

"You are silent, my friend. Has my offer offended you?"

"No sir—no. But you will pardon a father's feelings."

"I respect them—and I do not wish to hurry you. Take a day to think of my proposition, and to inform yourself respecting my character and position. I am a merchant. My name is Eugene Marmont, and I reside at No. 17 Rue St. Honoré, Paris. I will meet you at this spot to-morrow at the same hour, and shall then expect an answer. *Au revoir.*" He placed a golden louis in the hand of the soldier, and departed.

A little reflection convinced Bertrand that it was his duty to accept the merchant's offer. But cruel as was the task of reconciling himself to parting with his son, that of inducing Victor to acquiesce in the arrangement was yet more difficult. It required the exercise of authority to sever the ties that bound the son to the father. But it was done—Victor resigned his task to a little dog that was procured by the merchant, and after an agonizing farewell was whirled away in Marmont's carriage.

Years passed on. Victor outstripped all his companions at school, and stood at the head of the military academy; for he was striving to win a name and fortune for his father. The good Marmont, from time to time, endeavored to obtain tidings of the soldier; but the latter had purposely changed his usual route, and, satisfied that his son was in good hands, felt a sort of pride in not intruding his poverty and misfortunes on the notice of Victor's new companions. The boy, himself, was much distressed at not seeing or hearing from his father; but he kept struggling on, saying to himself, "*Courage, Victor—le bon temps viendra*—the good time will come."

On the death of Marmont, he entered the army as a sub-lieutenant, and fought his way up to a captaincy under the eye of the emperor. At the close of a brilliant campaign he was invited to pass a few weeks at the chateau of a general officer named Duvivier, a few leagues from Paris. The company there was brilliant, composed of all that was most beautiful, talented, and distinguished in the circle in which the general moved. But the "star of that goodly company" was Julie Duvivier, the youthful and accomplished daughter of the general. Many distinguished suitors contended for the honor of her hand; but the moment Victor appeared, they felt they had a formidable rival. The belle of the chateau could not help showing her decided preference for him, though, with a modesty and delicacy natural to his position, he refrained from making any decided advances.

One night, however, transported beyond himself by passion, he betrayed the secret of his heart to Julie, as he led her to her seat after an intoxicating waltz. The reception of his almost involuntary avowal was such as to convince him that his affection was returned. But he felt that he had done wrong—and a high sense of honor induced the young soldier immediately to seek the general, and make him a party to his wishes.

He found him alone in the embrasure of a window that opened on the garden of the chateau.

"General," said he, with military frankness, "I love your daughter."

The general started, and cast a glance of displeasure on the young man.

"I know you but slightly, Captain Bertrand," he answered, "but you are aware that the man who marries my daughter must be able to give her her true position in society. Show me the proofs of your nobility and wealth, and I will entertain your proposition."

"Alas!" answered the young soldier in a faltering voice, "I feel that I have erred—pity me—forgive me—I was led astray by a passion too strong to be controlled. I have no name—and my fortune is my sword."

The general bowed coldly, and the young soldier passed out into the garden. It was a brilliant moonlight evening. Every object was defined as clearly as if illuminated by the sun's rays. Removing his chapeau, that the night air might cool his fevered brow, he was about to take his favorite seat beside the fountain where he had passed many hours in weaving bright visions of the future, when he perceived that it was already occupied. An old man in a faded military uniform sat there, with a little dog lying at his feet. One glance was sufficient—the next instant Victor folded his father in his arms.

"Father!" "My boy!" The words were interrupted by convulsive sobs.

After the first passionate greeting was over, the old man passed his hand over his son's dress, and a smile of joy was revealed by the bright moonbeams.

"A soldier! I thought I heard the clatter of your sabre," said the old man. "Where did you get these epaulets?"

"At Austerlitz, father—they were given me by the emperor."

"Long live the emperor!" said the old man. "He never forgets his children."

"No, father. For when he gave me my commission, he said, thoughtfully, 'Bertrand! your name is familiar.' 'Yes, sire—my father served under the tricolor.' 'I remember—he was one of my old Egyptians.' And then—father—then he gave me the cross of the legion—and told me, when I found you, to affix it to your breast in his name."

"It is almost too much!" sighed the old soldier, as the young officer produced the cross and attached it to his father's breast.

"And now," said the young man, "give me your hand as of old, dear father, and let me lead you."

"Whither?"

"Into the saloon of the chateau, to present you to General Duvivier and his guests."

"What! in my rags! before all that grand company?"

"Why not, father? The ragged uniform of a brave soldier who bears the cross of honor on his breast is the proudest decoration in the world. Come, father."

Leading his blind father, young Bertrand reëntered the saloon he had so lately left, and went directly to the general, who was standing, surrounded by his glittering staff.

"General," said he, "*here* is my title of nobility—my father is all the wealth I possess in the world."

Tears started to the general's eyes, and he shook the old soldier warmly by the hand. Then beckoning to Julie, he led her to Victor, and placed her trembling hand in his.

"Let this dear girl," said he, "make amends for my coldness a moment since. A son so noble hearted is worthy of all happiness."

In a word, Captain, afterwards Colonel, Bertrand married the general's daughter, and the happiness of their fireside was completed by the constant presence of the good old soldier, to whose self-denial Victor owed his honors and domestic bliss.

TAKING CHARGE OF A LADY.

The steamer Ben Franklin—it was many years ago, reader—was just on the point of leaving her dock at Providence, when a slender, pale young man, with sandy whiskers and green eyes, who had just safely stowed away his valise, honorably paid his fare, and purchased a supper ticket, and now stood on the upper deck, leaning on his blue cotton umbrella in a mild attitude of contemplation, was accosted by a benevolent-looking old gentleman, in gold-bowed spectacles, upon whose left arm hung a feminine, in a bright mazarine blue broadcloth travelling habit, with a gold watch at her waist, and a green veil over her face, with the (to a timid young man) startling question of,—

"Pray, sir, will you be so kind as to take charge of a lady?"

The slender young man with the blue cotton umbrella blushed up to the roots of his sandy hair, but he bowed deeply and affirmatively.

"We were disappointed in not meeting a friend, sir," continued the benevolent-looking old gentleman, "and so I had to trust to chance for finding an escort to Fanny. Only as far as New York, sir; my daughter will give you very little trouble. She's a strong-minded, independent woman, sir, and abundantly able to take care of herself; but I don't like the idea of ladies travelling alone. If the boat sinks, sir, she's abundantly able to swim ashore. Good by, Fanny."

"Father," said the lady in the blue habit, in a deep and mellow baritone,— rather a queer voice for a woman, though,—"a parting salute!" She threw back her veil, displaying a pair of piercing black eyes, kissed the paternal cheek, veiled the black eyes a moment with a lace-bordered handkerchief, as her sire descended the gang plank,—his exit being deprived of dignity by the sudden withdrawal of the board,—and then placed her arm within that of the sandy-haired young gentleman, and began walking him up and down the promenade deck.

"Isn't this delightful?" said she. "O, what can exceed the pleasure of travelling, when one has a sympathizing friend as a companion!" And she rather pressed the arm of her companion. She was strong-handed as well as strong-minded.

Mr. Brown, for that was the name of the timid young gentleman with the sandy hair and the blue cotton umbrella, was not particularly susceptible, for he had already lost his heart to a sandy-haired young lady, who resided in New York; and, besides, he didn't like strong-minded women; so he asked, very unromantically, but sensibly, if the happy parent of the lady in the blue habit had purchased her a ticket.

"I believe—I am certain that he did not," was the reply. "Father is so forgetful!"

"I'll do it myself then, ma'am—if you'll excuse me a moment. What name?"

"Brown," said the lady.

"My own name!" cried the young man.

"Is it possible?" cried the blue beauty. "What a coincidence! How striking! charming!"

She made no offer of money, and Brown invested his own funds in a passage and supper ticket.

"You dear creature!" cried the lady, when he handed them to her, "you are very attentive. But there was no necessity for this supper ticket. I am the least eater in the world."

She said nothing about the cost of the tickets; and how could Brown broach the subject?

"There's that bell, at last!" she cried, when the supper bell rang; "do let's hurry down, Brown, for people are so rude and eager on board steamboats, that unless you move quick you lose your chance."

Brown was hurried along by his fair friend, and she struggled through the crowd till she headed the column and got an excellent seat at the table. Our sandy-haired friend had exalted opinions of the delicacy of female appetites; he had never helped ladies at a ball, or seen them in a pantry at luncheon time, and fancied they fed as lightly as canary birds. He was rather glad to hear Fanny make that remark about the supper ticket on the promenade deck. But now he found she could eat. The cold drops of perspiration stood upon his forehead as he watched the evidences of her voracity. She was helped four times, by the captain, to beefsteak—no miniature slices either, but huge, broad cubes of solid flesh. A dish of oysters attracted her eye, and she gobbled them up every one. Toast and hot bread disappeared before her ravenous appetite. Sponge and pound cake were despatched with fearful celerity. She took up the attention of one particular nigger, and he looked weary and collapsed when the supper was finished.

Yet, after all this, Fanny paraded the deck, and had the heart to talk about the "orbs of heaven," and Shelley, and Byron, and Tennyson, and Ralph Waldo Emerson, and Fanny Ellsler, and Schiller. Brown was very glad when she retired to the lady's cabin.

The morning he rose late, purposely to avoid her till the boat touched the wharf. He engaged a carriage and hunted up the lady's baggage; fortunately there was not much of it. This done, he escorted her on shore, and handed her into the coach.

"Now, then," said the one-eyed driver,—he had recently lost his eye in a fight, on the first night of his return from Blackwell's Island,—"where away? Oyster House, Merrikin, or Globe?"

"Where are you going, madam?" asked Brown.

"Where are *you* going?" asked the lady.

"To the American, ma'am."

"What a coincidence!" exclaimed the lady, rolling up her black eyes.

"American House, driver."

"All right—in with you!" cried the one-eyed man, as he pitched Brown headlong into the coach, slammed the rickety door on him, sprang to his box, and lashed his sorry steeds into a gallop. In due time they arrived, and a room was engaged for the lady, and one for her cavalier.

Brown went up town as soon as he had dressed, to see his sweetheart, taking particular care to say nothing of his namesake, the fair Fanny.

The next day he was promenading Broadway with Miss S., when he was confronted, opposite St. Paul's, by a furious man, with black whiskers, who halted directly in his path.

"Do you call yourself Brown?" asked the furious man, furiously.

"That's my name, sir," said the sandy-haired young gentleman, meekly.

"It's *my* name, sir," shouted the furious man. "John Brown. Now you know who I am. Do you know Mrs. Brown?"

"I don't know," stammered the unfortunate young man with sandy hair.

"Who did you come from Providence with? answer me that!" roared the furious man, getting as black as his whiskers with apoplectic rage.

"I—I took charge of a lady, certainly," stammered the guiltless but confounded young man.

"You took charge of Mrs. Brown, sir—Fanny Sophonisba Brown, sir, who has left my bed and board without provocation, sir,—*vide* the Providence papers, sir,—left me, sir, because I didn't approve of her strong-minded goings on, sir, her woman's-rights meetings, sir, and her nigger colonizations, sir, and her—but that's enough, sir."

Here Miss Sumker, who was a mild, freckled-faced girl, dropped the arm of her companion, and meekly sat down on a doorstep, and covered her face with a handkerchief.

"Mr. Brown, sir!" cried our poor young friend, finally plucking up a spirit.

"Go it, lemons!" shouted a listening drayman, as he hung over the scene from one of his cart stakes.

"Captain Brown," suggested the furious man, with smothered rage.

"Well then, *Captain* Brown," said Brown, 2d., spitefully, "the lady you allude to is a total stranger to me. She was put under my care by a benevolent-looking old gentleman, with gold-bowed spectacles, and she has already cost me ten dollars, money advanced on her account."

"All persons are forbidden to trust the same, as I will pay no debts of her contracting," said the furious man, with gleams of unmitigated ferocity and savage exultation.

"Then I'm done brown, that's all," said the young man, gloomily. "As for Mrs. Fanny Sophonisba Brown, I never want to see her face again. She is at the American House, and you can recover her by proving property and paying charges. And, for my part, I hope I may be kicked to death by grasshoppers if ever I take charge of a lady again."

This was the largest speech, probably, that the sandy-haired young man had ever made in his life. It was a regular "stunner," though. It convinced Miss Sumker, who had for a moment thought of withdrawing the light of her freckles from him forever, and who now hastened to replace her arm in his; and it convinced Captain Brown, who became suddenly as mild as moonbeams, shook his new acquaintance by the hand, and declared him a "fine young fellow."

But the drayman was disgusted at the affair ending without a fight, and expressed his feelings, as he laid the lash across his horse, by the single exclamation, "Pickles!" thereby insinuating that the nauseous sweetness of the reconciliation required a strong dash of acidity to neutralize its flavor.

The captain regained his strong-minded wife, and our sandy-haired friend went home with Miss Sumker, metamorphosed into Mrs. Brown, having "taken charge" of her for life.

THE NEW YEAR'S BELLS.

How the wind blew on the evening of the 31st December, in the year—but no matter for the date. It came roaring from the north, fraught with the icy chillness of those hyperborean regions that are lost to the sunlight for six months, the realm of ice-ribbed caverns, and snow mountains heaped up above the horizon in the cold and cheerless sky. On it came, that northern blast, howling and tearing, and menacing with destruction every obstacle that crossed its path. It dashed right through a gorge in the mountains, and twisted the arms of the rock-rooted hemlock and the giant oak, as if they were the twigs of saplings. Then it swept over the wild, waste meadows, rattling the frozen sedge, and whirling into eddies the few dry leaves that remained upon the surface of the earth. Next it invaded the principal street of the quaint old village, and played the mischief with the tall elms and the venerable buttonwoods that stood on either side like sentinels guarding the highway. How the old gilt lion that swung from the sign post of the tavern, hanging like a malefactor in irons, was shaken and disturbed! Backwards and forwards the animal was tossed, like a bark upon the ocean. Now he seemed as if about to turn a somerset and circumnavigate the beam from which he hung, creaking and groaning dismally all the while, like an unhappy soul in purgatory. The loose shutters of the upper story of the tavern chattered like the teeth of a witch-ridden old crone. But cheerful fires of hickory and maple were burning within doors; a merry group was gathered in the old oak parlor, and little recked the guests of the elemental war without. In fact, they knew nothing of it, till the driver of the village stage coach, making his appearance with a few flakes of snow on his snuff-colored surtout, announced, as he expanded his broad hands to the genial blaze, that it was a "wild night out of doors."

But on—on sped the wild wind, driving the snow flakes before it as a victorious army sweeps away the routed skirmishers and outposts of the enemy. Away went the night wind on its wild errand, reaching at last a solitary cottage on the outskirts of the village. Here it revelled in unwonted fury, ripping up the loose shingles from the moss-grown rooftree, and forcing an entrance through many a yawning crevice.

The scene within the cottage presented a strange and painful contrast to the interior of most of the comfortable houses in the flourishing village through which we have been hurrying on the wings of the cold north wind. The room was scantily furnished. There were two or three very old-fashioned, rickety, straw-bottomed chairs, an oaken stool or two, and a pine table. The hour hand of a wooden clock on the mantel piece pointed to eleven. A fire of chips and brushwood was smouldering on the hearth. In one corner of the room, near the fireplace, on a heap of straw, covered with a blanket, two little boys lay sleeping in each other's arms. Crouched near the table, her features dimly lighted by a tallow candle, sat a woman advanced in life, clad in faded but cleanly garments, whose hollow cheeks and sunken eye told a painful tale of sorrow and destitution. Those sad eyes were fixed anxiously and imploringly upon the stern, grim face of a hard-featured old man, who, with hat pulled over his shaggy gray eyebrows, was standing, resting on a stout staff, in the centre of the floor.

"So, you haven't got any money for me," said the old man, in the harshest of all possible voices.

"Alas! no, Mr. Wurm—if I had I should have brought it to you long ago," answered the poor woman. "I had raked and scraped a little together—but the sickness of these poor children—poor William's orphans—swept it all away—I haven't got a cent."

"So much the worse for you, Mrs. Redman," answered the old man, harshly. "I've been easy with you—I've waited and waited—trusting your promises. I can't wait any longer. I want the money."

"You want the money! Is it possible? Report speaks you rich."

"It's false—false!" said the old man, bitterly. "I'm poor—I'm pinched. Ask the townspeople how I live. Do I look like a rich man? No, no! I tell you I want my dues—and I will have 'em."

"I can't pay you," said the woman, sadly.

"Then you must abide the consequences!"

"What consequences?"

"I've got an execution—that's all," said the hardhearted landlord.

"An execution! what's that?"

"A warrant to take all your goods."

"My goods!" said the poor woman, looking round her with a melancholy smile. "Why I have nothing but what few things you see in this room. You surely wouldn't take those."

"I'll take all I can get."

"And leave me here with the bare walls."

"No, no! you walk out of this to-morrow."

"In the depth of winter! You cannot be so hardhearted."

"We shall see that."

"I care not for myself; but what is to become of these poor children?"

"Send 'em to work in the factory."

"But they are just recovering from sickness; they are too young to work. O, where, where can we go?"

"To the poorhouse," said the landlord, fiercely.

The poor woman rose, and approaching the landlord's feet, fell upon her knees, clasped her hands, and looked upward in his stern and unrelenting face.

"Israel Wurm," she said, "has your heart grown as hard as the nether millstone? Have you forgotten the days of old lang syne? O, remember that we were once prosperous and happy; remember that misfortune and not sin has reduced me and mine to the deplorable state in which you find us. Remember that my husband was your early friend—your schoolfellow—your playmate. Remember that when he was rich and you poor, he gave you from his plenty—freely—bountifully—not gave with the expectation of a return; his gifts were bounties, not loans."

"Therefore I owed him nothing," said the obdurate miser, turning away.

"You shall hear me out," said the woman, starting to her feet. "I ask for a further delay; I ask you to stay the hard hand of the law. You profess to be a Christian; I demand justice and mercy in the name of those sleeping innocents, my poor grandchildren, whose father is in heaven. You *shall* be merciful."

"Heyday!" exclaimed the miser; "this is fine talk, upon my word. You *demand* justice, do you? Well, you shall have it. The law is on my side, and I will carry it out to the letter."

"Then," said the outraged woman, stretching forth her trembling hand, "the curse of the widow and the orphan shall be upon you. Sleeping or waking, it shall haunt you; and on your miserable death bed, when the ugly shapes that throng about the pillow of the dying sinner shall close around you, our malediction shall weigh like lead upon you, and your palsied lips shall fail to articulate the impotent prayer for that mercy to yourself which you denied to others. And now begone. This house is mine to-night, at least. Afflict it no longer with your presence. Go forth into the night; it is not darker than your benighted soul, nor is the north wind one half so pitiless as you."

With a bitter curse upon his lips, but trembling and dismayed in spite of himself, Israel Wurm left the presence of the indignant victim of his cruelty, and turned his footsteps in the direction of his home. His *home*! It scarcely deserved the name. There was no fire there to thaw his chilled and trembling frame—no light to gleam athwart the darkness, and send forth its pilgrim rays to meet him and guide his footsteps to his threshold. No wife, no children, waited eagerly his return. It was the miser's home—dark, desolate, stern, and repulsive. Its deep cellars, its thick walls held hidden stores of gold, and notes, and bonds, but there were garnered up no treasures of the heart.

The miser's path lay through the churchyard, a desolate place enough even in the gay noon of a midsummer day, now doubly repulsive in the wild midnight of midwinter. The wall was ruinous. The black iron gateway frowned, naked and ominous. The field of death was crowded with headstones of slate, and innumerable mounds marked the resting-place of many generations. The snow was now gathering fast over the dreary and desolate abode, as the miser stumbled along the beaten pathway, bending against the blast and drift. A strange numbness and drowsiness crept over him. He no longer felt the cold; an uncontrollable desire of slumber possessed him. He sat down upon a flat tombstone, and soon lost all consciousness of his actual situation.

Suddenly he saw before him the well-known figure of the old sexton of the village, busily occupied in digging a grave. The winter had passed away; it was now midsummer. The birds were singing in the trees, and from the far green meadows sounded the low of cattle, and the tinkling of sheep bells. Even the graveyard looked no longer desolate, for on many of the little hillocks bright flowers were springing into bloom and verdure, attesting the affection that outlived death, and decorating with living bloom the precincts of decay.

"My friend, for whom are you digging that grave?" asked Israel.

The sexton looked up from his work, but did not seem to recognize the spokesman.

"For a man that died last night; he is to be buried to-day."

"Methinks this haste is somewhat indecorous," said Israel Wurm.

"O, for the matter of that," said the sexton, "the sooner this fellow's out of the way the better. There's nobody to mourn for him."

"Is he a pauper, then?"

"O no! he was immensely rich."

"And had he no relations—no friends?"

"For relations, he had a nephew, who inherits all his property. The young dog will make the money fly, I tell you. As for friends, he had none. The poor dreaded him—the good despised him; for he was a hardhearted, selfish, griping man. In a word, he was a MISER," said the sexton.

"A miser," faltered the trembling dreamer; "what was his name?"

"Israel Wurm," replied the sexton.

Graveyard and sexton faded away; in their place arose a splendid grove of trees—a clearing—a village school house. Two boys were sauntering along the roadside, engaged in serious, childish talk. One was fair, with golden locks; the other dark-haired and grave of aspect. Israel started, for in the latter he recognized himself—a boy of fifty years ago.

"Israel," said the golden-haired boy, "it's 'lection day to-morrow; we'll hire Browning's horse and chaise, and go to Boston, and have a grand time on the Common, seeing all the shows."

"You forget, Mark," said the dark-haired boy, sadly, "that I have no money."

"What of that?" replied the other; "I have a pocket full; and what's mine is yours, you know. Come, cheer up, you'll one day he as rich as I am; and then it will be your turn to treat, you know. I can afford to be generous, and so would you be, if you had the means."

Then the shadow passed from the face of the dark-haired boy, and a smile lighted up his countenance, and the two schoolfellows passed on their way together.

Grove and school house passed away, melting into another scene like one of the dissolving views. Israel stood before a huge illuminated screen, in the midst of a gaping company of sight seers. He could see nothing but a confused mass of heads, vaguely lighted by the rays from that vast screen. It was some kind of an exhibition.

"Now, ladies and gentlemen," said a strange voice issuing from the darkness, "we shall show you the wonders of the oxy-hydrogen microscope; natural objects magnified five thousand times. Look and behold the proboscis of the common house fly."

Israel gazed with the rest, and soon a huge object, resembling the trunk of a monster elephant, appeared on the illuminated disk. It passed away.

"Now, ladies and gentlemen," said the voice, "look well to the illuminated screen. What do you see now?"

"Nothing!" was the universal and indignant answer.

"I thought so," replied the voice. "Yet you have before you a miser's soul magnified five thousand times; a million such would not produce an image on the screen."

The illuminated disk grew dark and disappeared; then a lurid light seemed to fill all space; and soon huge billows of flames rolled upward, and writhed and twisted together like a myriad of gigantic serpents. Shrieks and howls of anguish issued from the fiery mass, but above all was heard the startling clangor of a bell.

"Halloo! who's this?" cried a voice that evidently issued from a set of powerful human lungs. The miser felt himself roughly shaken by the shoulder, and awoke.

"What's the noise?—fire?" he asked; for the bell he had heard in his dream now jarred upon his waking senses.

"Fire! no!" said the man who had awakened him—the butcher of the village. "It's the boys ringing in the new year. By the way, I wish you a happy new year, Mr. Wurm."

"A happy new year, Mr. Wurm," said the schoolmaster for he, too, was present.

"A happy new year," said Farmer Harrowby.

"And a happy new year" chorused a dozen other voices. It was great fun wishing a miser a happy new year.

"Thank you, neighbors; I wish you a thousand," replied Israel, cheerfully.

"How came you asleep there?" asked Farmer Harrowby. "Why, you might have perished in the drift."

"I was overcome by drowsiness," answered Israel. "I was very cold; I'd been to make a call on Widow Redman, and the poor soul was out of wood. By the way, farmer, the first thing after sunrise, I want you to be sure to gear up your ox team, and take a cord of your best hickory and pitch pine to the widow."

"And who'll pay me?" asked the farmer, doubtfully.

"I will, to be sure," answered Israel. "Have not I got money enough? Here—hold your hand;" and he put a handful of silver in the farmer's honest palm. "And you, Mr. Wilkins," he added, addressing the butcher, "take her the best turkey you've got, and half a pig, with my compliments, and a happy new year to her."

"And how about that execution?" asked the constable, who was round with the rest, 'seeing the old year out and the new year in.'

"Confound the execution! Don't let me hear another word about it," said Israel, magnanimously. "And now, neighbors," he added, "I owe you something for your good wishes; come along with me to the Golden Lion, and I'll give you the best supper the tavern affords. Hurrah! New year don't come but once in a twelvemonth."

- 267 -

We will be bound that a merrier party never left a churchyard, even after a funeral, nor a merrier set ever sat down to a festal board, than that which gathered to greet the hospitality of Israel Wurm. In the course of the evening, an old Scotch gardener gave it as his opinion that the "miser was *fey*." (When a man suddenly changes his character, as when a spendthrift becomes saving, or a niggard generous, the Scotch say that he is *fey*, and consider the change a forerunner of sudden death.)

"No, my friends," said Israel, overhearing the remark, "I am not *fey*; and I mean to live a long while, Heaven willing, for I have just learned that the true secret of enjoying life is to do good to others. I had a dream to-night which has, I trust, made me a wiser and better man. The miser lies buried in yonder churchyard; Israel Wurm, a new man, has risen in his place; and as far as my means go, I intend that this shall be a happy new year to every one of my acquaintances."

Israel was as good as his word, and never relapsed into his old habits. The widow and the orphan children were provided for by his bounty; he gave liberally to every object of charity. Hospitals, schools, and colleges were the recipients of his bounty; and when he died, in the fulness of years, the blessings of old and young followed him to his last resting-place in the old churchyard where he had dreamed the mysterious dream, and been awakened to a better life by the pealing of the NEW YEAR'S BELLS.

THE OLD YEAR AND THE NEW.

"O, this is beautiful—beautiful indeed!" cried a young and silvery voice, musical as fairy bells heard at midnight. "How white this snowy drapery hangs upon the roofs of these bright palaces!" and the speaker, a gay boy, danced trippingly along, following in the footsteps of an old, gray-bearded man who was tottering before him.

The old man turned. "You call that snowy drapery beautiful?" said he.

"Yes—it is like the raiment of a bride," said the boy.

"To me it seems a shroud thrown over the grave of buried hopes," answered the old man.

"But what are these joy bells ringing for?" said the boy.

"For a death and for a birth!" replied the old man.

"You speak riddles."

"I speak truth. The same sounds have a different import to different ears. To mine there is a death knell in these tremulous vibrations of the air."

"You are very old, father—and age has cankered you."

"A twelvemonth since, young child of Time," replied the old man, "I was like you."

"A twelvemonth! Your back is bent, your locks are silvery, your voice is tremulous. How is this?"

"Wrinkles and gray hairs are the work of sorrows, not of years. Eyes that are weary of the sight of suffering grow dim apace."

"But hark!" said the youth. "Hear you not that music—the peals of laughter that come from yonder illuminated house? It is a wedding festival."

"Yes," replied the old man, sadly. "A twelvemonth since, I heard the same sounds in the same house. There was music and feasting—it was, as now, a wedding festival. Where is the bride? Go to yonder churchyard. You will find her name inscribed on a simple stone. If you pass out of the city to the north, you will see some huge buildings of brick, towering upon an eminence. If you linger by the garden wall you will hear shrieks and curses, the howls of despair, the ravings of hopeless lunacy. The husband is there—the victim of his own evil passions—a raving maniac."

"Away with these croaking reminiscences!" cried the younger voice. "Let the music peal—let the dance go on. The wine is red within the cup."

"Yes—and the deadly serpent lurks below."

"Then the world is all desolate!" cried the New Year.

"No! there are green spots in the desert!" said the Old Year; "but beware of deeming it all fairyland! But a little while and you will follow me. But the end is not here—after Time, Eternity! There suffering and sin are unknown. There each departed spirit, after making the circuit of its appointed sphere, shall rise to a higher and a higher, while boundless love and wisdom illuminate all, radiating from a centre whose brightness no human senses can conceive."

The old man was gone. The joyous bells had rung his requiem. The young heir was enthroned—and with mingled hope and foreboding commenced the reign of 1853.